# READY OR KNOX

## (THE UNDERDOG SERIES # 4)

### BREA BROWN

WAYZGOOSE PRESS

Edited by Maggie Sokolik

Cover design by Keri Knutson, Alchemy Book Covers

Additional design by DJ Rogers, Book Branders

# ONE

## TAKEOFF

The captain announces we're third in line for takeoff, and we inch our way up the runway queue. Scout, nose pressed against the oval window, says, "Takeoff is my favorite."

Before I can respond, the woman in front of me turns and, peeking between seats, says, "Mine, too." Then she addresses Jet and me, like people usually do when our daughter is with us. "She's adorable!"

I smile tightly and mutter a "thank you," but Jet cheerfully continues the conversation from his position across the aisle. "She knows the drill. We have family all over the country."

"Oh, I can tell she's a pro at this. I have to admit, I've been listening and getting a kick out of her."

I suppress the urge to wrinkle my nose or roll my eyes, and instead keep my expression neutral. Of course, we had to be seated near the only chatty first-class passenger on the plane —other than Scout, that is. I hate being this tetchy, but if it were socially acceptable, I'd be wearing a sign today that says, *"My whole world is changing. Keep out of the personal bubble."*

The woman turns more fully in order to look behind her

and across the aisle at Jet. "Your little girl reminds me of my daughter when she was her age. About five, I'm guessing?"

Jet confirms the estimate just as the engines whine to a pitch that lets us know they mean business. I'm relieved when the flight attendant politely reminds our neighbor to face front for takeoff. With any luck, she'll fall asleep during the trip. Otherwise, it's going to be a long flight.

Scout won't mind, of course. Like her dad, she loves people, and people love her. She's the precocious child who draws positive attention from even the grumpiest of passersby. Nearly five years into her life, I'm used to being approached by people everywhere we go—they feel compelled to compliment her and us, as her parents, which is weird, in my opinion, but whatever. Jet loves the attention and eggs her on to say the funny things that tend to pop out when you get her talking about the subjects that interest her. Most of the time, I'm okay with it, or at least resigned, but there *are* still times when I long to have an uninterrupted conversation with our child in public. Today is definitely one of those days.

As the plane moves forward again, accelerating rapidly to get up to speed and achieve lift, Jet turns his head and tilts it a bit forward to see around me and watch Scout. She grins back at him at first but tries to suppress it, like the experience is no big deal to a veteran traveler like her. In spite of my foul mood, I chuckle at the two of them and laugh out loud when the wheels come off the ground, and our initial weightlessness makes Scout whoop.

We bank and climb before finally reaching cruising altitude. The welcome stillness and quiet cease as the fasten seatbelt light finally darkens, and the captain tells us we can leave our seats if we want. The flight attendant appears, taking drink orders and handing out snacks. When she arrives at our row, I ask for a water and almonds, while Scout selects apple juice and a granola bar. Jet orders what seems like one of everything. I expect him to pull a "Harry Potter," complete with accent (albeit a terrible imitation), and say, "I'll take the lot of it!"

After the attendant moves on, he says sheepishly, "I'm hungry."

I roll my eyes at the arrangement of food and snacks on his tray table. "No, you're not. There's no way you're physically hungry after that breakfast you ate at the hotel. You're bored."

"Definitely not bored."

"Nervous, then."

"Why would I be nervous? I'm not nervous. That's—"

I stare pointedly at his jiggling knee, which he immediately stills, placing a hand over it to ensure it remains motionless. When I look back up at his face, it sports the tell-tale wrinkled forehead and tightened lips of a worried man. "Because this is a big deal. Because this is outside your comfort zone. Because change is always a little unsettling. Because you're worried about how this is going to work and if we're going to be as happy in California as we were in Kansas City."

He waves off my speech. "Happiness is what we make it. It's all about attitude. If we have shitty attitudes, we're doomed from the start. As long as we stay positive." It's his turn to widen his eyes and direct a pointed look at me. "Everything will be fine."

I resist the urge to throw an almond right at his eye and instead open the book that's been sitting in my lap, ignored so far. Screw him with his "positive thinking" woo-woo bullshit. You can't magic away true worries and anxieties with unicorn farts and rainbows. Maybe you can for a while, but teeth-gritting your way through life, wishing things into submission, doesn't work. I agree that we have a choice about attitude *while* we're dealing with stressful or less-than-ideal situations, but how you feel or think about something doesn't change the actual circumstances.

What I needed him to say in response to my list of suggestions as to why he might be nervous was, "Yes, I do feel that way a little, but it's okay. It's okay if you feel that way, too. Together, we'll figure out ways to rebuild our life in California to be just as happy and rewarding as our life in Kansas City was."

That list wasn't a guess about his feelings; it was a recitation of mine. The worst part is, he knows that. He chose to lecture me, rather than reassure me. So, yeah. He can stick that bullshit up his fine, tight ass.

As I stew and pretend to read, Jet proceeds to stress-eat his way through his complimentary snacks.

After a few minutes, Scout taps my upper arm and points out the window. "Look at the clouds, Mommy. They're so fluffy and big, like snow! I want to go out and play in them!"

Placing my head close to hers, I say, "Wouldn't that be cool if we could?"

"But we can't," she says, suddenly wistful. "You can't walk on them, like they do in the cartoons. You fall right through."

"True."

"I like to pretend I can, though. Pretending is almost as good at the real thing."

"Almost." I turn my head and kiss her cheek, her flyaway curls tickling my nose.

"Sometimes I pretend I have a pet gerbil. When we get to our new house, can I have a gerbil?"

"We'll see," I say noncommittally to the oft-repeated request for the small rodent pet.

"I'll keep pretending I have one until I get a real one," she says blithely.

We stare out at the clouds until her eyes droop, and she slumps sideways against her seat back. I drape the blanket over her and recline her seat as far as it will go to save her neck from a lolling head.

While I watch her sleep, I consider that Bump has a point. Maybe pretending is close enough to the real thing until you can actually find something real to replace it. And maybe I've been looking to the wrong Knox family member for wisdom and reassurance.

Figures, considering she's been teaching Jet and me lessons since the moment of her debut into this world.

## TWO

## MAURA'S HIGHLIGHT REELS

*Replay #1: Nearly Five Years Ago*

"Ready?"

"Does it matter?" I panted back, lowering myself into the passenger seat and swinging my legs into the foot well.

"Well, I guess not. Ready or not, here she comes, right?"

"Yes. I can feel her head between my legs."

All color drained from his face. "What?"

"Not really," I amended so he'd be able to drive. He was no good to me unconscious. "Just. A lot. Of pressure."

I'd never given birth before, so I wasn't sure, but I feared we'd labored too long at home. I was so worried about being one of *those* women who shows up at labor and delivery with multiple false alarms that I overcompensated. But my water still hadn't broken, so I hoped it only felt like the birth was impending.

Turns out, we had plenty of time. More than we thought, anyway. Bump was on her way, for sure, but I wasn't dilated that much at all. At first, I was embarrassed by how wrong I'd gotten it and how big of a wimp I was. Then, when I realized it meant that I could still have an epidural, I was thankful.

I've seen the movies, and I knew I didn't want to go through a completely natural childbirth. "Screw that," might have been my exact words when my obstetrician first asked me if "natural" was going to be part of my birthing plan. Then I said, "My birthing plan is to feel as little of the main event as possible."

We spent the better part of a boring day at the hospital, waiting until it was convenient for the doctor to break my water to get things really moving. Bump was worth the wait, though. She was on the larger side, we were told, but she still seemed incredibly tiny to us—and vulnerable—but somehow wise. When she squinted at us through the jelly they placed on her eyes, it was as if she was saying, "I'm here now to teach you guys a thing or two about life. I hope you're ready."

Nobody's ever ready. Sure, we had all the gear known to man, everything money could buy. We had the fully kitted-out nursery. We'd even taken private instruction in our home about basic baby care, infant CPR, and first aid. Plus, it's not like we were novices with children; we felt like we'd gotten plenty of practice with nieces and nephews over the years. As we soon found out, though, we knew nothing. Nothing prepares you for the overwhelming love and fear that comes when they place your own child in your arms for the first time. Other parents can tell you that, and you can intellectually "get" it, but you don't truly *get* it until you experience it. Which is a shame.

I wish there were a way for everyone to feel that raw emotion. It would make us a much more empathetic species. Not everyone is cut out for parenthood or wants to reproduce, and nobody should be forced to be a parent who doesn't want to be one. However, if we all could experience that feeling at least once, regardless, to look into someone's eyes and be so connected to them that you'd give your life for that person, without hesitation, through some instinct that has nothing to do with logic or reason or choice, maybe we'd be more proactive when it comes to loving our fellow human beings. We all started this way, as a baby in someone's arms. If nothing else, we'd be more patient with the parent in the grocery store struggling with the tantrum-throwing kid.

In seconds, I saw a lifetime of moments, looking into those goopy eyes. Milestones flashed through my brain: crawling, walking, talking, the first day of school, learning to swim, splashing in the ocean for the first time, her first bite of sushi, learning to drive, graduating from high school... In the next seconds, however, I realized with crushing anxiety that none of those things were guaranteed to any of our kids, that so many things could happen between now and whenever to prevent any or all of that from coming to pass.

I tore my eyes from our new baby's face to see if Jet was feeling the same thing, but judging by his goofy expression, all he was thinking about was throwing the football with her in the backyard, or making more babies just like her. Because she was so incredible, he probably wanted to "collect" a hundred more.

Shaking, I transferred the baby to his arms, thinking maybe holding her would trigger in him the awesome but terrifying response I was having, but he continued to grin down at her with tears in his eyes and delight in every expression and move she made. She appeared even tinier in his massive hands.

It was all I could do not to snatch her back and say, "Mine.

Nobody else can touch her. We're taking her home right now, and we're never leaving the house. Ever."

A nurse, noticing my distress, brought it to the attention of the doctor, who was still between my legs, having just performed a bit of sewing on my undercarriage.

The doctor placed a calming, gloved hand on one of my knees and said, "You did great. Sometimes the adrenaline and anesthesia can make you a little shaky afterward. It's normal. Take some deep breaths for me through your nose."

I did, and the oxygen intake helped a bit with the physical shaking, but I was still shaken to my core.

"What should we call her?" Jet asked, seemingly from far away.

I turned my head slowly and focused on his lips as the words tumbled from them, but I had a hard time comprehending what he was saying. Eventually, it clicked that he was listing some of the names we'd discussed over the past several months, since we'd found out that Bump had girl parts.

In a stupor, I nodded, more as a way of acknowledging that I understood what he was asking, but he took it to mean I was approving the most recent name he'd suggested, "Scout."

I've always loved that name, since I first read *To Kill a Mockingbird* in middle school. And even though it was the character's nickname, I thought it would make a great real name for a boy or a girl. So it's not that I regretted the misunderstanding, but I also recognized right away that it would be a part of her origin story. *"I got my name because my mom was having a panic attack when my dad suggested it."*

Life sped up again as the breathing worked, and I came back to myself a little more each second, no longer feeling like I was moving and hearing everything from underwater.

Jet bounced the baby as she started to fuss. "Now I get to pick her middle name."

*Not Gloria, not Gloria, not Gloria,* I prayed.

"Audrey," he declared after a few seconds. "Scout Audrey Knox." Before I could point out that her initials spelled out "SAK," the phonetic equivalent of a quarterback's nemesis, he said, "It's perfect. She's perfect."

He was right.

Anyway, her initials seemed fitting, considering she'd probably knock us down and take our breath away over and over again in the coming years. Only, in this case, it wouldn't be such a bad thing.

## *Replay #2: Seven Months Ago, Last Christmas(ish)*

Shoulders-deep into a huge red velvet Santa sack, Scout giggled and squealed at the gifts inside, waiting in their original packaging. Jet and I watched from the floor a few feet away, at a good distance to capture candid photos of her reactions. She didn't seem to mind—in fact, she seemed thrilled—that we were doing this a couple of days early, since her dad would be traveling for a game on the actual holiday.

As for the sack, that was Jet's idea, a throwback to one of his childhood traditions. "My parents used to put all of our presents in it, and each year, we took turns being 'Santa' and handing out the packages on Christmas morning."

"That sounds sweet. Why don't we do that?" I asked on Scout's second Christmas when some of Jet's outlandish ideas gave me agita.

He thought about it for a second. "We could, but..." He sighed. "Each of us only got three presents, usually pretty small ones."

"So? Was it stuff you'd asked for? Stuff you liked?"

"Yeah! Well, everything except the itchy socks from Granny Knox." He chuckled. "Hey! That rhymes."

Determined to keep him focused, I said, "Well, Scout's an only child, so there will be plenty of room for *reasonable* gifts."

"True."

"And this way, you can be more thoughtful, rather than just throwing a ton of money at her and not considering what she actually wants."

That was the clincher. Jet loves nothing more than finding the perfect, unique gift.

The sack was a winner idea for me, because it saved me from wrapping gifts, and limited the size and type of presents Scout received. No ponies for this kid.

Last Christmas, we continued the tradition for the third year. Other than a few palettes of play makeup Scout had been begging me to let her have and some age-appropriate books about her favorite subjects—history, nature, and geography—I had contributed little to the gifting process. The other things —snow globes from cities he'd passed through for away games, the latest electronic devices "for learning purposes," a custom-fitted Chiefs football helmet, soft flannel pajamas emblazoned with arrowheads, and an authentic NFL football signed by Joe Montana (Scout's favorite player—after her dad, of course), among other things—were all Jet's ideas.

I was lining up the next photo, figuring the makeup was about to be dragged from the bag, when Jet said quietly so only I could hear, "I'm going to retire."

To say I was shocked would be an understatement. With a couple of years remaining on his contract, I figured I had to stick it out at least that much longer, playing the part of mostly-single parent for half the year and periodically during the other half. I wasn't even sure that would be the end of it. To be honest, I assumed he'd be seeking a contract extension, if not another full contract when this one was up. Like Drew McKnight, the self-proclaimed GOAT and pretty-boy quarterback of the New England Patriots, I expected Jet to play well into his late thirties and early forties.

When I managed to stutter some of that, he shook his head sadly. "Nah." Turning his attention back to Scout, who was rocketing two astronaut Barbies into space, he said, "I want to be able to walk her down the aisle someday—or not, if she doesn't want to get married. But you know what I mean. I want to be able to walk with her wherever. And talk. And eat solid food." He reached for my hand. "I want to do all that with you, too. Travel together. Goof around. Have fun without being in constant pain."

That season had been tough. He hobbled around on crutches, sat in ice baths, nursed swollen joints, and underwent testing for concussion protocols more than during any other part of his career. Not that he'd been a stranger to that stuff to begin with. I was thrilled that he recognized it was time to hang up the cleats, while he still had some say in the decision, without any nagging from me.

I squeezed his fingers. "That would be nice."

His brow crinkling, he looked down at his lap. "It may already be too late for some of that. I've pushed it pretty hard the past couple of seasons and made my body do things no one's body is made to do. But maybe not. I'm not going to keep going, pretty much guaranteeing I'll be a drooling mess before I'm sixty."

"Oh, gosh. Let's not think of that."

"I have, though, Maura. I do—all the time. I look at her, and—" He nudged his head toward Scout and sighed. "Anyway. It's time. I'll have to jump through some legal hoops on these rusty knees of mine, but Tom and I, with the help of a mediator, will figure all of that out. Don't worry."

"I won't. I mean, guys do this all the time. As long as we won't be homeless."

He waved that off. "Uh, no. Your theaters are safe, too."

"Then I'm not worried. I trust you."

Recently, we'd expanded The Knox into a chain, with locations in multiple Missouri and Kansas cities. I'd made my own arrangements to guarantee my non-profit mission wouldn't ever be put at risk by the whims of the NFL or anyone else, but it was nice to know he'd also taken that into account.

After snapping some more pictures of Scout unwrapping her gifts from Jet's parents, Gloria and Ned, and helping her rip open the packaging to play with them immediately, I turned back to Jet and said lightly, "So, this is it, huh? Last chance at that second Lombardi trophy and another hideous ring."

Raising an eyebrow at my snark, he said, "Yes, ma'am."

"No pressure, Number Fourteen." I hopped into his lap, turning sideways and wrapping my arms around his shoulders. "What's next, then? Announcing? Coaching? Loafing on the couch and eating chips all day?"

He shrugged. "We'll see. You know I've always wanted to booth announce, but that means more travel, and I don't know. That's less fun than it used to be."

"Yeah, it's one thing to leave *me* alone all the time, but now you have someone to *miss*," I said, my tone teasing.

"Stop it." Kissing me deeply, he made it known how he felt about that and only drew back when Scout giggled and made smoochy noises, mimicking our behavior with her new dolls.

We both crawled toward her and attacked her with kisses

and tickles, what she and Jet called, "Kissles," shelving more serious future issues in favor of living in the moment.

Less than two months later, after winning that second hideous ring, he stood at a podium and emotionally made his official retirement announcement, as promised.

### Replay #3: Three Months Ago

"How about unlimited free passes *and* refreshments for employees and immediate family members? We can give them a card, or something," Nina said, spitballing morale boosters for Knox Theater staff members.

I wrote it down. "Maybe. Could get expensive, though. And everything we give them takes away from the charities we sponsor."

"Not necessarily," she said. "Open up the vault, Ms. Moneybags. Take it out of your own personal account."

"It's not that I'm not willing!"

"I know. I'm teasing."

"I'm just not sure about the logistics of that. I'll have to talk to my brother about how it would work. We're supposed to keep personal and theater accounting completely separate."

"It'd be a write-off on your taxes, probably, too."

My head started to ache. "Let's come up with some other ideas, just in case we can't make that one work."

Lest I worry, she had a million more, each one stemming from her extensive turbulent past work experience, each one accompanied by an anecdote.

She was regaling me with yet another example of a time when an employer could have done better by her when Jet burst into the library I used as my home office at Fort Knox and said, breathless, "They want me."

"Uh, Nina?" I broke into her long-winded story, keeping my eyes on my husband. "I'm gonna have to call you back. On second thought, just email me the rest of your ideas. I'll see you tomorrow."

Without waiting for her to reply, I disconnected and set my phone on the desk while analyzing Jet's appearance. The sweat on his face and soaked-through shirt suggested he'd been down in the basement working out, but it was the first I'd seen him all day, so I couldn't swear to that—or provide an alibi, if pressed.

Actually, he looked a bit unhinged, and I knew he could run those stairs all day and not breathe any heavier than I was, sitting there, so either he sprinted from the gym down there, already winded from a workout, or he ran all the way from Scout's preschool after dropping her off that morning, bailing from his car due to necessity because someone was after him. Probably the former, the more I thought of it. I made a mental note to cut back on my true crime binge-watching.

"They want me," he repeated, panting, holding his phone up in his shaking hand. From what I could tell, there was a text or an email on the screen. "They saw my audition video, and they want me."

"Audition video?" I struggled to catch up, having no idea to what or whom he was referring. It was like I'd lost time, or something. Like I'd come into the middle of a TV show and missed the setup to the conflict. Did he mention an audition tape to me? No, I would have remembered that. Who were "they"?

"Champ, you're gonna have to back up and slow down. Maybe you *think* you told me something, but you didn't, so I'm lost."

He shook his head and swallowed. "No. I didn't tell you. I didn't want to curse it."

I blinked.

"Not because you're a curse! Or bad luck. Or anything like that. It's just, I didn't want to talk about it, in case— Well, in case they didn't want me. Because that would be embarrassing." He leaned against the door frame. "But they do. Want me, I mean. Tom just texted me."

"Who wants you? For what?"

"What?"

"Yeah, what?"

He laughed at what sounded like our attempt to imitate (poorly) an old comedy routine. "Oh, my gosh. I can't think straight."

Tamping down my irritation—and growing dread—I sighed and prompted, "I take it you got a job offer. In broadcasting, I guess, since you sent them an audition video? Where? With which network?" I forced a smile onto my lips, hoping it made it to my eyes. "Tell me all about it."

He flopped onto one of the couches, and I cringed at the possibility of sweat stains on the upholstery. Then I wondered who the heck I was, suddenly caring about things like upholstery. Before I realized it, I'd missed several seconds of his explanation.

"So they called Tom and said they loved my audition and would be stoked to have me come out there and tour the network. I asked if it was an interview, but Tom said, no. I already have the job, if I want it, and of course I want it. This is the one I wanted the most, because it's regional, which means I'd cover the games within a certain mile radius of home, and I wouldn't have to travel all over the damn country like some of these guys do, week after week. I mean, we'll still have to move out there, but that's something I've always wanted, to move back there, so I told them…"

Oh, shit. No. His voice faded out again as I processed what he was saying. He'd only lived two other places besides Kansas City, and he'd only ever talked about moving back to one of them: California.

I willed the blood to stay in my face, but he sat up on the couch and said, "Whoa, beautiful. You don't look so hot. I mean, you're still hot, but you look like you're about to barf. Are you okay? I told Beau to check all the lettuce and make sure it wasn't part of that recall, but maybe you ate some before he got around to it?"

"I'm fine," I snapped. "I— I didn't hear what you said at the beginning, which network."

He grinned. "*The* network, baby. Football Network. All football, all time. Every game, every week. Biggest staff of announcers in the business. And growing. Best equipment, best technology, best everything. Making the old networks look like dinosaurs. And gaining subscribers faster than any other outlet in the history of television."

"And they're located in…?"

"All over the place. That's the best thing. They had an opening in their West Coast market, which is what I auditioned for."

"I see."

"So that's why they want me to come tour their Culver City studio. It would be my 'home base.' I'd have an office there, and that's where I'd attend meetings and stuff, but I'd rarely have to actually go to that building during the season. I'd be covering the games for teams in California. That's it. Very niche."

"Niche. Yes."

"See, they save money not flying crews all over the place. They set people up geographically. It's better for families and for the network. And the fans, too. The fans get familiar with the announcers, and everyone on the crew gets to know each other, so it's a more family-like atmosphere. The announcers are experts about the regional teams they cover, too. I mean, I'd still have to study the visiting teams, obviously, but it's a lot less prep work. Football Network thinks fans want more passion from the booth, someone they can relate to, someone who's rooting for the same team they are."

"What if two California teams play each other?" I asked stupidly, really the last thing I cared about.

He rubbed his chin. "I don't know. I hadn't thought of that. Maybe Erin and I will flip a coin before the game, or something. Or we'll each pick a side." He tapped his chin. "Huh. I guess that's something I'll have to ask during my tour. And, obviously, it'll be hard for me when the Chargers or Raiders play the Chiefs, but I'll figure out a way to deal, I guess."

I pushed back from the desk, suddenly fighting the impulse to run from the room, from the house, from the whole thing. Before I could say anything, though, he practically yelled, "Oh, my gosh, Maura! I almost forgot to tell you the best part!"

He leaped from the couch and rounded the desk, perching on the corner of it, trapping me between him and the wall shelf to my left. The tang of his sweat, normally a heady scent that I didn't mind—even sometimes enjoyed, depending on the context—repelled me. I scooted my chair as far away as I could before it bumped into the shelf, setting a vase and a movie reel bookend rattling. I lifted my arm to steady each of them in turn, keeping my attention on Jet's hopeful—almost desperate—expression.

He wanted so much for me to want it as much as he did. He was selling it to me. And he was afraid I wouldn't buy it, that I'd refuse to go with him.

That realization broke my heart. How could he think that?

I inched my chair closer to him once more and threaded my fingers through his. He squeezed back and grinned. "My booth partner is Erin! You know, Erin Matheny, the sideline reporter?"

I actually perked up a bit at that news, not having to fake my enthusiasm for the first time in the conversation. "A woman? Wow. Really cool. Erin Matheny, huh? I've always liked her style. She seems nice."

"She is. Super-nice. She always asks about you and Scout. She was the sideline reporter who interviewed me that first game after Scout was born."

"I remember." I sounded—and was—surprised at that recall, since those days tended to be fuzzy.

"She was so happy for us, she almost started crying when I told her, before we went live. I told her she needed to keep it together, or we'd both be blubbering on national TV."

"You never told me that."

He laughed. "Probably would have cried telling you. Man, I was a wreck."

"Lack of sleep will do that to you."

"Yeah, but it was more than that, you know. I was so *happy*. I mean, I was already happy, but then I was even happier, happier than I thought was possible or even fair. Like, what had I done to deserve so much damn happiness? You know?"

"Yep."

"At the same time, though, I missed you guys like crazy.

Erin just *got* it. She was the only one who really seemed to understand how torn I felt. It was weird." He stared off vacantly into space for a few seconds, then blinked back to the present and smiled at me.

I stared at his hand in mine when I said, "Anyway. Um, California, huh? When do we leave?"

"So you're okay with that?"

I shrugged. "Where you go, I go, champ. It's part of the deal."

"I mean, we could probably make it work if I lived out there during the season and here in the off-season, but it would be so much better if you and Scout came with me. I want you two with me every day."

"We're a family. I wouldn't dream of living separately like that."

He stood and pulled my hand to bring me up with him. "I was hoping you'd say that."

"You doubted I would?"

"Figured I had a fifty-fifty shot."

"But you were going to take the job, regardless." It was a statement, not a question. I knew the answer, and I have to say, it hurt a little.

"This is the next phase of my plan." He nudged my nose with his.

I knew, going in, that this was part of his dream, just as big a part of it as playing the game and winning Super Bowls. Probably bigger, when I thought about it. A larger portion of his life, potentially, anyway. Some of those guys in the booth have been around forever! They've been announcing many times longer than they were players. But when we talked about this in the past, it seemed so far in the future, so abstract. How did we get there so fast? I wasn't ready for that phase. I thought I had more time.

Jet could barely stand still. "Good. Then it's settled. We're movin' to C-A!"

Leaning back, he rocked me forward until my feet came off the ground. I relaxed into his smiling kiss and thought with a mixture of dread and excitement, *California, here we come.*

Then my next thought was, *I need to Google how close we'll be to Gloria.*

## THREE

## WELCOME TO LALA LAND

The next thing I know, the flight attendant is leaning down close to me, telling me to put my and Scout's seats in the upright positions to prepare for landing. I do so while blinking and yawning. Needless to say, I didn't get a ton of sleep last night, in a strange airport hotel, anticipating today's departure. Bidding farewell to the only city I've ever called home and embarking on this new chapter of our lives has been an emotional challenge, to say the least. It's one I haven't always met gracefully.

It's not like I didn't know this day would someday arrive. This has always been on "The Plan," which Jet laid out in great detail for me on our first date and has reiterated many times over our eight-year relationship. Saying yes to his marriage proposal meant being fully on board, which is why I rejected that proposal multiple times before finally agreeing. I haven't taken The Plan lightly. It's as solid as the vows we took down in Belize when we eloped.

Here's the thing about the brain, though: it's plastic. When life goes a certain way for long enough, it conveniently forgets a lot of things it's been told in the past. It thinks, "This is our life, and our life is like this, and our life will always be like this, even when it's no longer like this. It's how life is."

Then you wake up one day, and you're told life is about to change. Even then, your brain doesn't quite get it. It only understands the parts it wants to understand.

It's all happened so fast. All I thought about for a while was how great it was going to be to have him around more, to not plan our lives around game schedules. To celebrate Christmas on the actual day now and then. I forgot to imagine this: moving thousands of miles away from "home."

When I pop a piece of gum in my mouth to take care of both my breath and my ears, Jet's hand appears in my line of sight. I drop a piece in his palm and offer one to Scout, too, who shakes her head sleepily and rubs her eyes.

The plane descends, bit by bit. Jet thanks me for the gum and asks, "Did you get a good nap?"

"Yeah," I say brightly, hoping to make up for my earlier bad mood. "You?"

"Nah. Too torqued." He blows a bubble and grins. "I'm so excited! This is the last time I'll have to make this trip for a while. We'll finally all be under one roof again, and life can get back to normal. Or we can figure out our new 'normal.' You know what I mean."

"I do."

"I'm pumped to see the new house in person, not just in pictures."

I level a skeptical look at him. "Like you haven't already. Please. Truth time, champ. In the weeks you've been out here by yourself, with nothing to do, you haven't driven the half hour from Culver City to scope it out?"

"I told you I'd wait, so we'd all see it in person for the first time together."

"I know what you told me. I'm asking if this will be your first time seeing it."

He sighs. "Well, it would have been irresponsible to buy a place sight unseen."

"Ah-ha!"

"But I only did a couple of drive-bys. I never went inside."

"Hmmm…"

"I mean it. I knew it would be much more fun to see it all together for the first time."

Since he's an even worse liar than I am, his earnestness eventually convinces me.

Then I turn my attention to Scout. "What about you, Bump? You excited to see the new house?"

She nods, still looking dazed from her long nap.

Jet leans forward to tell her, "This plane is like a time machine. We've been on it for three hours, but it's only an hour later here than it was when we left Kansas City!"

"That's because of time zones, silly, not a magic time machine plane," she says with a sleepy grin as we hear and feel the landing gear emerge with a clunk. She folds her little hand into mine. "I know you don't like landings, Mommy, so you can hold my hand."

I wrap her little paw inside both of mine and say, "Thanks."

"Who's going to hold my hand?" Jet asks nobody in particular, a silly pout in his voice.

I'm sure his new friend in front of me would, I almost say, but instead I reach across the aisle. He threads his fingers through mine. "Thanks, beautiful. Here we go. Everyone ready?"

———

After waiting in baggage claim for about a half hour, then enduring a thirty-minute ride from the airport, we stand in the driveway of our new house. It's not even ten o'clock local time, but our internal clocks are telling us it's closer to noon, and it's already been a full day.

As soon as we cross the threshold into the entryway, however, Scout soars into her second wind. "Oh, Mommy and Daddy, look at it! It's beauty-ful!"

She's right. A gorgeous house, it sits in a lush, gated, hilltop neighborhood in Pacific Palisades. For me, it's love at first in-person sight, and to walk through the front door together for the first time perks all of us up, even this exhausted, apprehensive grownup.

For several minutes, we stand in the entryway, surveying the open-plan layout of the living room, dinette, and kitchen. To the immediate left of the front door, a pair of doors open to a study, where I'll spend a lot of time running The Knox Theaters from afar. A door in there accesses the one-stall garage where Jet will store his precious crimson Corvette.

To our right is the formal dining room, then one of two hallways on either side of the kitchen that leads back to a powder room and the secondary bedrooms. Off that hallway are also the pantry, laundry room, and access to the main garage, where our everyday cars will go.

We advance further into the bright, airy house like astronauts on a strange planet. The white walls, built-ins, kitchen cabinets, and square columns pair nicely with the espresso flooring, ceiling beams, and trim. As we walk through, Jet jokes he'll need to wear sunglasses inside with all of the skylights and windows. The interior decorator we hired made sure to provide splashes of color in the decor and furnishings, but I love the house's overall clean look and lines. It's a wonderful contrast from the gloom of closed-up Fort Knox.

Motorized sliding glass panels separate the main house from the covered patios, which offer an additional sitting area and kitchen. More sliding glass panels can be lowered to protect those areas from the elements. Otherwise, almost the entire back of the house can be open to the pool area and the ocean breezes.

When Jet pushes the buttons to trigger the glass panels to retract into the ceiling, Scout hops up and down and claps her hands. "We live outside!" she says breathlessly.

Without pausing long, though, to survey what must seem like just another boring living area with a rock fireplace and kitchen with a grill and pizza oven, she tugs on our hands. We allow her to propel us through the doorway between the kitchen and dinette and down the other hallway that leads to three of the house's four bedrooms. There's hers, of course, plus an adult guest suite with pool access and a kids' guest suite that connects to her room through a walk-in closet.

Scout and I furnished her room together in a theme of her choosing: sea life, namely turtles, in a color scheme of varying shades of turquoise and sand. A fishing net hangs in the corner, ready to receive her beloved plushies when they arrive on the moving truck. Jet sits on her bed and tests its bounce. Then Scout informs us of the names of the sea turtles on her wall decals. "The big one is Jade, so it can be a mommy or a daddy, and the little baby ones are Charley, Coral, and Chase."

She starts to name the numerous turtle silhouettes on her area rug, but runs out of ideas halfway through, so Jet stops her and says, "You can think about that later, Bump. Show me your mermaid bathroom."

Gladly, she runs to the attached room and slides aside the shower curtain so he can see the *pièce de résistance*, the glass tile made to look like mermaid scales.

"Whoa! That's so cool!" Jet says, giving our daughter exactly the reaction she wanted. "Did you pick that out?"

"Yep!" she says proudly as we file back into her bedroom.

"Dang. You did a good job. This whole room is totally awesome."

"I think so, too," she says.

I ruffle her hair. "I'm glad you like it, baby girl".

"I can't wait until my plushies get here. When will they get here?"

Jet picks her up. "Tomorrow, Bump." She pooches out her bottom lip, so he pokes at it with his finger. "Oh, come on. None of that. We'll find things to do to pass the time, like… play in the pool." As soon as he says it, he flings her over his shoulder in a firefighter's carry and runs her, giggling, through the house and onto the sunny patio. "You packed a suit, right?"

Face red with blood, she says, "Yeah."

He sets her on her feet and pats her bottom. "Change into it, and meet me back here in…" He pretends to calculate precisely how long it should take, counting on his fingers and whispering the numbers. "Seven minutes."

"Seven?" she checks, already running for her rolling suitcase in the foyer.

"Seven. No more, no less." Stretching, he threads his fingers behind his head and stretches his elbows outward, arching his back, closing his eyes, and inhaling deeply.

I join him, ducking under his left arm and wrapping both of my arms around his waist, weaving my fingers on his right hip. "It's amazing."

"Isn't it? Almost perfect."

"Almost?"

"I wish we could see the ocean."

"Hmm." The mature vegetation offering our yard the privacy we wanted also blocks out the ocean view he desperately desired, but it's a short drive to the nearest local beach. "You can still smell it," I say, taking another deep breath to demonstrate.

He agrees begrudgingly, following my lead and sniffing the air, but on the next breath, he adds, "I already miss my SUV, too."

"You do realize you just told a child not to pout about her beloved toys, and here you are pouting *heavily* about your pitiful SUV-less life."

"That's different."

"Hardly. Anyway, one-point-five cars per household driver is plenty extravagant."

"Says you."

"Says pretty much everyone. Get over it, Knox. Or trade in one of your other cars for an SUV. It's hardly a brain-buster."

He steers me toward the water's edge by my shoulders. Planting my feet is fruitless, since he's infinitely stronger than I am, so he drags me closer to the pool, shrieking (me) and cackling (him) the entire way. "You're about to test the water for Scout and me in all of your clothes, smartass."

"Jet, no! My phone's in my pocket!"

"Oh, no! Then you'd have to live without something *you* love. How will you cope?"

In a last ditch effort to save myself—and my phone—I hop and cling to him like a deranged koala. If I'm going in, he's coming with me. It works. He halts his progress and adjusts me higher over his hips, my legs wrapped around his waist, ankles hooked behind his butt. He can't pry me off if he wants to. His changing expression tells me he doesn't want to, anyway.

Quietly, he says, "I love you, beautiful."

"I love you, too, when you're not bullying me."

"You call this bullying?" he asks, softly kissing my lips.

"Mmmm, I'm not sure. Do it again." He does. "More," I whisper, pressing myself even more tightly against him and leaning into his kisses, tasting him as I grip the back of his hair.

As the make-out session intensifies, he moans into my mouth and mutters against it, "Scout's gonna be back any second."

Regretfully, I dismount and back out of shoving range, not putting it past him to make one more effort to drench me. "You better go change into your trunks, champ. I hope you brought some baggy ones."

He winces and adjusts his pants. "Yeah, thanks for that."

"You're welcome. Any time."

For good measure, I smack him on the butt as he passes by me to retrieve our luggage from the foyer. Then, with anticipatory glee, I practically skip into what sold me on this place, the master suite I never knew I wanted.

It's everything the pictures promised, and more, featuring a sitting area with windows on three sides and skylight for maximum sunshine, direct patio access, and separate his and hers walk-in closets. The centerpiece of the bathroom is an elegant soaking tub, lit by a crystal chandelier (I'm not kidding) and flanked on either side by gleaming his and hers vanities. Behind the tub is a shower *room* for two—or six, if that's your thing. It's not ours, but if that ever changes, we have the perfect shower for it.

What *is* our thing is coffee. Therefore, the morning bar with built-in cabinets, mini-fridge, microwave, and full coffee station intrigued me more than any other feature of the house. I have to admit, when the real estate agent first described it to us, I scoffed at its seeming superfluity. I warmed toward the concept when I saw the pictures. Now that I've seen it in person, I'm totally on board and no longer scoffing. We are going to be best friends. I won't even have to leave the bedroom to get my first hit of caffeine or a light breakfast to eat in the sitting area or out on the patio or in the soaking tub. It'll be especially handy when Gloria's visiting, and I want to avoid waking her and prolong my first encounter with her in the morning. Yeah, I've already thought that far ahead.

When we first started looking at houses out here, my top priority was simplicity. The morning bar illustrates how quickly that flew out the window when Jet got involved. In the end, I caved. Working long-distance from home while juggling stay-at-home mom duties is going to be a big enough change; going back to unheated bathroom floors seemed like an unnecessary sacrifice.

"You like?" Jet asks, emerging from his closet in his swim-suit and finding me stroking the gleaming surfaces of the morning bar.

"I love," I say dreamily, eliciting a chuckle.

He motions with his head in the direction of the pool. "You gonna swim with us, or do you want some time alone with the espresso machine?"

I glare playfully at him and say through clenched teeth, "I'll be right there."

Before either of us can move, however, the doorbell rings. "What the...?" I wonder aloud.

Jet's face brightens knowingly. "I'll bet that's Richard and his family, here to welcome us to the neighborhood."

"Richard? Richard Valentine? Your boss?" I touch my travel-limp hair, tucking stray strands behind my ears and visualizing how my makeup-free, stress-pimply face must look right now. Maybe not as bad as it feels. But not good. "I wasn't expecting to see anyone today. I—"

He pats my butt on his way past me. "You look awesome, as usual, beautiful. Anyway, they know we landed about five minutes ago. I'm sure they're not expecting glitz and glamor."

Paralyzed with panic, I stand between the bedroom and the bathroom, unable to decide if I should attempt a five-second damage control session in front of the mirror or if actually seeing myself will only make things worse. After a couple of thrumming heartbeats, I chicken out and follow my husband without the appearance check. First impressions are over-rated, I tell myself, not believing it for a moment. In the last seconds before Jet swings open the front door, I swipe my fingers across my overgrown eyebrows and paste a smile on my cracked, chapped lips.

On our doorstep stands Richard, every bit the weekend version of the southern California man in his khaki shorts, designer t-shirt, and Docksiders, hair slicked back and nails perfectly manicured. Beaming beside him is the woman I assume is his wife, her long, blonde hair pulled up into a tight, sleek bun. A white sleeveless pants romper with gold sandals perfectly accentuates her not-too-deep tan. Full, red lips (definitely injected) and long, red fingernails (acrylics) and toenails round out the look. Although she's smiling, there's not a wrinkle or dimple to be found on her face. She's a walking Botox commercial.

In stair-step fashion, two daughters round out the group.

The youngest is a clone of her mother with a few of their father's features thrown in as nature's proof of paternity. The oldest looks supremely bored, to the point of mutiny, her eyes glued to her phone, which she taps and swipes away at with her manicured thumbs. I know from Jet that the oldest is Richard's child from his first marriage. Her dark beauty instantly marks her as the progeny of the man before us and Italian supermodel Vivica Rossi.

Richard extends his hand and shakes first Jet's, so hard that he yanks Jet across the threshold onto the front stoop, then mine, more gently, and says, "Hey, there! Wanted to be the first to stop by and say hi, or is it 'Howdy,' where y'all are from?"

"Thanks, Richard. 'Hi' works just fine." After all of the introductions are made, during which I learn that Richard's wife is Kiki, and the two girls are sixteen-year-old Paris and five-year-old Larissa, Jet moves aside and chuckles. "Come on in. Sorry I'm so... under-dressed." He motions to his swimming attire.

"Oh, you're fine!" says Kiki in a tone that pings my rarely used jealousy radar. She coughs delicately and amends in a less lascivious tone, "You're fine. We're not staying long. Just wanted to welcome you." She extends a bottle of wine I hadn't noticed, and I take it from her.

Scout runs up behind us in her swimsuit and peeks between our bodies at our visitors.

"And who's this?" Kiki asks, her pitch rising at least two octaves. "What a cutie-pie!"

"This is Scout," Jet says, shepherding her gently forward.

Richard turns to his wife, "Scout will be starting at Ursuline in August, like Lissy."

"That's right! Did you hear that, Larissa? I'm sure you'll be the best of friends."

Larissa's cold, silent appraisal suggests otherwise.

Scout waves. "Hi. I'm Scout. I have a mermaid bathroom. Wanna come see it?"

Larissa wrinkles her nose and rolls her eyes, but we're all saved from an awkward rejection by Kiki, who tugs on Paris's shoulder and says silkily, "Like I said, we won't keep you. Some other time, definitely, though, Scout! We're just over there." She points to a massive stucco-and-tile villa's tower we can see over the houses directly across the street from us. "Not quite on the same street, but still close."

Richard watches his household's feminine contingent back away and waves off his wife's less-than-subtle silent entreaties to come with them. "I'll be right there," he says, turning back to Jet and me.

"Thanks for coming over to say hi," Jet says.

"And for the wine," I add, lifting the bottle. I'm nowhere near a wine connoisseur, but I assume this one is of a higher-end price point than the ones I usually imbibe—not that it's hard to outprice my typical brands.

Richard beams. "You're welcome. Of course!" He claps Jet on his bare shoulder. "I'm happy for you that your family's finally joined you, and you're getting settled in, making yourself at home here. There's no better place on Earth than right here." He turns to me. "You'll see. You'll fall in love like everyone else does."

I tug on my earlobe and hope my smile doesn't seem too forced. "I can see why people do," I say as diplomatically as possible without committing myself. "It's beautiful."

"You picked a beauty of a home, too," he says, gesturing toward the inside. "Kiki was the seller's agent, so I guess I have you to thank for some of the money in our bank account." He winks.

"Yeah, thanks for giving me the heads up about this place," Jet says. "And Ursuline Academy for Scout. You've been a huge help. We really appreciate it."

"Don't mention it, man. Just… be as big a stud in the booth as you were on the field, and we'll call it even."

With an eager-to-please grin, Jet shakes Richard's hand. "You got it. I won't let you down."

## FOUR

## MAURA'S HIGHLIGHT REELS

*Replay #4: Five Years Ago*

*"What the small-town police force didn't know—couldn't imagine—at the time was that the body of the missing woman was literally right under their feet, buried in the sand underneath the climbing rope on their training course behind the station. The killer was taunting them, trolling them, daring them to try to catch him. Police Chief Ronald Weymeyer—"*

I flinched, my eyes flying open, as the left can of the noise-canceling headphones came away from my ear, bringing a rush of cooler air to the side of my head.

Jet smiled tenderly at my reaction and whispered, "Sorry. Didn't mean to scare you." He gently removed the headgear completely and set it on the nightstand.

I glanced down at the half-latched, milk-drunk newborn at my breast and verified she was almost finished with breakfast. Second breakfast, technically. But who was counting?

Podcasts were my salvation. They got me through every uncomfortable feeding, and I even found one I could play through the overhead speakers that soothed Scout to sleep. She liked Oprah's voice more than mine, I suspected. Who could blame her, though? I was partial to podcasts of the true crime variety, myself. I just wasn't sure if it would permanently damage my child to let her listen to them, even at that young age.

While tucking away my built-in portable feeding system, I held back emotion as Jet planted a long, lingering kiss on our sleeping daughter's soft spot. Then he turned his head and kissed my lips. Still whispering, he said miserably, "I don't want to go."

"You have to," I murmured back, although I wanted to clutch at the front of his shirt and hold him there in our bed, begging him to stay, to not leave me alone with such a massive responsibility so soon.

*I'm not ready. I can't do this!* every part of me screamed.

"I've got this," I lied magnificently.

He straightened but remained seated on the side of the mattress. "I know you do, beautiful. I want to have it, too."

"You will again. In roughly…" I closed one eye and did the math. "Forty-five hours." I stroked the bridge of the baby's nose as she stirred at our voices, now at normal volume.

"This season's going to suck."

Assuming he was referring to the mass exodus of retiring veterans after the team's latest Super Bowl appearance (and loss), I said, "It's a rebuilding year. Maybe some of the new guys will surprise you, though. Only one way to find out: preseason."

"No, I mean, being away from you and Bump—I mean, Scout," he amended at his use of the unisex pregnancy nickname the baby couldn't seem to shake, to my dismay. "It's gonna blow."

"Oh. Yeah." I swallowed the lump in my throat. "We'll get through it, though. No choice, right?"

"Right."

He sank for more kisses, and I chuckled. "You're going to miss the bus, champ."

With one last sniff of newborn head, he groaned and rose. "Yeah, yeah. I'm going."

I lifted Scout's tiny hand for a wave. "Bye, Daddy. No heroics. It's just the pre-season."

"Got it."

"Come back to us in one piece, please."

Crossing the room, he turned in the doorway for one last look at us and paused, as if committing the scene to memory. I quickly forced the corners of my mouth to rise. "Love you!"

With a choked "Love you, too," he ducked into the hallway.

I held my breath and counted his footsteps down the stairs. I waited, tensed, for the amount of time I estimated it would take him to get into his car and drive away. After a reasonable interval had passed, I relaxed into the pillows and gasped for air while I fought off the tears.

Damn hormones. Still raging. I pressed my lips and nose to the top of Scout's head, where Jet's lips had been so recently, and breathed in her baby scent, the air hitching in my chest on every inhale.

She sighed peacefully in her sleep, punctuating her exhale with a guttural grunt that helped joy punch a pinhole through my sadness and panic.

"You're stuck with me now," I said against her silky black hair.

I eased my arm out from under the swaddled newborn and settled her onto the mattress. Rising, I winced at the tenderness I still felt every time I moved, but I looked down at the person Jet and I made, and everything else disappeared. It didn't matter that my boobs felt like they were about to burst or that I had stitches in a place I thought only inept gymnasts, clumsy cyclists, or parkour enthusiasts needed. It didn't even matter that I was scared to death at the possibility of failing at my most important job, to-date. Failure wasn't an option. Quitting wasn't, either.

"We've got this," I whispered to the stirring baby, thinking maybe if I said it enough times, it would be true.

She half-smiled in her sleep, and just when my heart was about to melt at how much her mouth looked like Jet's, she grimaced and farted.

I giggled and shook my head. "Yep. Just like your daddy."

### *Replay #5: Five Years Ago*

When Jet came home after the longest forty-eight hours of my life, that first weekend away from Scout and me, he scooped her up from her bassinet in the library, where I had been trying to read to pass the time as I waited on his return, and held her away from his body, her head in one of his massive hands and butt in the other, gazing adoringly into her face.

"Hey, there," he said to her. "Did ya miss me?"

The sleeping baby didn't respond, but we *had* missed him, so much that at times, for me, it was a physical ache. I blamed the hormones. After all, it's not like the separation was a new thing for him and me.

At that time, we'd been together three years, all of it marked by the various milestones of the football pre-season, season, post-season, and off-season. Those *our* four seasons.

When we found out I was pregnant, we knew the timing of Scout's birth—right before the start of another football season —wasn't going to be perfect, but I had no idea it would be *that* hard. For all of us. I was convinced that Scout could feel the difference, too. While Jet was gone, she was fussier, less content to sleep alone in her bassinet, and harder to soothe.

I watched their reunion through a waterfall, eventually breaking down completely, covering my face in both hands as if that would hide my outburst.

Almost immediately, the couch cushion next to mine dipped, and sobbing, I sagged against Jet's solid body. When I lowered my hands and opened my eyes to apologize, he shushed me. Cradling Scout in one arm, he wrapped me in his other and kissed my wet cheek. "Oh, beautiful. It's going to be okay."

"It *is* okay!" I wailed. "It's fine. Better than fine. Our life is p-p-p-perfect!" Again, the tears overwhelmed me.

Scout, picking up on my distress, woke and fussed, each grunt becoming more and more indignant until she, too, succumbed to a full-scale fit. Her cries triggered my breasts to open their levees—quite painfully, I might add—so I reached out for her and latched her to one of them.

Jet sighed at the two of us. "That is one of the prettiest pictures," he said, somewhat sadly.

I had a hard time believing that a red-eyed, snotty-faced me was part of a pretty anything, so I asked him to get the box of tissues from my desk. When he came back with them, I pulled one from the top and mopped my face with my free hand.

"Babe, it'll get easier," he said.

"Don't call me babe," I reflexively shot back with a weak pretend scowl.

"There she is. That's better."

Through more tears, I said, "I'm sorry," my voice breaking on the last word.

He knelt in front of me and kissed my knee. "There's nothing to apologize for."

"It's the hormones."

"I'm sure."

"No, really. They're intense. It's awful. I feel insane."

"Maybe you should call your doctor and—"

"Not *that* insane."

"You never know, though. O'Doyle's wife had that depression some women get after having babies."

"Post partum."

"That's it. It was serious. She went on medication, though, and it helped a lot."

"Betsy had a reason to be depressed, though. They have, like, a billion kids."

"It only takes one."

"*And* she's married to O'Doyle."

"Fair point." Though he remained smiling, his forehead crinkled seriously, and his eyes locked with mine. "Still. Call the doctor, just in case." When I opened my mouth to object, he cut me off. "For *me*. I'll worry about you when I'm not here."

"You don't have to worry. I'm not going to *do* anything."

"I know *you* wouldn't, Maura. But if you're not feeling like yourself— Please. You don't have to feel this way."

I patted his hand and promised him I'd call the doctor first thing in the morning.

When I did, she asked me a series of questions over the phone to determine if I was a danger to myself or others. According to her, I wasn't. Nevertheless, she offered to prescribe me something to ease the depression while my hormones regulated. I declined, even though she reassured me I could continue breastfeeding with no worries. Instead, I made an appointment to see her in person in a week.

When I hung up the phone, I said to an expectant Jet, who'd been listening to my side of the conversation, "She says I'm normal."

"I'd like a second opinion."

I slapped his shoulder.

"Ow!" He rubbed the spot. "But you're going to see her next week?"

"Yes. I still can't drive, so I scheduled it on Wednesday when you can take me."

"Perfect. Thank you."

"You're welcome."

I never went the chemical route to ease my symptoms, but I did agree to counseling. I went every other week, my appointments coinciding with one of Scout's afternoon naps. She slept at my feet in her car seat carrier while I sat in a leather-and-chrome chair and cried to a stranger about loneliness and feelings of inadequacy as a mother, a wife, and a business owner. It was completely self-indulgent but cathartic. It worked.

After about eight sessions, the counselor released me from her care, checking in on me once a month to make sure I wasn't teeth-gritting my way through life. I wasn't. By then, I truly was more content and no longer resisting my feelings—good or bad. Merely acknowledging them and moving on was a game-changer for me. No more brooding. No more shame. Acceptance brought peace. It made me a more confident caregiver. I wasn't so uptight and worried all the time. It left a lot more time for fun and love and just enjoying Scout at every stage.

Through technology, I shared videos and pictures with Jet so he didn't miss anything when he was away from home. And when he was home, we were intentional with our time together as often as we could be, with Scout as the lynch pin.

It's incredible how one little bundle of limbs and organs can completely change your entire world—a world you already thought was pretty damn near perfect—for the better.

Most days.

*Replay #6: Five Years Ago*

A couple of weeks later, newborn Scout experienced her first NFL game—on television, that is. Obviously, she didn't do much watching. Who knows how much babies can even see from a digital screen like that? But the sights and sounds of football were going to be a big part of her life, so it was time to introduce her to them.

I clicked on the television and tuned into the banal pre-game chatter of the third pre-season match-up. There was the usual speculation about the rebuilt team, the effects of a Super Bowl loss on the psyche of the returning players, the attitudes of the fans, and Jet's mega contract (a topic that took forever to die).

Then things turned a little more personal, as if by this week, the announcers were sick of talking about the same things and needed some juicy material to gnaw on.

*"Knox also became a first-time father in the off-season, just a few weeks ago, in fact. Ben, you and I can both attest to how that can affect a player."*

Ben chortled. *"Yeah. We try to downplay it, right, because you* leave everything else in the locker room when you take to the field, supposedly. But it doesn't really work that way. Stuff off the field always has some effect."

"True, true. But Knox is a veteran and a professional. I don't expect it'll be that much of a factor, do you?"

"I have one word for him: nanny."

The two sexists chuckled at their clever banter and pitched it to commercial, promising the game would start after the break.

I kicked my foot against the floor to get Jet's easy chair rocking and muttered down to Scout, "Don't listen to them. They're old farts with no idea. Probably sat in a waiting room when their wives gave birth—if they were even there at all—and never changed a diaper in their lives. I bet they were glad, not sad, when it was time for them to go on the road every week, escaping their responsibilities at home. Your dad's not like that. He'll play harder to make us proud. That's how he operates."

She grunted and clawed at her face.

Gently, I drew her hands down and held both of them in my own. "I was skeptical, too, when he first told me that. But it's turned out to be true." I kissed her nose. "You and I are an inspiration, not a distraction."

Her response was to fill her pants, which was exactly the reply those announcers deserved.

The commercial break was over by the time I finished changing her diaper, and as promised, kickoff occurred. The starters played the entire first half, as is typical of that third practice game, before handing it over to the second stringers. Relieved when there were no heroics or showing off, I relaxed when Jet removed his helmet for the last time and switched to a visor while he caught his breath on the bench, gladly accepting a water bottle from one of the sideline crew and squirting a healthy stream into his mouth.

I finished nursing Scout for about the millionth time that day (again, like father, like daughter), and was just about to heave myself to my feet to use the bathroom when I heard my husband's name. I zoomed back into the television screen. Like a silly teenager with a crush, my heart actually skipped when he appeared on camera, all smiles for Erin Matheny, everyone's favorite sideline interviewer. I perched on the front edge of the recliner to hang on his every word.

*"We're here with Chiefs quarterback, Jet Knox. Jet, what are your hopes for this season, knowing that the guys you made so many post-season runs with are no longer here, and you have so many new teammates to get to know?"*

*He chuckled, lifted his visor a few inches, and wiped sweat from his forehead. Settling his hat again, he said, "I dunno. We just play. Of course, my hope is that we get the job done and have a lot of great seasons ahead of us. But building relationships takes time, you know? We have a good vibe already, but we're going to have to work hard to get to know each other. That's pretty normal."*

*"Do you feel like this team has what it takes to get the job done, to get you back to the big show?"*

*Shrugging, he frowned thoughtfully while grasping his pads up near his collarbone. "We have an awesome team with amazing talent and some great new plays that really take advantage of our strengths. We'll see. We'll see. It'll be fun to watch, no matter what."*

*"You also have a new teammate at home, I hear. Congratulations on the birth of your daughter."*

*His grin returned. "Yeah, thanks! She's— Oh, man, she's somethin' else. Not too big on night sleeping yet, so if you see me napping on the bench, you'll understand."*

*She pulled the microphone back. "Jet Knox gets up in the middle of the night for feedings and diaper changes?"*

*"Heck yeah, I do! I'm a dad. That's what dads do. I love it. Well, maybe not the really dirty diapers—they're no fun—but you take the good with the bad."*

*"A real team player, huh?"*

*"Absolutely. It's the least I can do." He looked straight into the camera and blew it a kiss. "Hey, Scout, Maura! Love you guys! See you in a few!"*

*"We'll leave it there, guys," the reporter said into the camera. "That's one happy quarterback who seems pretty optimistic about this season and life in general. Back to you in the booth."*

The shot switched to the action on the field, but the commentators remained focused on Jet's words, mostly what he said about his new teammates and how he had his work cut out for him this season on the field. Then they chuckled about how it sounded like he had his work cut out for him at home, too, as the series ended, and they threw to commercial.

Still warm and glowing from the shout-out, I gazed down at Scout, who blinked up at me as she tried to focus on my face. "See? Your daddy loves us." She wiggled and kicked her legs, her face screwing up into a pre-tantrum grimace.

I hurried her to the nearest diaper bag. "Yeah, you're wet and don't care. But someday, it'll matter to you."

It mattered a lot to me.

### Replay #7: Two-and-a-Half Years Ago

"It's a boo-tiful day…" The creepy whisper brushed against my cheek.

I batted it away and groaned. "Jeeeeetttt."

"It's your turn," he mumbled back.

"You owe me infinite turns," I replied, referring to all the times I'd been the only parent home while he traveled during football season.

He rolled over, smacking his lips and adjusting his head on his pillow. "Starting tomorrow. I promise."

A tiny finger poked me right under my eye, in the bag I could feel forming there from too many late nights and early mornings in a row. "Mommy," Scout hissed. "Time to get up."

"Go tell Daddy that, sweetheart. He loves getting up early."

"Don't come over here, Scout," Jet said. "I'll yawn my dragon breath in your face."

She giggled. "Daddy!"

I pushed against his shoulder and felt it shake with his suppressed laughter.

"If you get in this bed," he continued with his disgusting threats, "I'll fart and trap you under the covers."

Of course, that immediately resulted in the nearly three-year-old calling his bluff, scrambling onto the mattress—kneeing my crotch in the process—and nestling between her father and me. She pressed her face into his back, between his shoulder blades. "Fart, Daddy! Fart!"

"Don't do it, Jet! I'll mule kick you."

"Should I do it, Bump?"

Scout giggled but didn't answer otherwise.

He twisted to look over his shoulder at her. Big mistake. The first rule of negotiating with a toddler: don't make eye contact. They'll get you every time with their melty eyes and poochy rosebud lips. "Get up, Daddy. It's a boo-tiful day."

"How do you know? It's still dark outside!"

"Every day is boo-tiful, Daddy."

"Well, it'll be beautiful an hour from now, too. With sun."

"I'm hungry! Where's Bobo?"

Ah. The truth finally emerged.

"It's Bobo's day off," I said, purposely repeating her adorable nickname for our personal chef and drawing her closer to me so I could kiss her strawberry-scented dark curls. "We talked about that last night."

"Waffles, Mommy," she said, poking me in the chest. "You said."

"Oh, my gosh. You did. I heard you."

Whoever decided it was a good idea for us to be parents was wrong. So, so, wrong.

Resigned to getting up, I kissed her velvety face and swung my legs over the side of the bed. "Fine. I figured it would be after sunrise, but…"

"Yay!" While she navigated the bed and slid onto the bench at the foot of it, she said, "C'mon, Daddy! Mommy's making waffles! With booberries."

"I do like booberries," he said, still not moving.

Scout giggled. "L's were her most challenging letters to master, but she never got upset when we teased her about it. Instead, it seemed to serve as a reminder for her to slow down and try again. She liked nothing better than to use the opportunity to correct *us*, too.

On cue, she said, "They're buh-loo-berries, Daddy."

"Blueberries. Right. I love blueberries."

"Wet's go, then! Hurry up!"

By the time I finished using the toilet, they were both gone. Torzi, trying to sleep on the chair by the window, gave me the side-eye and a long-suffering snort. "Trust me, I know," I said to him. "You're not the only one feeling old this morning, Bub."

The previous two years had been one big blur of baby gear,

toddler gear, and kids' gear, mixed in with the usual cycle of off-season, pre-season, season, and post-season activity. Diapers and bottles and strollers, replaced by potty chairs and sippy cups. And still, I wouldn't go back and change any of it.

Okay, maybe I would have gotten more consecutive hours of sleep that first year. But from what I'd been told over and over and over again by other parents—mostly mothers, who *love* to kvetch and one-up each other with childbirth and parenting horror stories—we'd been lucky with Scout. She fell into a regular pattern of sleep within the first two weeks of her life and had always been okay with sleeping in her own bassinet, crib, or bed. Still, even when a newborn is sleeping "well," that's a max of four hours between feedings. And since she was born right before the season started, I did most of it alone those first few months.

I considered getting a "night nanny," but by the time I finished agonizing over how ridiculous that felt, she was sleeping through the night, and it was a moot point.

A "before sunrise" nanny was more appropriate as she got older and had the freedom to get out of bed whenever she wanted. However, the phase of sweet wake-ups was one I was secretly okay with lingering for a while.

I took the back stairs to the kitchen and found Jet and Scout waiting expectantly at the island, her bright-eyed and wide awake, him yawning and grinding his fists into his eye sockets. On my way past the coffeemaker, I overrode the automatic brew setting to get it started right away, rather than an hour from then, when it was set to kick on.

"Orange juice, please!" Scout sang.

While I was in the fridge getting the orange juice, I collected the blueberries, milk, butter, eggs, and heavy whipping cream, too, and slid them onto the island. As I got a cup for Scout, I swept through the other cabinets for a mixing bowl and the waffle iron, then rummaged through drawers for a whisk, spatula, and utensils. I dropped the armload of gear on the island and said to Jet, "Don't move. I've got this."

"I'm just staying out of the way," he said sleepily.

"Oh, is that what you're doing? Because it looks like you're waiting to be served."

He slid the container of orange juice closer to him and plucked the cup from the mixing bowl. "Here. I'll pour her juice."

"So helpful of you."

"I'm a team player. You know that."

"Mmm-hmm."

His job finished, he capped the bottle and plunked his elbow on the counter, jamming his fist into his cheek and closing his eyes.

Scout loudly gulped down her first serving and slammed her small plastic cup on the bar like a pub patron. "More, pwease!"

Jet obliged, smirking at me as if proving a point about his helpfulness.

I rolled my eyes and turned away from them to hunt down the dry ingredients for the waffles. The toughest thing to find was the white flour. Beau only cooked with the whole wheat stuff, but when *I* made breakfast, we did it right. By "right," I mean "as unhealthy as possible."

I finally found the good stuff, shoved at the back of the pantry, behind a stack of emergency canned goods Beau would never stoop to serve us and that were probably outdated. The white granulated and powdered sugars were back there, too. He thought he was so smart.

I came back to the kitchen with two bags of white stuff and wiggled my eyebrows at Jet. "Lookie what I found."

He perked up at the sight of the flour and powdered sugar. "Well, well, well. Hello, my old friends."

"Now that it's the off-season, you can eat this without worrying."

Rubbing his hands together, he hissed, "Yesssss. Don't forget the booberries," while I mixed all of the ingredients together to make the waffle batter.

I dumped in some of the tiny, navy blue berries and continued stirring. "There. Lots of booberries."

Before our daughter could correct us, we said together, "Buh-loo-berries!"

She nodded proudly at the two of us, and it was all I could do to resist rounding the island and smothering her earnest face in kisses.

## FIVE

## FAMILIAR, BUT DIFFERENT

When I awake before sunrise, completely disoriented and unsure of my surroundings, to the sounds of a doorknob rattling, I shoot up in bed and shake Jet's shoulder.

"*Mph mph mph*," he muffles into his pillow from his prone position.

"Jet," I hiss, still shaking him, after recalling where we are. "Something's wrong."

He groans and rolls over. "What?"

"Someone's at our door."

We both remain motionless, listening.

"I don't hear anything," he finally says, more than a little irritation in his tone. "You were probably having one of your crazy-ass dreams." He moves to tug the covers more fully over his naked body and roll over again, but the rattling resumes, freezing him in place.

"Mommy! Daddy!"

Both of us spring into action, scrambling from the bed, running in different directions when we realize our dressers are empty, but we also don't remember where we set down our luggage. Is my closet on the left or the right?

"Mommy!" The doorknob rattles, and she adds banging to the racket.

"I'm coming, sweetie!" I yell, finally finding my suitcases and rooting through them for the one pair of pajamas I packed.

Jet stumbles past the closet doorway, wrapped in our comforter.

"What are you doing?" I ask.

He doubles back. "Opening the door for Scout."

"Like that?"

"I'm covered."

"Yeah, but—"

"Daddy! Mommy! Why is your door locked?"

"Why *is* our door locked?" I ask.

"I locked it last night. Just in case Scout got up and tried to come in here while we were... you know."

After we tucked in our daughter last night and read from her favorite children's historical book about Pompeii, she didn't want us to leave her.

"I'm scared," she said, a sudden development I didn't quite believe. Nevertheless, Jet and I spent the next ten minutes reassuring her about the traffic noise from the nearby street, the unfamiliar sounds of neighbors, the rarity of coyotes in a neighborhood as populated as this one, the impossibility of said rare coyote gaining entrance to the closed-up, locked-down house, and myriad other worries manufactured to prolong bedtime and possibly procure an invitation to sleep with us for the first night.

Fortunately, Jet and I were on the same page about that being a hard "no," and we stood firm. I turned on her bathroom light and the hallway lights so she wouldn't have to lie in the dark or wake up not knowing where she was. Then we gave her a final kiss, turned on her white noise machine in an attempt to drown out some of the unusual ambient noise that she claimed was bothering her, and headed toward our own room on the other side of the house.

We didn't even make it past the kitchen before she was calling for us again.

In the end, Jet agreed to go back to her room with me to settle her down, and this time, we sat with her until she fell asleep. Jet rubbed her feet and legs while I played with her hair. It took twenty minutes, but when she finally gave it up, she was out cold.

Fizzy bubbles swim through my veins, most rushing to one particular area of my body, as I remember what happened next. Like horny teenagers, Jet and I ran, giggling, on tiptoes across the house to our new bedroom, where we proceeded to christen it. And the bathroom. And sitting area. Yes, it would have been traumatic, indeed, for Scout to have walked in on any of that. Locking the door was a good call.

Obviously thinking better of greeting our daughter in a bedspread with nothing on underneath, Jet crosses the hallway that separates our closets and opens his carry-on duffel bag, efficiently digging out a t-shirt and shorts. He shucks off the coverlet, leaving it in a heap in the middle of his closet, and slides on the shorts before yanking the t-shirt over his head. Smoothing down his hair, he reappears in the doorway to my closet and asks, "Is this better?"

"Yes. Now, if I could just find something to put on."

"Take your time," he says, catching his breath. "I've got this."

"Tell her I'll be right there, and I'm so sorry she got scared and couldn't get to us."

Shaking his head and chuckling, he waves off my message. "I'm sure she's fine. There's no need to be *sorry*."

"Waking up in a brand new place is disorienting and scary for a little kid. Tell her I'll be there in a sec."

"Yeah, yeah…"

"And I *am* sorry!" I call after him.

For someone who was so ambivalent about motherhood, I did an immediate one-eighty as soon as our daughter was born. I can't imagine life without her. I barely do remember it before her. It's like she's always been around. Even though being a mom is the hardest, most exhausting thing I've ever done—and "hard and exhausting" have never been two of my favorite things—it's the best part of my life. Truly.

Even at 5 a.m. on a Saturday.

———

"I want a turtle backpack, but all they have are these ones, and they're for babies," Scout whines at me, crowding against my side at my desk as we look online at the preferred retailer for Ursuline Academy's school supplies.

I've finally turned my full attention to her after multiple stall tactics that worked for a surprisingly long time as I sat on the phone with Nina, discussing the possibility of an assistant manager for her at the Kansas City Knox Theater. Now that I'm no longer local, she'll be taking on some of the off-site responsibilities I used to handle. We need someone in charge during her frequent absences and to handle the more mundane management duties.

The call took longer than I anticipated, considering neither she nor I were particularly eager to pull the trigger on a decision that would make this not-so-new arrangement finally permanent in our minds. Until our conversation today, we've both seemed able to trick ourselves into thinking I've been on a three-week vacation—or something. Officially changing our job descriptions takes it to another level, a level that feels almost as scary as that first step into franchising the theater a couple of years ago. This is real. This is happening.

What's also happening is Scout's entitled tone, which I don't appreciate at all. "These are your choices," I tell her, referring to the backpacks on the screen in front of us. Or you can go with something completely different. Look, here's a plain one in turquoise, your favorite color."

She sighs. "Yeah. I guess. I kind of have a new favorite color now, though."

"Oh?" This is news to me. I lift her onto my lap and kiss her temple, thankful she's dropped the whine. "What's your new fave?" I glance at the clock in the lower right corner of the screen, checking to see how long it'll be before Jet gets home and can take over the school supplies shopping chore.

"Teal."

"Teal?" I picture the color in my head and find it not all that different from turquoise.

"Teal."

"Aren't they almost the same thing?"

"It's easier to say."

"That, it is."

"It's darker, and more green."

"You're right. Very good. We can search for teal backpacks, then."

With her begrudging assent, I filter our search to narrow down our choices and, hopefully, expedite this process. Still, several dozen results pop up. Scout has to look at every single one before finally deciding on one we saw on the first page of results. I stifle my sigh, and we move on to the next item on the ultra-specific list sent to us by Ursuline.

Just when I'm about to run screaming from the room while clawing out my eyes, we hear the garage door open from the other side of the wall next to us.

"Dad's home!" I say, catching my near-hysterical tone and bringing it down a notch. "I bet he'd love to discuss the pros and cons of liquid glue versus glue stick."

Scout runs to the door where she knows her dad will appear and stands against the wall next to it, putting her index finger to her lip to implore me to silence.

To Jet's credit, when he comes through the door and she jumps out to scare him, like she's done every work day for the past three weeks, he pretends to startle. Each day, he's done something different, impressing me with his creativity. Today, he adds the flourish of a high-pitched squeal and pretends to stagger backward down the two steps that lead from the study into the garage. Scout collapses on the floor in gales of giggles.

"Oh, my gosh! You scared the poo out of me, Bump."

"No, I didn't!" she says through her laughter. "You knew I was going to do that."

He crawls up the steps, grinning slyly. "Okay, maybe I had an idea you would, but you were so much scarier than I expected!"

He has no idea what "scary" is until I set him loose on this school supplies list.

Grasping her ankle, he drags her toward him and tickles her until she claims she's going to pee her pants. Then he rises to his feet and picks her up, making her look little again up against him. With a tweak to her nose, he asks, "So, what'd you guys do while I was out working my butt off, huh?" He glances at the retail website on my computer monitor as he leans down to kiss my upturned lips. "Shopping? Figures!"

I disconnect my laptop from its desk dock and hand it to him. "And now you get to continue the fun. School supplies. The list is in my email."

Tucking the computer under his free arm, he adjusts Scout on his hip. "Goody. Chiefs everything! Done."

Scout laughs. "No, Daddy! We have to get what they tell us to get."

"Don't deviate from the list," I say in my best schoolmarm tone.

He kicks closed the door to the garage and sets Scout on her feet. "How hard can it be? It's kindergarten. Crayons, paste, safety scissors—"

"All brand-specific. From a very particular school-approved online retailer. And no paste. Glue only."

"What are they going to eat for snack?" He winks at Scout, then stage whispers, "Don't eat the paste."

"She won't, because she won't have any. Modeling clay, yes."

"Don't eat the modeling clay, either," he says, still whispering.

She wrinkles her nose. "I'm not a baby! You don't have to tell me that."

"Right. Good. Well, I guess I can check 'the talk' off my back-to-school checklist." He draws a check mark in the air in front of himself.

For someone who's supposedly worked all day, he's full of energy. I wish I could say the same. I'd suggest that he take care of dinner, but that would stick me back with the school supplies list, and I've had my fill of that.

They follow me out to the kitchen, asking at nearly the same time what we're having for dinner.

I bite down on the inside of my cheeks to prevent snapping, then answer, "I'm not sure yet. Whatever's easiest, probably." It's not their fault I'm tetchy because of what's going on at The Knox, so I'm determined not to take it out on them. That determination, however, is almost as wearing as the original stress.

As is typical, Scout assumes a much more easygoing attitude with her father, and thanks to this cooperation, they've ordered everything on the list before I've finished cooking. He shuttles her off to play in her room, which she does without complaint or argument, another benefit of being the dad.

"I'll be right back," he says to me, then disappears into our room. Soon, he reemerges in a t-shirt and shorts, rubbing his hands as he approaches the kitchen. "What do you need me to do?" he asks.

"Set the table?" I say distractedly.

"You got it."

While he clangs around in cupboards and drawers, I continue my unnecessary watchful study of the mixture of meat, rice, beans, cheese, and tomatoes in the skillet on the stove in front of me.

"That smells awesome," he says close to my ear a few minutes later, startling me. "You okay?" he asks on a chuckle, looking into the pan and plucking a tomato chunk from the top of the mixture. "You seem quiet."

"I'm fine," I answer in a way that every husband knows holds the opposite meaning.

He freezes, mid-chew. "What happened? Did I do something dumb?"

I laugh at his sudden seriousness and paranoia. "Nothing. And no. I'm tired. It's been a long week. School supplies shopping didn't help."

"I told you to save it for me. I love crap like that."

"I know, but Scout was eager to do it, and I ignored her all afternoon, so when she brought it up for the millionth time, I just went with it."

"Gotcha. Well, we knocked it out like that." He snaps. "Now you have the rest of the evening—and the weekend, if you want—to relax."

Since he's trying so hard, I decide to have mercy on him. "Yeah. Relaxing will be nice."

"You sure there's nothing wrong?"

If I voice my biggest worry right now—that I'm becoming obsolete in my own life's mission, so far removed from the action—I'll cry, so I turn my attention to spooning servings of the taco-seasoned ingredients into the tortilla-lined bowls Jet has so helpfully placed on the counter next to the stove.

Injecting as much cheer as I can muster into it, I say, "Dinner's ready!" and hope he doesn't notice—or care—that I haven't answered his question.

Whatever the case is, he lets the matter drop and carries two of the bowls to the dinette table, calling for Scout when he passes the hallway to her room.

As the conversation centers once again around our daughter and how "super-awesome" kindergarten is going to be and how excited she is to start school, my melancholy and panic pass.

Change is okay. Everything's going to be okay.

## SIX

## COFFEE, TEA, AND KIKI

The invitation came via courier—sort of. Paris Valentine screeched into our driveway in her aquamarine Porsche convertible one afternoon and, car left running with the door open, trotted to our front door on long, tan legs. I watched all of this from my desk in front of the window in the study like it were a movie.

The surreal experience continued as the teen unenthusiastically handed me a heavy-stocked envelope upon my answering the door. Before I could even thank her, much less open the envelope lavishly bearing mine and Scout's names and slide out the card inside, she was loping away again, folding herself into her fast car and shooting backwards from our driveway like she was fleeing the scene of a crime. Without another look my way, she burned rubber on the asphalt in front of our house and squealed her way from the neighborhood, leaving me to wonder if I'd imagined the whole thing.

The card in my hand was proof that it had happened,

however, and when I opened it, it revealed a foil-embossed invitation that said:

*You're cordially invited to tea. RSVP*

Drawn in beautiful calligraphy underneath those words were:

*Maura & Scout,*
*Please join Larissa and me (Kiki) tomorrow at 2:00 p.m. for a*
*girls' tea party!*

In a more natural but still precise and lovely handwriting below the calligraphy was, "Call and let me know if this day and time works for you, or if we need to reschedule. —Kiki."

Tucked into the envelope was a business card with about a dozen ways to contact her. With quite some trepidation, I chose the mobile phone number and called to accept.

Arriving at this moment, therefore, was as simple—however strange—as that. All red-tiled roof and pale yellow stucco, the Valentine house looks like the headquarters of a Colombian drug lord, which is fitting. Instead of cocaine or heroine, though, Kiki and Richard are peddling something else, something you sometimes can't buy with all the money in the world: belonging. Personally, I could go without, but it means a lot to Scout at this time in her life, so I'm willing to subject myself to something I never would have bothered with in a million years, were it just about me: a good old-fashioned tea date.

My instinct to dress up was a rare stroke of inspiration that panned out, so Scout and I are decked out in sundresses and sandals, looking like we're heading to the racetrack for Derby

Day. The only things missing are some outrageous hats. I balked at any headwear. That was a fortunate call, considering our hosts aren't sporting any, either. For once, I got it just right. My powers of observation are paying off.

I've seen women like Kiki around town, but she's the first one I've actually met and talked to. Her kind are fairly unapproachable. They give off "Don't engage me," vibes in public and definitely aren't the type of people you strike up a casual conversation with in line at the store or coffee shop. They tend to travel in pairs or packs, too, which multiplies their standoffishness exponentially. Overheard conversations among them—and they make sure they're overheard—usually center around "the help" or "the industry" or the latest cosmetic procedures they've sought. Terms like microblading, coolsculpting, and mesotherapy, among others, abound. (I've looked them all up, and I'd be lying if I said I wasn't tempted by a few.)

Included in some of their ranks are celebrities, but I've recognized very few, surprisingly. I thought I'd be bumping into actors everywhere I went around here. Not so. Or if I am, they're doing a great job of flying under the radar.

For the most part, the most glamorous people I see seem to be that increasingly rare breed of "women who lunch," although not much lunching is going on. Eating is counterproductive to their goal of looking fabulous all the time. Maybe the term should be updated to "women who exercise" or "women who chat."

Now, if only I could figure out what to chat about. I've already complimented the house and their outfits, the delicate tea service, the tea, the cucumber sandwiches, and the scones. I'm out. Unfortunately, Kiki seems content to watch me squirm. She simpers over her teacup and occasionally offers me more tea or food, but otherwise, she's not at all eager to fill the silence.

Before it becomes too awkward, Scout rescues me—sort of —by saying, "Did you know that whales barf after every time they eat?"

I smile tightly and say, "Scout, sweetie, this is probably not the best time to talk about that, when *we're* eating."

She frowns. "It's not a big deal. It's just that their tummies can't break down stuff like squid beaks, so they come back up sometimes."

"Grosssss!" Larissa yells.

"Sometimes, though, it stays inside them, and after they eat lots of squids and stuff, they make this blob of stuff that comes out their behinds." She sets down her teacup so she can use both hands to demonstrate. "It has a fancy name: 'Amber-griss.'"

I place a nervous hand on her knee. "Okay, thanks for the info, cutie. I think we get it."

"Why I said that is because I can smell that you're wearing perfume," she says to Kiki. "It smells very pretty, too."

"Thank you," Kiki says graciously through her own forced smile.

"And," Scout continues, "people who make perfume pay lots and lots and lots of money for ambergris, because they use it in perfume."

Kiki's mouth slowly slides downward. "Really?"

"Yeah! It's waxy, so it helps the smell of the perfume stick to your skin longer."

"Ugh, Mom! You have whale poop on you!" Larissa squeals, equal parts delighted and repulsed.

"That's enough, Scout," I say more firmly now, but Kiki clears her throat and tilts her head.

"And where did you learn about this… *ambergris*, Scout?" she asks pleasantly, as if we're talking about the weather or the price of milk.

"YouTube," Scout says matter-of-factly, reaching for another scone. I don't stop her. Maybe if she goes back to eating, she'll stop talking. She takes a bite and, spraying crumbs, elaborates, "Kid's science video."

In one breath, I chide my child for talking with her mouth full and apologize to Kiki and Larissa for the shower of food particles, which I try to pluck from Scout's dress and the small table we're perched around.

"No need to apologize," Kiki says brightly and tightly with a belated chuckle. "Children do learn the oddest things nowadays, don't they?"

"Scout loves animals, don't you?" I say. "Just nod until you're finished chewing," I add in a rushed mutter.

She complies.

"Larissa does too! Something in common!"

Larissa wrinkles her nose. "Not like that, though. I like cute animals, not nasty, puking whales!"

"Even the cute animals do gross stuff," Scout says, having polished off her scone. "Like koala babies, they—"

"Nope!" I place my hand over her mouth, and she freezes. With a nervous chuckle, I say, "I've heard this one before, and it's— We're not going to talk about it right now. Or ever."

Kiki blinks. "Well, now I'm intrigued."

"No, no. It's—" I shake my head. "Anyway, school starts in about a month, right everyone?" Removing my hand from Scout's mouth, I daintily and discreetly wipe it on my cloth napkin. "Are you excited?" I direct this question to Larissa, hoping she'll provide some more mundane conversational fodder.

Instead, she shrugs and says in a bored tone, "I already know what it's like, because I went to pre-kindergarten, and it was BO-ring."

I can't help but laugh at the way she says it just like Scout and Jet do when they're teasing me about my unadventurous ideas of what constitutes a fun weekend.

"Now, now." Kiki shoots me a warning glare, presumably for encouraging her daughter's bad attitude.

I clear my throat and pretend to wipe my mouth.

Refocusing on her daughter, Kiki says, "We've talked about this, darling, haven't we? How attitude is important? Thinking positive thoughts produces positive feelings, which makes us happy. And other people like happy people, not sad sacks."

"Sad sacks!" Scout giggles. "I wonder if Daddy was a sad sack when he got sacked when he played football. Then he'd be a sacked sad sack."

I squeeze her hand, thankful for the mood lightener. Larissa rolls her eyes. Whether she's rolling them at us, her mother, or both, I can't be sure.

Kiki releases a tinkly laugh that sounds about as real as her lips look. "Scout, you're a clever girl. I can see where your little jokes and factoids might get you in trouble in school, though. You have to learn to keep some thoughts *inside* your head."

"Why?" she asks, suddenly serious, her eyes latched to Kiki's face.

"Well, because it's not necessary to tell everyone what you're thinking all of the time."

"Why not?"

"It can be disruptive."

"Why?"

Kiki defers to me with a sigh and a shake of her head that she tries to soften with wide, bright eyes. "Mom? Want to jump in here?"

I do, but nothing I can think to say to this woman at the moment seems appropriate in front of children. Tamping down my rising irritation and anger, I draw Scout into my lap and kiss her cheek. "You'll learn when it's time to talk and when it's time to be still and listen. That's part of school."

"Will the teacher yell at me if I don't do it right?"

"No!"

"Maybe," Kiki intones.

I blanch. "She better not."

Kiki shrugs as if she still thinks it could be a possibility, and I shouldn't shield my child from it.

Scout buries her face in my neck. "I don't want to get in trouble."

"You won't, sweetie. Being smart is a good thing. Your teacher will tell you nicely when it's time to be quiet. Just be yourself."

"Okay," she says with a sniffle.

I'm about to figure out a way to extricate us from this social situation when Kiki claps her hands sharply and says, "Okay, great! How about you girls go upstairs and play in Larissa's room so your mommies can have a little chat?"

Before I can make any excuses to leave, the kids scramble away from the table with Larissa babbling excitedly about "ten thousand Barbies."

Kiki and I are alone.

———

Much later, Jet, Scout, and I sit next to a teeming playground, furiously licking ice cream cones before they can melt into sticky rivers onto our hands and clothes. Even in the weakening, setting sun, with an occasional relieving breeze, we're losing this battle with the confections. Scout and I are, anyway. Jet's keeping up just fine.

His eyes seem glazed over, and he's barely said more than a sentence or two since emerging from the study before dinner. When Scout and I left for our tea party, he was shut up in there on a conference call about the network's coverage of upcoming team training camps, and he was still on that call until moments before dinner. I've asked him twice if he's okay, and he managed a weak half-smile and some muttered reassurances both times.

The second time, he elaborated a little more and said, "It's just a lot, you know? I mean..." He never finished that thought, and I didn't push him on it. I get it. New jobs are overwhelming.

A teetering triple-scoop of butterscotch ice cream in a waffle cone seems to have perked him up, though, and he finally takes the bait Scout's been dangling in front of him for the past two hours, trying to get him to show some interest in what she and I got up to this afternoon.

"Oh, yeah! The tea party!" he says, biting off part of the top edge of his cone to expose more ice cream. "How'd that go? Was it fancy?"

Scout practically throws her ice cream on the picnic table in favor of giving this conversation her full attention. I catch it at the last second and cast around for some napkins to set it on, in case any of it survives long enough for her to come back to it.

"Mommy didn't like that I talked about whale poop."

"So… not fancy, then?" He glances at me to check my reaction.

"It was pretty fancy until then," I say, licking a runaway drip of mint chocolate chip. "Whale poop tends to bring down the fancy factor."

He turns back to Scout. "Why'd you even bring that up, Bump? That's kind of a weird thing to talk about at a tea party."

She shrugs, seeming unconcerned about her social faux pas. "I dunno. Nobody was talking, so I just said the first thing I thought about."

"And that was whale poop?"

"I watched a YouTube video of it this morning while you and Mommy were still in bed."

"I see."

"Animals do a lot of gross things—even the really cute ones, like gerbils."

"Yes, they do. People do a lot of gross things—even the really cute ones." He pokes her in the side to get her to flinch and giggle.

"Can I *pleeeeeaaaaaase* get a gerbil for my birthday?"

He glances at me for backup, which I provide with a wide-eyed, panicked head-shake. Instead of answering her, he pretends to concentrate on where he's going to bite next on his cone and asks, "So, what else did you talk about at the tea party?"

Before I can reply—or more accurately, dodge the question in front of Scout—she readily does. "Well, I wanted to tell them about how baby koalas eat their moms' poo sometimes, but Mommy stopped me."

"Steering clear of all poo talk was probably for the best."

"Then Larissa took me upstairs to her room, and we

played with about a billion Barbies. She has *everything*, Daddy. All the playsets and houses, pools, cars, campers, clothes. And the dolls... So many of the dolls! But not any of the chubby ones."

While Jet splutters at that information, I pick up Scout's destroyed dessert and throw it in the nearby trash can with my own napkins and paper cone wrapping.

"Larissa's mom says the chubby Barbies are gross, and she won't buy them for her. So I have some dolls that Larissa doesn't have!"

None of this information is new to me, as I heard all about it on our walk home. It was a distraction from the thoughts and information already pinging through my head, although I don't know if I would necessarily call it a "welcome" one. It did give me a reason, however, to set aside everything else and put on my "Mom" hat for a much-needed talk about body positivity.

"The chubby Barbies aren't fat, or anything," Scout continues while Jet tries to moderate his amusement at our daughter's main takeaway from the encounter. "They just look like some of the normal people we know. Like Aunt Gidget and Gigi."

If it were possible for butterscotch ice cream to shoot from someone's nose, Jet would have done it. He mops his red face and blows his nose with one of the rough brown napkins from the ice cream shoppe.

"Are you okay, Daddy?"

Eyes streaming, he clears his throat and wraps the remains of his cone in his soiled napkins. "I'm fine," he says, still choked. "Went down the wrong pipe."

I weakly pat him on the back. "There, there," I say mildly. "Scout, why don't you go run around with the other kids for a while before it gets dark and we have to head home? Just stay where we can see you."

She kisses Jet on the cheek as she scrambles off the picnic bench. "Feel better, Dad. I'll be right back."

He waves her off and lobs the ball of napkin and cone at the nearest trash can, making it. "Still have the accuracy," he says proudly with one last cough.

As soon as I'm sure Scout's out of earshot, I say to him, "We need to plan a birthday party for her. A big one."

"What? That's, like, a month away."

"Three weeks. The party would land the weekend before school starts. That means invitations have to go out *now* if anyone's going to show up."

With something between a smirk and a grimace, he points out, "My family doesn't need invitations, and I'm pretty sure their calendars are clear."

"Not for your family; for Scout's classmates."

"Her class— School hasn't even started yet. She doesn't have any classmates."

"Sure, she does. The class lists have been finalized. We know who her teacher is. Kiki's the PTA President. She can get me the home addresses of all the kids."

"Okay… Seems a little shady…"

"I'm not going to sell the information or use it to break the law. Just going to send some cute invites. And follow them up with emails."

Keeping his eyes on our daughter, he glances at me through his peripheral vision. "You seemed relieved that this year, her birthday would be a quiet thing, with only my parents and Gidget's family there. Why the sudden change in game plan?"

"The playbook as we know it has been blown up, Jet, now

that we live here. People here don't throw lame family birthday parties."

"I'm sure some do. And they're not lame!"

"Well, they're secondary. You have a big blowout for friends, then maybe dinner and some cake for family."

"I take it you learned this from Kiki."

"Some. But it's obvious. Everything's bigger, better, fancier here."

He sighs. "Okay, so we invite everyone from her class—"

"From *both* kindergarten classes."

"What? Why?"

Channeling Kiki, I explain, "We don't want to leave anyone out! She'll be moving up through the school with all of these kids. They may not be classmates this year, but they could be next year."

"Right. Okay. Then the entire kindergarten population comes over for a pool party? Some games? Twister, pin the tail on the donkey? Maybe break a piñata?"

I shake my head and reach for his hand. "No, Jet. Think bigger."

"Bigger than a piñata?"

"Much, much bigger."

"How many dollars bigger?"

"Since when do you care about how much something costs?"

"Since I'm no longer banking a few mil a year. And—"

I wait.

His ears redden, but he shakes his head. "Never mind."

"We have more money saved up than we could ever spend in multiple lifetimes."

"Yeah, but—"

"But what? What would you rather spend it on than

making sure your daughter has the best fifth birthday party ever *and* goes into kindergarten with friends galore?"

"I don't think you can buy that."

"We can, with Kiki's school database. I'll have to come up with the rest on my own, but I know exactly where to look for ideas."

"Great. So all you need from me is…?"

"Cooperation. And your attendance on the big day, of course."

"Which will be?"

"The Saturday before the first day of school."

He groans. "Babe, that's, like, two days after my first broadcast."

"I know. You'll be home that weekend. It's perfect."

"But—"

"All you have to do is show up. Trust me. I've got this."

## SEVEN

## MAURA'S HIGHLIGHT REELS

*Replay #8: Five Years Ago*

Head in hands, hands clutching hair, hair pulling painfully at roots, I stared at the baby monitor on the breakfast bar and whispered, "Please. Please, stop crying. Please." I'd tried everything I knew to try, everything that had worked so well in the past two-and-a-half months. Inexplicably, however, Scout was changing the rules on me. Nothing worked. Not rocking, not feeding, not diaper changing, not anything. She didn't have a fever or any other signs of illness or injury. I finally had to carefully lay her in her crib and walk away, afraid of the impulse I had to shake her and say, "Just tell me what's wrong!"

Nobody told me that was going to happen. I was led to believe that the baby you brought home from the hospital and got to know those first couple of weeks was the baby you had. None of the experts or fellow moms said anything about sudden about-faces in personality. I had no idea that the sweet, laid-back baby girl I'd so fallen in love with would one day wake up and decide, "Contentment is boring a-f. It's time to shake things up around here." Nobody had warned me this was possible.

Or had they, and I'd just forgotten? I tried to quickly scan the index of topics rattling in my brain. Diaper blow-outs, umbilical cord care, spit-up, chapped nipples, confused days and nights... The words bounced around, but I couldn't focus on any of them long enough to figure out if they were relevant. The crying was too much, too distracting, too psychologically painful for me to concentrate on anything but the noise.

Jet would be home soon, traveling back from an early-afternoon away game in Foxborough, Massachusetts. At least, I assumed he would be home soon.

Sometimes, particularly after losses like the one they'd suffered that day, he wasn't in a particular hurry to get home. He and some of the guys would hash stuff out in one of the meeting rooms at the training facility, drawing x's and o's on the electronic whiteboard into the wee hours of the morning, trying to figure out where they'd gone wrong and how they could avoid the same mistakes in the future. He said it helped to do it "while the pain is still fresh." Typically, he texted me when these sessions were going to take place, but sometimes he forgot or thought a text would be more disruptive, assuming I'd already gone to bed. I hadn't received a text from him one way or the other, so I had no idea when to expect him. That only added to my stress and frustration.

My aching boobs streamed the rejected milk that had nowhere to go but into the front of my robe as Scout wailed, their typical signal to get things flowing. If I trusted myself on the same floor as the hysterical child, I'd stand in the shower. I didn't, though. I needed to stay down here, physically far away from her while I figured out my next move.

I certainly wasn't at a loss for what to do from a lack of information, all gleaned from conversations with Mom, Deirdre, and Cyndi, plus the stack of books next to my bed. Not to mention the unsolicited stuff from Gloria, who—I had to admit—was the most experienced of the moms I knew, besides Nina.

Nina!

Feeling guilty, I turned down the volume on the monitor and fumbled for my phone in my bathrobe pocket. It was late, but I knew she'd still be up, grabbing some "me" time after her hectic evening routine of dinner, last-minute weekend homework help, and bedtime routines.

Remembering that made me pause for a minute with my finger above the button on the screen that would connect me to her. I never called her for anything less than an emergency at that time, understanding how precious her evening solitude was to her.

It *was* an emergency, though. What if Scout never stopped crying? Could she dehydrate? I couldn't see any symptoms of illness or injury, but could she be hurt internally? How would that have even happened? Suddenly, the most terrifying of topics sprang to mind: viruses that caused brain swelling, cancer—babies could get it, right?—congenital diseases so far not detected. The list went on and on, like movie credits, the longest, most horrifying credits ever.

That banished the last of the doubt about calling Nina. It was either that, or I was taking Scout to the emergency room, and I only wanted to do that as a last resort. I'd probably text Jet before I did that. Maybe. Unless I could get there and back before he got home, so he wouldn't be the wiser.

As soon as Nina picked up, I said, "She won't stop crying. How do I make her stop crying?"

Nina chuckled. "Yikes. That's always a good time."

"It's not funny. Please help me. I'm losing my mind. She's been like this all weekend."

"Yep."

"What do you mean, 'yep'?"

"I mean, 'yep, they do that.'"

"Since when? Nobody told me that. I mean, I've been told about colic, but she's never had that before."

"If this is her first long crying jag, I doubt it's colic."

"Then what the eff is it, Nina?"

In rapid-fire, she went through the typical baby checklist—peeing, pooping, eating, sleeping—and some tricks for getting that last one to happen more regularly and for longer periods of time, like lavender baths and baby massage, both of which I'd already tried multiple times to no avail.

"What's she wearing?" she asked finally.

"Wearing?"

"Yeah. What kind of clothes or pajamas is she in?"

"Some zippered, footie thing, like all babies wear."

"Does it fit her properly? Not too big, not too small?"

"Yes. I think. I'm not in the same room with her, so I can't be a hundred percent sure or take measurements or anything, but I don't remember it being too loose or too tight when I put it on her after her bath. It's the same as all the other ones like it."

"Mmm-hmmm," Nina said. "She's got a bunch of the same type that you put her in?"

"Yes. Oh, in fact, they fit her perfectly. I remember now, because she went up a size this week. They're brand new."

"You've washed them, though?"

"Yes! Obviously. I'm not a moron. I know you have to wash new baby clothes. And before you ask, I used the same detergent we've always used. She doesn't have a rash, or anything."

"No, we already ruled that out. That's not what I'm getting at. Is she still crying?"

I turned up the volume on the monitor so Nina could hear it as well as my boobs could. "Okay. Um, when's Jet going to be home?"

"I don't know."

"Can you text him and ask?"

"I guess… I don't like to bother him."

What I didn't tell her was that I never texted him. Ever. I was supposed to have all this stuff at home under control and let him do his thing out there in Football Land with no interruptions or distractions.

Up until then, there'd been no need for SOS texts. I *did* have things under control. Scout and I had a routine and an understanding. We were a team. We had been until that weekend, anyway. That weekend had been an entirely different story, one with only unhappy endings if I didn't distance myself from her for a little while.

Nina said, "You're not 'bothering' him by asking him to be a parent and partner."

"I know, it's just— It's a rule I have. For myself."

"Completely unnecessary, I'm sure. Never mind. Do you think you can handle being in the same room with her without throttling her?"

"I don't want to thrott—"

"Yeah, you do. It's normal, so don't think you're the first mom who's ever felt it. You're not that special."

I laughed too loudly in my relief. "Oh. Well, yeah. I've stepped away for a few minutes, so I think I can manage, if what you're about to tell me to do might get her to stop."

"Good. I hope so. If not, you set her right back down and leave the room again, ya hear?"

"Yes. Okay. Hang on. Let me get up there."

I took the back kitchen stairs up to the bedroom hallway, where I was greeted by Torzi, pacing outside Scout's nursery door. He growled at me in disapproval when I opened the door and slipped past him. "Stop judging me," I said to him.

"What was that?" Nina asked.

"Nothing," I said, embarrassed that the baby's crying hadn't drowned out my "conversation" with the dog. "Okay, now what?" I shouted into the phone, plugging my outside ear so I could hear her.

"Put me on speaker so you have two hands to deal with Scout."

I did as told, setting the phone on the changing table.

"Now undress her, down to her diaper. Change it if she needs it."

Again, I followed her directions.

"She's dry," I said. "Like I told you, I've changed her a million times, and I can hardly get her to eat enough to wet her diapers. I'm so worried, Neen."

"We definitely need to take care of that. But let's get her happier first. Is she mostly naked?"

"Yeah."

"Okay. Now, you take off your clothes."

"What?"

"Just— Trust me, okay? Do it."

"All of them?"

"As much of them as you did with her. Down to your panties. Naked from the waist up."

As I shucked my sodden robe, I said, "This is weird."

She ignored me. "Now, pick her up and take her somewhere you can lie down with her on your chest, skin-to-skin."

The double bed in the room for anticipated restless nights, a bed we hadn't had to use until that weekend, beckoned, still unmade from the night before. I carried the phone and an already-quieting Scout over to it and lay down on my back, situating the phone on the nightstand and the baby between my breasts.

"Should I pull the covers over us?" I asked in a near-whisper, not wanting to disturb the first peace I'd experienced in a long time.

"If that's what's comfortable and she likes it. She might want the air on her back. Try it."

I did, and she nuzzled closer to me, sticking her two middle fingers into her mouth and sucking on them.

"Yeah," I said to her. "There you go. I won't even pull them out right now."

"What's she doing?" Nina asked.

"Not crying," I said. "And sucking her fingers."

"She'll be rooting for milk in no time."

"I'm empty, so I hope not too soon."

"You have some in the fridge, though, right?"

"Yeah."

"Even better. Jet can feed her, and you can get some sleep."

"If Jet's home by then."

"He'll be home by then."

I didn't ask her how she knew. I didn't care. All I cared about was that my baby girl seemed okay again. Finally.

After a few minutes of silence, when I was sure my voice wouldn't crank up the tears again, I said, "Nina, why the heck is this working?"

"Babies love it."

"Okay, but she loves eating and sleeping and baths and massage, too, and none of those things worked."

"None of those things were her momma, relaxed and calm."

"It can't be that simple."

"It usually is, though, unless there really is a medical problem. Also…?"

I waited.

"Throw those pajamas away."

"What? They're brand new."

"She obviously hates them."

"But she would have hated any pajamas this weekend, right? She's going through a growth spurt or something, maybe? Something that's upsetting to her for a reason she can't figure out?"

"Maybe," Nina said. "Those pajamas weren't helping, though. I bet there's a seam or tag rubbing her somewhere. Swift was really sensitive to stuff like that. I had to keep her in gowns forever. She hated having her feet covered."

"Weird."

"Babies *are* weird. They're even weirder when they get to be kids."

"Yeah, but at least they can tell you what's wrong."

"Oh, you are in for some *fun* if you think the ability to talk means she'll actually talk to *you*."

I kissed the top of Scout's head. "She will. We're going to be best friends and talk about everything." When I rubbed her back, she arched it and grunted.

A few minutes later, Nina said, "Well, I'm going to let you go. Jet's home."

"He is? How do you—?"

"You may have a silly rule about texting him, but I don't. I told him to get his ass home and tell me when he got there."

"Nina!" I tried to inject some outrage into my tone—quietly, without disturbing Scout—but it fell flat due to the gratitude I was actually feeling. "Thank you."

"Any time. You know that."

Jet appeared in the doorway of the nursery, looking harried and worried. "What's this I hear about trouble in paradise?" he said softly, lowering himself to his knees next to the bed and palming Scout's head.

"I'll let you guys go," Nina said. "Here's hoping you get a restful night." My phone beeped to let us know she'd hung up.

"Looks mighty happy now," Jet said. "Not that I blame her." He craned his neck and kissed my lips. "Why didn't you call me? I was just yakking with some of the guys about pass protection when Nina texted me."

Eyes filling, I said, barely above a whisper, "I didn't want you to know that I couldn't handle everything."

He pressed his forehead to mine. "Ah, beautiful."

"I know, it's stupid."

"Not stupid, but silly. When's the last time she ate?"

"A while ago. I couldn't get her to, no matter what I tried. I was so worried…"

For the first time, I noticed he was holding a bottle of breast milk. Swiftly, he pulled his sweatshirt and undershirt over his head and wiggled his fingers at me. "Hand 'er over. It might not be as good as cuddling with you, but I'll try my best so you can get some sleep."

"Really? You have to be so tired after—"

"I got a good night's sleep last night in a silent, pitch-dark hotel room. We don't have anything quite that restful, but the blue room gets pretty dark."

I lifted the baby and handed her to him. "Sounds amazing."

"See you in the morning," he whispered, bouncing gently and offering the bottle to Scout. She took it and started sucking lustfully. "Whoa, whoa," he said. "It's not going anywhere, Bump. Slow down."

I grabbed his plain white t-shirt from the floor and slipped it on. The last thing I heard as I closed the door behind me was him saying, "What's the deal, huh? I thought we agreed you'd be nice to your mom when I wasn't home."

## Replay # 9: Six Months Ago

In the dark of The Knox Theater's only screening room, staring blankly ahead at the white, dormant screen, I absorbed the silence to my very core, hearing it ring in my ears. The cleaners had recently finished for the week, so the permeating smell of buttered popcorn competed with the pleasant but not overpowering scent of lavender and tea tree oil. That oddly comforting bouquet was the only stimulus in the room, other than the kiss of the leather armrests under my fingertips.

It was the first time my brain had been somewhat at rest since Jet told me about his new job, and I was thankful for the peace. I was in my happy place, my natural habitat, my sanctuary. It was so sacred to me that we stopped holding board meetings in there. It meant the screening room still felt special and new to me, newer and more exciting than any house would ever be. I decided *everything* that happened in there. It came straight from my head, my fantasies, into reality.

It was time, however, to say goodbye.

*No, Maura. That's a sappy, melodramatic story you're telling yourself. This place will still be a part of your daily life, no matter where you are. You won't be able to sit in these seats and stare at this screen, but you're still going to be in charge, still making those same decisions. Pull it together.*

Inhaling a deep, shuddering breath, I took my tough-talking advice and said out loud, "It's just a setting change."

The door that led to the lobby opened, letting in a wedge of light. Soon, Nina's head appeared as she ascended the ramp to enter the room. The rest of her body followed as she rounded the end of the short wall and scanned the room for me.

Finally locating me, she said, "You always sit somewhere different when you come in here."

"I like the different perspectives."

She threaded her way down the row and lowered herself slowly into the seat next to me. "So."

"So."

"You've told everyone in your family?"

"Yep."

"And Jet's family?"

"Uh-huh."

"What about Rae and Ana Paula?"

"Not yet. I'll tell Rae in person at our next yoga session."

"Really relaxing."

"Right? I can't chicken out, though."

"She'll be pissed she was the last to know. Do you think she'll find out through other channels before then?"

Still staring straight ahead, I let myself imagine those consequences for half a second. "Let's hope not, or I'm in deep shit."

"Sorry. I didn't mean to give you one more thing to worry about."

I reached over and took hold of her hand in her lap, moving it to the armrest between us and squeezing. "Oh, it's nothing I haven't already considered, but I can't worry about everything, you know? I have so many other things to think about."

"Like this place?"

"Yeah."

"What, exactly, *does* this mean for The Knox?"

"Honestly, I have no idea."

"Oh." She let go of my hand.

"Yeah. 'Oh.'"

"Soooo…"

"Sorry. It's a sucky answer, but that's all I have right now."

She contemplated that for a while. Then, in typical Nina fashion, she went into Mom Mode. You can't be mother to six kids, ages seven to sixteen, without learning to skip the drama and the fretting and go straight to getting shit solved. You'd never survive a week.

Half-turning in her seat, she said, "Well, I guess the biggest change will be that you're not here, physically. But we have the technology, right?"

"Yep."

"Maybe this means more expansion for the franchise. You open a theater out in California, and there you go! A new home base. That's exciting!"

"I'd have to research that. I don't know what the market is like out there. Maybe it's already been done."

"But maybe it hasn't. Or it hasn't been done like *we* do it."

"We'll see. I'm not sure how the West Coast fits into our brand."

Nina waved that off. "Our brand is whatever we make it. Flyover country doesn't have the monopoly on practical giving. If anything, it might be easier and more lucrative on the West Coast. Liberal-minded people *love* to feel like they're making a difference. The easier the better. What's easier than going to a movie?"

"I said I'd research it," I snapped, then immediately apologized.

"It's okay. You have a lot on your mind. I can take that piece of it off your plate, if you want me to."

I shook my head. "Nah. There's no rush on it. It'll be a good distraction once we get settled out there and Scout's in school all day. I'm sure I'll find time somehow, somewhere."

She stood. "I wish you were more hyped about this. It could be a lot of fun. A new adventure."

"It's happening, no matter what. Not sure I can manage 'hyped,' but I'm determined to try to make the best of it."

"Are you?"

I looked up at her. "Sure! What choice do I have? There's no use being mad and miserable."

"True." She edged her way back to the aisle. "You gonna be in here for a while?"

"Yeah. Just a little longer."

"Take your time. Just keep in mind, we have a showing in here in…" She looked at her phone. "…twenty-eight hours. So, you probably need to be out of here by then."

And to think I hadn't wanted to hire her. What would I have done without her?

*Replay #10: Five Months Ago*

A week after Jet returned from his tour of the Culver City studios and it was official that he and Erin were Football Network's newest West Coast announcing team, I decided it was time to tell Rae about our impending departure from the only city she and I had ever lived in. I chose the end of my private yoga session with her in the in-home studio her wife, Ana-Paula, designed and had built for her in their backyard as a recent anniversary gift.

"This is bullshit," Rae grouched when I made my announcement immediately after saying, "Namaste." "You're just going to follow behind him, like a good little wifey?"

I breathed deeply through my nose for four beats, held it for four, and released it before replying, "It's not my favorite decision he's made without discussing it with me, and I wouldn't put it like that, but yes."

She rose from her mat and started rolling it into a tight tube I could never quite duplicate. I'm sure she redid my pathetic attempts after I left each week. "Wait a minute. He didn't even discuss it with you?"

Oh, gosh. Why did I tell her that? It kind of slipped out, but it kind of didn't. I knew it would be like pouring Miracle-Gro on kudzu, but I said it anyway. Why? So someone would be on my side, of course. My secret side. The side nobody knew I was on. The side of "pissed off and deeply disapproving." Someone needed to say what I could only say if I wanted to make the situation even more unpleasant than it already was. I knew I could count on Rae, feminist curmudgeon extraordinaire. Still, I needed to be careful. It was great to hear someone else voice my feelings, but I couldn't appear to be agreeing with them. Not to anyone. Not even Rae.

"Well, of course we've discussed it. Several times over the years. So he didn't need to talk to me about it when the actual situation arose, because I always knew this was coming."

"More bullshit. That's not how it works."

"It is," I argued, keeping up my phony side of the conversation, one I'd had with myself many times in the past few days as I'd wondered if I was justified in being miffed about what was happening. I joined her at her eye level and retrieved my mat from the floor.

She snatched it from my hands and commenced rolling it expertly. "No, it's not. Shit changes. Shit *has* changed. Have you discussed this since you bought The Knox and turned it into a huge chain?"

"It's not a huge chain, and no, we haven't talked about it that recently. Because there was nothing to talk about. It's always been part of 'The Plan'—"

"And nobody and nothing gets in the way of Jet Knox's almighty plan, right?"

I gulped. "Right."

"What about your plans?"

"My plans are…" I clear my throat. "More flexible. I can work my plans around his plans."

"Bullshit." She lobbed the mats toward a corner where several others were already rolled and stacked. Then she grabbed two neatly folded white towels from a bamboo shelf next to her and handed one of them to me.

"Okay, I get that you think this is bullshit. You're on the record with that. Several times." I patted the sweat on the insides of my elbows and wiped behind my neck before dropping the towel into a nearby hamper and returning to stand facing her. "Now I need you to be my friend and tell me it's going to be okay."

Hands pulling on the ends of the short towel around her neck, nostrils flared, and lips all but invisible, they were so tightly pinched together in a straight line, she stared at me for a few seconds. Her fury on my behalf was genuine, originating so clearly from loyalty and love that it brought tears to my eyes.

"I knew it," she said quietly, without the usual self-satisfied tone she used for that phrase. "Come here." She pulled me into a damp hug, the dewy skin of our arms and shoulders tacky against each other.

With horror I found myself sobbing into the towel around her neck like a little kid. Like Scout when she doesn't get her way about something she desperately wants and has foolishly set her hopes on, despite our warnings to the contrary. She knows what the result is going to be, but she doggedly refuses to believe it until it actually comes to pass, and then it's just as painful as if she's been blindsided.

"I don't want to go!" I wailed.

"Well, no shit. This is your home. Your life is here. How can he not see that?"

"He does!"

"Even worse. He knows, but it doesn't matter. All that matters is what *he* wants."

"No, it's not like that." This time, my defense of him was real. I withdrew from Rae and wiped my nose on the back of my hand. She wrinkled her nose in disgust but didn't offer me her towel or a tissue, so I swiped my hand against my buttery yoga pants and hoped it didn't leave a snot streak. Then again, I didn't really care. "He offered to move out there alone, so Scout and I didn't have to be uprooted, but—"

She snorted and rolled her eyes.

"No, really. He meant it." A tear trailed onto my lip. I

licked and wiped it away. "He said he could live out there during football season and with Scout and me here the rest of the year."

"Oh, wouldn't he just love that?"

"What?"

"Freedom and bachelorhood for half the year and family life the other half!" She shook her head. "Oh, my gosh. They're all the same. Pigs."

"That's not what he had in mind."

"Yeah, he did, Maura. Don't be an idiot."

I blinked and gasped as if she'd physically slapped me.

Noticing my reaction, she softened and explained patiently (well, her brand of "patiently"), "It was a win-win proposition for him. If you go with him, he gets his way, his precious plan intact, and—like always—everything and everyone submits to his will. If you don't go with him, he still gets his way, his precious plan intact, *and* he gets a bonus new lifestyle—for half the year, anyway—*plus* his wife and daughter are waiting for him when he wants to play the dutiful husband and father again. Just when that's getting old, it's time to go back to California to live it up like a horny college student."

"You— You know Jet's not like that."

"They all are, sister."

"Not him."

"Not yet. But give him a chance. Now I see exactly why you're trailing after him. Shit. All those California babes, throwing themselves and their perfect, surgically bestowed bodies at him with no spousal supervision? I wouldn't let A-P go off without *me*, either."

"I trust him!"

"Uh-huh."

"I do! You should have seen him when he thought I might

take him up on the offer to live separately. He— he was terrified."

"So commercial acting about car insurance and razors really *can* teach you a few things. Good to know."

"It wasn't an act, Rae!"

"You know what? I get it. You have to tell yourself all of this to sleep at night. I probably shouldn't have said anything, should have just patted you on the back and said, 'There, there,' like you wanted, and complimented you for being such a great partner. Loyal, supportive, submissive, selfless. All the things the League tells guys to look for in a spouse. Someone who looks good on your arm—and is great in the sack when she's not birthing your babies—but won't be a spoiler when it comes to your career or the NFL's plans for your career. Bravo. You've done it. You're the best." She slow clapped.

Before I even knew what I was doing, I pulled back my arm and swung it forward, slapping her full force on the left cheek.

She stopped clapping and closed her eyes, but she didn't otherwise react or move. At first. Then, she slapped me back just as hard. Maybe harder. She's strong. And I didn't blame her. I deserved it. You get what you give, right? But it hurt like a sonofabitch. I couldn't take it as stoically as she did.

"Motherfu—" I hissed, bending at the waist and holding one hand to the burning side of my face. Everything she'd said echoed in my mind as I recovered with my nose near my knees, and my anger bloomed in direct proportion with the hand print on my cheek.

Rising to my full height again, towering over my more diminutive "friend," I pushed her backward with my free hand to her chest. After stumbling a couple of steps, she regained her balance and ran at me, both of her flat palms hitting me in my solar plexus, knocking me on my ass on the wooden floor, as well as knocking the air from my lungs.

From my vulnerable position, I raised my legs and kicked out, scooting across the floor on my butt as she fled from me. I managed to make glancing contact with her knee as she yelled, "Stop it, you stupid Stepford wife! Gender traitor!"

That popped me back on my feet, and I went at her again, this time just randomly flapping my hands in the vicinity of her arms and chest. "Shut up! Just shut up!" I screeched.

She put her fists up in a defensive boxing posture, jabbing out at me occasionally when she saw an opportunity. With each jab, she added a verbal blow. "You. Can't. Have it. All. You. Won't. Be able. To Juggle. It all."

"I can. I will. You've never believed in me. But I can do things, too, Rae."

She blinked a few times as my fingertips made contact with her face again, close to her eyes. Out of breath, she backed away and rubbed her left eyelid. I must have gotten her, I thought. Good. I hoped for an infection that swelled it shut and wept green pus.

While I was contemplating the grossest thing I could wish on her watery eye, she panted, "Because you're a loser. You always have been. Always were. You met Jet and got to act like a winner next to him, but you're still the same as you always were: all talk, no game."

"How— How can you say that? I— I've done things. The job fairs and the theaters…" It sounded pathetic, even to my own ears, so I shifted approaches. "I've been there for *you*."

"Yeah, that's your excuse. You're always too busy supporting someone else to be your own person. Too busy finding other people careers to have one. Too busy standing by your man to stand on your own."

"That's— that's not fair, and you know it."

She placed her hands on her hips and sneered. "Now you're too busy pretending to be the perfect wife and mother to follow through on something that could have finally propelled you to the next level, given you purpose, shown people you do have a reason for existing."

"Why? Why are you saying these things?"

She shrugged as if she didn't care how much she was hurting me, as if our years of friendship suddenly meant nothing to her because I wasn't doing what she thought I should do, the way she thought I should do it. "Because they're true. And I think it's about time someone told you. I'm tired of enabling your co-dependent bullshit. Maybe nobody else is, but I am."

I frantically gathered my purse and shrugged on the coat I needed out in the real world, where it wasn't artificially tropically warm. On my way through the door, I said what I probably should have said to her a long time ago—and many, many times, in fact: "Fuck you, Rae."

Unfortunately, it came out on a sob, not forcefully and confidently, like I wished it would.

"Get out," she said. "Run after Jet to California. You'll fit in well out there with the rest of the flakes."

## EIGHT

## PARTY PLANNER

It's true that our lack of social life here in California originally had us thinking small for Scout's fifth birthday, with Jet's parents and sister's family at the house. Since Scout's cousins are her favorite people, I was sure it would be plenty of fun for her, and that was all that mattered.

When Kiki got wind of it, though, you would have thought I'd told her we were skipping Scout's big day altogether this year.

After she dismissed the girls to play upstairs, that weird, assessing silence descended again. For lack of anything better to talk about, I pounced on the topic of school again, which led me to think of the first day of school, which lands close to Scout's birthday. That train of thought took me to babbling about the family party we had planned, to which I hastily invited Larissa when I noticed Kiki's horrified look.

She stopped my monologue with a hand to my knee and said, "But Maura, birthday parties are the perfect networking opportunities! You're totally squandering one of the best, most effective ways to meet and influence people."

"Oh, well, we're not all that interested in—"

"Plus, what a great way for Scout to meet all of her classmates before the first day of school! You can't just throw that away!"

"We don't even know who her classmates are yet." Despite not being hungry at all, I plucked another scone from the tea tray and bit off the corner.

"Exactly!"

"So how do we invite them?"

That's when she nonchalantly offered to invade dozens of people's privacy.

Because I'm a decent person, I balked at first. My objections fell on deaf ears, though. Kiki already had her phone out and was tapping away, her long, red thumbnails a blur.

"No, no, no," she muttered while swiping. "A family party will never do!" She clicked her tongue. "Especially not when the timing is so perfect!"

"I don't know if—"

"Trust me, Maura. Scout will be an instant loser if you continue this little hermit act of yours. Is that what you want?" Pausing in her PTA espionage, she lowered her chin and looked at me through the tops of her eyes.

"No! Of course, not!"

"Only the truly, truly eccentric can get away with hiding away like that. Otherwise, you have to get out there, especially if you have kids. You have to open doors for them!"

"Right. Which is why we're sending her to Ursuline."

"That's the absolute bare minimum, sweetie. Ground floor. Ugh. Don't be one of *those*."

"Those what?"

"Those people who half-ass everything in life but expect the same results the rest of us hard workers get. Raising kids is hard work. It takes just as much sweat equity as fixing up a house for resale or... or... building a business! You have experience with that, with your little theater chain, right?"

*Little theater chain?* In other circumstances, I would have bristled at that characterization of The Knox, but my brain was too busy trying to process everything else Kiki was saying —and finding ways it didn't—couldn't—apply to me.

"I don't really see the connection between running a business and being a mother."

"Oh! How can you not? It's obvious!" She set her phone down and wiggled her hips in her chair. "Done. I emailed you the mailing and email addresses of every parent in the incoming kindergarten classes."

"Clas*es*, plural?"

"Oh, yes. You can't afford to be exclusive yet. This invite— by snail mail, darling—has to go out to ev-er-y child entering kindergarten this year."

"But that's— That's a lot of kids, right?"

She waved off my concern. "Only fifty, or so. And not all of them will accept, obviously."

"Obviously."

"Right. You've left it pretty late."

I winced, but considering I hadn't been planning to throw a party, I wasn't really guilty of what she was accusing me. For some reason, though, that defense didn't spring to mind in the face of Kiki's single-minded mission to make me Pacific Palisades' newest socialite.

"What you need to understand, though, is that Scout's not going to be shut in a classroom all day with the same twenty-four classmates. She's going to see the students from the other class in the lunchroom and on the playground. She might be in classes with them in subsequent years. Ursuline goes all the way to twelfth grade, you know. There's no starting over once you've set a foot wrong at Ursuline. Each step has to be perfect."

I gulped. "That can't be—"

"It is, though. I don't know how things are where you're from in Kansas, but here, image is everything, even with kids. *Especially* with kids. Kids are the ultimate extension of one's image."

Instead of continuing to argue that I don't care about image, I simply corrected her about my state of origin—which she brushed off as, "even worse." While she rattled away about all the ways reputation and connections mattered, a tiny voice taunted me, "You might not need any of this, but Jet does." Suddenly I was doubting everything I thought I knew about life.

I didn't have time for a panic attack, fortunately. Kiki had moved on to Phase 2 of her argument:

"Five is a milestone birthday, too! You can't throw together a lame-o family party for the fifth birthday." She poured both of us more tea and sipped at hers daintily.

When I claimed ignorance of the age five being any more special than four or six, she sighed and rattled off, "The first, fifth, thirteenth, sixteenth, eighteenth, and twenty-first. Those are the biggies. You simply *have* do do something special to mark them. Otherwise, it looks like you really don't care."

I guess my parents didn't care. Knowing for sure this wasn't true, I took a deep, stabilizing breath and merely said, "I see."

Then I listened with everything in me to the anecdotes Kiki reeled off about children's parties she and Richard have been to through the years, hoping to cull some good ideas.

When Scout and I left the Valentines', my head felt like it

was full of bees. Kiki's parting words to me were, "Check your email for those addresses. You're welcome!"

Skepticism still remained throughout the rest of the afternoon and evening, even as I tried to convince Jet at the playground that this was definitely the way to go.

After a good night's sleep, however, I was fully on board, feeling like I did when I finally got my inspiration—usually at the eleventh hour—for one of the job fairs at The Career Center. I could do this. I could plan the most epic kid's birthday party Pacific Palisades has ever seen. Well, maybe not, but possibly the most epic kid's birthday party *these* invitees have ever seen, if they don't know any celebrities' kids.

Jet's still not sure.

"Holy shit. What happened in here?" he asks upon his first sight of Party Planning Central, the formal dining room we've yet to use for anything other than collecting dust. I barely glance up from stuffing envelopes with the invitations I picked up from the print shop this afternoon.

Acting like the room always looks this way, I merely say, "I needed a place to spread out and get organized."

"*This* is organized?"

He's right that our dining room looks like a Staples storeroom was hit by a terrorist with a vendetta against office supplies, but I won't give him the satisfaction of anything more than, "I know what and where everything is, and that's all that matters."

He sits across the corner of the table from me, still in the business casual attire he must have been wearing while covering Chargers training camp today and for the past several days.

"How'd it go?" I ask him in an effort to distract. I'd hoped to be done with this by the time he got home, but Scout was unusually uncooperative at bedtime, probably angling for a way to stay up until Jet got home.

He yawns. "Exhausting. I think I was less tired when I was the one working out on the field at camp."

"Doubt it. I remember how you'd come home and collapse."

"I guess I'm tired in a different way now. Mentally tired." He snags my inspiration binder before I can react. Oh, well. He had to find out sometime.

"A chocolate fountain, Maura? Really? For kindergartners? You realize we'll be mopping up syrup—and puke—all day, right?"

"Too bad. You only turn five once."

He turns the page to the next vendor flyer I've impaled on the binder's rings. "Turning the back patio into an arcade? That's cool, but there are going to be a *lot* of people packed into this place. And I'm not sure virtual reality and the pool are a good combo."

Fold, insert, seal, stack. Fold, insert, seal, stack.

"Don't be such a worry wart. We'll do the VR on the front lawn and driveway, if it'll make you feel better. Oh, that reminds me: I need to call to set up valet parking. Nobody wants their Bentley scratched." I pause my assembly line to add a note to the ever-growing to-do list on the legal pad next to me.

"Did you really book a deejay? Where are we going to put him? Isn't that going to be kind of loud? I mean, what about the neighbors?"

*Where was I? Oh, yes.* Fold, insert, seal, stack.

"*She* will be set up near the outdoor kitchen. There's plenty of room over there, plus that way she can be heard both inside the house and in the pool area. If the neighbors complain, we'll just invite them to join us. The more the merrier!"

He flips another page and groans. "I'm not sure an open bar at a kids' birthday is appropriate."

"Parents have to get through the day somehow. You and I will stay sober, obviously, to supervise everything."

Pushing the binder away, he slumps in his chair, legs straight in front of him, and scrubs his face with both hands. "This is spiraling out of control, Maura. I don't understand why it has to be so—"

"Hey. It's all good. I've got this."

"You say that, but—"

"You doubt me?"

Letting his arms go limp, he blinks at me while I straighten my four even stacks of stuffed invitations, ready for address labels—if I can locate them.

"No. Of course not. I know you *can*. The question is, '*Should* we do this?' It's too much. She still so little. What's left after this? How do we keep topping this year after year?"

"By the time she hits her next big milestone—thirteen—there'll be all kinds of new stuff to do."

He groans again.

I cast about the table, searching for the labels, finally finding them when I lift the binder that Jet set on top of them. Ugh. I wish he wouldn't touch anything; he's messing up my system! More seriously, I say, "Listen. This isn't just a kids' party, okay? This is a social event for us, too."

"That doesn't make me feel better, knowing we're using our kid to show off to a bunch of snotty rich people."

Through clenched teeth, I continue, "Like it or not, your new career path requires a social standing of sorts. Your boss will be here. This isn't only about impressing a bunch of five-

and six-year-olds; now, it's about showing people that we're here to stay. We're embracing this sometimes over-the-top way of life."

"It surprises me you'd want to embrace that. You're the last person I thought would."

Even though it feels like a rebuke, I shrug it off. "When in Rome…"

"Rome was way less over-the-top than this party is going to be."

"This will help Scout, too. She's going to be the youngest kid in her class—by a lot." Kiki's little list came with birth dates, too, although I'm not about to tell Jet that.

"So?"

"So, it matters at this age."

"She would be so bored in pre-K," he says what we've already discussed a thousand times.

"I know. I absolutely think we're doing the right thing having her skip it. The academic side of it will be a piece of cake for her. But socially? I don't know, Jet. I mean… she thought whale puke was appropriate tea party conversation."

He chuckles. "She's four!"

"Exactly. She's smart and funny and odd in a way that amazes and scares me sometimes." I peel off the first address label and line it up with a ruler/level combo before pressing it down on the envelope in front of me. Perfect. Next.

Jet watches me with unfocused eyes. "It's downright mind-boggling to me. She knows shit I didn't know until high school. Hell, she knows shit I don't know *now*. Thank God for Google." He shakes his head and stops staring.

While I precisely position and stick each label, I say, "Her best friends up until now have been her cousins, people who've known her since birth and are used to her sometimes-strange tangents. And even they give her the side-eye sometimes and say, 'Who cares?!' when she gets obsessed with stuff."

"That's just who she is, though. Throwing a huge party isn't going to change that."

"I wouldn't want it to. At the same time, though, she doesn't yet have the social skills to know when to back it off a bit and let others steer the conversation toward more typical childhood interests. What if she's teased? What if she has trouble making friends? It hasn't been a problem for her so far in life, but what if the kids at Ursuline Academy aren't as accepting?"

"I doubt she'll be the only weird kid there. 'Weird' is the new normal."

"But what if her brand of weird isn't?"

At that thought, my hands shake so much that I have to take a steadying breath before I can apply the next label, and even then, it's not as straight as the others. Still acceptable, but… I push back from the table a few inches and shake out my hands, then rub the back of my tense, aching neck. I've been sitting here since finally getting Scout to bed hours ago.

Jet shrugs it off. "She'll be fine. Everyone who meets her loves her. You know that."

Someone like him, who's always been able to make a lot of friends and charm people, takes it for granted. As one of those shy people who likes to fly under the radar, I more fully understand what it's like to be on the outside, looking in, especially when it comes to school.

"People love her because she's genuine and kind. All the flash of the party is for us—to impress the grownups. There are some things Scout and I have built in especially for her, to show off her best attribute—her empathy."

"Now *this* sounds more interesting. Tell me more."

I pick up one of the extra invitations on the paper-strewn table and hand it to him, watching as his eyes scan the text, and his face relaxes. Then I slide before him the half-sheet of paper that I folded into each invitation, a short form, asking for the guest's favorite color, song, activities, and interests, plus three things they like best about themselves.

"How are you going to use this information?" he asks, waving the form after he's read it.

My stomach flutters, and I sit forward, leaning across the corner of the table. "Yes, there will be a deejay with pink hair and sleeve tattoos, but that deejay will play each kid's favorite song and announce three positive things about that kid to intro it. Then he or she will be encouraged to lead the dancing for that song with Scout."

He rubs his chin. "Nice. What happens if someone doesn't want to do that, though?"

"Obviously, the dance is optional, but at this age, and with enough sugar in their systems, with so many other kids doing it, too, I don't think we'll have many who'll turn down the opportunity to feel like a rock star for three to five minutes."

"We'll see."

"And if they do? No biggie. The rest of us will dance to 'their' song and celebrate them."

He flicks the card in his hand. "I like that you specified 'no gifts.' One of my nightmares about this was the stack of stuff she'd be getting that she doesn't need. You know people will ignore it, though."

"That's where *this* comes in." I snatch my binder from the other end of the table and page through until I come to the flyer I want. Opening the rings, I slide the paper out and show it to Jet.

Anyone who chooses to bring a gift, despite our request to the contrary, will be directed to place it in a bright, festive bin marked for donations to a children's charity that takes gifts year-round and distributes them to kids around the country who have the misfortune of spending their birthdays in the hospital due to illness or accident.

"Nice," Jet says again. "Really clever touch."

"Thanks. But that's not all! We're going to give a hand-picked parting gift to each child, using the info on the RSVP about their interests and favorites so that we can show one of the greatest gifts you can give a person is to allow them to give to you."

He chuckles. "Deep."

"And true!"

"I totally agree. You know how much I love giving presents."

"Mmm. And I know you're not sure about the open bar for parents, but on the bar is going to be a fishbowl for donations to Scout's favorite organization, Ocean Conservancy. The 'looser' people get, the more they'll donate, I'll bet."

"Looks like you've thought of everything." He reaches over and hooks my elbow to direct me into his lap. "You're amazing."

"Our daughter is. And we're going to show all these kids—and their parents—exactly that."

## NINE

# FUMBLE

"Are you ready for this?" I ask Jet a week later, silently marveling at the enormous array of food in front of him on the dinette table. It's the Wednesday before the first pre-season game, which means he's gearing up to hit the road for his first booth announce tomorrow, a Thursday night game. Like any season, the last couple months of prepping and coaching and practicing have come down to this.

He chews and swallows his bite of high-protein flapjacks. "Ready as I'll ever be, I guess," he answers with a grin. He chases down a forkful of fruit with orange juice, followed by coffee.

I pat his shoulder before turning toward the kitchen in search of my own nourishment. "You'll be great."

"It's just a pre-season game," he says, but it sounds like he's trying to convince himself, not me, of its insignificance. "I'll have time to study on the bus up there, too. Easy-peasy."

"Absolutely." I disappear into the pantry, saying a little prayer while I select from the shelves a box of crunchy raisin bran and a can of my favorite nut mix to sprinkle over the top.

I don't have any doubt that Jet can do anything he sets his heart on; I've seen him do it time and again. Hell, he got me to marry him, and I swore multiple times to multiple people, including him, that I was never going to do that. Ever. Never ever. Yet, here I am.

He can also memorize like a beast. The guy had so many plays up in that head of his during any given season—different ones each season, too—that it was no wonder he often talked in sports metaphors. That's all he had room for. I couldn't have done it, and I don't know many other people who could. So when he—and our friend, Rae—joke about his lack of intelligence or his knocks to the head, that's all they are: jokes. He has an amazing brain—for certain things.

Words ain't one of 'em.

He's no etymologist or lexicographer, and he'd be the first person to admit it, although he'd never use those words. In fact, if I use "big words" in conversation or—heaven forbid—in an argument, he rolls his eyes and implores me to "speak English." In those instances, I might get frustrated, but most of the time, I don't give a rat's ass about his narrow vocabulary. It doesn't bother me that he overuses the word "awesome" and puts the word "super" in front of everything to make it superlative. In fact, that's one of the things I love about him. He doesn't pretend to be something he's not. He knows the sentences, "I love you," and "You were right," and that's about all he needs, as far as I'm concerned. With me, it doesn't matter.

In his new job, it matters.

It's always struck me as odd that game announcing was on The Plan, considering this self-professed "weakness" of his, but from what I've gathered, he figures his plain speaking is

an asset. Most football viewers aren't looking for Shake-
spearean prose from the booth. He has a point there.

But reading.

It's not that he can't read—he obviously can. Nor does he
have any disorders that make reading harder. His eyesight is
also excellent. The problem is inflection and pace.

When he reads aloud to Scout, it's stilted and monotone,
but fast. It's the weirdest thing, like he's trying to get through
the words as fast as he can. With some of her books, I can
totally relate. I rush through them, too, but I still vary my
inflection, as needed. Jet doesn't. He reads out loud like a
robot, like the personal assistant on my phone when I ask it
the weather forecast or to read the entries in my calendar.
Just last night, he read a story to Scout at bedtime and
sounded the same as always. If he reads from the
teleprompter like that, today's broadcast is going to be
painful.

I'm putting all my trust in the consultants and coaches
that work with the "talent" at Football Network. Surely, they
wouldn't allow Jet to go on the air reading like Mr. Google.
Plus, if he says it'll be "easy peasy," I should believe that,
right? Maybe I should prepare to be wowed by his performance. Maybe I should have more faith in his abilities. I'm
still going to pray, though. There's no harm in covering all the
bases.

I emerge from the prayer closet/pantry with my breakfast
fixings and set them on the island at the same time Jet arrives
to place his dirty dishes in the dishwasher. Pouring cereal,
nuts, and milk into a bowl, I smile at him again.

"You look more nervous than me," he says astutely.

"What?"

"What?" He nudges me playfully.

"Well, I'm not nervous at all, so you must be flat-lining," I lie.

He shrugs. "I'm prepared."

"Oh, good," I say, sounding way too relieved. "I mean, that's great. I'd expect nothing less from you."

"Erin's been helping me."

"Perfect. She's a veteran."

"Yeah, that's why they put her with me, probably."

"They know what they're doing. And so do you, I'm sure."

He points to my cereal. "You better eat that before it gets soggy."

"Huh? Oh, right. Yeah." I slide a spoon from the drawer and dig it into the flakes.

Dropping a kiss on my forehead, he steps around me. "Better get going. Gotta catch the bus at eight."

"Don't forget to say goodbye to Scout."

"I don't want to wake her up."

"Tomorrow's her actual birthday."

"I'm aware of that. I'll be back in plenty of time for the big bash on Saturday, though."

"That's not the point. I'm afraid she's going to be really disappointed she's not getting that gerbil for her birthday. You'll only be adding to the upset if you don't kiss her goodbye."

He sighs, but his lips turn up proudly as he reverses course to walk down the hallway to our daughter's room. As I pull up a stool to the island and sit down with my breakfast, I hear their murmuring voices but not the content of the conversation.

Scout love-hates goodbyes, even short-term ones. They're something we've all gotten really good at over the years, however. Unfortunately.

When she was really little, it became a tradition that no matter how sad we were each week after Jet left, I'd say to Scout, sometimes through both of our tears, "We've got this." At first, I said it strictly for my own benefit, but as Scout grew and began to understand the world around her, it became a reminder to both of us that goodbyes are part of life, and we're strong enough for anything life can lob our way.

———

My phone buzzes on the desk next to me while I take a break from putting the finishing touches on the birthday party to watch Scout model the cute sun dress and sandals she—and her stuffed animals—have chosen for her to wear over her swimsuit on her big day.

She moves on to a comparison and contrast of the French braid versus the crown twist for the first day of school in two weeks—neither of which I'm good at and both of which will add several frustrating minutes to our nervous morning. When I glance at the insistently-buzzing phone's screen, I expect to see Nina's face. What I see instead makes me recoil.

"It's Gigi," I say lightly to mask my ambivalence. "Calling to wish you a happy birthday, I bet."

Scout swipes her finger across the screen like a pro and places the phone against her ear with a breezy, "Hey, Gigi!"

I turn back to my laptop while I listen to the largely indistinct high-pitched squawks through the earpiece our daughter has learned to hold a few inches away when conversing with Jet's mom. Mostly, I try to focus on which vendor to call next to verify delivery the day after tomorrow, but occasionally, I catch a word like, "pretty" or "popular" and clench my teeth.

It hasn't escaped me that I'm reinforcing those shallow

qualities with this weekend's party. An almost-five-year-old isn't going to grasp my more complicated motives or appreciate the nuance built into my plans. I'm actually counting on her not to see it as anything more than a huge party to celebrate her birthday and maybe distract her from the fact that she's not getting the top item on her birthday wish list.

Soon, I hear the typical wrap-it-up phrases from Scout, so when she hands me the phone after saying, "Bye-bye, Gigi! Love you more!" I nearly set it down without a second glance, but Scout stops me cold. "She wants to talk to you."

Instead of whining, *"Whhyyyyyyy?"* like I want to, I pat her hand and say, "Oh. Okay, sweetie." Then loudly enough that I'm sure Gloria can hear me, I add, "I won't be long. Then we can finish choosing your hairstyle."

So much for "nuance."

While Scout skips away, presumably to get yet another vote from Torzi, I close my eyes and submit to my mother-in-law's mobile summons. "Hello, Glo— Mom."

"I'm worried about Jet."

"I'm fine, thanks. And you?"

She ignores my manners prompt and merely repeats—or possibly answers, "I'm worried about Jet."

"Why?"

"Why?" I hold the phone a couple more inches away from my ear. "Are you even watching the game?"

Although it's recording and firmly on my long to-do list for later, she's the last person to whom I'd admit the truth in this particular case. "Yep."

"I can't hear it through the phone."

"I turned it down when you called."

Either buying it or deciding it's not worth arguing about, she asks, "What do you think so far?"

*Shit!* "Uh, well… I mean—"

"I know you don't want to say anything negative, and I don't either. Trust me. It's breaking my heart to listen to this." Her choked voice bears this out. "In fact, I think today's performance is worse than that god-awful season preview they did, but I chalked that up to him being uncomfortable in the studio with the teleprompter. Am I being overly critical?"

"You? Hypercritical? Never."

"Be serious."

I swallow and say, "He's just finding his feet."

"He needs to find them—fast. At this rate, he's going to find himself out of a job before the regular season even starts." I can practically hear her wringing her meaty hands.

"It's not *that* bad." *Please, God. Tell me it isn't that bad.*

"Thankfully, that Mexican girl stepped in."

"Erin?" I supply distractedly and weakly. "I don't think she's Mexican."

"She looks it. Anyway, it's obvious Jet's humiliated. He's hardly said two words in the past several minutes. Which is probably a good thing, come to think of it. He seems to forget he's wearing a mic and doesn't have to shout. Do you think he's going to get fired?"

"No!"

"If he can't handle these piddly pre-season games, how's he going to keep up in the regular season? Or the post-season?"

I gulp. "He'll be fine. I'll, uh, work with him at home, or something."

She *tsks*. "Oh, Maura, really. What are you possibly going to do?"

First, I'm going to watch that train wreck of a game. Then I might know better. But probably not. To her, I say, "I'll figure it out. He'll figure it out."

"He's never struggled like this with anything. Except multiplication. He was terrible at that. 'Seven times eight is fifty-six, Jet!' I can't tell you how many times we had to go over and over that. He probably still doesn't know it."

"I'm sure he does Gloria! Geez."

"Only because it's a multiple of seven, which is important in football. You know what I'm saying, though."

"If I didn't know better, I'd think you were calling your son stupid."

"I am not! I'm simply saying when things don't come naturally to him, he checks out."

Oh, no, no, no, no, no. There will be no checking out here. We're all in. I'm basically running a busy non-profit remotely, just a notch above doing it from my basement—and only because we don't have a basement. Before bed every night, I expand my Spanish vocabulary. "Organic" is my new middle name. I've even acquired a taste for avocados, although if I eat one more, I'm going to turn into one. I'm working my ass off to embrace the California lifestyle. So nobody's checking out of anything or anywhere. I left everything and everyone to follow him out here. I'm a medical marijuana card and one surfing lesson away from going completely "native," as my friend Colin would say.

Not to mention, I have four dozen kids and their parents, most of whom I don't know, arriving at our house in two days, and school starts in two weeks. For better or worse, this is our home now.

"I have to go," I say now to my mother-in-law, stuffing down the panic rising in my chest.

"Don't tell Jet I said any of this. He's so sensitive lately.

But I wanted to at least convey my worries to you. Of course, Ned thinks I'm overreacting, and Gidget thinks I'm being mean. I figured you would understand the most where I'm coming from. Surely, you're just as worried as I am."

"I have every faith that things will be fine. He's still figuring it out. Not everyone starts their new job in front of a national audience."

"Every job he's ever had has been in front of a national audience. That's definitely not the problem."

"Then nothing has changed there. And he has producers and consultants to work out the kinks. We just need to be silently supportive."

"Yes, yes. Fine. I suppose."

That's the closest I'm ever going to get to her admitting I might be knowledgeable about something, anything, so it's a good time to end the conversation.

"Okay, then, Gloria. We'll see you Saturday at the party."

"Of course. I'll be there—along with half of Southern California."

Right before I disconnect, she puts in her vote for the crown twist for Scout's first day of school hairstyle.

Right. Priorities.

———

Sleep eludes. Too many things banging around inside my skull. Did I confirm every vendor for Saturday's party? I check each one off a mental list to make sure, then do it again, in alphabetical order this time, so I know I haven't left anyone off. Yes. Everything is set. Tomorrow—that is, later today, Friday—my grocery order will be delivered, and I can get most of the food prepped ahead of time and stored in the fridge. I'm also expecting the cleaners, even though it's not our usual week, to arrive and spruce up the main areas of the house and any bathrooms the guests will be using.

Knowing I've done all I can to be as prepared as possible, I try to distract myself with the game I should have watched live, like I told Gloria I was doing. My plan, in fact, had been to turn it on as soon as I got off the phone with her, but I chickened out. I just couldn't make myself do it. If it's as bad as she says it is—and there's no reason to think it isn't, considering she would never unnecessarily criticize her golden boy—then do I really have to see it? I get it. It was painful.

Plus, I'm sure Jet will be his harshest critic and will give me all the gory details from his perspective when he gets home later. That all seemed like reasonable justification to remain in the dark about the specifics and avoid as much vicarious embarrassment as possible.

The more I thought about it, though, the guiltier I felt. It was his first-ever booth announce. Good, bad, or ugly, it was a big deal, a milestone in his career, and as his partner, it was my duty to share it with him. I couldn't go back in time to watch the game live, but it was recorded. The least I could do was watch it before he got home. That way, I'd know exactly what he went through and could be a better support, if needed.

So I watched. I'm still watching, actually, although it's the fourth quarter—thank God—so I'm almost finished. My humble opinion of Jet's performance lands somewhere between Gloria's assessment of "train wreck" and a Jet Knox "super-awesome." It's not the worst rookie broadcasting job I've ever suffered through. A lot of retired guys can't cut it. They have the knowledge but can't stick the delivery.

Only the truly good ones stick around—like Dallas's

former quarterback, Lorenzo Walker. He transitioned to broadcasting so seamlessly, it felt like he'd been in the booth forever by the end of his first season. He's still one of my favorite announcers. He's the perfect blend of funny, down-to-earth, knowledgeable, and entertaining. I see that same potential in Jet, although he may have to work just a little bit harder to cultivate the skills it will take to get there.

The interaction between him and Erin is actually pretty good for new partners. They seem relaxed with each other, for starters. Most of the time, they truly do sound like two friends, both avid fans, discussing their favorite game. In the way of content, she intuits when the moment calls for a bit more filler—stats, player back stories, and the like—and readily provides it; he excels at the play-by-play and at predicting what the offense is going to do next. There were a few times when I was downright impressed—and proud—at how well he knew exactly which play was being run, like he was still the guy receiving the calls through his helmet.

So there's hope and a lot of promise, but there's also a ton of room for improvement. As I predicted/worried, his delivery is rough when he has to read something. He may need to enlist the services of a private coach, someone to give him pointers and help him smooth things out a bit. He's lacking polish. That's hardly unusual for a newbie. It's not a fatal flaw, if he quickly remedies it.

One thing's for sure, though. He's not nearly the "stud" in the booth that he was on the field, and he has a long way to go to get there—if that's even possible. Frankly, at this point, it's hard to imagine. That doesn't mean I can't hope and dream for it, though.

"Hey." He startles me by suddenly appearing a few feet in

front of the chair where I'm curled up. He perches on the edge of the matching chair next to mine.

I fumble removing my earbuds and closing the lid on my laptop before he can see what I'm watching. "Oh, hi! You're home."

"I believe I am," he says wearily. "What are you still doing up? I thought for sure you'd be sound asleep by the time I got back."

Glancing at the clock on the fireplace mantle, I wince at the position of the hands. "Oh, shit. I didn't realize how late it was. I was having trouble switching off my brain and sleeping."

"That's never a problem for me. So, whatcha watchin'?"

"Nothing! I was listening to music and reading some Yelp reviews of The Knox."

"That's probably not going to help you sleep."

"They're all good, except one or two that complain we don't play first-run films, but those people are clearly missing the point, so…"

"The internet is such a great hiding place for trolls," he says around a yawn, tousling his hair to release it from its TV-perfect style. "That's why I don't go on there. I definitely won't be reading viewers' comments about my broadcasting performances."

"Good call!" Realizing I sound a little too eager, I tone it down. "That is, nothing good comes from that. If you want helpful, honest feedback about how you're doing, hire a consultant who's a professional in the business."

There. Wow. It was surprisingly easy to lob that bit of advice in there and make it sound general, not in response to anything specific.

He rubs his chin. "Today was really hard."

"It'll get easier."

"Did you watch?" Before I can answer, he groans. "You did. I can tell by the pity in your eyes."

"It's not pity! And of course, I did. It was your first booth call."

"I sucked."

"No, you didn't."

"You don't have to lie, Maura."

I set the laptop and earbuds on the coffee table in front of us and move to sit sideways on his lap. Bracing my hands on either side of his face and squeezing his cheeks, I say, "I'm not lying." I place a peck on his squished lips. "You're new. Even veteran broadcasters have to shake off the rust, and—"

"There's no rust for me to shake off." Because I still have hold of his face, it comes out muffled. I let go. He settles back farther in the chair and rests his head under my chin, against my chest.

"Okay, different analogy: you're like a— a…" I choose something he can relate to. "New car! You have to break it in those first thousand miles or so, right? Everything's a little tight. Needs to be babied a bit."

"First *thousand* miles? I'm screwed. I'm going to look like a complete ass on national television every week. That is, if they don't fire me." He turns his head, burying his face between my boobs and inhaling.

Letting my head fall back, I sigh at the recessed lights in the ceiling, noticing one is burnt out and absently wondering how the heck we're going to change it. Do we even own a ladder that tall?

"I thought," he says, interrupting my musing about the mundane and bringing me back to the tougher problem at hand. After a pause, he draws his head back and looks up at me, then starts again. "I thought it would be easy, you know? I can memorize stuff. I've memorized how many plays over the years?"

"Thousands."

"Thousands. Exactly. And this is just sitting around talking about football, right? I can talk about football all day."

"Yes. We've tested that theory."

He squeezes his fingers into his eyes. "But it's not that simple, you know?"

"Nothing ever is."

"I'm fine when I'm allowed to just talk. But when I have to say something specific or read from the 'prompter, I'm all, *'beep boop beep boop.'*"

In spite of my best efforts, I crack up at his self-aware robot impression.

"Or I get tongue-tied. And then I can't recover."

"It wasn't as bad as you think. It feels worse than it was, I'm sure."

He drops his hand and blinks down at me. "Well, you watched. You tell me. Be honest! If you weren't married to me or didn't even know me, and you were watching today, like a normal viewer, what would you have thought?"

"I can't be that objective!"

"Try."

Inhaling deeply through my nose, I replay in my mind some of the most uncomfortable parts of the broadcast I just watched. "I'd think…" I exhale, squirming. "I'd think, 'This guy is new.'"

"And awkward."

"Mmm, maybe a little. But cute."

He rolls his eyes, but a crooked smile sneaks through. "Oh,

come on. I'm not on camera that much. Thank God. That would make this ten times worse."

I snuggle up to him. "Doesn't matter. I know what you look like, especially when you're concentrating. You're cute. More like, *hot*. Totally hot. Like, 'I don't care if this guy sings the alphabet, off-key, and forgets some of the letters; I could look at him *all* day.'"

"Stop objectifying me."

"You know you love it, champ." I run my hand up his chest and dot him on the chin with my index finger.

He sucks in a breath through his teeth. "Be serious."

"Oh, I am. Extremely serious." I wiggle my hips to grind my butt against his stiffening crotch. Breathing warmly against his jaw, I whisper, "And we seriously need to get to sleep. Busy day tomorrow." With a silly kiss on his cheek, I stand up and sashay away from him, toward our bedroom.

He quickly follows, catching up to me right before I reach the door. Hooking me around the waist, he turns me to face him, walking me backward into our room, kicking the door closed behind him. "I think sleep can wait a few more minutes, don't you?"

"Definitely," I answer, nudging my lips against his.

"This isn't a pity-screw, though, right?"

"Absolutely not. This is an 'I'm-married-to-the-hottest-sports-announcer-ever' screw."

"I'll take it," he says with a chuckle as he tugs off his clothes and backs me up to the bed.

## TEN

## PARTY TIME

For someone who was so reticent about nearly every extravagant idea, Jet sure is enjoying all aspects of the party. Now *I'm* the nervous one, anxiously overseeing each detail, fluttering from front lawn to living room to kitchen to patio to pool area to backyard, making sure everyone is having a good time and nobody is barfing, crying, or endangering themselves and others.

While Jet and Scout lead the dancing, I tidy the abandoned areas of the house and front yard to mitigate cleanup later. When half the party moves to the pool for a rousing game of Marco Polo, I ready the towels for when the game ends or the kids tire of it and exit the pool. Then I check on the rest of the guests in their various places: parents mingling with each other near the bar; kids in the front yard experimenting with virtual reality; more competitive guests trying to one-up each other on the arcade games; and still others continuing to dance or suck down as many chocolate-covered marshmallows, strawberries, pretzels, and pineapple chunks as their tiny tummies can handle.

After checking the bathrooms to make sure we're still good on toilet paper and hand soap, I bump into Scout in the hallway. "Hey, you. Having a good time?"

"The best, Mommy!" She hugs me around my waist and looks up at me. "Thank you for my party."

"You're welcome, sweetie. Glad you're enjoying it. Everyone else seems to be having fun, too."

Jet peeks his head through the doorway from the outdoor kitchen. "There you are, Bump! Come on! We're about to play some water volleyball."

"Coming. I just wanted to check on Torzi to make sure he's not lonely."

"He's fine," I say, steering her back toward her dad. "Go play. Before you know it, it'll be time to wrap things up and send everyone home with their presents."

As they hurry back to the pool, I hear Jet say, "If you ride on my shoulders, you can hit some sick spikes."

I wish I could follow them, but one of us has to keep everything moving smoothly. The bathing suit I'm wearing under this sarong is part of a costume. The role: carefree hostess of an effortlessly amazing house party.

Noticing the fruit supply running low at the chocolate fountain, I fetch more from the fridge and start cutting up the rest of the pineapple. Kiki Valentine, dressed from head to toe in white linen, arrives in the kitchen, taking a seat across from me at the island. Without even realizing why I'm doing it, I suck in my tummy, stand straighter, and start chewing on my comparatively thin lips while I command my knife-wielding hands to remain steady. Knives and nerves aren't a good combination.

Since meeting her, I've been awestruck and more than a bit intimidated by Kiki. She's so polished and together. A successful real estate agent, her face is on several billboards, buses, and bus stop benches in the greater Los Angeles area. There's no escaping her toothy, charming grin, which serves as an invitation to call her with all of your real estate needs.

As soon as the Valentines arrived today—not too early, not too late—Larissa made herself at home, taking charge of Scout's attention and demanding to know the day's schedule of events, like a tiny dictator in a purple polka dot sun dress with matching bikini underneath. She's been at the center of every activity so far, almost as if she's the birthday girl.

Richard said his hellos and gravitated toward the bar, where he's been ever since, aggressively networking, glad-handing, and drinking.

Mindful of the pooling fruit juices, Kiki leans conspiratorially across the island and says, "Fabulous shindig, Maura."

"Thanks." Focusing on the sharp knife and curling my fingers away from the blade, I say, "A lot of it is thanks to you. I couldn't have done it without that list."

"Shhhh," she glances around, making it seem as if she's casually taking stock of the other guests while adjusting her earring. "That has to be our little secret."

"Right. Sorry. Well, we do appreciate it."

She waves off my gratitude but her simper indicates she's well aware of her contribution and hopes I don't forget it.

"And thanks for coming. Summer must be a pretty busy time for you." I pop a piece of pineapple in my mouth and savor its sweetness. It's the first food I've had all day.

"Every season is a busy time, but yes, summer is even crazier. I'll pull back a little with school starting up and our babies entering kindergarten. Can you believe it? It seems like just yesterday." She blinks her impossibly long eyelashes rapidly, as if staving off tears, but her eyes remain clear and dry.

Meanwhile, a huge lump forms in my throat. I clear it away with a swallow and manage, "It really does."

"There's no need to worry, though. Scout will fit in just fine. She's such a darling girl! You must be so proud."

"We are. She has a heart of gold." I scrape the pineapple chunks into a bowl and the scraps into the trash, then rinse the knife and my hands, patting the moisture from them with the towel over my shoulder and moving on to the strawberries.

"Well, this party will be talked about for a long time, I can tell you that, and parents will be trying to top it for years to come, I bet."

"I hope it hasn't come off as ostentatious," I say with a wince and chuckle that I hope convey some measure of modesty. "We just wanted everyone to have a great time and get to know each other."

"This has been a wonderful opportunity to remind all of these kindergarten parents about PTA, too," Kiki says with a sly smile. "It'll be great to have some new blood like you."

Why do I suddenly feel like a minnow being approached by a school of sharks led by Kiki? I push back the paranoia.

"Of course, we'll be involved in PTA, as our other obligations and schedules allow. We're pretty busy, too."

Now her large red lips tighten across her bright white teeth. Her eyes deaden. "We're all busy, hon. That's just the way life is. But we never make the children pay for that, right?"

"Right! Absolutely not. I just meant—"

She perks back up. "And we're ready for you! Jet, too! We

have lots of dads. Not just gay or trans dads, either. Like, actual dad-dads."

"Gay and trans dads *are* 'dad-dads,'" I say as sweetly as possible.

"Right. But you know what I mean. Straight men are also into PTA here."

"That's... great." *And not all that unique.* "I'm sure Jet will want to participate as much as I do. Maybe more so." *Definitely more so, considering I don't want to do it at all, and this conversation isn't motivating me further.*

Strawberries de-topped, I gather them up and drop them in the bowl on top of the pineapple. After washing my hands of the sticky juices, I motion with the bowl toward the fountain in the open area between the kitchen and living room. "I just need to..."

"Of course! Sorry. You're hosting the kindergarten gala of the century here, but I couldn't let the afternoon get away from me without having a chat with you. We need to get the girls together again soon for a play date."

"Sure."

"Fantastic. With Richard and Jet working so closely together, and with us living so close, it seems natural that our families would see a lot of each other socially."

A visceral dread floods my body, but I manage a polite, "Absolutely," that sounds just as fake to my ears as half the bosoms in this room.

"Plus, Richard just loves Jet. That's all he talks about lately. 'Jet Knox' this and 'Jet Knox' that." She holds her hand like a privacy flap next to her mouth and stage whispers, "I think he has a man crush!"

When all I can do is laugh nervously, she continues, "But that's good for you, because as long as Richard likes someone, they don't have to be the best in the biz to make it." Now, she looks more pointedly at me. "If you get my drift."

Sensing she's referring as politely as possible to Jet's less-than-stellar start in the booth, I blush and stammer, "Uh, y-yes. I think I d-do." The heavy fruit bowl slips a bit in my damp hands, so I readjust my grip while trying to shake off the feeling that everything she says is calculated. I'm ashamed at myself for my suspicions. She's done so much to try to make us feel at home since moving here, and without her, I wouldn't have had any way to invite our guests to this party. There's something about her, though, that makes me uneasy.

Not having the immediate opportunity to examine it further, I brush it aside for now and chalk it up to reverse snobbery.

She wiggles her crimson-tipped fingers at me. "Well, then. Toodles!"

*Toodles*, indeed.

———

Well after Scout voluntarily turns in for the night, tired from her social duties and hoping, no doubt, to avoid helping with the cleanup effort, Jet and I remain awake and busy. The deejay and bartender immediately packed up their equipment and settled up with us after the last guest left. A few hours later, the party rental supplier picked up and hauled away the VR, arcade games, and chocolate fountain. Now we're left with a house more wrecked than anything my brother and I ever dealt with after hosting drunken high school high jinks when our parents went out of town for the occasional weekend.

I'm not ashamed to say that my first reaction and temptation when faced with the destruction was to, simply, move. My second idea was to call the cleaning service back. Of course, they're closed until Monday. Living with this mess until then is unthinkable. Right?

Since Jet repeatedly asked me to reconsider the messiest part of the party plans—to no avail—it's only fair that I'm the one to deal with its aftermath. Chocolate and fruit juice drips, splatters, and spills outline where the fountain stood minutes ago. With a bucket of hot, soapy water, a plastic scraper I normally use to clean the pizza stone or the cast-iron skillet after a particularly messy dish, a sponge, and a washcloth, I drop to my hands and knees at the furthest sticky spot I find—remarkably close to the white couch, many yards away—and start scrubbing.

Jet smirks at my position but refrains from saying, "I told you so." Instead, he chooses the more passive-aggressive, "Don't forget those," while pointing at the formerly white columns all the way out on the patio, now smeared with fudgy hand prints. "And those…" He holds up his index finger and twirls it in a large circle around his head, gesturing to every white wall in the space around us, also intermittently painted with brown goo.

I want to cry, but I merely breathe deeply through my nose and say, "Got it. Thanks."

He takes a large black trash bag from under the sink and methodically makes his way through the house, shoving paper plates, plastic cups, napkins, wooden fondue sticks, and other detritus into it, whistling as if it's the best time he's had all day.

After several minutes of working the exact same five-foot circle, I eventually see the futility of spot-cleaning a floor that needs a complete mopping. Since I can't mop the walls and columns, I transfer my attention to them. Fortunately, the smears wipe off the glossy paint relatively easily, although the sheer number of them will prove time-consuming.

Jet comes back from the pool area with the full trash bag in one hand and the canvas bag of wet pool towels in the other. "Done with the floors already?" he teases on his way through to the utility room to drop off the laundry.

"Har har," I crow when he appears to be out of earshot.

"I heard that!"

*I heard that,* I mock silently, sponging four chocolate stripes that had to have been deliberately put there by someone dragging their fingers along the wall.

When he re-enters the kitchen after taking out the trash, he cheerfully pours the leftover fruit into separate zipper bags and stores them in the fridge. He sprays the counters and wipes them down, singing one of the kids' "theme songs" quietly under his breath and shaking his hips and butt to the beat.

What is his deal? If nothing else, he should be tired from the physical activity. He was all over the place today, dancing, swimming, tossing the football with a couple of the sportier parents, carrying Scout around on his shoulders, playing in a pinball tournament, supervising (and trying out) the virtual reality experience, and eating his own weight in fruit, chocolate sauce, and cake. You name it, he did it. And while I waited for the party supply company to pick up their equipment, he took the gifts some guests just couldn't resist bringing to the Happy Birthdays donation center in town, rushing to get there before they closed for the week.

Now he's bee-bopping around like party cleanup is his jam.

Hoping I don't sound too bitchy about it, I finally ask, "What are you so peppy about?"

Surprised, he stops mid-lyric and stares at me for a minute, grinning. "It was a fun day. You know how I am. I love stuff like this. Being around people pumps me up."

Ugh. Extroverts.

Accurately reading my silence, he says, amused, "This party was *your* idea. I was totally cool with having a few kids over for a cookout and a pool party or whatever, but no! You had to suddenly go all Kardashian on me and blow the place up for a bunch of five-year-olds."

"It's a milestone age!"

"Sure. So rent a bouncy house and *maybe* hire a clown."

"Clowns are creepy."

He doesn't argue with that. Rather, he merely pitches his soiled paper towels in the trash and kicks off his boat shoes, setting them out of the way in the laundry room.

"Anyway," I say, when he pads barefoot back into the room, "it was a raging success."

"Of course it was! You served booze to the parents and unlimited sugar to the kids. You gave a whole new meaning to 'party favor' with those gifts you got each guest. Shit, that deejay got even the shiest kids dancing and out of their shells. Theme songs for each kid? Brilliant."

I blush. "Thanks."

"You're welcome. So my question is, why aren't *you* peppier?"

I move down the wall and dip the sponge into the soapy water again, wringing it out before scrubbing at what I hope is strawberry juice. "I. Am. Blinking. Shattered. As Colin would say."

With a sympathetic chuckle, Jet walks over to me. "Aw, beautiful. Here, let me help." He takes the bucket and sponge from me. I continue to wipe the latest clean spot with the wash cloth to clear any leftover residue. "I'll scrub, you wipe."

"Thanks."

"Of course. We're a team."

"The chocolate fountain was a mistake."

"Like we tell Scout, mistakes are important; we learn from them."

I groan. "Oh, I've learned."

With stronger hands than mine, he makes much faster work of the stains, and we move quickly from the living area onto the patio.

We work in silence for a few minutes, and then he says, "What really brought all this on? And stop it with the 'milestone' reason. Did you lose a bet with Scout? Is she blackmailing you? Was this an elaborate bribe? Spill it."

"We don't do bribes."

"I know we don't. So, what's the deal?"

I shrug and pretend swabbing wet spots on columns takes much more concentration than it does. How can I tell him the truth, that I did it to impress his boss (and his boss's wife)? That after the season preview broadcast a couple of weeks ago, I panicked a little at how bad he was on-air? That Thursday night's pre-season game only amplified those fears and solidified my resolve to throw this bash in an effort to show how well we could fit in, how dedicated we were to making friends and putting down roots here?

I can't. Despite his self-criticism the other night, he still has faith in himself that he can do this, if for no other reason than it's part of "The Plan," and he always follows through on his plans. I can't be the one to shatter that. I won't be.

I sure as hell am not going to admit, either, that I succumbed to good old-fashioned peer pressure when I was lame-shamed by a mom who has her shit so together, it could be sold as perfume additive. That trade secret's safe with me.

Who knows if the plan even worked, anyway? It was a desperately improvised ploy, after all. I didn't talk to Richard more than to say "Hello," "How's it going," and "Goodbye." Now that it's over, it seems naive and a bit ridiculous to think that one afternoon at our house would convince a dollars-and-cents guy like him that Jet's an indispensable part of the broadcast team, just because he's fun and kind and funny and wonderful. Guys like Richard don't care about that; they only care about the bottom line. If Jet's inability to perform—on-air, that is—costs the network money, he'll be gone without a second thought about who he is as a person—who we are as a family.

Then again, Kiki said Richard's been swayed before by charm over talent. If we can inveigle our way into a safe social position...

"It was to help Scout make friends," I finally answer quietly, wringing out the washcloth in the soapy bucket.

"Wow." Irritation creeps into his voice. "Here I am, scrubbing shit off the walls with you, and you won't even honestly answer my question. Nice."

"That's the truth!"

"Maybe part of it, but I'm not that stupid. A pool party would have done the trick. Scout is an awesome kid. She doesn't need over-the-top tactics to make friends. She's not like you." He freezes, mid-scrub.

I try to avert my suddenly pale face and stinging eyes, but since I'm standing right next to him, it's impossible to hide my hurt.

"Oh, my gosh, Maura. I'm— I didn't mean it like—"

"Okay." My choked voice lets him know it's anything but.

"I just meant because you're—"

"A loser?"

"No! One of those people who isn't good at making friends. I— I can't remember the fancy word for it right now." He scrubs in double-time, leaving me behind as he puts more distance between us, probably to get out of testicle-punching range.

"I think the word you're searching for is 'loser,' and there's nothing fancy about it."

He sets down the bucket and hurls the sponge into it. Bubbles float up between us. He waves them off. His sun-pinkened nose flares. "No, it's one of those five-dollar words you use all the time, something you call yourself. Intro-something."

"Introvert."

"Yes!" He looks relieved. "Introvert. Scout isn't an intro-vert. She's more like me. She likes being around people and making friends. People *want* to be friends with her."

"Right. Unlike me." I drop my rag into the water after wiping the last of the cleaned spots.

"Maura, that's not what I meant. You're purposely taking it the wrong way, to make me the bad guy, when you're the one who won't tell me what the hell's going on."

He bends down to pick up the bucket and takes it to the outdoor kitchen, dumping the murky water into the sink and rinsing out the sponge. While the bucket refills, he stomps into the storage closet, where he finds a mop and floor cleaner. Back at the sink, he turns off the water and hefts the bucket and the mop into the living room, wiping back and forth on the floor as if he's doing a trendy, new, intense cleaning/workout program.

I cling to my hurt to mask my guilt. "I know I don't fit in

here. I wanted to try, though. I don't want Scout to pay for having a mom like me." I stop, fearing I've laid it on too thick.

My fears are confirmed when he doesn't rush to reassure me. Still, I wait. He says nothing but rubs so hard at one chocolate stain, I'm worried he's going to take the varnish off the wood floor.

"Would you?" I take the mop from him and set it in the bucket. Pulling the plastic scraper from my pocket, I kneel down and gently, gradually peel the dried, waxy chocolate blob from the plank. As soon as I move out of his way, he continues his soggy charge across the room, stopping now and then to point to other spots that need the scraper's attention.

When several minutes go by without him saying anything, I say lightly, as cheerfully as possible, "I just wanted Scout to see some familiar faces on that first day of school, to have some friends already. She seemed to make a good start on that today. I saw her talking and laughing with a couple of kids as they sat beside the pool. That's promising."

He points to a row of caked-on drips at the base of the kitchen island. While I scrape, he stews. Inadvertently (I think) splashing me with mop water as he goes behind me, cleaning what I've started, he finally says, "None of that explains what motivated you to plan a party that had to have been a nightmare for you. All those people and all that noise and all this mess when you could have picked a few kids from the class list and hosted a much more traditional thing."

"That wouldn't have been fair. Think of the kids who had been left out. It would have created resentment between those kids and Scout, right out of the gate." This much is true, at least. I feel on much firmer footing arguing the scale of the guest list than the scope of the activities.

"Still…"

"It just got out of hand."

"I'll say."

His constant criticism about a day he thoroughly enjoyed combines with my frustration at failing to justify the day's activities without telling him the full truth, so I snap, "You know what? I'm really tired, and I pretty much planned this whole thing and did all the work on the front end, so I'm gonna leave this with you and go to bed."

I throw him the scraper, which he snaps cleanly from the air. "What? It was your idea! Of course, you planned the whole thing and did all the work! I tried to help, I tried to convince you to tone it down! I didn't have time to organize such a circus, with everything going on at work."

"Yeah, because you're the only one juggling a career."

"I didn't say I was, but this was your idea, your choice!"

"That's never stopped you from butting in and taking over before." I stride toward our room, hoping he'll let me have the last word. For once, he does, probably left speechless by my shameless gaslighting.

I'd feel worse about that if I thought the truth would hurt him less.

## ELEVEN

## FIRST DAY FIASCO

Scout's first day of kindergarten starts with a fit when she wakes to find her much-anticipated crown twist didn't hold up overnight, and there's no time for me to fix it. I pull her hair back in a simple half-up, half-down twisted ponytail—still adorable, especially with the waves left by the wet braid from last night.

I prepared her for this possibility when I tucked her in, and she seemed fine with it at the time, but she's five. Now that it's a reality, she's not nearly as receptive to it. She whirls on me and rips down the first half of the inferior hair twist.

I throw up my hands and say, "Wear your hair down, then."

"Noooo! It'll get in my eyes, and I won't be able to see, and I'll get runned over or something!"

I turn her around by the shoulders and begin again on her hair, saying to her in the mirror, "Then be still. If you pull it out again, you're getting a normal ponytail, and that's that."

"Noooo!" She pinches her eyes closed and wails through a square mouth, shaking her head back and forth. I gently plant my palm on top of her head to steady it, and she wails harder. "Oww!!!"

Jet pokes his head into the bathroom. "What's going on in here?"

"Just the usual dramatics."

"Mommy's being mean at me!"

I sigh but don't bother to refute the claim. Scout is typically a laidback child, unless we have to be somewhere at a certain time, especially early in the morning. Since I'm not the most chipper of morning people, either, especially before my first cup of coffee, we butt heads a bit. Jet knows the drill.

Now, he observes the hairstyle I'm attempting and says, "I can take over."

Of course, he can. He'd love that, wouldn't he? To jump in and be the big hero? That's been his role in our family dynamic from Day One. When Maura can't cope, bring in the big guns.

It'd be nice if he'd acknowledge that sometimes *I'm* the hero. *I'm* the one who dries Scout's tears and distracts her from missing him when he's away from home. *I'm* the one who'll be stuck at the PTA meetings and volunteering at weekend events when he's out of town, working. *I'm* the one who sacrificed her career and entire social life—such as it was —on the altar of Jet's Plan. And if he only knew what I'm willing to do—and have done so far—to keep his dream of booth announcing alive.

But no. None of that *can* be known. I'm an unsung hero, the introverted friendless loser with nothing better to do than smooth the way for everyone behind the scenes.

I will say that Jet has bent himself into a pretzel to make up for the other night. All day yesterday, he tried to dote on me, offering to fetch me drinks, massage my back and feet, cook dinner, and entertain Scout so I could have some of that solitude that loners like me crave so much. I took him up on that final offer, if only to be left alone for an hour or two. The rest were politely rebuffed, including the one he made last night in bed. The one thing he hasn't done, however, is apologize.

I'm too tired to keep punishing him. "Doing" is his love language. Since I'm fed up with this activity anyway, I slide over to give him access to Scout but warn, "This isn't her first choice, but we don't have time to redo the one she wants."

"No biggie," he says eagerly. "This works for now, right, Bump?"

Unbelievably, with her dad at the controls (pulling her hair a lot harder than I would, I'd like to add), she nods and sniffles.

I roll my eyes and mutter, "Coffee," as I escape the bathroom and head down the hall to get breakfast started.

Another one of my grand plans for Scout's first day of school is a full, healthy, protein-packed, brain-feeding meal to start Scout's formal education off right: poached eggs, turkey bacon, avocado on whole wheat toast, and a blueberry smoothie.

When she sits down at the table, however, she stares at her plate and crosses her arms over her chest, saying with a scowl, "I wanted Froot Loops."

"Froot Loops?" Jet says in his most cajoling tone. "Froot Loops? You have this in front of you, and you want Froot Loops? Look! Avocado toast! You love avocado toast!"

"It looks like smashed boogers."

Jet snickers but quickly recovers and sobers. "Come on, Bump. You're being a butt. Eat your breakfast."

She turns up her nose. "No. It's gross. I don't like eggs like that."

Still standing near the stove, I offer, gripping tightly to the spatula—and my last shred of patience, "I'll make scrambled eggs for you."

"Yuck. I hate scrambled eggs. I wish Bobo was here instead of you."

Tears prick my eyelids, despite my knowing that both things have been said merely for effect and out of spite. With a deep, steadying breath, I set down the spatula in the sink and, to the sound of Jet reprimanding Scout and commanding her —to no avail—to apologize, I leave the kitchen and trudge into our bedroom to get dressed.

When I come back a few minutes later, Jet's eating both his and Scout's prepared breakfasts. Our daughter's drinking the milk from what I assume was a bowl of Froot Loops, judging by her smug glare over the rim of her bowl when she lifts it to drink the unnaturally-colored leftover milk. I make no comment and carefully moderate my movements as I calmly collect the dirty dishes in the sink and pour myself another cup of coffee. Without a word, I take it out to the patio, where I drink it alone, looking out at the tropical shrubbery swaying in the ocean-scented breeze.

As soon as Scout runs to her bathroom to brush her teeth, Jet joins me, standing next to my lounge chair. "I had to give her something. We couldn't send her to school hungry, and she wasn't going to eat what you made."

"Whatever. It's fine." Sip, sip, sip.

He inhales and holds it so long that I look up at him, squinting through the sun. Finally, he says exhales, breathes in again, and says, "I'm sorry about Saturday night."

"It's fine," I say brusquely. "We were both tired."

"Yeah, but—"

"Forget it. I'm sorry, too, that I put the worst construction on what you were trying to say." *And that I won't be completely honest with you about the reason for such an over-the-top party.*

I drain the rest of my coffee and rise from the chair, turning immediately to reenter the house and continue our morning.

He gently snags my hand on my way past him and reels me against his chest, kissing my cheek. "Breakfast was delicious."

"Thanks."

"And for what it's worth, I like you way better than Beau. Much easier on the eyes, for one thing."

I attempt a smile but worry it comes out more like a grimace.

He backs off, but his tone remains bright when he says, "Okay! Let me just check on Bump's progress and try one more pep talk, and we'll be ready."

"Sounds great."

I follow him as far as the kitchen, where I pour the rest of my coffee down the sink. Then I busy myself loading a few stray dishes into the dishwasher and wiping down the counters.

When Jet and Scout still haven't reappeared several minutes later, I poke my head into the opening of the hallway and bellow, "Let's go! We're going to be late!"

After a slight pause, Scout emerges from her bedroom, her dad right behind her, and walks toward me, head down. When she reaches me, she stops and says, "I'm sorry, Mommy," before burying her face in my belly.

I hug her tightly with one arm and place my other hand on the back of her head, stroking her neck with my thumb. "You're always forgiven."

She pushes away from me to run to the refrigerator to get her lunch satchel, containing the Ursuline-approved bento box, then continues on to the laundry room, where her backpack hangs on its hook by the door.

"What did you say to her?" I ask Jet as we walk together toward the garage.

"I told her it's okay to be nervous on the first day—I always was for the first game of the season—but if you're a jerk to all of your teammates, you ruin their first game, too, and nobody plays well."

A sports metaphor. Of course. I can't help but take comfort in his predictability.

He tugs on my hand. "Come on. We still have the drop-off line to survive."

As the three of us climb into the car and fasten our seat belts, I say to my teammates, "We've got this."

———

As Scout's bouncing head disappears into the building with several dozen other adorable bouncing heads, I squeeze the steering wheel and ask Jet, who practically has his face pressed against the car window, "Are you crying?"

"My eyeballs are a little sweaty," he says in a choked voice as I pull away and exit the parking lot.

Although parents are welcome to accompany their children, especially kindergartners, into the school on the first day, Scout insisted she could walk in alone. We didn't want to make her second-guess her own confidence, so we respected that and said breezy goodbyes in the car, forgoing our own need for prolonged hugs.

It's not about us. This is her journey, her life. She's ready for this part of it. We've done a great job—in spite of ourselves—preparing her for this day and instilling in her the confidence to walk into that building on her own, not gripping our legs and wailing, but holding her head high and meeting her new adventures with the same steely determination her dad showed every week as he ran out of the locker room and through that tunnel onto the field. We should be proud of that.

Jet clears his throat. "Uh, you gonna go?"

I flinch and press down the accelerator to advance through the light that's not going to get any greener.

"She's going to be okay," he says.

"Oh, I have no doubt about that," I reply with a chuckle.

"We'll be okay, too."

"Yep."

"It's crazy, though, isn't it?"

"Yep."

"I remember exactly what I thought the first time I held her." Pausing, he rubs his eyebrow but pushes on through a tight throat. "I thought, 'Holy shit. This is even better than winning the Super Bowl.'"

"Imagine that."

"It seems obvious, but until then, I really couldn't imagine it. I'd told myself it would *probably* be true, but until you feel it for real, you can't predict how much better it is. She wasn't real to me until I saw her and held her and kissed her. And then it was like a helmet to the chest. With no pads."

"So that's what that feels like."

"Yeah. Except it didn't hurt. It knocked the wind out of me, though, for sure." He blushes. "Sorry. I'm getting all mushy over here, and it's probably not helping things."

I reach over and take his hand. "It's okay. We're allowed. It's a big day."

Inserting a teasing tone into his voice he says, "Okay, then. Spill it. What were you thinking the first time you held her?"

"So many things."

"Tell me a few."

"Glad I wasn't pregnant anymore, for one."

"Sure, sure."

"Glad that I survived childbirth. Because I wasn't sure I would."

He winces.

"Amazed at how beautiful and perfect she was and that we made her."

"Yeah," he whispers.

"But when I looked down at her, I also saw this day. Lots of others. Big, momentous days and ho-hum normal days, too. Splashing in the pool, playing on the floor, eating ice cream, even arguing over hair. It all flashed across her face when I looked down into it. It was overwhelming and scary, but it was also exhilarating. I couldn't wait to experience it all with her. With you. At the same time, I didn't want it to happen too fast." At yet another red light, I turn my head and blink at him, sending tears down my cheeks. "It's happening so fast."

He swallows audibly. "I know."

I choke back a sob and return my attention to driving. Neither of us says anything the rest of the drive home. Or in the garage as I park the car. Or as we walk into the quiet house, absently greeting Torzi on our way to the patio.

I collapse face-down on one of the fully-reclined lounge chairs and think, I can sleep until it's time to pick her up, and that will make the day go by more quickly. Then I remember that life is already passing too fast, and I don't want to do anything to make it go by any faster.

Jet kneels next to my head and kisses my shoulder. "You okay?"

With a big breath and a brave smile, I turn my head and answer, "I'm fine." I sit up, forcing myself to think of something—anything—else.

My brain immediately throws up what we just witnessed at the school, all those kids with fresh haircuts or perfectly styled locks in their stiff, clean, and trendy new clothes, posed with their chalkboard placards, announcing their grade and age. After taking the obligatory pictures, the parents mingled with each other, chatting happily about who knows what in their yoga clothes and sunglasses. Even without their makeup and in their huge shades, I recognized a few from prime time television, something Jet and I were told to expect, as Ursuline is one of the most popular schools in the area for that segment of society.

That's what I'm up against, though: moms who mingle with celebrities—because they're also celebrities or are married to them—and look elegant even in messy ponytails and fitness clothes. Moms who are always on trend *before* the trend is a trend, because they *set* the trends. Moms with glamorous careers and lives, insiders to a world I've dreamed about my whole life.

Ten years ago—ironically, before I'd met Jet—I would have thought this was *the* life. Living in California, close to where so much of the movie magic that I love happens? Dream come true. Bumping into stars while browsing produce in Trader Joe's? Heaven. In theory, it was what I wanted back then. I was also terrified of it, though, which is why I never actually tried to make it happen. And now, now I'm so different from that job counselor with stars in her eyes and a vast movie collection I regularly used to escape reality. Or maybe I'm not all that different, at my core, but I'm self-aware enough to realize I was never really cut out for this. Living here has only underscored that fact.

I don't fit in. At all. I have no desire to do so. I *could* do it, easily, at least on the outside. I could buy the expensive clothes and accessories, cut and color my hair in the latest style, drive a flashier car, eat more avocados, eat *less*, overall, and socialize with the wives of Jet's co-workers, who would introduce me to their social circles, who would introduce me to *wider* social circles, until I, too, was assimilated. But then what? I make their interests my interests until there's no more me left at all? I've worked hard to make myself who I am. A lot of existential angst went into it, not to mention blood, sweat, and tears. I'd prefer not to be a social outcast and have *no* friends out here, but if I can't find my own tribe of people like me out here, then I'd rather be a loner.

"Did you see those moms on the front steps? They were all so... perfect."

Jet transfers himself to the lounger next to mine and sits on the side of it, elbows braced on his knees. "Ah, yes. The Front Step Brigade."

I laugh.

"We don't have to compete with those other parents, you know," he says seriously.

"I wouldn't dream of trying."

"I catch myself doing it, comparing myself to other guys, other dads."

"You stack up just fine."

He shakes his head. "It's been so long since I've lived here —and even when I lived here, in this state, I didn't live *here* in

L.A.—that I've forgotten what it's like to be surrounded by so many people—beautiful people—every day, everywhere you go."

"Yeah, because in Kansas City everyone's so hideous?"

"No! That's not— I— You know what I—"

I crack up at his bumbling. "Calm down. I'm just giving you a hard time."

"What I meant was, even the 'ugly' people out here are so…" He searches for the perfect word. "Sparkly. And petite. I feel like such a giant. I'm used to being one of the tallest people no matter where I go, but in Kansas City—"

"Midwesterners are corn-fed and stout."

"Yes! Here, I'm not just taller, but I'm *thicker.*"

"Yeah, baby!" I say with a lecherous growl.

"Anyway," he continues, "I catch myself looking at my co-workers or other dads at the school and think I'm not tan enough, I'm not cool enough, I'm not young enough, I'm not graceful enough, I'm too big and clumsy, my teeth aren't white enough—"

"If your teeth get any whiter, champ, they'll glow in the dark. Don't even think about it."

"You know what I mean, though. It sucks to feel 'less-than.' I never felt that way growing up."

"Because you were a native. Now you feel like an outsider. It'll all come back to you. I, on the other hand…"

"Culture shock can screw with you."

"You felt it in Kansas City, too, when you first got there?"

He looks up, squinting in the sun. "Nah. Everyone's so friendly there. Sure, there were some things that I was like, 'What the heck?' but nothing huge. Their obsession with barbecue is a little weird."

"Don't you badmouth barbecue."

Straightening, he raises his hands in front of his chest. "I'm a convert!" His hands drop to his lap. I move to sit beside him on his lounger and thread my arm through his, so we're linked. "Anyway," he continues, "after so long in New York, I had to get used to people smiling at me again."

"Smiling is our favorite. It's rude not to!"

"At first, I thought everyone was laughing *at* me."

Resting my head against his shoulder, I say, "I miss smiley people. Like, real smiles. Smiles that reach the eyes."

He pulls back a bit so I can see his face and demonstrates an L.A. smile, wide and toothy, but dead-eyed. "You don't like this?" he asks through clenched teeth.

Wheezing, I hide my eyes against his forearm. "Oh, it's so scary!"

He holds the look. "Did I nail it?"

"Please stop."

"Okay. I'm done." He laughs with me, but as soon as I'm sure his face will remain "normal," he immediately resumes the expression.

"Gaaaa!" This time, though, I don't hide from it. I lean forward and kiss it away. Hard.

His lips relax against mine, and his eyes droop. To steady us, he lets go of my hand and cups my face.

I rest my wrists on his shoulders and comb my fingers through his hair, pressing my forehead against his. "I miss Kansas City."

"Me, too," he says, surprising me.

I pull my head back. "You do?"

"Yeah. Don't get me wrong. I like it here. I love my job and our house and the weather—gosh, the weather!"

"Right?"

"But it doesn't feel like home."

"It will eventually, though, won't it?" I ask, desperation thick in my voice.

"Probably. Because home is where you and Scout and I are. Together."

I stare into his eyes. "Agreed."

After a few seconds of silence, he kisses me again, then withdraws and says, "Come on. Let's do something to take our minds off things for a while."

I roll my eyes. "Let me guess."

"When was the last time we had the whole house to ourselves, huh?" His eyebrows wiggle. "Would be a shame to waste the opportunity."

His suggestion, coupled with the kisses he's now placing all the way up my right arm, appeals more than I'd like to admit. Taking him by the hand, I lead him inside.

TWELVE

SEPARATION ANXIETY

My nethers are still buzzing when my phone does the same
from my shorts, somewhere far away on the living room floor.
At first I ignore it, assuming it's Nina, forgetting I took the
day off. Then, through my endorphin-crazed brain, I
remember that a piece of my heart is wandering around this
cruel world outside my body, and I'm the primary contact on
all of her emergency forms.

I practically launch off Jet, prompting a sharp gasp and
grunt from him, and dig through the pile of clothing on the
floor next to the coffee table. I grope frantically through
pockets until I locate the device. Sure enough, "Ursuline
Academy" flashes on the screen, and I answer it breathlessly
with my internal organs all crowding to leap into my throat at
once.

"Mrs. Knox?" says a cheerful voice.

"This is she," I squeak, scrambling for the cashmere throw
on the back of the couch and wrapping it around me, as if she
can see me.

"This is Rosario Nuñez, guidance counselor at Ursuline

Academy. Before I say anything else, I want to let you know that Scout is just fine."

"Okay." I can breathe now, but my brain is still shouting that something's not right. Otherwise, the counselor wouldn't be calling.

Jet sits up and scoots to the edge of the chair, blinking up at me. I mouth, *"The school,"* which has him reaching for his shorts and brings him, hopping as he pulls them on, next to me. I put the phone on speaker, so he can hear, and hold it between us.

"She's a bit upset right now, so her teacher sent her to spend some time with me."

My ears zoom in on the background noise and isolate the weeping, something I should have noticed and recognized right away. My heart skitters. "Oh, no. What's wrong?"

"This is completely normal and really common on the first day, especially for younger kindergartners. In fact, the whole first week of school, I'm pretty busy with separation anxiety cases, but…" She takes a deep breath. "Scout's been with me for a while now, and nothing I say seems to be soothing her. So I told her we'd call you. Sometimes hearing a familiar voice helps, and maybe you know what to say to calm her."

I nod dumbly, then hurry to inform her, "My husband—her dad—is here, too."

"Oh, good. I'll put her on the line right now." Her voice dims slightly as she holds the phone away from her, presumably handing it to our daughter, and says, "Scout? Your mommy and daddy are on the phone and want to talk to you, Sweetie."

Her sniffles and sobs come through at full volume, and she says, her voice tiny and snot-swollen, "Hello?"

Jet struggles to poke his head through his t-shirt. "Scout? What's the matter, Bump?"

Her response is to cry harder, saying through her tears, "I w-want to c-c-come home!"

My heart breaking at how small and vulnerable she sounds, I nevertheless manage to keep my voice steady and upbeat when I reply, "But you were so excited for school! What changed?"

"I w-want you and D-daddy."

Jet and I exchange anguished looks. While we scramble for the right thing to say, we murmur indistinct things at the phone. Then I finally land on something more concrete. "Sweetheart, you have to stay at school so you can learn and make a million friends and all those things we talked about all summer."

"I d-don't w-want to."

"But you have to," Jet says. "It'll get better, I promise."

"I w-want to c-come home."

While I blank, Jet continues to try to reason with her. "You can't right now, though."

"Why not?"

"Because school is your job, just like Mommy has the theater, and I go to work every day, too."

"You're not at work now," she says.

Damn. Nothing gets past that little booger.

"No. Today's a special day," he says. "I stayed home so I could take you to school and pick you up again later. See? Just a few more hours, and we'll be together again."

"I want to see you now!"

He sighs and rubs his face. "The first day is hard. It's a big change. But you can do it."

She begins crying again, this time softer, more resigned. Crushed.

"You can have a gerbil," I blurt.

Jet widens his eyes, raises one eyebrow, and slackens his jaw.

I ignore his face-pulling and say while looking at the phone, as if pleading with the device, "If you stop crying, and you're a brave girl and go back to your classroom, we'll get you that gerbil you've been asking for— and we'll get up a little earlier tomorrow and put your hair up exactly the way you want it."

She sniffles.

We wait, holding our collective breath.

"Okay," she finally near-whispers.

Jet and I exhale at the same time.

"We love you, Bump. You can do this," Jet says.

"You've got this," I remind her.

I can picture her determined expression as she nods, although she doesn't reply verbally to our pep talk. Finally, she says, "Mrs. Nuñez wants to talk to you again."

Crisis averted, I sigh and rub my forehead. "Okay, sweet girl. Put her on. Have a great rest of the day!"

After some rustling, the counselor returns to the phone. "So much better. What did you say to her, in case I need to reinforce later?"

Blushing, I admit, "I bribed her."

"Effective."

I'm relieved she sounds more amused than disapproving of my Band-Aid measure. Then she reassures us that Scout's emotional response to her first day is typical and not anything to worry about and promises to call again if there are further episodes.

When we disconnect, I collapse on the couch and pull my knees up to my chest, resting my forehead on them. Jet stands in front of me and rubs my head.

"She's fine," he says.

"She's too young. I knew she was too young."

"She's not. You heard the counselor. It's common."

"Especially with the *younger* kindergartners. She said that, too."

"There are lots of younger kindergartners who also went to Pre-K and probably still have a hard time adjusting to the all-day routine."

"She wouldn't have."

"We don't know that."

I look up at him, suddenly full of shame at what we'd been doing while our daughter was suffering, scared and feeling alone. Without another word, I shrug off the blanket and walk naked to our room, close myself in the bathroom, and cry while drawing a hot, steamy bath.

———

At afternoon pick-up, Scout and I are subdued while Jet is falsely cheerful, and we all attempt to pretend like nothing unusual happened today. Jet receives one-syllable, gray answers to his admittedly cliché questions like, "How was your day?" ("Fine.") "What was your favorite part?" ("Recess.") "Do you like your teacher?" ("Yes.") "Did you make any new friends?" ("Maybe.")

I expect her to be excited about the promise of her new gerbil, figuring it will be one of the first things she talks about on the way home, but she uncharacteristically doesn't even bring it up. It's probably just as well, since I'm experiencing major parental remorse over it.

Jet tried to reassure me that the bribe wasn't a big deal, in the grand scheme of things. However, unlike my brother and his wife, Deirdre, who could probably roll out a scroll the length of a football field with all of their parenting do's and don'ts, Jet and I have two simple rules: no corporal punishment and no bribes. I blew it today.

My husband disagrees. In typical analyst fashion, he studied the replay while I soaked and sobbed. At lunch, he said, "Hon, you did the best you could with what you had. The play was busted, the blitz was coming for you, and you threw up a prayer."

I rolled my eyes at the sports metaphor but couldn't help admitting it was pretty brilliant, the more I thought about it.

Problem is, this isn't a football game. It's not a game at all. This is our life, our child. She's in her most formative years. The things we do now will have lasting consequences. Everything we do and say matters. We're teaching her how to treat us, how to treat others. Today, I taught her that she can get whatever she wants if she cries long enough or seems pathetic enough. I taught her that Mommy (and Daddy) will swoop in and rescue her when life doesn't go the way she thinks it will.

But mostly, I taught her that *things* fix everything. If you're sad, buy something. As long as you have the money to acquire stuff, you can have the happiness.

Ugh.

Eventually Jet gives up on making conversation, and we finish the ride home in silence. When we alight from the car in the garage, he jerks his head at the bikes on the nearby wall racks.

"Wanna go for a ride?" he asks Scout, handing me her

backpack and lunch sack, making it clear I'm not invited. Which is totally okay with me. The last thing I want to do is struggle-bus up and down the hills in our neighborhood.

Her eyes brighten, and she grins while nodding.

Schlepping her bags while Jet takes down the bikes and sets them on the driveway, I say, "I'll just, uh, sort through all of these first-day-of-school papers and make dinner. Fish tacos, right, Scout? That's what you said you wanted?"

*Because if material possessions don't solve everything, food will take care of the rest. Sigh.*

"Yeah!" Still in her sun dress, she climbs onto her bike. "With extra chip-tolt-a-lay sauce, please!"

Jet jogs over to me, snagging the cycling helmets from their hooks on his way. Voice lowered, he says, "Hey. I can look through those papers with you later. You do whatever. Relax. Shop online. Swim. Read a book."

"But—"

"I'm just gonna let her blow off some steam and maybe get her to tell me what the deal is, why she's so down on school, after only one day." Helmet settled on his head, he lets the straps dangle. "I figure a little exercise will do her some good, clear her head."

Despite my doubts, I still nod. He's trying. Gotta give him points for that.

"I guess I'll do some research on gerbils."

"I don't think they're complicated."

"You know we're going to end up taking care of it, though. I want to know what I got us into."

He backs away, grinning. "You might be surprised. See you in a bit."

Turning to Scout, he plops her helmet in place, and they fasten their straps while discussing which direction to ride in.

I watch them pedal as fast as they can on the level driveway to pick up momentum for their first hill, only feet away from the house. Jet manages, but at the top of the rise, he sets down his bike in someone's front yard and doubles back to pull Scout the rest of the way by her handlebars, both of them giggling during the arduous climb. It's probably the best workout he's had in weeks.

———

Hours later, during my nightly Spanish lesson, I sit propped against the headboard, staring into space, hearing but not listening to Juan (the sultry-sounding instructor) through my earbuds. I'm distracted, anxiously waiting for Jet to get out of the shower so I can ask him what he and Scout talked about on their ride.

At dinner, she was much more like her usual self, chatting exuberantly about one of her favorite topics, the ancient volcanic eruption that obliterated Pompeii. She complimented the fish tacos. She ate everything with no complaints. She chattered about gerbils and speculated about the different fur colors she might have to choose from.

The one time she reverted to her earlier gloominess, when Jet said, "Bath time," it was her token, "Aw, man!" objection to anything that takes times away from playing or any of the other things she'd rather be doing.

He provided his part of the script: "Come on. We worked up a sweat on our bikes, and you have school tomorrow."

"I don't want to go to school!"

Pointing in the direction of her bedroom, through the walls, he said kindly but firmly, "Go. We talked about this."

She lowered her head, and her voice wobbled when she said, "Okay," and complied.

As soon as she was gone, I said sincerely, "Nice."

He merely shrugged and changed the subject.

Around my memory, Juan babbles more complicated words and phrases, things I could actually use every day, but I can't focus.

The day's events and emotions soon prove too draining. To the sound of the running water slapping against the shower tiles, my eyelids droop, and I fall asleep sitting up with the lights still on.

What feels like seconds later, Juan's voice fades. I wake to the tickle of the buds being plucked slowly and gently from my ears. Jet smiles down at me and sets my phone and the listening devices on my bedside table before switching off the light and sliding into his side of the bed.

Sinking under the covers and digging my head into my pillow, I cuddle up to his back and whisper, "*Te amo.*"

"I love you, too," he replies immediately. "So does Scout. You're a good mom."

The statement is a balm to my scorched ego, like aloe on a sunburn, and my eyes well. I press my forehead between his shoulder blades and inhale his freshly showered smell through his soft t-shirt. "Thank you. You're a good dad. The best, really."

He reaches back and grabs my hand, pulling it over his side and braiding his fingers through mine. "Oh, I wouldn't go that far."

"I would. You always know exactly what to say to her to calm her down. I'm so jealous of that. You keep your cool, and most importantly, you don't break our rules. You don't have to resort to bribes, like I did today."

He clears his throat. "About that…"

Rising on my elbow, I prop my chin on his upper arm to look around his shoulder and down at his profile. He blinks straight ahead while I wait.

Finally, he says, "I promised her another gerbil."

"What?" I can't help but laugh at his miserable, yet sheepish, expression spotlit by the moon.

When he sighs and rolls onto his back, I adjust so my elbow isn't poking him in the chest but remain half on top of him, looking down into his face. Transferring one hand to my lower back, he rubs absently and says, "I caved, too. We went on our bike ride, and we stopped to rest, and, like I told you I was going to do, I tried to get to the bottom of what her problem is at school. Is there a kid who's mean to her?—I'll kill 'em."

I snicker.

"Is the teacher a jerk? Does the lunchroom smell bad? Do her classmates? Is the feng shui all wrong in the classroom? I mean, what is it? Let's figure it out and fix it."

Already knowing the answer—that he can't fix everything —I nevertheless refrain from comment.

"She couldn't pinpoint anything. All she had was, 'I don't like it.' Then she said she was never going back, and if we took her back, she'd just cry and cry and cry and sit down in the counselor's office until we came to get her."

The improbability of her actually following through on such a threat is the only thing that saves me from abject despair and frustration. "How do you reason with that?" I say, resting my head on his chest, under his chin.

"My parents would have told me, 'You're going, and if you raise a stink, we'll beat your butt.'"

"Not an option."

"No. Of course not. They probably wouldn't have, either, but I wasn't about to test them."

I imagine Scout in that same scenario and know she definitely would call our bluff.

When I say as much to Jet, he says, "Oh, she'd know right away it was a fake. A bad one, at that."

"So you promised her another gerbil?" His fingers twine through my hair, pulling it away from my neck. My eyelids sag as goosebumps rise.

"It's more like I agreed to her terms. After I told her she'd get used to school and would make so many friends she'd eventually like it, she said, 'I'll go to school and won't cry if I can have *two* gerbils, a boy one named Joey for Joe Montana, and a girl gerbil that I will name Ruth, like RBG.'"

"Wow. RBG, huh? Gotta love that spunk."

"Yeah. Well, I told her to keep dreaming, because there was no way we were going to have a boy and girl gerbil, unless we wanted to be overrun by baby gerbils. She folded her arms over her chest and said, 'Then I will cry and cry and cry forever.'"

"Shit."

"So I negotiated a little. I told her she could earn two gerbils of the same sex with a full month of gripe-free school attendance."

"A month is a long time for a five-year-old."

"Wait for it. She came back with, 'Two weeks.' I said, 'Three.' She said, 'Deal.' I figure by then, she'll be over whatever this is, we'll all be used to the routine, and she can have her damn gerbils."

"Oh, man. It's come to this: negotiating with a tiny terrorist."

"Well, this is it," he says with determination. "No more.

She gets her buddy gerbils, we get a stress-free school year. The score's tied, and we're back to our original game plan."

Judging by his soft snores a few minutes later, he actually believes that. I, on the other hand, lie awake for a long time, thinking, *Oh, mierda.*

We might be screwed.

## THIRTEEN

## PTA QUEEN

Ursuline Academy holds its Parent-Teacher Association meetings in its vast, opulent library. The first time I stepped in here, during our tour of the school, was a surreal experience. It felt like I had stepped onto the Hogwarts campus, and Hermione was going to zoom around the corner at any second, carrying a huge stack of dusty tomes, searching for the perfect spell to get her friends and her out of their latest pickle.

The dark wooden shelves and tables gleam with lemon-scented polish. The spines of the books on the shelves, although varying in height, thickness, and color, line up perfectly at the same spot, about an inch from the edge of each shelf. They look built-in, like they're part of the shelving unit. But they're real—I checked. The librarian or custodian must come through here at the end of every day with a ruler to adjust them. There's no way the students keep them that tidy.

Today's visit brings to mind a different movie, with so many adults milling about, chatting about their recommendations for cleaning services, raving about their new cars' advanced tech, and sharing the latest celebrity and Hollywood industry gossip. I can't stop thinking about Ron Burgundy in *Anchorman* bragging to Veronica that his apartment is filled with leather-bound books and smells of rich mahogany. This is exactly what he meant. I breathe in the lemon-scented polish, wood, paper, leather, and binding glue. The only thing missing—and rightfully so—is a snifter of scotch in my hand.

Every time I glance around, I see more details, too: the tiny lamps with green glass shades and brass beaded pull strings on each table. The tall wooden ladders attached to rollers on tracks so the librarians and the older kids can reach the higher shelves. It's all so stereotypically "fancy library" that it would be comical if it weren't so impressive.

Of course, it's also kitted out in the latest tech, but I have to really search for it to spot it. Leaning back in my chair, I see the electrical outlets and USB jacks mounted under the tables. Students bring their school-issued laptops with them when they come here, so no bulky desktop monitors or processing units spoil the room's sleek elegance. During my school years, we had one small section of desks with hulking, whirring computers for online research and catalog searches—if we were too lazy to use the card catalog. The card catalog in this library, with its little drawers and shiny brass handles, seems deceptively necessary with such a lack of visible technology, but I bet it hasn't been touched, other than to update it and clean it, in forever. In fact, I wonder if the students are even taught how to use it.

Sitting and fidgeting next to Jet at one of the solid, sturdy wood tables, waiting for the first PTA meeting of the year to start after this, the second week of school, I try to distract myself by wondering if I could locate a random book in this place using only the card catalog. The answer ("Maybe?") doesn't instill much confidence, so I move mentally along to who has to dust all of this wood and leather. That doesn't work, either. My answer, the school's custodian, is too simple and obvious and doesn't lend itself to any imagination.

I'm annoyingly nervous, as if I'm at a fancy party full of influential movers and shakers, not a private school PTA meeting. None of the famous parents are even here. Unless you count Jet. I don't, because he's my husband. And here in California, a former All-Pro quarterback of a rival football team who regularly kicked the asses of these people's favorite teams isn't particularly fighting off hordes of autograph seekers. People have been polite, for the most part, but he's not given the royal treatment here like he was everywhere we went in Kansas City.

Every once in a while, Jet will receive recognition from someone who still appreciates his storied college career. At Scout's party, one of the parents said he and his husband are both University of Southern California alums, and they remember exactly where they were when the Trojans won the National Championship during Jet's tenure with the team. Today, though, nobody has any warm recollections of college days gone by to share. The vibe in the room is decidedly tense —or is that just me?—and expectant.

I recognize a few more parents from Scout's party, so we nod and wave at each other. A fellow classroom mom says hi to me as she passes by with her complimentary gourmet gluten-free cookie and fresh-brewed coffee. Otherwise, Jet and I are definitely part of the newb crowd, each of us keeping to ourselves and taking in the atmosphere, unsure of what's going to happen next.

The Front Step Brigade (or FSB), in contrast, gathers near

the doors of the library, chatting and laughing like they're at a cocktail party in one of their own homes. They remind me of a strange breed of long-legged cranes that congregates at the entrances to buildings and rooms, assessing everyone who passes. At the center of their flock, or construction, is the queen crane, Kiki Valentine.

Jet sits back in his chair, folds his arms over his chest, and sighs. "When the heck is this thing going to start?" he grumbles.

As if she's heard him, Kiki, clipboard in hand, strides to the podium in front of the tables and chairs and beams at us. "Hello, hello, Ursuline parents!" There's a murmured reply as everyone—even the FSB—finds chairs and settles in. "I see some new faces out there, which is *marvelous*, of course! In case you don't know me, I'm Kiki Valentine, Ursuline Academy's PTA President. If you didn't pick up an agenda and you want one, raise your hand, and my lovely assistant, Taniya, will pass one down to you." She giggles as one of the FSB wanders the room, handing out green sheets of paper.

I look down at the one on the table in front of me. Introduction, old business, new business, upcoming events, Q&A, dismissal. Seems pretty straightforward. Maybe this won't be so bad after all.

A mind-numbing ninety minutes later, I've had to nudge Jet awake twice, and my butt may be permanently asleep on this beautiful, but unforgiving, chair, but we're still talking about upcoming events. As we finally move on to the question and answer portion, I vow to throat-punch anyone with questions.

Sure enough, one of the FSB volunteers for an assault by raising her hand as soon as Kiki opens the floor. While I imagine doing the deed, this potential victim asks when we'll be getting our assignments for Oktoberfest.

"Oh, my goodness!" Kiki places a perfectly manicured hand on her forehead. "I totally skipped over Oktoberfest in the upcoming events list! Where is my head? Thank you so much, Julia, for reminding me."

She makes a big show of shuffling through her notes, pressing her big red lips together, then blowing her platinum bangs from her Botoxed forehead. "Ay-yi-yi. So much to talk about tonight, guys! Oktoberfest! Here we go. This is our first big PTA fundraiser of the year, so it's all hands on deck." She lifts the clipboard sign-in sheet for this meeting. "With your email addresses here, I'll send you assignments for bringing food and manning tables or game booths. Everyone will help set up and tear down. October twenty-sixth, people! Clear your calendars, if you haven't already! It'll be here before you know it."

Jet leans close to me. "I'm pretty sure I'm out of town that week."

I shrug, feeling like this whole thing has been a scripted farce, and I'm being punk'd. Before I can say anything, though, Kiki adds, "Everyone! I'll need dress and pants sizes. Gentlemen, that's especially important for the lederhosen, but ladies, the dirndl dresses are pretty unforgiving, too, so be accurate!"

"I'm definitely out of town that week," Jet mutters, shaking his head. "Uh-uh. That's not happening."

While stifling hysterical laughter, I inadvertently draw Kiki's attention. "Maura Knox!" She grins at me, and I notice with guilty satisfaction that she has lipstick on her right front tooth. "You'll be in charge of wardrobe. I'll send you a list with phone numbers and emails, so you can track down sizes and make sure everyone has what they need for the day."

"But I—"

"Thank you so much!" she says sweetly before firmly moving on. "Everyone, if you have any other questions, just email or call me. I'm afraid we've gone quite a bit over time on this meeting, so we need to wrap it up. Thanks for coming! We'll be in touch!"

With that, she steps down from the podium and power walks from the library, Richard trailing after her, his eyes down on his phone, where they've been the whole meeting.

"What just happened?" I ask Jet while everyone else stands up and makes their way for the doors.

"I'm pretty sure you've been volunteered to be some kind of German seamstress."

"I'm not doing it alone. You're totally helping," I say.

"I'll be out of town," he repeats.

"You'll be home plenty of the time leading up to that weekend."

He claws his hands down his face. "Is it too late to come out of retirement?"

———

Days later, I'm still not quite sure what happened at the end of that meeting. One minute I was dozing, the next I was being called out and assigned costume director for a school fundraiser.

Costume director. For a school fundraiser. What freaking wormhole have I fallen into?

Jet, of course, thinks it's hilarious. He's obviously convinced he'll be putting forth zero energy into this effort. He's wrong. If veteran PTA members are clamoring for assignments about this Oktoberfest in early September, that means it's a big deal. I can't—won't—be going it alone with the lederhosen and dirndl dress distribution.

Fortunately, I'm no stranger to the concept of Oktoberfest. My people are good Germanic stock, mixed with a bunch of Nordic stock. And some eastern European stock. Plus, some Ashkenazi Jewish DNA, which was a pleasant surprise to all of us when Mom went through her "finding her roots" phase. My point is, the Kansas City community knows how to do Oktoberfest. I'll admit, I've never gone so far as to wear a traditional dirndl dress, but I'm familiar with them, having seen them at local celebrations. I've come across fewer men in traditional lederhosen, but the costume variation was popular at festivals among waitstaff.

Just because I've been known to be an avid participant of such events doesn't mean I'm at all interested in helping organize one; however, if this is what it takes to be the model parent of a school-age child, I'm all in. I'm not going to half-ass this like I used to do with so many other things in life. This is important.

That determination wavers a bit—a lot—when the first email (and second through fifth emails) from Kiki arrives. It's information overload. Directions to the storage facility where the costumes are kept. Information about the dry cleaner the school has a contract with so I can get all of the stored costumes "freshened." Contact details and map to the costume shops that will help us if we need additional garb. Online shops that will "do in a pinch," if the local stores run low on stock or don't have the sizes we need.

The worst, though, is the spreadsheet with names, phone numbers, and email addresses, plus blank spaces for measurements. This isn't just a "small, medium, or large" situation. This is a "bust, waist, hips, thigh" situation. And I have to get those numbers from more than a hundred people. Nearly two hundred, in fact, because it's numbered by student, not parent, and Ursuline parents, whether still together or not, are expected to work together for the good of the children.

I click the 'x' to close the spreadsheet and close my eyes, breathing slowly through my nose like they teach in that meditation app I tried once. It worked so well to relax me then that I promptly fell asleep. With each inhale, I tell myself I'll take it one task at a time. With each exhale, I tell myself I have plenty of time. It's not having a sedative effect today, but at least I'm no longer on the verge of a panic attack.

This is how Jet finds me, sitting cross-legged on the floor when he rolls his suitcase through my study toward the garage. I hear him, but I keep my eyes closed, repeating my mantras.

"Since when do you meditate?" he asks, a grin in his voice.

"Since Kiki. Shhh."

"Ah. You got the emails."

I open one eye. "Yes, *we* got the emails."

"But *you* opened them."

"You need to open them, too. I'm not doing all this alone, Jet."

"I know!"

"I'm serious."

"I know!" He gestures to his suitcase. "But I'm kind of walking out the door to announce a game in San Francisco this weekend, so I'm not going to screw with it right now. I need to focus."

That's true. He does. He really, really does. Oh, gosh. I need to do some more nose-breathing.

"Are you going to be okay?" he asks, sounding more annoyed than concerned. "It's just a school fundraiser. If everyone makes it out to be something bigger than it really is, it won't even be any fun."

"You do know it's 'FUND-raiser,' not 'fun-raiser,' right?"

He levels a playful glare at me. "Yes, smartass. But it's not the end-all, be-all of everything. Nobody's going to die if someone's lederhosen are too tight."

"You never know. I've heard from many a guy that constriction down there can lead to nasty consequences."

"Many a guy, eh?"

"A few. Plus, they always warn on those commercials about erections lasting too long. I'm sure tight lederhosen would be equally dangerous."

He laughs and waves off my half-serious suppositions. "You're being silly."

"I just want to nail this, you know?" I fling my legs straight in front of me and lean back on my arms. "I want to be one of those parents who really rocks the whole classroom volunteer thing."

"You want to be the PTA queen?"

"No, that's already taken by Kiki."

"Queen Keek."

"Yes! Queen Keek. But I want to make Scout proud. I don't want to be one of those slacker parents who expects everyone else to do the work. I'm going to be the slack picker-upper."

"Sure, sure, sure," he says, gripping his suitcase handle. "But take it from someone whose mom was all up in school business and politics: kids don't see it the same way the parents do. It's not that great having your mom around all the time."

"You think Scout won't want me around?"

He shrugs. "I can only tell you how I felt. Sometimes I

wished there was somewhere I could go where my mom wasn't. School should have been that place."

"Well, it's not like I'm going to be there every day. But I'm going to pull my weight."

The way he purses his lips and raises his eyebrows slightly tells me he thinks the two are inextricably linked, but he says, "Okay. Just sayin'. Don't take it too seriously. The only time Scout's going to notice your efforts with school stuff is when it embarrasses her."

Oh, gosh. He's right. Little kids don't feel proud of their parents for working hard; they expect it to the point that they don't notice it. Until it becomes overbearing. Like Gloria. I will *not* be like Gloria.

It will be tricky, indeed, finding the right balance.

## FOURTEEN

## PILING ON

She calls after—and sometimes during—every game now. As if it's not painful enough to simply watch and listen, Gloria feels like she needs to wallow in Jet's performances with me. I'd screen her calls, but she'll just keep calling. Hell, I wouldn't put it past her to drive up here to sit next to me on the couch and talk about it, if I continued to ignore her. So I answer, and I listen, and I hate how right she is with her often brutal criticism.

He's bad. He's really, really bad.

"He's not getting better, and this is the regular season now!" Gloria says, practically squawking, the panic rising in her voice.

"First regular-season game," I say, always finding some way to qualify and justify. "Everyone's nervous for the first official game."

"Maura, what are you going to do?"

"What am *I* going to do?"

"You said you'd help him. Whatever you're doing isn't working."

That's because I've done nothing. What can I do? If I suggest he practice with me at home, that gives away how terrible I think he is at his job. If he's already aware of that—and I'm guessing he is—that will only make things worse. If he's unaware—which is also possible—I'll destroy whatever confidence he has, and he'll probably perform even worse. It's a lose-lose.

Plus, what possible expertise do I have to offer? None. I have no idea what he's going through or how to improve the situation. I've never studied broadcasting or media. I'm not a performance coach or consultant.

"He has people for that at the network," I finally say to Gloria.

"They should be fired," she says. "He's a gorgeous, wonderful man. If they can't get him up to snuff, then they can't help anyone."

While I'm not so sure "gorgeous" or "wonderful" have any bearing on announcing abilities, I'm not about to say so and appear to contradict Gloria on any of her compliments.

"I really need to let you go, Glo— Mom."

"No, don't make me watch this alone!"

"What's Ned doing?"

"He can't bear to watch at all."

Shit. Poor Ned. Poor Gloria. Poor Me. Poor Jet.

"Well, I'm about at that point," I say.

"No, no, no. You and I have to watch. We don't have a choice." If it's possible, she sounds even more despondent than before.

"Yes, we do, Gloria. In fact, I think it might be bad for your heart to subject yourself to this every week."

"I'm his mother, and I stand by him no matter what. As his wife, you need to do the same." Her voice hardens. "Although

I have to say, I'm not surprised you want to bail when things get a little rough."

I can feel the color creeping up my neck, but I keep my voice steady. "I'm not 'bailing' on anything."

"If you don't watch, you are."

"I don't want to watch with *you*." Immediately, I regret being so candid.

After a short silence, she says quietly, "Oh, I see how it is."

I sigh. "I'm sorry, Gloria, but you're stressing me out."

"Oh, heaven forbid precious Maura gets stressed out," she says. "Stressed out Maura runs away. She runs away from a wedding. She runs away from her business. Run, run, run, Maura!"

"Goodbye, Gloria."

I hit the button to hang up on her, knowing full well there will be consequences for that.

I don't care—right now.

———

Preparing for an upset husband, I've fixed his favorite comfort food for a late dinner, spaghetti and meatballs, following his mom's recipe, one he's had written down for ages but that Beau wouldn't touch with a ten-foot pole and I've stubbornly ignored since I became in charge of meal prep. Despite our contentious call earlier and my hanging up on her, there's one thing I can't deny Gloria knows best: food—especially when it comes to her youngest kid. I even used white pasta and added in a dripping loaf of garlic bread. The salad's loaded with artichoke hearts and avocados, just like Jet loves it.

When he walks into the house and through the study and living room wearing a huge grin, I blink in surprise. Before I can figure out what it means, though, Scout and Torzi ambush him. He kneels down for hugs and scratches the dog behind the ears.

"Hey, gang. How's it going? Oooh! Lovin' the hair, Bump. Did Mommy do that?"

Scout nods. "It very hurt, but it has to be tight so I can sleep with it like this, and it will still be pretty in the morning."

"You'll still be pretty, no matter what," he says. "Even after I do this…" He wraps his hands around her torso and tickles her ribs.

"Daddy!"

Torzi barks at the tomfoolery.

Between giggles, she asks, "When are we going to get the gerbils?" even though we've told her a thousand times.

Jet stops tickling and tweaks her nose. "Thursday after school, Bump. It's in my calendar."

"I can't wait!" she squeals, hugging him around the neck.

After she lets him go, he rises to his feet and approaches me, sniffing the air. "Oh, my, my." He points to the bubbling pot of sauce on the stove. "Is that what I think it is?"

"What do you think it is?"

"My mom's spaghetti and meatballs?"

"You got it."

He rolls his eyes in ecstasy. "Oh, beautiful. What did I do to deserve this?"

Casually, I avoid his eyes and stir the sauce. "First regular-season game, right? I figured you'd worked up an appetite and would want to…"

…*eat your feelings.*

…*disappear into this red sauce and never resurface.*

…*pretend like you're a kid again, with no worries.*

"…celebrate."

He grabs me in a silly side hug and plants a huge kiss on my cheek. "You're the best. This is perfect."

"There's salad and garlic bread, too. And wine."

Lots and lots of wine.

"I'll crack that open right away," he offers, striding to the wet bar in the dinette. He whistles to himself while he selects a bottle of red and uncorks it.

A few minutes later, when we're all seated at the table, he raises his glass in a toast. "To great days," he proposes.

"To great days," Scout and I echo, holding aloft our glasses of milk and Merlot, respectively.

The dinner conversation centers around gerbils, so I get no further clues from Jet about how he thinks his first day in the booth went. When the gerbil line of conversation dead ends a surprisingly long time later, Scout switches to another of her favorite topics, the future—every hope, dream, and fear she has about life. Like father, like daughter. Always thinking ahead.

Finally, future Scout graduates from university with her Ph.D. in history, and the meal ends. Present-day Scout runs off to spend some quality time with Torzi before bed while Jet and I clean up the kitchen. I figure this will be when we'll have time to chat, and he'll drop the Mr. Joviality act and tell me how he's really feeling about his performance today.

But after she departs, and we've been working side by side for a few minutes at the sink and dishwasher—him rinsing, me stacking—he catches me surreptitiously watching him and winks at me with a grin.

I can't take it anymore. "So? How do you think it went?" I ask, careful to phrase it in a way that doesn't give away my own opinion.

"It felt great!" he says non-specifically.

"Really. No bugs in the system? No issues reading the prompter?"

He considers the questions but eventually says, "Nope. Well, there are always little things that first game that don't go quite as planned. Same in the booth as on the field."

"Okay. Like…?"

He shrugs and hands me the last plate, then swivels to lift the stock pot and saucepan from the stove. "I dunno. Little things. Stuff the people at home don't even notice but that we can feel." He returns to the sink, extends the spray nozzle, and rinses the saucepan. "Like, I jumped my cue once or twice coming back from break. Erin lost her place on her stat sheet and called a player by the wrong name during a penalty call. Dumb stuff. We'll get better."

"Ah. So, Erin thought it went well, too?"

"She wasn't as pumped as I was. This is old hat for her."

"Being in the booth isn't."

"No, but talking to thousands of people live is."

"True. And the producer and director? Richard? Everyone seemed satisfied?"

"Yeah! Everyone told us we did awesome! What did you think?"

Finished with the final pot, he turns off the water and waits for me in the resultant silence. I focus on perfectly nesting the large stainless steel item in the dishwasher before dropping in the detergent pod and fiddling with the controls, as if it takes all of my concentration. Finally, I say, "Oh, it seemed like a typical broadcast. Hard to get excited about the game, since I hate both of those teams." I smile and wink at him. "Sort of a snoozefest."

"Yeah, lots of new guys out there, too, which is why Erin

was having a problem. I'm lucky that I actually know some of them from practice squads and benches. A few have played as substitutes for injured players. Some were new to me, too, though."

Realizing I've been holding my breath, I exhale as quietly as possible and smile at him. "No matter what, I'm sure you're relieved to have that first one out of the way."

"Definitely. The jitters at the beginning of a season are about as reliable as death and taxes." He pulls his loosened tie the rest of the way off and drapes it over his shoulder. "In fact, the only thing I have left to do is to hit the showers. Wanna join me?"

I smile wanly at his offer. "I would, but it's a school night, and someone's still up and needs to be tucked in and all those pesky things."

"Torzi can do it," he says, walking backward across the living room and beckoning beguilingly.

"Raincheck."

"Suit yourself."

As soon as he disappears through the door leading to the master suite, I relax my shoulders and breathe normally for the first time since talking to Gloria.

Gloria.

She's a first-rate alarmist, and she's got me all worked up, too. I watched too much of that game with her. After a while, all I could hear were the mistakes, the awkward pauses, the stilted reading, the stuttering and bumbling. Life through Gloria-colored glasses sucks. She's too negative, too critical. According to her, the world is always coming to an end.

This is Jet's retirement all over again. When he left the game as suddenly as he did, rumors swirled. Everything from him being sick to Scout or me being sick to him having a second family in Canada and going off to play in the Canadian Football League. It was bananas. Nobody could accept that he wanted to stop abusing his body and spend more time with his family—the only one he has, here in the U.S. That explanation was too simple but, at the same time, improbable. Nobody leaves before their contract expires unless they've suffered a career-ending injury—or they're forced out. Technically, neither of those applied to Jet. Barring more injury, he could have easily played a few more years, if he'd wanted to. He just didn't want to anymore. I can see how that would be difficult for fans to accept and they'd seek out bigger, deeper, more sinister explanations.

But his mother? She called to ask him about each and every whisper she heard. It became a game with Jet and me. He'd see her name and face on his phone and say, "Get ready." Then he'd try his hardest not to react too strongly to whatever she said, so I wouldn't get any hints about her latest worry. After he'd disconnect, I'd have to guess the tabloid headline that she believed enough to ask about. I was pretty familiar with all of the theories, and Gloria's penchant for fake news, so I was damn good at that game.

She's probably surprised—and somewhat disappointed, particularly after today—he hasn't emigrated to Canada by now to be with his Canadian woman and play in the CFL.

The difference this time is that I'm on the outside, looking in. I don't know what's unfounded worry and what's reality. Is Jet performing exactly as the folks at the network expect him to be performing at this stage of the season and his new career? On the other hand, what if everyone at Football Network is too embarrassed for Jet and afraid to tell him he's bad? Erin seems like a pretty straight shooter, not to mention a consummate professional who wouldn't spare feelings at the expense of her own quality work product, but maybe she's been instructed to treat the All-Pro QB with kid gloves while he learns the ropes.

Are Gloria's—and my—expectations too high? What about other viewers, though, the ones who didn't give birth to him or aren't married to him? Surely, they're complaining. People are ruthless and have zero tolerance for sub-par work, especially in the entertainment industry. Honing your skills is something you do on your time, not theirs. When they're sitting down with a beer to watch their favorite team play, they don't want to be bothered by a bumbling broadcaster. This is something they've been anticipating for months, since the season ended for their team in January or February. I know, personally, what it's like to be distracted by bad announcers. It negatively affects the entire experience.

Football Network's patience isn't going to last forever in the face of furious fans. Nor will Richard Valentine's.

## FIFTEEN

# THUNDERSTRUCK

The house looks and smells how you'd expect a gerbil breeder's house to look and smell, with the overpowering odor of cedar chips and the underlying scent of rodent urine and excrement.

Scout has chosen two males, one gray-and-white, the other full black, litter mates that Scout names Joey and Pompeii.

We listen patiently while Ms. Gerbil Expert explains how to feed and care for Joey and Pompeii and keep their cage clean. She recommends *The Gerbil Care Handbook* by the American Gerbil Society (I am not making this up) for handy reference at home but also gives us her card, offering to answer any of our questions, as needed.

Then she solemnly hands to Scout the small plastic carrier with the bright red slotted lid and handle and says, "They're all yours. Be good to them."

I imagine Joey and Pompeii saying, "So long, suckers!" to the others they're leaving behind as their adoring new owner carries them away. But really, who are the biggest suckers here? It's definitely the adult bipedals following the victorious child, murmuring sweet nothings to her new best friends through the slotted lid of her pet carrier.

At our next stop, the pet supply store, a sales associate helps us pick out a huge glass and metal terrarium with a wire mesh lid to go with it. Plus thirteen tons of food, bedding, toys, fur powder, multi-colored plastic houses with connecting tunnels, and a wheel. These rats are going to live better than I do. Russell (as his name tag states) probably rubbed his hands with glee when he saw us walk through the door, two hapless parents and the proud new mama of two long-tailed fur babies, still riding like royalty in their plastic gerb-mobile.

Several minutes and hundreds of dollars later, strong, strapping Jet staggers through the house under the heft and bulk of Joey and Pompeii's bachelor pad mansion, while I juggle the shopping bags with all of the other purchases for the rodents' new life of luxury. In Scout's bedroom, Jet sets down his awkward armload, then picks it up again when our daughter changes her mind—twice—about where she wants the tank to go. While Jet pours paper bedding into the terrarium, I assemble the exercise wheel and play sets.

Scout keeps her nose pressed to the side of the carrier, watching the gerbils' every move and providing a running commentary. "Mommy and Daddy are making your house nice and cozy. You're going to love it."

I have an alternate monologue running through my head. *"See those chumps over there? They're my parents. Super-easy to manipulate. I have them wrapped around my little finger. The trick, though, is to make them think* they're *in control. You'll get the hang of it. Just be your cute little self, and soon they'll be serving you, too. Cleaning your cage, giving you unlimited refills on your water bottle, protecting you from the dog, buying you new stuff, keeping you well-stocked with cardboard to play with and chew on… There's really no limit to their devotion. Sure, they'll act fed up once in a while, but just twitch your cute little nose and look up at them with the biggest eyes you can make, and you'll be back in business."*

"Now, Scout," I lecture out loud. "You'll have to keep their cage clean and give them food and fresh water every single day. On Saturdays, you'll need to help us switch out their bedding and clean the inside of the cage."

"Uh-huh. Okay."

"I mean it. They're *your* pets."

She finally tears her eyes away from the new loves of her life to train them, wide and earnest on me. "I know, Mommy. I love them and will take care of them forever and ever."

Or two-to-four years, the average lifespan of one of these things. But whatever.

"When you take them out of the cage to play with them, Daddy or I need to be around. You'll have to hold them somewhere with a door, to keep Torzi away."

I don't trust the dog not to eat Scout's new friends the first chance he gets. While that would seem advantageous for me, we'd have a traumatized child, and I suppose that's worse than cleaning out a cage once a week. Maybe. Time will tell, I guess.

I snap the last piece together on the second play set and position it precisely where Scout wants it, after conferring with the gerbs, of course.

Jet steps aside so Scout can access the short step stool that makes her tall enough to reach down into the cage. He loosens the lid on the carrier, but she insists on being the one to dump Joey and Pompeii—not so gently—into their brand new abode. We watch as the rodents stand exactly where they're placed, as if uncertain what to do first—stimulation overload. Finally, Joey burrows into the bedding and cautiously roams the rest of the cage, pausing now and then to rest on his back legs, nose twitching as if he's sniffing the air.

"He likes it!" Scout says, dragging her nose across the glass as she follows his every move.

Pompeii eventually follows his brother's lead, sniffing the wheel and climbing gingerly into it.

"Look! Pompeii's going to get some exercise," she says with a giggle.

I tap her shoulder with the water bottle. "Go fill this, please, so we can show you how to hang it from the wires on the lid. Then you can give your friends a treat."

"I wanna hold them!" she says, skipping toward the bathroom.

I glance at my phone, dismayed by how much time this venture has stolen from the afternoon and evening.

Noticing my frown, Jet says, "I'll hang out in here with them for a while, if you have other things to do."

I bite my lower lip. "Are you sure? I really do need to finish up some stuff I had to stop when we left this afternoon."

"I'm sure." He demonstrates to Scout how to hang the water bottle and opens the box of treats for her to give one each to Joey and Pompeii. When the giggling girl is occupied once more with her new favorite pastime, gerb-watching, he turns back to me. "Go on. I've got this."

I kiss his lips and the top of Scout's head. As I exit the bedroom, I hear Scout say, "Can I hold one of them now? Pleeeeeaaaaase?"

Passing Torzi in the hallway, I mutter, "Don't even think about it." As if understanding me, he turns and follows me to the study, where he settles in the chair by the bookshelf. I hope he's okay with no longer being top dog, so to speak.

———

Among her many talents, Nina always knows when I'm sitting at my desk in the study, concentrating on Knox business. I've accused her of planting a hidden camera in here, tracking my cell phone, and witchcraft, all of which she vehemently and with great amusement denies. Tonight is no different. Her intuition hits about an hour into my diligent activities, between responding to emails and disbursing last week's profit to its volunteering charity.

It's nearly ten o'clock where she is, about the time she'd have said goodbye to tonight's crew and locked up. I picture her arriving at her car and waiting until she's seated inside with the locks engaged to hit the button to call me. Nina doesn't cut corners on personal safety. She and I have seen enough movies where men accost distracted women. It's mid-September, so the nights are chilly in KC. She's sitting in her locked car with the defoggers and heater on full blast to take the edge off the nip in the air. Might as well call me to catch up while she waits for things to heat up.

I answer, expecting her to complain about one of the part-timers or dish some spectacular (or spectacularly bad) numbers from tonight's showings at various locations. The last thing I'm expecting her to say, in a strange, detached voice, is, "It's gone."

"Nina?" I look at the phone to double-check that it's really her picture and number on my screen. "Nina, what's wrong? What do you mean, 'It's gone'? What's gone?"

"I'm sorry. We got everyone out safely, and the firefighters tried to save it, but…"

My brain struggles to catch up. "Wait. 'Save it'? Firefighters? What's happened?" For lack of anything better to do, but in order to do *something*, I stand and pace between my desk and the window looking out on the driveway, front yard, and street.

"The theater. Here in KC. It's… gone. By the time we got everyone out and accounted for and the firefighters arrived, it was fully engulfed. I don't— I have no idea how— It just… poof!"

"No."

"I know. I can't believe it, either, and I *saw* it."

"Are you okay? Is everyone okay? You said everyone got out, but were people hurt? Burned?" I put my hand to my forehead. "Oh, my gosh, Nina. You all could have been killed!"

I scramble to think of which charity had the Kansas City location booked tonight but can't get my thoughts to cooperate. "Who— Which group was there volunteering? Oh, shit. How terrifying!" I collapse into my desk chair, almost missing it but catching myself before falling to the floor.

Nina's talking again. Something about how all the volunteers were able-bodied adults, staff from a local nursing home for Alzheimer's patients. The film was *The Notebook*, so the audience was adult, too, mostly people on dates.

"Oh, thank God." That spot of good news helps to quell my panic. "What about injuries? Are you okay?"

"Everyone evacuated calmly and got out quickly. I have a little smoke inhalation, because I did a final sweep of the bathrooms, break room, and screening room to make sure everyone was out and I was the last one to leave."

"A 'little smoke inhalation'? Is that a thing?"

"Yes, it is," she says defensively on a laugh-cough. "It's minor. So stop worrying. Nobody got hurt. But the building, the theater…"

"I don't care. I mean, I do care, but that's the least of my worries." It's technically not a lie. It *is* the least of my worries. That doesn't mean it's not a big worry, though. The others are just gargantuan.

"Where are you right now?" I ask, suddenly needing to know, desperate to adjust my earlier mental picture of her to something just as safe, if not as humdrum, as her warming-up car. "Home? Hospital?" I rummage in the middle drawer of my desk for a pen and scrap of paper. "What do I need to do, other than get there as fast as I can? Who do I need to call? Anyone? The fire marshal wants to talk to me, I'm sure. I can also take care of calling the insurance company."

Nina sighs and coughs. "Just get here first. That would be amazing. It's— it's all starting to hit me now, and I can't stop shaking."

"You're in shock. Geez. Tell me you're at the hospital."

"I am. But they're about to release me. I have to get home to the kids."

"Do you need to stay there, though? Is there anyone I can call for you? I'm sure Cyndi or any of the board members would gladly stay with the kids tonight if your sitter needs to go. Oh, the board members. Do they know? Shit, Nina." Instantly overwhelmed, I plunk my forehead against the desktop and try to make the cool pressure of the wood against skin and skull soothe me.

"You're the first call I've made. It'll be on the news tonight, I'm sure, so some of the board will find out that way. I hate that."

"I'll call them all. Conference call them. Text them. Whatever. Don't worry about it."

I lift my head as Jet appears in the doorway to the study, already talking before realizing I'm on the phone. "Scout's ready for bed and wants a kiss," he says, his playful expression fading as he takes in my obvious distress. "What's going on?" He crosses the room in three strides.

With a shaky hand, I put the phone on speaker and set it down on the desk so he can hear what Nina's saying. I take notes while Nina tries to figure out what she needs from me most urgently. Then I say, "I'll be there as soon as I can. Jet leaves tomorrow for a game, but I'll call Gloria to stay with Scout and— Anyway, don't worry about that. I'll be there in the morning. Stay at the hospital and get some rest. One of the board members will stay with your kids tonight. I'll text you who they should expect so you can let them know. Probably Colin. Everyone loves Colin."

"They do." And like that, she's weeping. "I was so scared."

My eyes fill as I listen to her process some of her experience, but she chokes off a sob, swallows and says, "No. I want to go home. I want to be with my family. I need to let them know I'm okay. They need to see me. I need to see them. And touch them."

"Okay."

"My usual sitter can stay with them until I get home."

"All right. If you're sure."

"I'm sure. Just— just get here, Mo, okay? I don't want to do this alone anymore."

I sniff and swipe away the stream of tears that's tickling the side of my face. "Got it. You gave my number to the fire marshal?"

"Yes. She'll be calling you."

"Then focus on you now, okay? I've got the rest."

"Thank you."

"Don't even," I warn kiddingly. "I'm the one who should be thanking you. Love you, Neens. Take care."

It's not until I hang up the phone and am in the middle of explaining to Jet what happened that Scout comes to find us.

She lingers in the doorway. "What's taking so— What's the matter? Why are you crying?"

"There was a fire at the Kansas City Knox," I say brightly, as if the building were a silly Billy for going up in flames. "No big deal, really. I'm just crying because I'm so glad everyone's okay."

She wrinkles her nose. "That doesn't make any sense."

Jet sweeps her into his arms and holds her tightly to his side. She rests her head on his shoulder. "Don't worry, Bump. Everything will be okay."

"Is it all gone or just a little burned?" she asks, her chin already puckering as she anticipates the worst, based on my reaction.

Jet, rubs her back. "Sounds like it's all gone."

She buries her face in his neck and cries hard. I come around the desk and share the task of rubbing her back, whispering that it's okay, but I'm jealous of her freedom to grieve the building she loved. I don't have that luxury. My focus has to remain on less emotional things. I have to pretend I don't care so much about the property and everything it symbolized for me over the years. But I do. I care a lot.

————

The plan was to sleep on the way to Kansas City and arrive semi-refreshed and ready to get shit done as soon as the tires hit the runway and my feet hit Midwestern soil. My brain has other ideas. At forty thousand feet, it decides it's a great time to run through a list of things I may have forgotten to pack, do, or remind Jet to tell his mom when she arrives to stay

with Gloria while both of us are away—in separate locations—
this weekend. I keep up a continuous stream of texts to Jet as
the latter part of that list grows. It's like I'm live-tweeting the
horrible show in my mind called, *Gloria Ruins Everything*, while
I imagine all the stuff that can go wrong in my absence.

When the episode titled, "Car Line" ends, and I've texted
everything I can possibly think to text about that complicated
before- and after-school procedure, Jet replies, "Please stop
worrying. Everything will be fine. I love you. Stop texting."

Got it. He's trying to get a few hours of sleep before he has
to get up and get ready to leave, himself. He'll be gone for
only a couple of days, but Gloria will be staying at our place
the whole time I'm away so he can maintain his normal
schedule at work. Nothing will be changing for him, really. If
anything, he'll have it *easier* with me gone and his mom there.
Gloria will insist on doing *everything* home- and parenting-
related. In his off-time, he'll be allowed to loll on the couch
watching endless episodes of all of his favorite football reality
shows.

And the food. They'll eat meat and starch every night for
dinner, with nary a vegetable in sight. Gloria will bake and
bake and bake. Sweet rolls and cookies and cakes. Oh, my.

Oh, gosh. I can't think about that.

Instead, I move my brain along to catastrophizing the fire
recovery. Maybe the blaze will be ruled arson, and I'll be
blamed for it, like so many other people who torch their busi-
nesses for the insurance money. Of course, I didn't, but I'll
have to prove my innocence. My reputation will be dragged
through the media. My life will be put under the microscope.

Even if the fire marshal declares the blaze an accident, she
could decide I was negligent, depending on what caused the
fire. Faulty wiring? Not my fault, right? A dirty popcorn

popper would be, though. It's my responsibility to make sure everything's kept in tip-top shape and working order to minimize danger. Have I been doing enough to ensure my customers' and employees' safety? I thought so, but if I'm questioning it now, maybe I haven't been. I'll have to pull up all the inspection and health and safety documentation.

What if everyone who had been at that screening of *The Notebook* sues me?

At that exasperating, terrifying thought, I whip off my eye mask, pluck out my earbuds, and kick off my blanket. Moving from my flat bed to an upright seat, I turn on the overhead light and pull my trusty laptop from its bag in the neighboring seat. If I'm going to be awake, I'd better be productive.

Compiling the documentation I'll need to prove—to myself, if nothing else—that Nina and I have been on top of every safety regulation and code helps ease my mind a bit. Then I do the same for the other Knox Theater locations and relax further—until I think of the next thing I may have screwed up or neglected in my complacency and absence.

Breathe in, hold, breathe out. Breathe in, hold, breathe out.

I've got this.

## SIXTEEN

## "HOME"

When we land in Kansas City, I'm supposed to take a car to my parents' house, where I'll be staying during my time here. They're on another cruise, a month-long riverboat sail through Europe. I texted them separately from the rest of the board after our call last night to let them know what was going on, and they offered their house as base camp. I'll definitely be doing that. Starting later today.

For now, I can't even muster the energy to go farther than the closest hotel. I check in online on the shuttle from the airport and barely have to speak to the person at the front desk, other than to get my key. In the room, I park my suitcase, take off my jacket, peel back the top coverlet and fall, fully clothed, into the bed. In seconds, I'm asleep, face down in the pillows.

My alarm wakes me too soon. The phone chimes from my jacket pocket on the chair between the bed and the window. Even in this small room, it seems impossibly far away. I let it tinkle its annoyingly cheerful tune and try to ignore it, but it's set to increase in volume the longer it plays, so I eventually heave myself to a sitting position and fumble the now-blaring device from the pocket. Rubbing my stiff neck, I groan at the early hour on the display and disgustedly push the phone away from me. I need to get moving. People need me.

Just when I've almost convinced myself they don't need me quite yet, and I can probably get another hour of sleep, the phone buzz-bings from across the mattress.

I flip it over and see a text from Nina. *Still on for 8:00 at the theater?*

With the dispatch of a text, I could easily push back the time of the meeting. I want to. In fact, if it were up to me, I'd never visit the burned-down building. Dread spreads through my entire body, starting in my stomach and flowing all the way to the tips of my fingers and toes. I looked at some of the news coverage online last night. Is it really necessary for me to see it in person? And what about Nina? Is it healthy for her to go back there so soon? She spent half the night in the hospital, for crying out loud.

It's that thought that convinces me I'm being a coward about the whole thing. The woman who was the last one out of the building, who inhaled its smoke, and who spent time in the hospital afterward for her troubles, is ready and willing to take me to the scene, because she knows it's important for both of us to physically stand in its presence, to take in the sights and smells and sounds. It'll help us say goodbye. It'll bolster our resolve to rebuild.

I reply, *I'll be there. You sure you're ready?*

*Ready as I'll ever be*, she immediately fires back.

That makes two of us.

———

Seeing my beloved flagship Knox Theater reduced to charred rubble is something I'll never forget it, as long as I live. Every hint of smoke scent will bring it back. Every fire engine's siren or news story of a business fire will bring on a wave of empathic sorrow, knowing how the owners of that building will feel when they see the aftermath, all those dreams and aspirations and ambitions and plans seemingly gone in a literal puff of smoke.

Those things aren't gone, of course. They never resided at a particular address or in a specific structure. When you first see that wreckage, though, it's hard to remember that. They seem one and the same, fused like the melted metal strewn here and there among the blackened brick and wood.

The popcorn cart is what did me in, though. Among all that unrecognizable damage, the damn thing was still standing—mostly. Sure, it was misshapen and upended, but there it was, plain as can be, some of its red paint gleaming as if nothing had happened, the cracked glass casing still holding fluffy—albeit burnt—popped kernels. I pointed it out to Nina, and she chuckled. That chuckle turned into a full-blown laugh that morphed into a sob, and soon we were holding each other on the opposite sidewalk, crying as passersby edged past us with curious stares.

The fire marshal arrived soon after we did. She told us in a no-nonsense way that it appeared to be a freak lightning strike that started the fire. Odd, since it never even rained last night, but it was plain as day that's what happened. She even showed us the exact place it had hit and how the fire had started and spread quickly from there.

"Lightning is a more common cause than people realize," she said, shaking her head. "White hot. A fire from it spreads like crazy, too. By the time you realize there's a fire, it's too late. You're lucky it didn't spread to any of the surrounding buildings, other than some smoke damage."

After that proclamation, she said she'd send me a copy of her official ruling and told us a dozer would be there as early as mid-morning to push everything into a pile. Firefighters would be on hand to douse everything again and make sure there were no lingering embers that might reignite. Then she left Nina and me to discuss the logistics of settling things with the insurance company as quickly as possible so we could clear the site.

What a mess! Still, I was relieved that the cause of the fire was an act of God, not a result of my—or anyone else's—negligence.

I've spent the past two weeks with my phone seemingly fused to the side of my head. When I'm not on the phone with the insurance company or contractors, I'm in offices and conference rooms, sweet talking city officials to expedite my rebuilding permit. Our goal is to get our furloughed part-timers back to work as soon as possible, as well as reschedule the charities who have come to rely on the funds they raise on their service nights at the theater. I haven't had to schmooze this many people since Scout's birthday party. The only difference is I'm not the one doing the cleanup this time. The entire process, however, is somewhat like rolling a pistachio up a sandy hill—with my tongue. It's exhausting.

I wish I had more time and energy to appreciate my hometown during the best part of the year—the start of football season. Fall has been and always will be my favorite season, and this year, Chiefs fans are drunk on their team's reigning champions status. If only Jet could be here to see it and feel it. There's nothing like knowing you've helped caused such euphoria in so many people. I hope he gets a taste of it once in a while when he encounters the occasional West Coast Chiefs fan, rarities that we are. We do exist, though. And when we happen across each other out there, look out.

Here, we're a lot less rare—as in, we're everywhere—obviously, and it's nice to see the ubiquitous red and yellow car flags and bumper stickers and window clings. It's still surreal to see our last name on so many people's backs, and I wonder how long it'll take for Jet to be usurped as this area's favorite quarterback. So far, the new guy looks good, but he's still in that weird place where fans aren't ready to commit to liking him, in case he blows up spectacularly. If he takes them to the post-season in his first year, that'll rapidly change.

For now, though, Knox jerseys still outnumber his by a lot. Jet was careful to retire the "right" way, at the top, before any nagging injuries could affect his weekly performance and damage his trust with fans. His unexpected departure was a kick in the gut for some, but he explained himself well and quickly earned the public's forgiveness and understanding.

He's still so fondly thought of around here, in fact, that some fans have started an online fund to help the charities whose fundraising weekends will be postponed during rebuilding. The board has also received emails from numerous people asking how they can help the guy who's given back so much to this community, in both time, money, and things you can't measure as easily, like hope and joy.

Putting our last name on the theater was something I agonized about when we first opened; I didn't want it to seem like I was capitalizing on something that wasn't mine by birth but rather by what some would say was total luck. A selfish part of me didn't want to share the project, either. It was *my* idea, *my* hard work to get it up and running, *my* tenacity that's kept it going and growing. It was also *my* name by then, and it was a name I was proud of. I would have been a fool not to piggyback off such a winning brand. That name recognition was a key to our early success. I'm okay, therefore, that sometimes Jet gets more credit for what goes on with the theater than he actually deserves. Everything Jet Knox touches turns to gold.

Well, almost everything.

Now, as I shovel an early fast food lunch down my throat at Mom and Dad's lonely kitchen table before a scheduled confab with Nina, my phone rings. My heart dances like a middle schooler's when I see the picture lit up on the display, and I answer breathlessly, "Hey, champ."

"Hey yourself, beautiful," he says, his cheerful voice the best thing I've heard all day. "How you holding up?"

"Barely," I say.

"Nah. You're a brick."

"One of those cardboard ones. You know, the ones Scout had when she was really little, for building and knocking down? Hollow on the inside, easily flattened underfoot."

"Oh, come on now. Catch me up. What's the latest?"

I relay the piece of new that's most on my mind right now, an available building Nina ran across by pure chance and thinks might work as a temporary location while we rebuild.

"That's great news!" he says. "And really unexpected! How is Nina, by the way?"

"Still coughing. Crying at the drop of a hat."

"Aw, man. I hate that. Maybe you both should cool it for a couple of days now that you've gotten the urgent stuff figured out."

"I just want everything back to normal as soon as possible."

"I know, Maura, but there's no rushing something like

this. You're just going to get frustrated and burned out, pun totally intended."

"Yeah, yeah."

"Oh, gosh. I got the 'yeah, yeah.' That means I should probably let you go." He says it with both a hint of the jocular and a pinch of hurt.

I clutch the phone more tightly. "No, don't! I didn't mean it that way. It's— It's really good to hear your voice." My throat tightens.

"You can hear it some more if you watch the game this afternoon."

"Oh, crap! You're about to go on, aren't you?"

"Not for a few more hours. Time difference and all."

"Oh, yeah. I forgot. Do you think the game'll be televised here, though?"

He laughs. "Uh, yeah, it better be. The Chargers are playing the Chiefs."

I rub my neck, which is sore from the not-so-supportive daybed that's still in my childhood room, where I've been sleeping. "Duh. I knew that. I'm all messed up. Can't think straight."

"I bet. How've you been sleeping?"

"Some."

"Get a nap this afternoon, before the game, maybe."

"Then I won't sleep again tonight."

"Man, I hate that cycle," he says.

"Have you heard from your mom yet today?" I ask. "I'll call Scout this afternoon, like I always do, but is everything going okay there?"

"I've gotten a few texts, yes."

Knowing that means he's been bombarded. "Sorry she's bothering you. I told her to call *me* when you're traveling."

"She's not bothering me. You're too busy to be dealing with that kind of stuff, anyway."

"You're busy, too."

He scoffs. "It's not a big deal. Takes two seconds to answer a text. Don't worry about them or me, okay? Just take care of you and focus on what needs to be done out there, so you can come home. We miss you."

"God, I miss you, too." Speaking of crying at the drop of a hat… With greasy fingers, I swipe tears from my cheeks, then reach for a napkin to scrub away the residue. "I want to come home. You've been so patient and understanding. You're the best."

"I try. I love you, beautiful."

"Oh, I love you, too, champ."

We end the call, and I feel better for having talked to him. I even throw away the rest of my lunch, filled now with something more nourishing than salt, grease, and carbs.

———

My goal is to be back in Pacific Palisades before Mom and Dad return from their European travels. It's not that they would mind hosting me; I just draw the line at falling into that surreal wormhole that takes me back to the exact living arrangements we shared when I was growing up. It's been bizarre—and uncomfortable—enough, sleeping on the old daybed; to have them back home with their way-too-familiar routines, sleeping down the hall from me, would be a serious mind-fuck. I can't handle any more of those.

Plus, my family needs me. I hear a strain in Jet's voice that wasn't there the first two weeks of my absence. He has questions every night about something, usually school-related but not always.

"What's this about a field trip you said you'd chaperone?" *Oh shit.*

"Students can dress up for the class Halloween party. What's Scout going to be this year?" *Uhhhh...*

"Where do you keep the passports? I need mine for the Mexico City game next weekend." *The safe! I know the answer to that one!* "What's the combination, again?" *Ooh! Another answer I know!*

It's funny, I used to go it alone all the time when he traveled non-stop from August through January. And I didn't have Gloria there cooking my meals and doing my laundry. Thank God. I'd have gone insane. Granted, Jet was never gone for weeks at a time, but I still didn't have to pepper him with questions every time we talked while he was away. I handled things.

Being away has shown me several things: a) if I die suddenly, Jet—and by extension, Scout—is screwed; b) I'm not allowed to die first, which sucks; c) women are the lynch pins of society; d) all it takes is one hiccup in life for one's "system" to go to shit.

On cue, Gloria calls as I'm wrapping up an evening with Cyndi, Colin, and the kids. I've noticed I'm staying later and later at their house or my brother's, delaying the time when I have to go back to Mom and Dad's empty place. Turns out, introverts *can* get enough of being alone.

I mouth a goodbye to the Bennetts and give one-armed hugs to Mikey and Gracie before turning my full attention to my mother-in-law's voice on the phone. In my rental car, I switch on the hands-free and sit in the driveway with the engine running, shivering a bit as the interior slowly warms up.

"Is everything okay?" I ask first, always on alert for problems.

"You tell me."

I shake my head, confused. "Sorry?"

"Are you ever coming home, Maura? You know I'm glad to stay as long as I need to, but do I need to stay much longer?"

An inexplicable shame floods my body, making my extremities tingle. "Uh, not too much longer. We're finally making progress with Planning and Zoning, so I can probably head home soon. Why? Is something wrong?"

She sighs. "It's *wrong* that you're away from your family for so long."

The shame quickly mutates into irritation, then anger. I wonder if she ever had this conversation with her son when he was traveling every single week for months at a time, year after year. Somehow, I doubt it.

As I organize my thoughts, searching for a polite enough one to verbalize, she continues, "Scout needs her mama. Jet needs his wife. They're getting *crabby*."

I can't help but feel a hint of satisfaction at these revelations. It's especially sweet hearing Gloria admit it.

"I see," I say, trying to hide the smile from my voice. After all, it's kind of mean to delight in other people's misery. "Well, like I said, I'm trying to get things moving here as fast as I can. It's not really up to me, though."

"Surely you can do all those things from here. You don't have to be *there*. What do you pay that Nina woman for?"

"Not stuff like this," I say. "Listen, Gloria. I appreciate that you're willing to level with me and tell me how much Scout and Jet miss me, but this is a pretty special circumstance, and

I'm going to need the two of them to step up and cope just a little longer."

She harrumphs, and I almost laugh out loud. Then she drops, "Fine, but I need you to call that PTA woman. What's her name? Tiki?"

"Kiki," I say with a laugh that does burble out this time.

"Yes! Kiki. Seems like a lovely lady. Really has her act together! I attended the PTA meeting last night and took notes for you and Jet."

"Oh, that's— Well, that wasn't necessary, but thank you." *I think.*

"You're welcome. I also signed you up for a few things. I wrote them all down on the refrigerator calendar. Jet said you'd put them in the one on your phone. I offered to do it myself, if he'd share your family calendar with me—"

"Oh, no!" I catch my panicked tone and chuckle nervously. "You don't have to go to all that trouble."

"That's what Jet said. Anyway!" she sing-songs. "After the meeting, Kiki approached me and told me to remind you about... Oh, darn. What was it? Something about Oktoberfest and German costumes or some such." She trails off again then, snaps, "I don't know! Just call her. She says she's been trying to get in touch with you, but you haven't been returning her voice mails."

Probably because I haven't listened to them. Because I totally forgot about them. Because I have more important things going on.

"Damn. She *has* called. I always mean to call her back, but..."

"Really, Maura." By Gloria's tone, you'd think I had committed a capital crime rather than simply forgotten to return some calls. But then, I'm sure Gloria was the Kiki of her day and relates much more to her than to me, the slacking peon.

"I'll deal with it," I say. "Thanks for the reminder."

"Mm-hm. I hope you think about the other reminders I've dropped on this call, too, the ones about your family."

"I haven't forgotten my family!"

"Are you sure *they* know that?"

Heart pounding, I say, "Jet is a grown-ass man, Gloria. He knows that two weeks apart doesn't erase an entire relationship. I'm not in Greece enjoying the nightlife and chatting up hot guys. I'm taking care of our business."

"And neglecting other business."

"Oh, for fu—" I snap my seatbelt into place. "Thank you, Gloria, for your concern. I'll do you a favor and *not* tell Jet about this conversation."

"Don't keep secrets for my sake. I think he'd be relieved that you know. As for Scout—you know, your daughter?"

I bite the inside of my cheek. "Yes, I'm familiar with her. Very."

"I'm calling while she and Jet are out on a bike ride, because I'm concerned about her. She's not eating very well, and I have a feeling she's not sleeping as restfully as a child her age normally does."

"Is she sick?"

At the mere thought of it, my own stomach does flip-flops, and my temperature rises. I got caught up in the conversation with Cyndi and Colin and didn't call her after school today, like I normally do. When I realized what had happened, I figured I'd just catch her tonight when Jet calls. Of all the days to miss our call...

"Maybe she's coming down with something," I say to Gloria. "Ask her if any of her classmates have been sick."

"She needs her mother."

This time, the statement doesn't bring any satisfaction. It brings tears. In a pinched voice, I say, "I know she does. But is that all, do you think?"

"I think that's enough."

"No, I mean, is everything going okay with school? How does the work she's bringing home look?"

"It's hard to glean anything from color-by-number and simple addition, Maura."

"But is it done correctly?"

"Of course. She's the smartest kid I've ever known. The problem isn't her brain. It's her heart. You need to come home."

I nod, shaking tears into my lap. "I will. I am."

"When?"

"As soon as I can."

She lets out a frustrated groan, so I rush ahead with a more definite, "I'll solidify some things with the contractor tomorrow and make my travel arrangements. I'll be home this weekend."

"Good. I'll let you tell Jet and Scout the good news yourself when they call you later tonight."

I grit my teeth and say through my tears. "Thanks."

## SEVENTEEN

## BABY TRAMP STAMP

By the time I land in L.A. and order a ride from the airport to home, it's dark outside, the brightly-lit windows of our house a beacon to this travel-weary, homesick soul. In the front entryway, I kick off my shoes.

"Hello!" I call out. Nobody answers or appears.

Torzi moseys into the kitchen, then stretches and shakes from his ears to his tail. I meet up with him.

"Hey, bud. Where is everyone?"

Jet offered to meet me at the airport, nearly insisted, in fact. But since I was getting in so late on a Sunday night, after he'd been working all day and getting Scout ready for the upcoming school week, I told him not to mess with it. Waiting one more hour for the three of us to be reunited wouldn't kill us, but it would make for a much less complicated evening for him.

I have to admit, though, I was kind of expecting them to be more anxious to welcome me home once I got here. Never mind. It's not all about me. How can I expect everyone to drop everything just because I'm coming home after being gone for three weeks? They've had to establish new routines without me, and I'm glad they have. That means my absence wasn't the miserable burden Gloria wanted me to believe it was. Sure, I hope they missed me, but she made it sound like I needed to get back to avoid a news-making disaster. Leave it to Gloria to exaggerate.

There are plenty of explanations for the not-so-enthusiastic welcome home, too. The game Jet announced was in Vegas today. Maybe he got home later than expected (likely). Scout spent the afternoon and dinner at the Valentines' so Gloria could get on the road and home before dark. Maybe Jet got caught up talking to Richard when he picked up Scout on his way back into town (even more likely). Maybe dinner took longer to make, eat, and clean up than Jet had planned (likeliest yet).

I look around the kitchen, however, and notice that it appears as if it hasn't been used since I left. That's definitely not the case, given that Gloria was here, but its fixtures sparkle and counters gleam, even in the dimmed under-cabinet lighting with the overhead lights off. Jet didn't cook in here tonight. The man can't make a sandwich without dirtying seven dishes and utensils, and he never thinks to brush off the crumbs or wipe down the counters unless I remind him.

That must be it, then. He and Scout went out to dinner, just the two of them, and service was slow, setting their whole evening routine back.

I tilt my head to listen, and determine they're in her bathroom, which makes sense considering it's bath time on a school night at the end of a weekend. Wending my way through the short hallways, I follow the voices. When I arrive at the bathroom, I lean casually against the door frame and cross my arms over my chest to observe, undetected, for now. I smile at the tableau before me, a dedicated dad caring for his adoring daughter, spending quality time together before bedtime.

Jet, in a gray t-shirt and red athletic shorts, kneels next to the bathtub, the pink bottoms of his bare feet and his wide back facing me and concealing my view from a splashing Scout, whom he chases with a washcloth. "Bump, we've got to get this off before your mom gets home. If she sees it, she'll—I don't want to even think about what she'll say. Or do."

I stiffen, no longer content and amused, angling myself to get a better view.

"Why, though? All my friends wear it!"

"No, they don't. Parker and Brynn and Neville don't. And the ones who do are—" He stops short of insulting her classmates. "You guys are still little. This stuff is for big kids."

"I'm a big kid!"

"Yeah, you are. My bad. You're a big kid about a lot of things. But not this. Now, stop fighting me and let me wash your face!" He manages to hold her head still with one hand and make contact with the rag-covered other one.

I clear my throat.

Jet startles, dropping the washcloth and letting go of Scout, who slides backward with the sudden absence of support to the back of her head. She catches herself on her elbows before submerging, and that's when I see her now-smeared face.

"Beautiful!" Jet springs to his feet faster than he probably ever thought possible again, after multiple surgeries. Soaked from his bathtub wrestling match, the front of his Chiefs t-shirt displays a darker gray than the back of it. "Hey! You're home!"

"I am, unless I'm a mirage." Refusing to take my eyes off our daughter, who suddenly realizes it's a good idea to take over the job of scrubbing her own face, albeit clumsily and inefficiently, I say, "What's up?"

Jet chuckles nervously and tries intercept me on the way to the bathtub with a hug, but I neatly avoid his embrace and step around him. When I remove the small terry square from Scout's hands, I shake it open and flat to inspect the pink, black, and yellowish stains on it, then look down at the raccoon circles under Scout's eyes. Makeup. Lots and lots of makeup. More than I ever wear in a week. I'm speechless.

One hand limp at his side, the other on the back of his neck, Jet looks down at his feet and says, "I didn't want to make a big stink about—"

"Oh, I'll make a stink about it."

"Maura."

I flap my hand toward the tub. "Look at her!"

"I'll take care of it. Next time Scout goes over there, we can politely explain that we don't want her playing with makeup. Have you eaten dinner?" He cups my elbow and steers me to the bathroom door. Insistently. Too insistently. "I brought home your favorite burrito platter from the taqueria. Why don't you go heat that up and eat, and we'll finish up in here?"

I glance over my shoulder at Scout, crouching now and splashing her face, her posture reminiscent of a scampering Smeagol in *The Lord of the Rings*. Water glistens on her spine, trailing down her lower back and—

I gasp and jerk my elbow from Jet's grip. "Oh, my—"

He closes his eyes and pinches the bridge of his nose. "Yep. Just great," he mutters to nobody in particular.

Hoisting Scout to her feet, I turn her away from me and

bend over so I'm eye level with the shooting stars and fancy script declaring her to be a "Super Star." I scramble for the wash cloth and rub frantically at the fake tattoo just above her heart-shaped butt.

"Ow! You're doing it too hard!" she cries.

Halfway through the job, when she's merely a "Star," I suddenly stop and drop the balled-up rag in the water before turning and storming out, speed-walking down the hall and through the kitchen and living room to our bedroom, slamming doors behind me. At the foot of our bed, I pace, nibbling at my thumbnail. Knowing there's nothing I can do to make it any better, I listen helplessly to Scout's cries drifting through the house.

By the time her crying stops, and Jet joins me in our room, I've given up my caged lion act, but only because my feet are killing me. Slumped on the bench at the end of our bed, legs straight out in front of me, I mop my own black-tinted tears with a sodden tissue. I stare at Jet's toes while he stands silently in front of me.

Finally, I say, "I blew it."

"Well…"

"What the hell, Jet? What. The. Hell?"

"Are you asking about the makeup, or the tattoo, or your reaction, or…?"

"I come home after being away for almost a month, and this is what greets me?"

His jaw flexes as he clenches his teeth, but he doesn't answer my rhetorical question.

"I thought she knew better than that."

"She's five."

"Still. We've talked about this since— her whole life!"

"You've warned her about lower back tats? I thought that talk was years away. Good for you for getting ahead of that."

I ignore his attempts to make me laugh. With a windy exhale, he sits down next to me and says, "It's not *that* big of a deal. We bought her makeup last Christmas, for crying out loud."

"Little kid makeup. Play stuff that hardly shows up when you put it on. Not— not— the entire contents of a Sephora!" I draw up my legs and pull them to my chest, resting my chin on my knees.

He tuts and rubs my back. "Come on. Calm down. This isn't how you want to be after being gone so—"

"Were you going to tell me?" If lift my chin to watch his face as he answers me.

"Of course!" he says earnestly. "I wish you hadn't actually seen it, but…"

"I don't want Scout to be friends with Larissa anymore. I don't want her going over there anymore."

"Oh, babe. That's…" He puffs his cheeks and blows out slowly. "That's going to be really tough. Scout likes going to Larissa's to play."

*And we have to suck up to his boss and family so you don't lose your job,* I think but just barely manage not to say.

Jet doesn't need me to contribute reasons, anyway. He continues, "She's been there a lot lately. The Valentines have been super-helpful while you've been gone. Playing over there was a good distraction for Scout when she was missing you."

My face flushes with a mixture of shame and rage. "So that's what this is about, huh? I had to go!"

"I know! Nobody's saying you didn't."

"And it takes a long time to straighten out everything I had to straighten out."

"Yes. It does."

"I came back as soon as I could. As it is, it's going to be complicated to do some of the stuff I need to do without being there, local."

"You didn't have to rush back."

I look sharply at him, freezing in the middle of wiping my nose. "You didn't want me to come home?"

"Of course, I did! When you could, when it made sense. Not because you felt like you *had* to." He pulls me to his side with one arm around my shoulders, and I finish mopping my face. "C'mon. Let's take a deep breath and regroup."

Hip-to-hip, we rest in silence for a few seconds, doing just that, until he says, "It was easy when all of her friends were family. Even when we didn't agree, we honored each others' wishes. Out here, it's a little different. We have to accept that she's going to be exposed to things and people who are different from us. That's a good thing!"

I scoff wetly.

He takes my hand, sodden tissue and all, and squeezes it. "You're exhausted, babe."

"Ugggggh."

Laughing at my reaction to the hated endearment, he nevertheless trudges on. "Let's have a redo, okay? You take a shower or eat or do whatever you need to do to reset, and we'll all meet back up in Scout's room for a bedtime story. How's tht sound."

I shrug. "Okay, I guess. I still blew it. I can't take any of that back."

"No, but you can apologize and promise to do better. It's important for her to see we know how to do that when we screw up. That way, she learns how to do it, too."

Groaning, I say, "God, you became an even better dad while I was gone. Fuck me."

"Trust me, I will," he says, wiggling his eyebrows. "Later."

When I crack up, he smiles and kisses my lips. "There," he whispers. "That's already better. I'm so glad you're home."

"Even like this?"

"Even like this."

## EIGHTEEN

## TRAINWRECK BREAKFAST

In order to not stir up such recently aggravated emotions, last night's apology when I tucked in Scout was rather generic. Now it's time for me to show some real courage and vulnerability.

On my way to the coffeemaker as I pass Scout at the island, slumped over her cereal, I place a glancing, tender hand on top of her head. While I pour hot, steaming coffee into a mug, I say, "Bump, I'm sorry about last night. I was tired, and it upset me to see you like that, but that was no excuse for hurting you. I didn't mean to."

She grunts something noncommittal.

I exchange glances with Jet as he breezes, whistling, into the kitchen and takes in the atmosphere. The whistling trails off, and his chagrined expression tells me he thought last night's glossed-over apology was the final word. I can practically hear his thoughts, and they consist of one word. "*Noooooooo.*"

Hoping to prove him wrong, that we can have this conversation without it blowing up, and we can all move past it, I lean onto the counter, across from Scout, and brace myself on my elbows, trying to get down to her level so she'll look at me. It's a good thing my hands are wrapped around this warm cup of coffee, because the chill emanating from her is fierce. A wise voice in my head tells me to leave it for now, to come back to it after school, when it's not so fresh. As usual, I ignore it.

"Scout, sweetie, do you understand why I was upset?"

She jams her fist into her right cheek and shakes her head, refusing to look at me and choosing, instead, to stare into her bowl of milk.

"We've discussed makeup plenty of times, haven't we? How it's okay when you and I goof around with it, but we only put on a little bit because you're already beautiful without it, and we don't want to cover up the pretty face God gave you?"

Looking more like her dad than ever, with her set jaw and stony eyes, she says nothing and doesn't move.

"And tattoos," I press. "They're fun, too, especially the fake ones. The one you chose was…" I swallow. "Really neat."

"Parker's mommy and daddy draw tattoos. Real ones," she says.

"Uh, yes. They do. For big people."

Jet places a decidedly warning hand on my shoulder, but I shrug him off while I try to find the right words. *No slut shaming. No slut shaming.*

"You probably don't know this, because you're— you're still so innocent and sweet, but where you put that tattoo was — Well, it was a little *advanced* for someone your age."

"Babe…" Jet says, clearing his throat.

"Hang on. I'm doing a thing."

"Okay, but—"

Through gritted teeth, I say, "Don't undermine me, please."

He steps back like someone cautiously moving away from the blast zone at a bomb site. I wait to make sure he's going to honor my request. When he goes about pouring his coffee, I take my cue and turn my attention back to our daughter.

"You know, we've talked about parts of the body that are more private than others. Nothing shameful about them, right? But they're the parts we keep covered by clothes when we're around other people. Unless we're being, um, sexy."

Finally, she looks up at me, unable to hide her curiosity about the topic.

I smile gently. "People tend to get tattoos where you put yours to be sexy. And five-year-olds are too young to be sexy, right sweetie?"

She wrinkles her nose. "Ew. Yes."

"I understand you didn't know that when you chose that spot. Maybe someone told you to put it there, and you thought it would be cool?"

Shrugging, she says, "Sort of. But it was my idea. We were watching *Trainwreck*, and Larissa told me—"

"Excusemewhat?" Jet says, coffee dribbling down his chin.

That tidbit has spiked my blood-pressure, too, but I want to hear the whole sentence, so I shush him as he joins us at the island, mopping his face.

"Go ahead, sweetie," I say to Scout, despite my nausea.

"When we were watching *Trainwreck*, Larissa told me the main girl in the movie…"

"Amy Schumer. Uh-huh."

"In real life, she has a tattoo on top of her butt, and it's really cool, and I like that girl because she's funny, and I thought it would be funny to have a tattoo on top of my butt, too."

"Y-you watched *Trainwreck* at Larissa's, huh?" I ask cheerfully. "Did Larissa's mommy and daddy know you were watching that?"

"Uh-huh. Larissa's mommy turned it on for us." She slurps the milk from her bowl.

Jet claws at his cheek, but I lay a steadying hand on his arm.

"But," Scout continues, after licking away her milk mustache, "she told us that we had to watch the normal version, not the *really* funny one. It was still funny, though."

"Oh, not the uncut version. In that case, what a great parent," Jet mutters.

I talk over him, saying in practically a yell, "I see! Well, that was probably for the best. Anyway! You should brush your teeth and get your shoes on, Bump. It's about time to leave."

After she skips down the hallway, Jet dumps his coffee down the drain. "Well, that explains the back tattoo," he says mildly, already over his shock and dismay and suddenly calm, as if everything's fine and settled.

Now that it's just the two of us, I open the release valve on my temper. "Does it? Does it, Jet?"

Confused, he closes the dishwasher and levels a wary look at me. "She's watched mature stuff with us before."

"Not *that* mature. And the key words are, 'with *us*.' Supervised. Where we've covered her eyes and ears during certain parts. Did Kiki and Richard stand behind the girls and cover their eyes and ears through that whole film? Because that's about what they'd have to do."

"I'm not thrilled they let them watch that particular movie, but at least now we know Scout wasn't trying to be sexy; she was being funny. 'Funny' is okay for a kindergartner. We like 'funny.' I'm funny."

I scowl.

"Not right now, maybe…" As I take Scout's lunch from the refrigerator, he begs, "Maura, please don't lecture her in the car about this. Just drop it, okay? It happened, it's over, let's move—"

"I'm not going to say another word to her about it, trust me."

His shoulders relax. "Oh, good. It wasn't her fault, and—"

"I *am* going to have a talk with our PTA President, though. I'll be waiting for *her* on the school steps."

"Oh, no. No, no. That wouldn't be a good choice, babe."

"Good choice? Do you think she'll be in a position to lecture me about 'good choices'?" I slip my feet into my casual slides in the garage and boom, "Scout! Let's go!"

"No," he says, trailing after me, "but she might get the school security officer to escort you off the property. You could be banned! And then what? Then— then I'd have to do all of the PTA stuff by myself! Let's regroup and, uh, think of a more level-headed way of dealing with this, m'kay?"

He pulls his Tesla's keys from the peg on the wall. "I'll take Scout to school today. You stay here and cool off."

"Cool off? I'll do no such thing. She needs to know that she crossed a line—a lot of lines!—yesterday, and she needs to know right away." Plus, I should probably do this while I have the courage. If I leave it too long, I'll talk myself out of the confrontation.

Before he can react, I snatch the keys from his hand, and in an attempt to evade him and retain control of the situation, I jog to the car, sliding behind the steering wheel. Scout, blissfully unaware of the situation, comes into the laundry room, lifts her backpack from its hook, and bounces her dad on the way to my car.

When she notices I'm not in my vehicle and joins me in his, she asks, "Why are we taking Daddy's car?"

"It's faster," I say.

Jet rushes to get in the passenger seat while I simultaneous press the buttons to open the garage and start the engine.

Scout claps. "Yay! Daddy's coming with us today!"

"Seatbelts," I say curtly, waiting just long enough to hear the obedient clicks before backing so quickly from the garage that it makes Scout squeal and giggle.

Jet says so only I can hear, "Calm down. And be careful with my car."

Ignoring him, I jam the shifter into drive.

———

On our way to the school, I notice with more than a little regret that I'm still braless. For the first time in five years, I'm grateful that my already modest chest shrank another cup size after I nursed Scout. Unless someone looks closely, they won't be able to see my "free birds" under my black t-shirt. I hope.

The whole drive, Jet talks me down at a volume inaudible to the backseat occupant while I attempt to carry on a cheerful, normal-sounding before-school conversation with her.

"I'm serious, Maura. Do NOT make a scene at the school. That will be much worse for our kid than any R-rated movie. Well, maybe not *any* R-rated movie, but definitely the one she saw."

"So, yeah! Another Monday, huh, Bump? Remind me what

your special classes are on Mondays. Is music today? You love music class. Or is Monday a gym day? I can't keep it straight. Oh, music *and* gym. That must be why I get confused."

"I swear to God, Maura, if you park this car at the school and get out, I will— I'll— I'll tackle you. In front of everyone."

"Hey, Bump, I packed your favorite fruit snacks in your lunch last night. Just something to brighten your day."

"Stay in the drop-off line, Maura. In. The. Line. Do not pull into the parking lot. Drop and go. We're going to drop her and go. And we'll call Kiki and Richard tonight to discuss— Maura! Unbelievable. Are you even listening to me at all? Please don't get out of the car. I'll walk her to the doors."

I shove the car into park, but he's already out, opening the back door for Scout and grabbing her hand as she says, "Bye, Mommy! Can you both drop me off every—" The slamming door cuts off her question.

I scramble out and jog around the front end, holding my breasts against my body with one arm while I reach out to hold Scout's other hand. My shoes slap loudly against my heels with each step.

Now that we're here, my determination is starting to flag a bit. I want to have it out with Kiki right away, but I underestimated how intimidating it would be with an audience. I scan the steps, hoping the Front Step Brigade isn't here today, for some reason. Divine intervention, maybe? But God's dealing with more pressing issues like—I don't know—sex trafficking or famines, so my prayer goes unanswered. I get it. It was short notice.

At the top of the steps, Scout lets go of both of us and runs for the doors. "Bye!" she yells without a backward glance.

"Bye! Have a good day! I love you!" Jet calls to the closing glass and steel.

"Bye! Love you," I say quickly, already turning to trot down the steps, where Kiki and her minions are stationed, at the halfway point of the flight. With each step down, I bounce a little too freely, so I cross both arms over my chest, pretending I'm cold and smiling nervously as I pull up alongside the edge of the group.

Despite those busted knees, Jet's still faster at stair runs than I am, especially in these shoes, so he arrives a half-second sooner than I do. "Kiki!" he bellows, startling one of the moms so much she sloshes coffee—or whatever's in that travel mug—down the front of her shirt.

"Shh," I say to him, grabbing at his elbow. "This is my show."

Risking my wrath, he completely ignores me. "We need a word," he says breathlessly when Kiki acknowledges his summons with a raised eyebrow and *Who me?* touch of her chest.

She exchanges quizzical glances and arch smiles with the others and says, "Okay, then," as she threads her way through the throng to get to us.

I clutch at Jet's hand, holding tightly and digging my nails —such as they are—into his palm. "Let me talk," I mutter. He attempts to wrestle his hand away, but he doesn't take his eyes off Kiki.

Still all forced beneficent smiles, she says, "How nice to see the two of you together again."

Jet shifts on his feet. "Uh, yeah. It's good to get back to normal. So, Kiki—"

"It's always wonderful to see parents make time in their busy schedules for their kids."

"We try," Jet replies, his tone decidedly cooler and demeanor stiffer.

Focusing on me, Kiki says, "You've been gone so long! It was delightful getting to know Gloria, but there's no substitute for parental presence and involvement. Yesterday, I could tell how excited Scout was at the idea that she might be your top priority again."

Jet begins to say something, but I inch in front of him and subtly scoot him aside with my leg. "Hang on a minute, champ." I tilt my head and furrow my brow. "Not that it's any of your concern, but she's always my top priority."

"I'm sure Kiki knows that," Jet says with a nervous laugh, grasping my shoulders and rubbing them like I'm a boxer in my corner, needing a pep talk. "What she probably meant was—"

"You've been in Kansas City for the past month, though, right?" she says, rejecting his interpreter services. "That can't have made things easy, and it's hard for a child to be separated from her mother for so long!"

"Three weeks, and it was an unusual, emergency situation, but yes. I just got back, which brings us neatly to what I wanted to discuss with you this morning."

"I'm all ears," she says drolly.

"I'm a bit concerned, Kiki," I say, hitting the k's in her name as hard as I can, "about some things Scout's revealed about the playdate at your house."

"Oh? Which one? There have been so many lately! Not that we've minded, of course. Anything to help." Her rapid blinking makes me want to punch her.

Jet mumbles something grudgingly appreciative from behind me that is barely audible.

"Yesterday's," I say, my back teeth throbbing with the amount of force I'm exerting on them.

"What about it? We love Scout to pieces. She's become like

another sister to Larissa. The girls had a marvelous time, as usual."

"Maybe *too* marvelous a time? We need to talk to you about some unacceptable activities that went down."

"Excuse me? 'Unacceptable activities'? That sounds like a serious accusation." She tries to edge farther from her posse, each member of which is no longer trying to pretend to do anything else but listen to our conversation, but Jet and I don't budge, so she can only move so far. The curious group moves with her, hemming her in even more than before. "I— I guess I don't understand. Did Scout say something happened? Because you know how little girls can be. They have such active imaginations at her age. In fact, I rarely give much credence to the things Larissa says. Don't worry, though. They outgrow it. Our oldest is a teenager and hardly talks at all anymore. Hahahaha!"

"It's not what Scout said," I reply, completely taking over and ignoring Jet's, "Honey," behind me. "It's what she came home looking like."

Now Kiki tosses her head back and laughs even louder. "Oh! The girls had so much fun with all of my old makeup." She directs her attention at Jet. "I would have washed it off for you, but I didn't want to interrupt their playtime. Then you arrived to pick her up, and…" She widens her eyes innocently. "You didn't seem bothered last night. I assumed— I mean, don't all little girls go wild sometimes, pretending they're all grown up? And it washes."

"Yes, it washes," I say. "So do temporary tats. But it's inappropriate for a five-year-old to have a tramp stamp."

"Yeah, so!" Jet jumps in. "I guess what we're saying is that maybe next time Scout's over—"

"Oh, there won't be a next time."

My steely vow elicits a scoff and fierce objections from Kiki, so Jet continues sweetly, "Maybe you could, uh, supervise the kids a little better and—I don't know—steer them clear of things like makeup and, um, lower back tattoos?"

She stares us down as if we're requesting something radical, like that our daughter not play with any electronic toys while under her roof, which makes me doubt myself for a second. Am I overreacting? Are we crazy and out of touch or too strict? Are our expectations unreasonable and prudish? I glance over my shoulder at Jet to make sure he's backing me up, and he smiles encouragingly at me, but his expression becomes almost apologetic his eyes slide back to Kiki.

Doubling-down it is, then, I decide, standing even straighter and letting my arms drop, no longer caring about the "girls" swingin' free. "And another thing, Keek. It's none of my business what you let *your* kids watch, but *Trainwreck* is, for sure, an unacceptable film to show to kindergartners. It's my business to make judgment calls like that, and that one's a no-brainer."

The crowd gasps and titters while Kiki blushes to the roots of her unnaturally blonde hair.

"So you might want to keep movies with a rating higher than 'G' shelved for the next playdate you host, which will *not* involve my daughter." With that, I turn on my toes and with as much dignity as one can display while supporting one's boobs with a well-placed forearm, and prance back to the parking lot.

## NINETEEN

## SHAME SPIRAL

When Jet catches up to me, I expect a lecture, or disapproving silence. I do *not* expect the round of applause I receive after he slides behind the wheel and pushes the ignition button. In fact, I take it to be a sarcastic slow-clap at first and say, staring resolutely out my window, "Just drive, please."

But he whoops and replies, "That. Was. Awesome."

I whip my head around to make sure I'm interpreting his statement correctly and that he's not being sarcastic. When it's verified, I say, "Awesome? Interesting. Because you were about as supportive back there as the invisible bra I'm wearing."

"What? I was all-in on the assist, babe. I was playing 'good cop,' which, let's face it, is much more natural for me, anyway. Not that you're a natural 'bad cop.' I just mean that I'm more comfortable smoothing things over. It's what I did in the locker room all the time when guys would fight. You know, try to bring it back down to a level that won't get physical." His gaze travels down to my chest. "Oh, damn. Lookie there. Well, I'm sure nobody else noticed."

Everyone else noticed. But it's California, so maybe I'll get a pass. Doubtful, but maybe. "Just drive," I repeat more forcefully. "They're all still staring at us."

He backs carefully from the parking space and exits the lot with a jaunty wave to the group of onlookers, which doesn't include Kiki. She must have high-tailed it into the building or to her own vehicle after our dust-up. Good. I hope she's as embarrassed as I am. Otherwise, this is all for nothing. Actually, that wasn't my goal, but I can't quite remember anymore what the aim of the conversation was. Oh, right… Makeup and tramp stamps and age-inappropriate movies and how I don't want our daughter messing with any of them.

It definitely wasn't about humiliating her in front of everyone after she pinged that nerve about my being away for so long.

She's right, though. I *have* been an absentee mom. Gloria said it, and now Kiki's confirmed it. For the past three weeks, I've put the theater above my husband and child, more focused on putting out metaphorical fires twenty-five hundred miles away for convenience's sake and refusing to compromise efficiency by doing what was better for everyone, which would have been overseeing cleanup and reconstruction from home. I chose to compromise my family's needs, instead. The worst thing is, I knew full-well I was doing it. It's not like I needed Gloria or Kiki to point it out to me. I was well aware of the choice I was making and decided it was worth it, or that it didn't really matter, neither of which were my calls to make. Did Scout think it was worth it? That being apart didn't matter? I doubt it. And if I'm honest with myself, I'd totally agree with her, in hindsight.

It's just… I was so in my element back in Kansas City. As out-of-place as I feel here, I feel even more at home there. The cooler weather was invigorating, a reminder that every year, every phase, every life has seasons and that it's not natural for weather or society or *anything* to be as homogeneous as it seems out here, at least in our social and economic circles. I didn't realize how much I've been craving interaction with people who *get* me and love me and want to be around me, not because of what I might be able to do for them, but because I'm simply *me*. Being with Colin and Cyndi and even my brother and Deirdre was utterly refreshing. Hanging around the kids was like putting on a comfy old hoodie, the Aunt Maura hoodie that's classic and never goes out of style.

I'm still more comfortable as an aunt than as a mother. I've been doing it longer, for one thing. For another, it's all the fun without any of the responsibility. The responsibility of parenthood some days is crushing, paralyzing. I keep thinking I'll get used to it eventually, and some days I manage to barely think about it. Most days, though, it's there, an ever-present nagging voice that says I'm not cut out for something so fucking important and that wonders who the hell ever sanctioned someone like me being allowed to reproduce.

Maybe God figured Jet would pick up the slack in our parenting partnership, so it would all end up okay. It seems to come so naturally to him, as effortless as breathing. He was born to be a dad. More than that, he *loves* it. Nothing about it is a chore for him. He approaches every facet of it like an adventure and acts like no matter what he's doing with Scout, there's nothing else he'd rather be doing. Only it's not an act. I've never once heard him complain or even seen him roll his eyes when they're doing something together. He doesn't rush through activities like I sometimes do, just so I can say we did them and I can move on to something more interesting to me. There's nothing more interesting to him than being with her. She's his ultimate passion project.

I need more. It has nothing to do with how much I love her (immeasurably); in fact, it seems to be directly correlated to that. The more I love her, the more I need things to distract me from the non-stop, heart-gripping fear that something terrible is going to happen to her and the absolute knowledge that I can't—and shouldn't—protect her from every negative thing that life will throw at her. My insecurities make it nearly impossible to be as in-the-moment with her as Jet always seems to be. My mind is constantly racing ahead to what could go wrong. Raising her can't be my passion project, because someday that project will be complete, and then what?

My passion project is the Knox Foundation. Its mission has no end. There will always be people and organizations who need the help that the foundation and its theaters provides. There's no fear, insecurity, or doubt when I'm leading its charge. I'm effortlessly good at it. I'm worthy.

So although I missed both Scout and Jet, I kept finding reasons to stay in Kansas City. They seemed like legit reasons at the time, at least as legit as coming home would have been. Each choice to stay or return always seemed like a wash, equally valid with the same number and severity of pros and cons. I justified my continued absence with the reassurance that Scout was in the best hands she could possibly be in with the best grandmother and the best dad in the world taking care of her. How could the absence of my completely average mothering even warrant notice? It couldn't. She was fine, and I was where I was supposed to be: touching the lives of people whose struggles I could actually positively impact.

The contrast between Kansas City Maura and California

Maura is painful. Here, I'm just a dork who bitches out other mothers in public.

Jet interrupts my mental beat-down with a sudden laugh as he goes over the last ten minutes in his head like a replay he can't stop analyzing. "I should be worried that you talked to my boss's wife like that, but I have to say, it was a huge turn-on. You were a fierce mama bear facing down another mama bear." He curls his hands into claws and quietly roars.

The same thing that turns him on makes me cringe when I picture what I must have looked like. "I can't believe I said those things," I mumble and blush.

Oblivious to my chagrin, he continues eagerly, still grinning, "Did you see the other moms' faces when you mentioned the title of the movie? Horror. They couldn't believe their flawless leader made such a low-brow mistake. Did I mention you were awesome?"

"I don't feel awesome. Can we stop talking about it, please?"

"Sure, sure." He pauses, and in a flirty mutter from the side of his mouth, says, "I'm glad I took the day off, because after that, I am horny as hell. Does that make me a bad person?"

"Maybe."

"Oh, well. Sorry, not sorry."

To my relief, he finally stops talking and drives silently for a few minutes, allowing me to return to my self-flagellating thoughts. The quiet doesn't last long, unfortunately.

"You know, Kiki made it sound like I was super-cool with the way Scout looked when I picked her up last night, but I was just as freaked out as you were. Well, maybe not *that* freaked out, but I wasn't feelin' chill about it, either. I must have a good poker face, or something."

His poker face actually sucks, but telling him that doesn't serve me, so instead I say, "If you were truly upset by Scout's appearance, Kiki would have known it. So either you weren't upset, or she's lying."

"Okay, then, she's lying. Because I wasn't like, 'Oh, wow. This looks great. I can't wait for my wife to come home after being gone for three weeks and see that this is the kind of shit that happens on my watch.'"

"For chrissake…"

"What?" He looks briefly at me as we turn into our neighborhood.

"I get it. I was gone a long time. Why does everyone keep bringing it up?"

He taps the steering wheel with his thumbs. "I wasn't saying it to make you feel bad."

"Well, I do, okay?"

"Why? Like you said, it was necessary. It's not like you *wanted* to be there that long."

When I say nothing to agree with that statement, he looks over at me again, this time more lingeringly. "Right? I mean, you *wanted* to come home, but it just wasn't possible."

Again, I remain quiet. This time he doesn't try to prompt a reply. We're parked in the dim, cool garage before I muster the nerve to look at him. His set jaw and white lips say it all. Poker face, my ass.

"I'm sorry," I say for what feels like the millionth time since stepping back on California soil.

He merely nods as a way of letting me know he's heard the apology. No acceptance of my apology seems forthcoming, however, so I rush on, "It wasn't a conscious thing. Well, I guess it kind of was. I knew the stuff I was doing could be done over the phone or by email or video call or whatever. But there were things not related to the theater that were keeping me there, things I haven't figured out how to do with technology yet, like maintaining connections with our friends and family. I wasn't ready to leave *them* again."

Unbuckling his seatbelt, he swivels at the waist and settles half-sideways in his seat, facing me. "So, let me get this straight. You were totally okay with only talking to Scout and me on the phone once a day, but that's not good enough for the KC peeps?"

"No! I missed you guys so much. You know that."

"I thought I did, but the way you're describing it, you missed us *less* than you've missed Colin and Cyndi and all those other people, and you didn't miss us enough to want to leave them and come home to us."

"That's not it at all."

"Sounds like it."

"Jet, I miss *home*. I miss the theater. I miss going to work. And yes, I miss hanging out with everyone there. I miss belonging."

"So it's all about you, huh? Never mind how Scout and I were feeling or how much we wanted and needed you back here. That didn't factor into your decision-making at all?"

"You guys were fine."

"Did we have a choice? What was I supposed to do? Bitch on the phone to you every night about how much it sucked to basically live with my mom again? Did you need Scout to cry when she talked to you, like she sometimes did when she talked *about* you to me? Would that have lit a fire under your ass?"

"She cried sometimes about me?"

"Uh, yeah. If 'sometimes' means, like, every night that last week."

"Why didn't you say something?"

He chuckles mirthlessly. "I thought you were working as fast as you could and didn't need us to make it any harder for you to be away from us. What an idiot, huh?"

"You're not an idiot."

"I sure feel like one, thanks to you."

"I didn't think you guys needed me or even missed me that much. I knew Gloria was spoiling you both and taking care of everything—"

"Not everything."

I roll my eyes. "The necessities. Plus, you had work, and Scout had school, and you both were so strong and upbeat on the phone! It really did seem like it was no big deal that I was gone, but it was a big deal for me to be back where I felt needed and known and understood by more than just the two people I live with."

He bites the inside of his cheek as he considers all of that, but it must not pass the sniff test, because he finally shakes his head and opens his door, getting out of the car without another word to me.

Something tells me his horniness is no longer an issue.

## TWENTY

## CATCHING UP

Jet's been quiet, or dare I say, "stony," since our heart-to-heart in the garage. Not that I blame him. I kind of hate myself, too, now that I've said out loud what I've been thinking and feeling for the past three weeks.

We haven't been intimate since I've been back from Kansas City. Barring those six weeks after Scout was born, this is the longest we've ever gone without sex since those early, torturous "no-sex-during-the-season" days of our relationship. For the past five nights, I've tried to make amends in the basest way possible, but all of my efforts have been thwarted. The first three nights, he was already asleep (or faking it) by the time I got in bed. The fourth night, I practically raced him in the bathroom so I could be waiting for him. While brushing his teeth, though, he suddenly remembered something urgent he needed to research for work, and *I* fell asleep waiting for *him*.

Last night, my last chance before he leaves for a game in San Francisco, I was determined. Despite the questioning looks it elicited, I not-so-subtly made sure he was always in view throughout the evening. When he announced he was going to bed, I agreed it was time. I spent the exact same amount of time that he did in the bathroom, even though he doesn't brush his teeth nearly as long as I prefer to do (yet he still has whiter teeth than I do—how unfair!). We simultaneously slid under the covers, which seemed like fantastic foreshadowing of things to come. The chaste kiss he gave me before he turned out his light quickly doused my optimism. He might as well have said, "Goodnight, Mother," as he turned on his side, facing away from me.

What. The. Heck?

I stewed on my half of the bed for hours after his platonic peck. Hours. The good news is, I was no longer sexually frustrated; I was decidedly turned off and pissed off.

I've been nothing but pure understanding all week about his anger. It's totally justifiable. I can't change how I feel, but I've apologized for how I chose to behave in response to those feelings. He claims he's forgiven me, but if this is his idea of forgiveness, it sucks. He's doing it wrong. You forgive and move on, right? Why is he still punishing me with pouty silences, dirty looks, and sexual abstinence?

The one thing we have in common, for sure, is that both of us are mad because we're hurt. He feels betrayed; I feel rejected. There's a fair bit of shame in there for me, too, but that's sort of par for the course. At least that feels somewhat normal. All I want is a return to normal. I'm determined to do my part to get there.

This morning, I feel worse than dead. At least dead is peaceful and restful. It would be amazing to loll in bed all day —with Jet, preferably (hey, angry sex can be hot; don't judge) —but with Oktoberfest a mere week away, I have way too much to do.

I spend the morning sorting through all of the lederhosen and dirndl dress orders that arrived in my absence. Through the magic of technology, I kept up with the ordering while gone, checking the inventory spreadsheet with the sizes Ursuline parents emailed to me. If we didn't have an appropriate size available, I ordered a new one right away, ensuring timely delivery.

Under ordinary circumstances, I would have been home to receive each shipment and open, sort, and catalog them individually, as they arrived, maybe two or three a day, tops, easily matched to each email request.

Like so many other plans and strategies of the past few weeks, though, the system went awry in my absence. Not knowing what else to do with them, Gloria and Jet piled the boxes and polybags on the floor and sofa in the study as they were delivered. There are dozens of them.

Armed with the spreadsheet of names and sizes, I slice my box cutter through tape and rip open the silver mailers with my bare hands, pausing occasionally to gulp cold coffee from the cup on the edge of my desk. Inside each box and bag is typically another plastic wrapping or bag of some sort, containing the individual costumes. It doesn't take long before I'm surrounded by a mini-landfill of cardboard, bubble wrap (why??? Clothes aren't fragile!), and plastic.

That's how Jet finds me when he pokes his head through the double study doors to say goodbye before leaving for this week's game.

"I'm gonna— Wow. That's…"

I wait.

"I have no words."

Remembering my vow to fix things between us, despite my sore feelings with him, I laugh as I lower the blade into the box cutter and set it on my desk. "Better find 'em before the game tomorrow."

He wades through the sea of shipping materials far enough to lean in for another one of his Puritanical pecks, but I grip the front of his shirt and yank him forward for something a bit more meaningful—with tongue. Ripping packages open makes me aggressive—and horny.

It doesn't take him long to relax and reciprocate with gusto, twining his fingers through my messy ponytail while I cup his butt cheeks in my hands and pull him against me.

When we separate, he winces down at me. "On that note, I have to get going."

I groan, refusing to let go of his derriere. "Can't you call in sick?"

"Uh, no. Nobody calls in sick."

"That's not healthy or sanitary. What if you had SARS? Ebola? Would those qualify you for a sick day? I'll call and pretend to be your doctor."

"Not sure I'm willing to fake any of those symptoms. Anyway, I can't let down Erin and the rest of the broadcast team." He steps back and adjusts the front of his pants. My hands fall away as he moves outside of my reach.

"Right. Of course. I was mostly kidding." I try to shrug off the less-than-subtle jab about dedication.

"I know. It's tempting, though."

Is it? I wonder. Even after such a relatively passionate kiss, minus the reflex physical response, he seems remote, detached.

"Well, it was worth a try," I say lightly, smiling as if nothing's wrong. "I probably have too much to do to be distracted by your sexiness, anyway, so get outta here." I wave him off playfully.

He half-turns to go, then pauses in the doorway, gripping the frame and looking back at me. "You should get Scout to help you with all this. You know how she loves sorting."

"You're right," I say, surprised I hadn't thought of it myself.

"Plus, it'll be something you two can do together. I don't know if you've noticed, but she hasn't been her usually peppy self this week."

I had noticed, but I assumed she was picking up on the tense vibe between Jet and me. Before I can figure out a way to say that that won't result in an argument right before he leaves, he says, "She really needs to spend some time with you." With that somewhat serious, almost rebuking remark, he pushes off the frame and walks away, lifting a hand in a half-hearted wave. "See you tomorrow night."

"Yes," I say faintly to his retreating back. "See ya."

———

Scout tries to decline my request for help, which leads to me trying to pretend it doesn't matter, which leads to obsessing about Jet's passive-aggressive digs at my recent absenteeism, which leads to a further determination on my part to spend the day with Scout, which leads to forcing her to help me, which leads to her doubling-down on her silence, which leads to two grumpy Knoxes working together on a not-so-pleasant task.

In other words, it's a perfect Saturday.

"Did you check off that last name?" I ask, already knowing she didn't, because I watched her stare into space and not react when I called it out.

"Yes," she says absently.

"Please double-check," I say as evenly as possible. "It was Veronica Hayes, Arya and Catelyn's mom."

"I checked it!"

Mustering my final drop of patience, I navigate the stacks of already-sorted and to-be-sorted dresses and lederhosen and peer upside down at the list on the tablet's screen. Sure enough, there's no mark next to Veronica's name. I jab my finger at it. "Right here. Please check her off."

That's when I realize there aren't nearly as many check marks on the list as there should be, given the number of costumes we've already inventoried. I turn the clipboard around to better view it, hoping that I'm mistaken. Nope.

"God— bless America, Scout." I take the tablet from her and start checking off names from memory, tapping all of my frustration onto the screen. "You've hardly checked off anyone!"

"I can't read very good!" she says, her voice wobbling.

"You know your classmates' names. You helped me with your party invitations just fine."

"This is the whole school, though. I very don't know everyone in the whole school!"

"They all have similar names. You read just fine when you want to. This is the job you said you wanted to do, so please do it."

"I don't want to do any of it! I *want* to play in my room with my gerbils and plushies." She stomps her foot to under-score the point.

My internal principled parent wars with my internal effi-cient businesswoman. I would work more quickly by myself, but if I tell her to go to her room, I'm giving in to her, in a sense. What's the ultimate goal? Completing this odious task as quickly as possible is only one part of it. Another part is reconnecting with my daughter. Is this the way to do it, though? It's both slowing me down *and* putting a strain on us.

I wave her off, pissing off the principled parent, hardcore. *Way to go, dillhole. Reward her for being a brat. Brava.*

Angering someone was inevitable. Hell, this whole house is stuck under a cloud of it lately. And it's not like dismissing Scout has pleased her. In fact, her scowl as she storms toward her room would indicate the exact opposite.

Exasperated, I slap the tablet against my leg, then hiss at the sting. "Shit," I whisper, referring to the entire situation.

Going back to the list, I check off a few more names I remember calling out, then backtrack through the piles, lifting the costumes on top of the stacks to dig down until I get to the names already crossed off weeks ago—by me—following my inventory of the storage unit and our existing stock.

With a sigh, I return to where I was in the process, pulling the next costume from the large box and matching it with a gender, size, and name on the list, then writing the name on a sticker that goes on the outfit, and setting the neatly-folded bundle on the "sorted" stack designated for the first letter of the person's last name. I check off that person.

Only a bazillion left!

Three more costumes in, I find my mind wandering to the point that I can't remember if I matched the last two to the correct size or put them in the appropriate alphabetical stack.

"Damn," I mutter, going back over my work to be sure. The last thing I need is to misplace someone's costume or assign a teeny-tiny dress to a big, strapping guy. With so many unisex names and the very real risk of incorrectly assuming someone's gender identity, I need to be more careful, or I'm going to end up with a mess, proving my ineptitude at yet another facet of life.

After multiple close calls and corrections, I throw the clipboard aside, rub my eyes, and stretch. This is obviously not going to be the quick job I thought it was going to be, not if I want to do it right. And I do. I refuse to be the weak link in the Oktoberfest chain like I've been the weak link here at home. That depressing thought deflates me further.

I round my desk and sink into my chair, kicking my slippers-clad feet onto the desktop and leaning back as far as I dare to go. I technically don't have time to rest, so to justify this little break, I pull out my phone and check my messages. Surprisingly, there are few. No texts at all. A few unimportant emails and even more spam. To generate some activity, I send a text to Nina to touch base. She texts back that everything's fine, and since it's a Saturday, there's no progress on the construction plans.

*Makes sense.* I tap back.

*Good to be home?*

It would be nice to confide in someone how terrible it's been so far and how lonely I feel and how scared I am that I've really screwed up, and I don't even know how I could have done anything differently, but she has enough going on.

I simply send back a thumbs-up emoji, the best friend of the vaguely positive and typically one I avoid. Jet overuses it, and I hate it. You can't tell anything from a freaking thumbs-up. Is it an enthusiastic thumbs-up, a sarcastic thumbs-up, a "fine, just leave me alone' thumbs-up? It's impossible to tell. The only thing worse in a text response is the letter K. Like, you care so little about the conversation that you can only muster a single letter for the lazy one-syllable reply that's not even a full word.

Jay-soos. I'm analyzing text replies now.

Reminded of Jet, I send him a smoochy Bitmoji and before

thinking too much about it, immediately enter, *Scout doesn't want to help. I tried,* and hit the button to send it.

After a few minutes, during which I imagine him composing a long, thought-out message, perhaps with some more ideas of how I can get through to her, or hints about what's wrong—other than the obvious—I receive back from him, *K.*

## TWENTY-ONE

# OKTOBERFEST

Sorting and labeling each costume was just the beginning of my gargantuan task. Now I have to distribute them. My initial idea was to hang them up backstage in the school's auditorium and have parents come pick them up at their leisure, but Kiki nixed that plan. The school's security policies wouldn't be conducive to parents wandering that far into the school unsupervised, so office staff would have to escort each parent to the auditorium. She also vetoed my backup ideas of leaving the costumes in the office or passing them out to teachers for the children to take home to their parents.

"We can't burden administration, staff, or teachers. They're too busy with other things."

Fair enough. I felt like a jerk for even suggesting it in the first place.

Her idea? Set up a table in the hallway outside the office before and after school every day this week and let parents know they can pick up the costumes or give instructions for their kids to pick them up. I can distribute any unclaimed kits at the beginning of the day Saturday as PTA members arrive to set up Oktoberfest.

This had involved taking multiple trips to lug boxes from my car, up the eighteen front stairs—I'd counted them every time—past the staring front-step brigade, and into the school, then back again, twice a day, because, in Kiki's words, "We can't expect the school to find a place for us to securely store these." Like my car is a Brink's truck, or something.

By Wednesday, I'd wised up and, without seeking approval from anyone, set up on the sidewalk next to the drop-off lane. As each car had pulled up, I'd yelled at the driver, "Do you still need your Oktoberfest outfit?" If they'd said yes, I'd quickly gotten their name and handed (sometimes threw) their wrapped kits through their open windows or the car doors as their children had alighted from their vehicles.

On Friday, Kiki and her front step friends waited until I'd hauled all of the remaining boxes—a disturbingly large number of them—onto the sidewalk before they sauntered down and asked for theirs and their spouses' costumes. Most of them. One woman said her lazy-ass husband could come get his himself. Chances of that happening? Zero.

Wouldn't you know it, I'm still carrying around his and many others this morning as Scout and I arrive at the school for the actual event. I'm going to set up in the parking lot with the boxes in my trunk, and people can come to me. I'm beyond caring if it looks like I'm doing something shady.

When I text that plan to Kiki, I do so without a hint of approval-seeking and park my car in the first spot I find. Turning to Scout, I say, "Here we are, kiddo. As soon as I get rid of these stupid— er, last few costumes, we can walk around and have some fun. Shouldn't be long. I'm closing up shop when the event starts. If people still need their stuff, they can text me or come find me."

She mumbles, "Okay. Whatever," as she continues playing a game on her tablet.

Despite my intermittent and admittedly half-hearted efforts to make things right between us, Scout continues to freeze me out. So does Jet. When he left for Mexico City yesterday, I tried to act like it was a goodbye like any other, going in for a kiss when he announced he was leaving. He dodged my lips so they landed on his cheek, their imprint to be covered up by Scout's kiss seconds later. Blinking, I couldn't hide my hurt at his rebuff, so he took pity on me and came back around to kiss my forehead. The kiss was firm and lingering, but it lacked any bodily contact and still didn't quite satisfy my craving for something deeper, something more redolent of his feelings for me, in spite of the current disquietude underlying our relationship.

Nevertheless, I gratefully received my platonic pecks and smiled him off, as usual, reassuring him we'd miss him but be fine. It was a routine I could do in my sleep, unfortunately.

Playing nice-nice with Kiki in our first one-on-one face-to-face interaction since the incident on the stairs is another matter. It's even more unnatural and difficult when she strides up to us in the parking lot, her fake, red smile pasted to her face, her eyes blank, her Botoxed forehead smooth, and says, "Rachel's sick, so I'm going to need you to be in charge of her booth today."

"I don't think so, Kiki. I promised Scout a day with just the two of us, and—"

"It's okay, Mom," Scout says helpfully/unhelpfully, her eyes still glued to her tablet. "I'm not very in the mood."

"Then we'll go home. You can't wait here in the car or wander around by yourself while I work a booth."

Kiki blinks earnestly. "Oh, it's safe! The school safety officers have volunteered to keep an eye on things, remember? A lot of students' parents will be busy, doing their part, so kids are going to pair up. Larissa will hang out with Scout."

"No! No, thank you," Scout says, surprising both of us. I expected her to jump at the chance to hang out with her friend outside of school, something she hasn't done since I've been home.

Kiki's smile fades. "Why not? You're friends!"

Scout's sudden vehemence falters, and I can see the polite, people-pleaser in her warring with something equally fierce but not as vocal.

"That won't be necessary, because we're not staying." I clear my throat in the face of Kiki's seemingly genuine confusion—or what I think is confusion; it's hard to tell when someone's forehead never moves.

"But we need your help, Maura! Think of the children. This is our first big fundraiser. It sets the tone for the whole year."

Scout tugs on the sleeve of my sweatshirt, her tablet finally forsaken in the face of confrontation. "Mom," she whispers. "It's okay. I'll stay with you."

"What's that, Scout?" Kiki asks in a sugary tone, bending down as if talking to a toddler. "You want your mommy to be a team player?"

Scout nods helplessly in the face of Kiki's pressure. "Of course, you do. You're a good girl." She reaches out to pat Scout on the head, but I pull my daughter closer to me and say, "We already have plans. We're busy."

"Never too busy for our children!" she says, straightening to her full height, not as tall as she usually is, since she's wisely forgone her usual three-inch spike heels for today's proceedings on grass, but still matching me inch-for-inch. We must look like two mama Sasquatches squaring off for battle, one protecting her precious young, the other standing in a power pose, hands on hips. "What am I missing? Have our girls had a spat? Larissa hasn't mentioned anything. We have a very open relationship. She's not one to complain or tattle, but I'm sure she would have said something to me if there was a problem."

It takes everything I have not to roll my eyes.

Knowing enters her eyes, which she tries to squint. "Now, Maura. I hope you're not letting recent events poison our girls' friendship. I've been very careful not to speak badly of you in front of Larissa, despite what you did."

"What *I* did?!"

"Well, yes," she says, hand to heart. "I was the injured party. You attacked me in public."

Scout looks up at me, her forehead crinkled.

"I didn't attack you!"

"Maybe not physically, but verbally. It was humiliating."

"Jet and I tried to pull you aside, but you refused to leave your support group. Your irresponsible behavior was an embarrassment to you, not anything I said."

Kiki gasps audibly. I want to smack her. Just once. One smack, packed with the anger and frustration of the past two weeks, much of which isn't even her fault.

That tiny bit of last-second insight might be the only thing that holds me back. I take a deep breath. "Listen, Kiki, maybe you and I can go for coffee or a drink or something soon and discuss things. To be honest, it's been a rough few weeks, and it would probably be better if we talked when I'm a little less frazzled from playing catch-up."

*Why? Why, why, why did I admit that? What the fuck?*

She switches from outraged to doleful so fast, I feel motion-sick. At least, I think that's what's brought on the nausea. It could be any of a dozen things right now, though. One would definitely be her pitying tone when she says, "Yes, your mother-in-law—delightful woman—told me all about your troubles in Kansas."

"Kansas *City*. Missouri."

"Right." She waves me off. "I always forget that, because it doesn't make much sense, and all those states in the middle of the country kind of blur together. But anyway, I realize you've been away a lot lately and, while I'm not familiar with that experience, because I make a point to stay local and available, I can sympathize with what havoc that must play on a family life. I can't even imagine being that far away from my girls and Richard, much less for such a long time! You must feel terribly stressed out and out-of-touch."

"I wouldn't go that far," I say, trying to interject some moderation into the tale she's spinning.

"You said yourself, you're frazzled." She drops a cold hand, so cold I can feel it through my sweatshirt, onto my upper arm and rubs it up and down. "I hate to delay your catching-up process further, but it's not the school's fault that your life is in a bit of upheaval right now."

"'Upheaval' isn't—"

She shakes her head, closes her eyes, and says, "Sh... sh... sh... It's none of my business. No need to explain." Opening her eyes, she smiles coldly. "What *is* my business, however, is today's event, and you're down as a substitute booth supervisor in case of illness, injury, or absence, so I need you to honor that commitment, m'kay?"

I clench my teeth and say through them, "I don't even have a dress."

"Oh! Well, that was poor planning, but..." She closes one eye and sizes me up. "No worries. Use Rachel's costume. You seem about the same size. Robust girls, the both of you." Pushing past me, she roots around in my trunk until she finds the dress with Rachel's name pinned to it. "Here we go! Poor thing said she's been too ill to come get it this week, and— sure enough!" She thrusts the folded costume at me. "One perfect German girl coming up!"

To prevent the dress falling and hitting the pavement, I instinctively clutch it to my chest as Kiki lets go of it.

She extends her hand to Scout, who automatically inter-prets the gesture as an order from an authority figure and steps toward it, away from me. "Scout and I will hand out costumes while you run into the school and change. The bath-rooms are open so we wouldn't have to rent any of those hideous portable potties." She shudders and grins. "Off you go!"

For a second, I debate standing my ground, but grudgingly, I spin on my the toe of my ratty canvas tennis shoe and march into the building. She has a point that I committed to being an alter-nate. Granted, I did so assuming I wouldn't be needed and that I'd be far down on the list of subs, given my intense involvement in pre-event planning. My assumptions were obviously wrong.

I should have known better. The hard workers always get more work, not less. Stupid me. I've forgotten a lesson I learned in elementary school and used to my advantage all through high school, college, and well into my tenure at The

Career Center. It's all coming back to me now, though, as I pull the dress up and slide my arms into the puffy sleeves, knocking my elbows on the sides of the tight toilet stall.

Kiki's right that the costume fits, girth-wise. Unfortunately, Rachel is a good six inches shorter than I am, not to mention, erm, chestically enhanced. After contorting myself and pulling at the garment to zip up the back, I yank it over my ass and stuff the baggy front of it with toilet paper. I emerge from the stall and groan at the reflection I see in the mirrors over the sinks. The length of this thing—or lack thereof—is obscene. I text that, with a selfie as evidence, to Kiki.

She texts back, "Hot-cha-cha! LOL. Looks fine. Don't be such a prude! I need to change, too. Hurry."

I could rip this off and tell her to shove it. I could refuse to go out there dressed like this. I could say, "Sorry, this isn't going to work."

I could do all those things.

But then again, isn't this the least I can do, considering how distracted and absent I've been lately? So the skirt's a little short. So what? Everyone else will be dressed like this, too. It's not like I'll be the only one. We're all taking one for the team. Hell, the guys have it worse, in those tiny shorts and dumb-ass suspenders. To make this all about me and refuse to be a good sport would be selfish. Haven't I been selfish enough the past few weeks?

Suck it up, I tell myself as I fluff my hair in the mirror and turn sideways to make sure everything is, indeed, covered. It is—barely. I have no legitimate excuses for refusing to do this, other than that I just don't want to. That's not good enough, is it? We all have to do things we don't want to do. That's called, "Life." It's what Jet and I tell Scout when she complains about cleaning her room. How is this any different?

With a sigh, I check one more time that the toilet paper is securely stuffed into and concealed by the dress, then grab my street clothes and exit the bathroom.

My fears about looking as if this is my professional uniform rather than a costume are confirmed as I walk back through the volunteers setting up stalls and get double-takes from nearly everyone. Plus, I'm freaking *cold*! Southern California has decided to pretend to be seasonal today, complete with overcast skies—hence my original wardrobe choice of jeans and sweatshirt.

When I return to the car, Scout brightens at my appearance. "Mom! You look like Alice in Wonderland!"

I smile back at her. "Yeah?"

"Uh-huh!"

"And that's a good thing?"

"Totally!"

I laugh, cheered by her enthusiasm and first show of approval toward me since I returned from Kansas City. "Okay, then. If you think I look good, then that's all that matters."

She nods enthusiastically while I adjust my skirt for the first of a predicted million times the rest of the day.

As Kiki steps past me, she says so only I can hear, "Report to the test of strength booth by ten, Alice in Sluttyland."

———

"Sick," my nearly-exposed, cold ass. After stewing about it for a while, I know without a doubt that Rachel had no intention of ever showing up. This isn't the first event she's flaked, so I know Kiki's not fooled, either, but it suits her purposes today—a weapon to use against me.

Feeling like a victim while severely under-dressed for both the weather and the circumstances brings on a whole new level of vulnerability. Some of the looks I've gotten from attendees—including, unfortunately, pubescent boys—have made me blush and sweat, which has helped with the temperature problem. Unfortunately, it's exacerbated the half-naked insecurities.

Scout's been oblivious, thankfully. She's served as my loyal sidekick all day, cheering for the participants and handing out prizes to those who can hit the bell by smashing the metal platform as hard as they can with the heavy mallet. For those who can't, she offers sincere condolences and encouragement that they'll be able to do it their next try. We've had many repeat visitors. I'm trying to choose to believe it's due to her rather than my skirt.

At the end of the afternoon, I wave across the lawn at Kiki and mouth, "See ya!" Before she can hustle her way over and demand that I help with cleanup, I usher Scout to the car and jump in like I'm fleeing the scene of a bank robbery.

"Seatbelt, seatbelt. Quick!" I say to Scout in the rearview mirror, checking the other mirrors and the backup camera before peeling out of our spot.

She giggles. "Mom! I'm not buckled in yet!"

"Get on it, then. Got it?"

"Yeah. Jeez. Why are we going so fast?"

I reach into the passenger seat for my sweatshirt, pulling it over my and and smoothing it down my body at the first red light. "I just want to get home. It's been a long day. I wasn't expecting to be out so long."

"It was fun, though, right?"

"Uhhh…" I laugh. "Fun? Well…"

Waiting, she says nothing. I check her face in the rearview mirror and see her smile fading by the second. Before it can disappear, replaced by the sour, disapproving expression I've been looking at all week, I quickly say, "I had a great time hanging out with you today. We were a good team."

Her beam returns. She wiggles a loose front tooth with her tongue. "Yeah! I think everyone liked our booth best."

"Certain people did," I mutter, then say more loudly, "I think you're right."

"Larissa's booth was lame."

"Oh? I guess I didn't notice where she was."

"She had this rubber ducky game, where you pick a duck and turn it over to see what prize you get. Bo-ring!"

I laugh. "You're right; that *is* lame. Where's the fun or challenge in that?"

"Nowhere. People liked our game much better."

"Fo' sho'."

"Oh, Mom. You're so *extra* sometimes," she says with a groan-giggle.

I'm not sure what that means, or if it's good or bad, but if it makes her laugh, I don't even care.

## TWENTY-TWO

## SCHOOL DAY BATTLES

Another Monday morning, another nightmare.

Scout woke in another foul mood, but these days, I manage it on my own. Jet looked suitably apologetic when he kissed me goodbye and scooted out the door. He also looked decidedly relieved. His parting words to Scout were, "Get it together, Bump. It's going to be a long year if you're going to be like this every single morning from now until June."

Unfortunately, she's okay with that. It won't make *her* year long. Jet suffers through, maybe, thirty minutes of it before he leaves for work. *My* life is the miserable one. *I'm* the one left to deal with it.

Now that she has her gerbils, we're back on the struggle-bus. The shift didn't happen immediately after they arrived. Jet and Gloria enjoyed good behavior from her while I was gone. But since I've been back, we've slowly slipped from cooperative into ornery. Fortunately, we haven't received any calls from school. Yet. Mornings, though, are absolute hell again. This morning is a particularly rotten one.

Hair: the crown twist she suddenly doesn't like all that

much, now that I've perfected it. She wants hair like Larissa. She'll need to take up her complaint with DNA. I can't Mommy Magic super-straight blonde hair onto Scout's head, and I'm not going to stand over her grumpy ass with a flat iron every morning. Not to mention the damage that would do to her hair at such a young age. So, no, she can't have hair like Larissa. There's the first fit.

Clothes: adorable, as usual, in my humble opinion, but that doesn't count for anything, obviously. Despite the cooler mornings, she insists on peeling off the leggings under her skirt and asks if we can *cut* her shirt to make it show her belly. That's a hard "no." Cue fit number two.

Shoes: Monday's school routine features an hour of gym class, so appropriate footwear is required. Scout suddenly hates all of her sneakers *except* her custom Chiefs runners, which invited all kinds of grief last time she wore them to school. Apparently, the Rams fans were merciless.

Jet tried to warn Scout the first time she wore them to school, but she was adamant, and a part of him was proud of that. But when it resulted in the inevitable razzing, her told her with a hug, "Aw, Bump. Sometimes you just have to let people be wrong and cheer for their lame teams. They don't know any better." That didn't lessen her hurt, but it did make her laugh.

I offered to talk to her teacher or the counselor or principal about it, but she panicked and said that would make it worse. Of course, though, the only shoes she wants to wear on gym days are the ones she's told herself she *can't* wear.

Today, after multiple suggestions, I eventually plunk a pair of rainbow Chucks in front of her and say, "There. These are pretty, fun, and match anything, plus they won't scuff up the gym floor or hurt your feet when you run in them."

She turns her nose up at them, but when I walk away, signaling that's my best and final offer, she slides her feet into them. Peeking around the door frame from the hallway, I watch her painstakingly tie the shoes the way Jet and I taught her over the summer: Criss-cross applesauce; one bunny, two bunnies; bunnies hug and play leap frog, then run away from each other. She even double-knots them this morning, having the bunnies hug and play leap frog twice.

I don't have time to pat myself on the back for that victory, though. Arguing and fit-throwing have made us later than usual, so I gather her lunch and backpack for her and urge her into the car.

At the school, in the drop-off lane, definitely the most stressful part of my day, I anxiously await our turn in the unloading zone. Jeremy, the drop-off attendant, in his neon orange-and-yellow vest, demands efficiency and compliance with the non-negotiable rules, which are posted on individual signs at each of the three unloading stations in The Zone:

1. Your vehicle *will* remain locked until it comes to a complete stop in the striped Zone.
2. Your child *will* remain buckled until the vehicle comes to a complete stop.
3. You *must* put your vehicle in *Park* before unlocking any doors.
4. Your child *must* be able to unbuckle their seat belt quickly and open their own door to exit vehicle.
5. Your vehicle *will* remain in park until your child closes their door and steps under the front step canopy.
6. You *will* immediately pull away into the left exit lane once this process is complete.

When you're doing it correctly, the entire process should take no longer than ten seconds. Any breaking of the rules, and Jeremy will blow his whistle and point sternly with his neon baton, identical to the ones used by airport marshals to direct planes on the tarmac. When that happens, you have to immediately pull out of The Zone and circle back to the parking lot, where the sloth-like parents and kids say their morning goodbyes.

You unlock your car before you come to a stop in the loading zone? Whistle and point *and* a safety infraction. Same with not putting your car in park or pulling away before your child steps under the canopy. Three infractions and you're banished from the drop-off line for the rest of the year. Shame, shame, shame. You turn around to help your child with her seat belt? Whistle and point. You open your door for any reason? Whistle and point.

Say your goodbyes and give your pep talks or reminders while waiting in the line *before* you get to The Zone, because once you're there, there's no time for chit chat or niceties; concentrate on the job and unload, period. If you linger too long, whistle and point.

Ursuline Academy doesn't play, yo.

Jet and I laughed at the whole process that first week (after we were safely away, of course), but I've come to understand in the intervening weeks that Jeremy's no joke. We're only a month into the school year, and I already have my first infraction. Trying to be as efficient as possible, I got flustered and did the steps in the wrong order, unlocking the car while it was still moving. He noticed. Before I could even come to a full stop, he whistled, finger wagged, and pointed his baton at the parking lot. My license plate is written on his clipboard in red with one "x" next to it. I've seen it, because after escorting

Scout into the building from the parking lot, I tried to plead my case with the guy on my way back to my car.

""No appeals," he said around the whistle in his mouth and with his eagle eyes trained on the cars currently in The Zone. "Do better next time. You'll get the hang of it." He whistled and pointed for another parent's mistake, bellowing, "Let's go, people! Keep it moving!" furiously waving his neon baton and almost hitting me in the head.

Defeated, I shuffled to my vehicle, realizing how ridiculous it was to argue such petty rules. Since then, Scout and I have been model unloaders, although I do little things in protest that Jeremy can't detect. Like, as I'm pulling away, I smile but mutter through clenched teeth and motionless lips, "You little fascist shit." Sometimes I scratch the side of my nose or my eyebrows with my middle finger. It's passive aggressive and immature, but it makes me feel better.

Today, though, Scout has other ideas. We pull into Slot #2 in The Zone, having already said our goodbyes and "love you"s and all that crap that Ursuline must not care about. I stop the car, put it in park, unlock the doors, and say, "Have a good day!" our signal that she's free to open the door. But she doesn't move.

"Let's go, Bump," I prompt, nervously glancing through the windshield at Jeremy.

"Let's go, let's go, let's go! Wake up, folks!" he yells.

"Is your buckle stuck?" I ask into the rear view mirror, not daring to pivot even a half-turn to check.

She says nothing and doesn't move.

"Scout!"

Whistle and point.

I sigh and mutter a mild obscenity under my breath, checking my left mirror and over my shoulder before pulling into the exit lane and turning into the slow-assers' parking lot of shame.

As soon as we're motionless, I whirl on her. "Dang it, Scout. What's the deal? You know the routine. Why are you so uncooperative this morning?"

Arms folded over her chest, she stares out the window and refuses to answer.

For a second, her cute profile, so dainty and fine-featured, distracts me, but irritation soon douses any tenderness. "If you don't answer me by the time I count to three, you're—you're grounded! One…"

"What does 'grounded' mean?" she asks, finally looking at me.

Good question. I know what it means, in theory. I experienced it plenty of times in my youth. I have no idea what it would look like for Scout, however, since we've never had to resort to it. On the fly, I answer, "I take away something you like—no, something you *love*—as punishment."

She frowns. "Like what?"

Shit. "Umm… Umm… Like your tablet!"

She shrugs. "Whatever."

Damn! Should have gone for the gerbils, but I didn't want to threaten something I couldn't deliver once it came down to logistics. How do you "get rid" of gerbils for a week? Lock their cage in a closet? Rent an off-site climate-controlled storage unit she can't get to? Sounds like a bigger punishment for Jet and me—schlepping out to some storage unit every day to feed and water the dang things—than it would be for her.

"I don't want to go to school today," Scout says, interrupting my musing. "Nobody likes me."

"That's not a reason to skip school. You still have to go. And I don't think that's even true. What about Larissa?"

"Especially Larissa. She calls me 'Baby.'"

I can relate to hating that nickname, although on a totally different level. "Because you're younger than everyone else?"

"I'm not! I'm five like them."

True, but most of them will be turning six sometime during the year. I suppose that's too fine a detail for kindergartners to grasp until it actually comes to pass, though.

"She calls me that because I cried on the first day."

"She's still harping about that?"

"Yes. And she gets Arya and Catelyn to do it, too."

Ah, yes. Arya and Catelyn, the *Game of Thrones* twins. There are a few Harry Potter characters in the class, too, but I can only remember Neville at the moment. I doubt anyone named after a Longbottom would be a bully. Probably the other way around. Plus, I met him and his dads at the party. Good folks. Neville's polite and sweet. Judging by some of the things Scout has said about him at the dinner table, he has a crush on her, too. The feeling might even be mutual.

"What else do they tease you about?"

She shrugs and looks down at her hands in her lap. "Just... stuff."

Suddenly, her refusal to hang out with Larissa at Oktoberfest makes a lot more sense, as does her behavior of the past couple of weeks. I thought she was still mad at me for being away so long and for the way I acted when I first arrived home, but maybe it hasn't been about me at all. In some perverse way, that brings massive relief.

Still, my heart breaks for the struggle she's having at school, one I had no idea about. "I don't understand. I thought you and Larissa were friends."

"We were, until..."

She seems to be searching for the right words or hesitant

to tell me what started the bullying, so I say, "It's okay. You can tell me anything."

"She says I'm a baby because I'm not allowed to wear makeup or fake tattoos or watch grownup movies."

Oh, shit. So it *is* sort of about me. More than sort of.

"Ah. I see. Well, I bet a lot of kids in your class have the same rules in their houses."

She shakes her head. "Uh-uh. They all laugh at me."

"All of them do?"

"Well, Larissa and Arya and Catelyn."

"They might seem like the whole class, but that's only three kids."

"But everyone else starts laughing when they do."

Group think. Great when used as a force for good; terrible when used as a weapon.

"Well, Bump, it sounds like the first step is showing them you're not a baby."

"I try! But you won't let me have hair like them, and none of my clothes look like theirs. I'm the best in gym class, so they make fun of my shoes. I'm awesome at recess, but they tell everyone not to play with 'the baby.'"

To her credit, she doesn't cry when she explains this; her anger is too hot for tears.

"Why would you even want to have hair and clothes like them?"

"So they'll think I'm cool and not a baby!"

"They're not cool, though, honey. They're bullies." I unbuckle my seat belt and open my door. "Come on. Let's go inside. We're going to talk to Mrs. Nuñez about this."

With both hands, Scout grabs the grip next to the door handle. "No!" she screeches. "We can't tell anyone. Larissa said if I tattled on her, she'd be even meaner!"

"That's a classic bully move. It's not going to work." I open her door with her still attached to it, half inside, half outside for a few seconds until she lets go and scrambles back to a sitting position, still buckled in.

"Mommy! Pleeeeease!!!"

The abject terror in her face at the thought of my intervention softens my resolve. I remember that feeling well. Now, as the adult in this situation, I suspect Larissa, the little holy terror, would cry like the baby she accuses Scout of being if confronted with her bitchery, but I can't guarantee she'll stop bullying my daughter or that it *won't* get worse the minute the teachers and administrators have turned their attentions elsewhere. The last thing I ever wanted when I was school age was for my parents raise a stink about something. I doubt Scout's strategy of flattering Larissa into liking her is going to work, either, but I understand how that's a safer plan. And I'm proud of her for thinking of it on her own.

Kneeling next to Scout's open door, I kiss her elbow. "Hey. It's okay."

"It's not okay! She—she says she'll have her daddy fire Daddy if I tell anyone."

It feels like every biological process south of my neck screeches to a halt. My brain, on the other hand, fires off so many thoughts and feelings and reactions at once that I can hardly spit out the word, "Wh-what?"

Now the tears do flow, followed by great, heaving sobs.

All I can do is kneel there and hold Scout's hands, because I have to give it to that little asshole, Larissa: she's struck gold with that particular threat. Something tells me it's not the first time she's used it, either. I imagine a bunch of Football Network employees' kids in Larissa's wake, terrorized at company functions and playdates, blackmailed into silence.

I motion for Scout to slide over so I can perch next to her while I let her take her time calming down. In the meantime and to hasten the process along, I reassure her—quite woodenly—that Larissa doesn't have that kind of influence over her dad. But does she? I don't know. She might very well have Richard wrapped around her finger. Even a good kid like Scout has her moments and manages to elicit the occasional bribe—ahem, *gerbils*—from parents with rather firm stances on such things. Larissa strikes me as the type who rarely hears the word, "no"; hence, the backlash when a kid like Scout doesn't comply with her every demand.

I'm at a loss, though. I have no idea what to do in this situation. As an adult, I should know. I don't. All I keep thinking is, "Never negotiate with a terrorist." That's okay for foreign policy (debatable), but it's not particularly helpful in this instance.

The bell rings, signaling the start of the school day. Shit. Now she's tardy, on top of everything else.

At the risk of triggering another dam break now that she's finally stoppered this one, I say, "Maybe your dad can say something to Mr. Valentine about—"

"No! Please, don't tell Daddy." She doesn't cry, but her crinkled chin and downturned eyes tell me tears aren't far behind if I continue that line of thinking. "I don't want him to know. It'll make him embarrassed."

Hmm. Just when I think Scout's picking up more from me than I thought regarding her dad's job performance, she says, "Larissa says her daddy calls my daddy names, that he's the worst announcer in the world. As long as I don't tell on her, she says she'll say nice things about Daddy and tell her daddy that he'll get better. If I tell on her, she'll be mean about Daddy, too, and her daddy will fire him."

Damn. We're dealing with a five-year-old sociopath who knows exactly what she's doing. How the hell…?

Jeremy, on the way to his car after terrorizing the last of the parents in the drop-off line, stops next to us. "Is there a problem here?" he asks softly, surprising me with his gentleness.

I smile weakly at him. "Just a little wobbly this morning. Thanks for checking."

He nods sympathetically. "It happens," he says. "Have a nice day."

I blink at the difference in him as he moves on. Maybe it's the vest. Currently, it's draped over his arm. I watch him stow it and his baton and whistle in a small crate in the back of his SUV. Like a police officer or firefighter, the uniform may transform him into a different person, someone who has to detach emotionally in order to do his job efficiently. Or maybe it's just the setting. Out of his sphere of control, he's not as confident.

Sphere of control. Yes!

I pivot to face Scout. "I have an idea."

She wipes her dripping nose with the back of her hand, so I pull a travel packet of tissues from the backseat console and give a few to her.

"I won't say anything to your teacher or anyone else at the school about this. Not yet. But we're not going to sit back and do nothing, either."

Scout sniffles. "What can we do, though? Be mean back at her?"

I shake my head. "Nope. You're on the right track with being trying to be nice to her."

The kindergartner slumps. "I am? It's not working, though."

"That's because here at the school, she's kind of a big deal. Her mom's the PTA President, and a bunch of Football Network kids go here. She feels like the big cheese."

A slow smile spreads across Scout's face. "A big, stinky cheese."

I laugh. "Yep. So we're going to invite her over to our house, where she's just another kid, and we're going to show her that kindness isn't weakness." That's all I have at the moment, so I pray she doesn't ask me for details.

Fortunately, my prayers are answered. She nods resolutely, tightening her jaw and flaring her nostrils just like her dad used to do before taking the field for that one last drive to win it all.

I raise my hand for a fist-bump, which she readily returns, and remind her, "We've got this."


Jet arrives home late from work to find two fired-up home teammates, which seems to both surprise and delight him. His drawn and slightly harried expression quickly transforms to one of beaming bemusement as he steps from the laundry room into the kitchen.

"What's going on in here?" he asks, immediately interested in the array of baked goods cooling on racks on the island. He snatches a snickerdoodle as if expecting to have his hand slapped and eats it in one quick bite before either Scout or I can rebuke him.

When we simply watch him enjoy the cookie and wait for his appraisal, he slows down his chewing to actually taste it. He sets his duffel bag on one of the island chairs and drapes his garment bag over it, moaning appreciatively and giving us two thumbs up as soon as his hands are free.

Scout claps. "I told you they were good, Mom." She explains to Jet, "Mommy said they didn't taste as good as her grandma's."

"Then grandma's must be pretty magical," Jet says, his mouth already full with the next one, "because these are the best cookies I've ever had."

Scout levels a "told you so" look at me, and I shrug. "Okay. I trust you guys. You're the cookie connoisseurs."

Jet rounds the island, and on his way to pluck a no-bake cookie from its platform of a wax paper-lined plate, he hooks me around the waist and pulls me in for a cinnamon-sugary kiss. A real kiss. One that has Scout hiding her eyes and making gagging sounds.

I pull away first, sensitive to our daughter's discomfort, but Jet keeps my body up against his with a firm arm while he inhales the no-bake cookie. "Mmmm. Wow. That one's good, too," he muffles through the chewy oats, peanut butter, and chocolate and surveying the counter for his next victim.

Savoring our physical closeness, I watch him savor a large chocolate chip cookie one bite at a time. When he's finished, I lick a crumb from his bottom lip, satisfied by the change in his eyes right before I break away, saying, "Let me get you some milk to go with your 'dinner.'" He grins at the implication that he's allowed to eat as many as he wants.

As he loads up a "sampler" plate, he inquires about our days, and just when I'm about to gloss over what sparked our rekindled solidarity, Scout surprises me by telling him about the bullying at school. She leaves out the parts referring to him and his job, casting occasional glances my way as if to make sure I understand she wants to keep that between the two of us, but everything else spills from her like chocolate from a fondue fountain. Her account is matter-of-fact, and she even lets him in on our plan to win Larissa over with a playdate including plenty of non-baby activities. I gauge his reaction throughout, wondering when he's going to go into protective-dad fix-it mode, but he's either unconcerned or stuffing down his feelings with sugar, because he simply nods now and then or makes approving noises.

Finally, she takes a breath and pauses long enough for him to respond more fully, so he says, "Sounds like you two have it all figured out." He visibly struggles to finish his last cookie— a raspberry thumbprint, the recipe of which had also been handed down from my grandmother. I tense a bit at his terseness, but he smiles at both of us after gulping down his milk. "Bullies suck, don't they?" he asks.

Scout covers her mouth and widens her eyes, pretending to be outraged at his "cussing."

"They do suck," I say.

"My strategy was always to just ignore them, but from what you've said, Bump, this is pretty hard to ignore. And you don't want to tattle. I get that. But it's okay to let a teacher know, especially when things get so bad that you don't want to go to school."

I almost scoff out loud at the idea that he was ever bullied. Popular jocks aren't vulnerable like other kids. He was beloved by all, from his first day of kindergarten until he moved that tassel from right to left on his graduation cap. I keep my skepticism to myself, though, recognizing that he's offering other options to our daughter if our plan fails. It won't, obviously, but it's good for him to feel like he's contributing.

Scout simply says, "Okay," to his advice, then changes the subject back to baking. "We're going to make all of these kinds of cookies for the bake sale. We were trying them out first, though."

"You'll have the busiest table, for sure."

"Just like we had the best booth at Oktoberfest."

I clear my throat and hide my blush by cleaning up Jet's dishes and going to work packaging the cookies in labeled air-tight containers.

"So, how was your day?" I ask, remembering the not-so-happy look on his face when he first walked in.

He inhales deeply through his nose and holds it for a few seconds, then after a loud release, says, "It's just good to be home." He wipes his lips and leans back against the counter, his eyes focusing on mine and holding them.

"I'm glad," I say, packing as much meaning as I can into those two words. "It would be nice to get back to normal around here."

"I agree," he says, making me want to cry with joy.

Scout, oblivious to any subtext in our conversation nevertheless must feel some easing of the tension between us, because she suddenly hops down from her perch at the island and rushes her dad to wrap her arms around his waist, resting her head against his bulging belly.

He groans but returns her squeeze. "Careful, Bump. My food baby's about to burst."

She giggles and gently pats his tummy, then presses her ear against it again. "It's making noises."

"Cursing?" he says with a rueful chuckle. "Or maybe just asking, 'Whyyyyyy?'"

We all laugh at his self-imposed misery. Then Scout stacks the tins and explains the reasoning behind the order in which she's stacked them. It's all a lot more complicated than it seems, a system based on the complexity of the recipes with provisions for nutritional value—or lack thereof.

Jet and I exchange a proud, amused glance over her head, and I feel a surge of hope that everything's going to be okay.

————

I'm a little less Zen about things with Jet a few hours later, when Scout's zonked, and we're attempting to relax in the hot tub. Jet earned this soak with some laps in the pool first. I simply showed up for the good part.

Still slightly out of breath, he flicks water from his face and summarizes what he's learned from Scout tonight with, "So, we're killin' her with kindness, huh?"

In spite of my apprehension, I say confidently, "Yup. Did you get any great brainstorms during your swim to help us accomplish our mission?"

He shakes his head with a grimace. "Nope. You know how I get. I zone out. No thinking. Just moving and breathing and counting strokes."

Must be nice, I think but don't say.

"Scout seems pretty excited about the stuff the two of you have thought up so far. It's probably better to go with that hold back some plays, just in case. You don't want to show her everything you've got—yet." He straightens his arms out to the side and rests them along the edge of the spa.

"Oh."

With a tender smile, he kicks a little water at me. "You're throwing everything you've got at her, aren't you?"

"No. Maybe. I mean, I'll think of something else, if it doesn't work. But it'll work."

"I'm sure it will."

"Don't patronize me, Number Fourteen."

"I'm not!" He pulls his arms in and crosses the small bubbling pool in a crouch, kneeling in front of me and taking one of my hands. "It was good to see the two of you working as a team again."

"We're not a team without you," I say, moving a lock of his hair from his forehead.

"I'm in." Parting my knees, he floats between them so he can reach up and bracket my face with his hands, his thumbs drawing wet swathes across my cheeks. "There's no team I'd rather be a part of." He pushes his feet against the bottom of the hot tub to rise higher in the water, bringing his face even with mine and softly kissing my lips.

At my first taste of him, I instantly want more. How does he do that to me, even after all this time together? I slide forward off the ledge seat so that we're chest-to-chest, bobbing in the bubbles, steam rising around us as we kiss again. And again. Each time, our lips press harder, our tongues probe more deeply.

"I've missed you so much, Maura."

"I've missed you more," I say breathlessly, nearly frantic with my need to consume him, to have him devour me. This intimacy and affection is what I've been craving since my homecoming. I don't need an explanation—beyond what I already know—for his recent coolness; I don't need an apology for it. I just need this. Finally getting it makes me so weak in the knees and lightheaded that I'm grateful for the buoyancy of the water and the solidity of Jet's body.

Drowning is still a definite possibility.

## PLAYDATE PLAN

Scout insists she and Larissa are too old for "playdates," so I'm not allowed to call it that out loud. That's what it is, though. It's a forced socialization exercise. I just keep telling myself it's only for a few hours, and I continue to remind myself that there's an actual goal here: to get Larissa to lay off Scout at school.

How am I going to do this? I have no idea. Despite all my big talking, there's no plan, really, other than "be really nice." That was always my mom's advice. When I was a kid, it struck me as fake. Now that I'm an adult, that hasn't changed. What has, though, is that I realize sometimes you have to take the roundabout way into someone's good graces, especially when that someone has a certain influence on your life.

A part of me today thinks that we're caving to Larissa, giving her exactly what she wants: power. She's five, though. I mean, really. How power-hungry and diabolical can a five-year-old be? At best, she's a sociopath-in-training. In the sleepless nights since Scout's revelation about the bullying, I've perhaps given more credit to and built up Larissa's behavior into something bigger than what it likely is: a bratty kid picking on another kid because she can. If nothing else, she'll start to feel bad—even if she doesn't understand why—when she's a jerk to Scout. She'll remember how nice we are to her, and the guilt will outweigh whatever satisfaction she normally gets from terrorizing someone.

In my head, it makes perfect sense. Now that we're doing it, I'm a lot less sure. I could be giving Larissa just another opportunity to have access to my daughter for further torment.

Kiki meets Scout and me at the front door. "Oh, Maura. Thank goodness!"

Given our history, it's an unexpected greeting. Her relief at our arrival seems a bit out of proportion for a simple child pick-up, too, but I smile uncertainly at her and say, "Finally, someone appreciates me."

She doesn't hear me, doesn't understand my joke, or doesn't think it's funny. Regardless, it's like I never said anything as she leads us through the house, bulldozing through rooms and stuffing things into a glittery duffel bag. "You'd be an absolute lifesaver if you could take Larissa for the weekend. I have a mini-conference to attend, starting this afternoon and going through tomorrow evening, Richard's out of town again—with Jet, fact—and our oldest daughter just stormed out, leaving us with nobody with watch Larissa! Nothing to worry about, of course; you know how teenagers are, thinking the world revolves around them." She smiles and places her hands on her hips, shaking her head as if to say, "Kids!"

"Oh. Well, I—"

"I'm sure she'll be no trouble. She and Scout get along swimmingly, am I right, Scout?

Scout nods but shrinks next to me, signaling how she really feels about a whole weekend with the girl who makes her school days a living Hell.

I give her a tighter side hug for reassurance but keep my focus on Kiki. "Right, it's just—"

"Exactly. It's just for the night, really. And tomorrow morning and afternoon. Early evening, at the latest. Richard or I can swing by your place to pick her up."

The more I think about it, though, the more I delude myself that this could be a good thing. It'll be the perfect opportunity for the two girls to have some extended one-on-one time on Scout's turf and get to know each other better. Plus, maybe it will put me back in Kiki's good graces after bawling her out in front of everyone and bailing on Oktoberfest cleanup. This may not be exactly what I want, but if I'm being mercenary about it, there's no denying Kiki will owe me, big-time, for the favor.

"Sure," I say lightly. "We're just hanging around the house this weekend. We'd be happy to have Larissa." That last sentence comes out through teeth clenched a little tighter than I meant, but it's like my body didn't want to release the lie.

"Oh, good!" Kiki grabs her purse from the trestle table and bellows for Larissa that it's time to go. She thrusts the sparkly duffel bag at me. "Everything she needs is in there. Change of clothes, toothbrush, hair accessories."

I grab the surprisingly heavy bag and shoulder it with an embarrassing amount of effort.

"She doesn't eat gluten, and we're NSNF at the moment, trying to do a cleanse. Larissa!!!!"

I shake a finger in my ear to get it to stop ringing after that latest summons. "NSNF?"

"No sugar, no flour."

"Oh, that's—"

"It's not as hard as it sounds. Stick with veggies and meats. Natural sugars from fruit are okay, too. Just steer clear of pre-packaged foods and read labels."

"Okay."

"Larissa, let's go! You're going to make me late! And Scout and her mom are here."

In a t-shirt, tights, and a mini skirt, Larissa plods down the stairs in her heavy-soled shoes and whines, "Why can't I just stay home by myself? I'm totally fine."

Kiki smiles shakily. "Oh, darling, this will be so much better. You're going over to have a sleepover at Scout's!"

Larissa wrinkles her nose as if that's not much better, but with a roll of her eyes, she leads the way out the front door, muttering on her way past Scout, "Weekend at Baby's house. Great."

———

By the end of the twenty-minute drive from her house to pick up some dry cleaning and bring it back home, I've already had my fill of Larissa-darling. "What kind of car *is* this, anyway?" "It smells funny in here. Did you fart, Baby?" "What are you wearing, Baby?" "What are we even going to do? I bet your house is so boring without all the party stuff."

It's going to be a long weekend.

On our way into the house from the garage, I turn and block the doorway, looking down on her. "Larissa, sweetie," I say in the nicest tone I can manage, "don't call Scout 'Baby.' She doesn't like it."

"But that's her nickname."

"No, it's not. In this house, you will not call her that."

Larissa rolls her eyes and sighs. "Fine. Whatever."

I stand aside to let the girls file in past me. Scout, her face aflame, says, "You didn't have to say anything, Mom. I'm used to it."

Instead of arguing with her, I let her lead the way to her room, hearing Larissa ask, "Do you have anything un-lame to do here, *Scout*?"

Scout replies sunnily, "Yeah! Wanna race gerbils? You can pick which one you want. They're both fast."

I smile sadly at my sweet child's attempts to play the good hostess and please her unpleasant guest. My smile fades, though, when it I realize how much their interactions remind me of Rae and me. Having a frenemy like that can lead to years—decades—of drama. And trauma.

I don't want that for Scout.

Moving out west has not only distanced me physically from Rae, but also emotionally. She'll always be a part of my life—she and Ana Paula are Scout's godmothers, plus they're on the board of directors for The Knox Foundation—but she's no longer *in* my life like she used to be, and that's for the best.

She's taken our move west so hard that we haven't talked as friends since. The distance between us has crystallized for me what an unhealthy relationship she and I have had over the years. I'm not willing to keep modeling that for my child, and I'm not willing to keep accepting it for myself.

If Larissa and Scout ever get beyond their current dynamic —and that's a big "if"—I'll be keeping a close watch for similar patterns and coaching Scout on healthier responses.

For now, I'm content to let the girls play independently, although I make frequent trips down the hall and eavesdrop at the door to check on things. So far, so good. Care-giving and supervision are the parenting skills at which I excel; I usually outsource entertainment to Jet. The things that entertain me generally don't appeal to young children. They're what Scout calls, "BO-ring."

The original plan for today consisted of a couple of hours of entertainment, which is all Scout and I brainstormed. Suddenly, we have to fill about eighteen hours not taken up with eating, sleeping, and movie-watching. Gerbil races aren't going to occupy them for much longer, especially when the actual race participants stop cooperating, which is inevitable. There's swimming, of course. Scout also has toys typical of kids her age: Lego and Barbies and action figures. Something tells me, though, that Larissa's not typical and won't want to play with those things for very long. Arts and crafts keeps Scout busy on rainy weekends, so we'd already planned to pull out all of that stuff: markers, crayons, scissors and glue, plus jewelry-making and other crafty kits. What else does Scout like? Reading, but that's pretty solitary. I can't imagine the two of them sitting quietly, both absorbed in a book. I mean, I *can* imagine it—it's a dream come true—but I don't think that's particularly realistic.

I search through my immense personal catalog of films and write down a few options for the girls to choose from later, before bed. This is an area in which I am an actual expert. I even throw in a couple of PG movies so I'm not accused of only offering "baby" choices but cap off the selection at six, not wanting to overwhelm. They'll surely be able to find something that appeals and they can agree on with the variety I'm offering.

That's pretty much all we have here at the house. Obviously, we could venture out for entertainment. This area's chock-full of interactive museums and parks, not to mention the beaches and piers. I had planned on working most of Sunday—The Knox isn't going to design and rebuild itself—but maybe I can squeeze in a bit of both that and cruise directing.

Next, I weigh my laziness against my somewhat pathetic urge to impress when it comes to dinner options. With delivery services nowadays, the choices are endless, and we tend to take advantage of them on the weekend, to give us a break from the rotation of my admittedly limited (for now) recipe repertoire. Larissa's dietary restraints pose an additional challenge and pretty much rule out my cooking. I'd have to stock up on all new ingredients to even attempt a no-sugar, no-flour, gluten-free meal. Delivery, it is. Fortunately, L.A. is the place for "GF" restaurants. We're spoiled for choice there. Another one of my worries falls to the wayside.

A clunk, yelp, and brief, cut-off cry bring my attention back home. Torzi and I both sit up on our respective couch cushions and cock our heads toward Scout's room, where the noise originated. I listen so hard, my ears ring, but I don't hear anything else. That doesn't mean I relax, though, like Torzi does, falling back onto his side and scrubbing his head against the upholstery to regain the most comfortable position he can.

I set down my phone and tiptoe down the hallway, as I've done several times already. Outside the door, I stand with my back pressed against the wall next to it.

"And remember, you're not going to tell anyone, Baby, or your dad's gonna get fired, and you'll be poor and homeless."

"You broke it. What am I s'posed to tell my mom when she asks what happened?"

"*You* broke it. Or say your dumb dog did."

I can hear the tears in Scout's voice when she says, "Okay. She's gonna be so mad, though."

"Are you gonna cry about it, Baby? Really? Lame!"

When I'm feeling homicidal probably isn't the perfect time to reveal my presence, but I can't let the taunting go on any further. I move into the doorway and take in the scene: the broken plaster on the floor, the other half in Scout's hands, the tears on her face, and Larissa lounging smugly on Scout's bed.

"Oh, no!" I say, kneeling down to pick up the other half of the cast Jet and I had done of our hands and Scout's feet when she was a newborn. "What happened?" I look directly at Larissa when I say this, trying to force her to be the liar.

She merely shrugs. "I guess Scout's clumsy."

I turn to Scout. "You can tell me the truth. I already know it."

She shakes her head, terrified to say the words.

"Larissa, why did you break this?" I ask, maintaining eye contact with Scout.

She scoffs. "I didn't! Geez. Rude!"

"I heard you two talking, so I know you did. Now I want to know why." I take the half from Scout's hands and merge it with mine. It, fortunately, broke cleanly at one of the thinner places, where all of our hands intersect. I might be able to glue it or to find somewhere that can repair it professionally. Even after I've assessed the damage, Larissa hasn't replied. I look pointedly at her, signifying that I'm still waiting.

She glares back coldly. "I don't have to answer you without a parent present."

"Excuse me?" I laugh. "I'm not a cop."

"You're acting like one."

Gritting my teeth, I inhale deeply to maintain my composure. It's obvious this kid is an apt pupil and has a teenage sibling.

Scout pulls on my arm. "It's okay, Mom. We can fix it, right? It was an accident. She didn't mean to break it."

"Yeah, since I didn't break it at all."

"Please stop lying to me, Larissa," I say, softening in spite of my frustration and anger. "It's pointless, okay? I know the truth, and I'm not even all that mad that it got broken. Accidents happen. I get it. What irritates me is being lied to."

She rolls her eyes.

"What enrages me is hearing you threaten Scout and using her love for her dad as a way to get her to do what you want her to do."

That gets the girl's attention. For a second, I see the panic in her eyes before she slackens her lids once more into an unimpressed glower.

Setting down the broken plaster cast on the dresser where it originally sat, whole, I walk to the bed and lower myself onto the foot of it, still out of reach of Larissa but close enough that I can speak more quietly, and she'll hear. "I know what you've been saying to Scout at school. You know, bullying can get you in big trouble."

"Are you threatening me?"

"No!" I sigh. "No, Larissa, I'm not. I'm just pointing out to you something that maybe you didn't think about. If a teacher heard you, you'd be sent to the principal's office, and your parents would be called, and it would be a whole, big thing."

She laughs. "Oooh… Call my parents. Big whoop."

"And you might be kicked out of Ursuline."

"Whatever. I hate it there, anyway."

"I don't think you do."

"Mom." Scout shakes her head tersely at me from her position across the room. "Don't. It's not a big deal. Larissa's my friend. Right, Larissa?"

This time, the girl scowls at Scout. "You tattled, Baby."

"I didn't mean to. I—" She shifts from foot to foot. "My mom asked me why I didn't want to go to school, and—"

"You tattled."

I slap my hand down on the mattress. "Enough!"

My sudden outburst startles both girls. Scout stares at the floor. Larissa's cheeks flush, and she sits up on the bed for the first time, but she remains disturbingly void of any outward signs of contrition.

"This ends now," I say firmly and scoot closer to our guest. "You don't have to threaten Scout for her to be your friend."

She snorts. "I don't need—"

"I'm not finished. You don't have to be a jerk to get people to respect you at school, either. Fear isn't the same as respect. Think of all the friends you'd have, how popular you'd be, if you were nice." For the first time since I've walked into the room, she drops her cool-girl facade, so I think I'm getting through to her—finally. "You want people to *want* to be around you, not to *have* to be around you, afraid that if they're not, you'll do something to them—or someone they love." I put my arm around her shoulders, and she doesn't shrug me off, so I squeeze her a little closer to me. She surprises me by sagging against my side. "Right?" I say, waiting for some sort of verbal cue that she's understanding what I'm saying.

She nods, which is good enough.

Looking down at her perfectly straight part, I continue gently, "Remember Scout's party? Everyone had a great time, not because they were threatened into being here, but because we welcomed them here and made them feel special. They had fun. Did you have fun?"

She nods again.

"It makes me sad that you think it's better to scare people

into being your friends than it is to treat them kindly."

All I get in response to that is a sniffle. I squeeze her again. "So, I'll make you a deal, okay? You stop torturing Scout with your threats about her dad's job, and we'll start over. Clean slate. No grudges."

"Okay," she says in a small voice.

"Because you don't have to be like that, sweetie. Isn't it exhausting? Just be a kid. Play. Have fun." *Eat gluten and sugar.* When she lifts her face to me, I smile down at her. It's remarkable how pretty she is when her face isn't screwed up with hatred and disdain. She smiles back, even. "Yeah? Do we have a deal?"

"Yeah."

"Great."

"I'm sorry."

I laugh and pat her on the back before standing to go. "You're forgiven. For everything. Just do better from now on. That's what we tell Scout."

"I'll pay for that broken thing with my allowance, too," she adds sweetly.

I pick up the cast on my way to the door. "Well, unfortunately, this thing is priceless, but I appreciate the offer. How about you pay it off in kindness? You start being nicer to people, and we'll call it even."

Her grin widens. "Deal!"

For the first time in several minutes, I look over at Scout, who still appears worried and terrified. I walk over to her and kiss the top of her head. "Relax, Bump. It's going to be okay."

She doesn't answer.

To both of them, I say, "Let's get our suits on and go swimming to work up a good appetite for dinner. Cannonball contest? Crazy hairstyle competition? Make funny faces underwater and see who laughs first? Any of that sound like fun?"

Larissa springs from the bed and lunges toward her duffel bag by the wall. "I know how to dive," she says.

"Good. You can teach Scout. I'll meet you two outside in five minutes. Don't get in the pool without me."

As I exit the bedroom and close the door behind me so they can change clothes with some privacy, I smile to myself. Damn, I'm good.

Halfway through our viewing of the original *High School Musical*, Jet texts to see how the playdate went. I tell him it's still going and quickly explain the situation, to which he texts back a laugh-crying emoji. I send back a middle finger and a heart-kiss emoji, then put my phone face-down on the cushion next to me. I want to stay present with the girls, so I tune back into baby-faced Zac Efron dancing and singing in his track suit.

It's crazy how young everyone looks in this film. My mind wanders down the rabbit hole of all the other things in which I've seen the actors since—network TV shows, for example, and adult-targeted movies with mature themes. It's surreal to watch such innocence, knowing some of their futures. My memory strays to a particularly tantalizing image of Efron in the silly *Baywatch* remake. Wait. Was it supposed to be silly? Not sure, actually. I don't think I ever saw it, just drooled over the pictures of him in his swim trunks, shirtless and shiny. The Rock wasn't anything to sniff at, either, but Efron ticks more boxes for me: those eyes… that chest… those arms…

The phone buzzes and lights up again, this time actually ringing. Larissa, who's been on her best behavior since our little chat—just call me the brat whisperer—looks over her shoulder at me from where she and Scout are lying on their bellies on the floor. Scout continues to ogle Efron, without a single glance my way.

"Sorry," I whisper, turning the phone over, planning to reject the call. Whoever it is can text like a normal person, if it's that important. Kiki's name fills the screen, however. With the brightest tone I can muster, I say to Larissa, "It's your mom," then answer, "Hello?"

"Maura, it's Kiki."

"Hi, Kiki. How's the conference going?"

"Oh, you know how these things are. Fun at times, boring at other times, overwhelming, exciting."

"Sounds eventful."

"It is. I wanted to call before it got too late and check in. I trust everything's going well."

"Just fine," I say, motioning Larissa to join me on the couch. "She's right here if you want to talk to her."

"If it's no trouble. I don't want to interrupt anything."

"Not at all. Here she is."

I hand over the phone, pause the movie, and say to Scout, "Hey, let's go outside and put up all the pool toys."

She provides the expected groaning complaint at the suggestion, but I lead the way without arguing back, so she follows. On the lit-up pool deck and patio, we gather the foam noodles, rafts, and inflatable toys from our swimming session, stuffing them haphazardly into the storage container against the back of the house.

"How do you think it's going?" I ask, revealing my secondary motive for dragging her out here.

She bats a beach ball at me, and I catch it. "Okay, I guess. More funner than I thought it would be."

"Same. Things have been a lot better since we had that talk, don't you think?"

"Yeah. She's nice when you're around."

It's true that I haven't left them alone since the broken plaster incident, but I'd hoped the turnaround in Larissa's attitude was because I'd gotten through to her.

"Do you think she'd be mean again if you two were alone together?"

"Prolly."

"But she's been so sweet ever since!"

"That's how she acts with teachers, too."

My heart sinks, but I refuse to lose all hope. Maybe this is different. Maybe something I said really did make her rethink the way she treats people.

"I'll try to always be with you two, okay? But if she does say or do something mean again, and I don't notice it, let me know."

"I don't want to tattle," she says, struggling with the last item, an inflatable shark that's twice her size and doesn't fit into the container with all of the other pool paraphernalia.

I take it from her and strap it with a bungee cord to the top of the now-closed container so it won't blow away. "It's not tattling. And I won't get onto her about it—unless it's really bad. I just want to know if she's faking."

"She is." The sad confidence in my daughter's voice breaks my heart. She's been here before. She no longer has any hope that things will improve.

"Then we'll keep trying, right, Bump?" I open my arms to her, and she walks into them, wrapping hers around my midriff and pressing her ear to my belly. "It might take a few more days like this, but we'll show her how much better it is to be nice—for real."

She says nothing in reply. I don't blame her for doubting that. I don't believe it much, either. But it's all I have.

## TWENTY-FOUR

## BAKE SALE IMBROGLIO

I'm not a wino, but I do a good impression of one after a girls' weekend with two five-year-olds.

Richard and Jet, who had been together at the Rams game Jet had been calling, got to the house at the same time. They joked about caravaning from the airport and how, next time, they'll coordinate better and carpool to shrink their carbon footprints.

Next time.

I may not be ready for a "next time" for a while. While there were no major incidents for the rest of the weekend, I was on alert for any tells that Larissa might be putting on a show for my benefit. The girl is good. If Scout hadn't made me look more critically at her behavior, I would have missed some of the cues. Nothing big, just certain phrases not ringing quite true, certain tones missing the mark, sometimes trying too hard. I acted like I didn't notice, though, partly to keep the peace, partly to let her go on believing she has me snookered. As long as *I* know she's full of shit, I won't let down my guard. Embarrassing as it is, I have to admit I would have gone on believing our little heart-to-heart had worked if it hadn't been for Scout's heads up. Played by a kindergartner.

By the time I finished flattering Richard with how lovely and well-behaved his daughter was, and he left with Larissa, every last drop of gasoline had evaporated from my internal fuel tank. It was only seven o'clock, but I could have gone straight to bed right then.

With one look at me, Jet immediately took charge of Scout's bedtime routine. I took charge of a bottle of wine under the stars next to the pool. Jet found me later, having taken only two sips from my glass before conking out. Calling me his "adorable wino," he escorted me to bed, dumped my wine, and put away the leftover bottle.

It took me two days to fully recover, which is pathetic, but true. Recharging after the weekend was harder and worse than any hangover I've ever experienced. I couldn't get my brain to quiet. It insisted on analyzing and reanalyzing every word, expression, and action I'd witnessed from Larissa, wondering what was really going on behind those ice-blue eyes. It felt somewhat ridiculous giving so much credence to a child's thought processes, but she's so much like her mother that trying to figure her out felt like figuring out a corner of the puzzle that is Kiki, too.

Scout bounced back from our extended time with Larissa more quickly than I did, a testament to both youth and her built-up tolerance. I've had to remind her multiple times, however, that we aren't going to be homeless if her dad loses his job. A five-year-old's worst nightmare, that scare tactic was particularly savvy on Larissa's part. The prospect of homelessness when you're a kid and don't understand how income and money works, let alone how much of it your parents have is terrifying.

It's kind of terrifying, no matter how old you are or how unlikely the notion is.

Right now, though, I'm focused on something a lot less existential: keeping all of the baked goods in the backseat of my car from toppling, sliding, spilling, or collapsing as I make my careful way up and down hills and around curves from our house to Ursuline. Jet and Scout left the house at the same time I did in a separate vehicle and are probably already at the school, wondering where the heck I am. They lost me at the first curve and never looked back.

It's probably just as well. Nobody wants to be associated with the driver who's holding up traffic, eliciting horn blasts, rude gestures, and loud insults from other motorists. But the cookies, cakes, brownies, and sweetbreads must arrive intact at any cost. Even the most careful packaging and packing can be foiled by these twists and turns. Not on my watch, though.

I turn painfully slowly into the school parking lot at last, with several in the line of cars behind me shouting and honking their good riddances. Jet pushes away from the back of his car, where he's been leaning, waiting, a bemused smile on his face as he lifts Scout down from where she's been sitting on the trunk. After I pull into the space next to him, I open the back doors so we can start transferring the goodies inside.

Leaning into the backseat from opposite sides, we come face-to-face. "Make some friends?" he asks wryly.

I blow my bangs from my forehead as I survey the totes of foil- and plastic-wrapped plates and plastic containers. "The important thing is that nothing shifted."

"Including the traffic."

"Shut up." I playfully push his face away and admonish

him to be careful as he lifts the stiff, rectangular canvas bags from his side and hands one of them back to Scout.

When I remind him it's going to take more than one trip to unload the car, just as it did to load it, he says, "No, it won't," and hooks several totes' handles onto his fingers, somehow keeping them all level, his tongue poking from the corner of his mouth. "Let's go," he says, his voice straining as he leads the way, power-walking across the parking lot and lightly trotting up the front steps.

Scout and I trail behind him, her with one tote, me with one in each hand. When we get inside, he's already set down his bags on and around the table that's been assigned to us in a surprisingly prime location. Right next to Kiki's.

Great.

The Queen herself stops gushing over him and switches to gushing about him when Scout and I arrive with our paltry-by-comparison contributions to the merchandise. "Your husband just carried in an epic amount of stuff," she announces, as if we had no idea. "Handy guy to have around, huh?" She tries to nudge me, but I step sideways just in time, managing to make it look natural and inadvertent while I go about arranging and setting up our table.

He beams at her while wiping his forehead with his forearm.

"He'll do anything to avoid retracing his steps," I say, shaking my head while he massages his abused fingers.

After draping our table with a simple rust-colored cloth to match the Thanksgiving theme of the sale and set out the pre-approved price list from one of several of Kiki's emails about today's event, I begin lifting out and unwrapping the baked goods, instructing Scout where to set everything for maximum aesthetic effect (a.k.a., wherever it will fit). Jet collapses and folds each tote as it becomes empty and slides them under the table, hidden from view by the drop cloth.

When everything has been unloaded, Scout stands behind the table, and I back up into the middle of the gymnasium to get a far-off view of our display. I shout a couple of last-minute adjustments, which Jet quickly makes, and give my team a thumbs-up when it looks good enough. I'm proud of our efforts—until I start to look around at the other tables.

While the items Scout and I baked—with some help from Jet, if you call licking the beaters "helping"—look like the typical results of a parent-child effort, the other tables may as well be set up for photo shoots in a national magazine. Everything is picture-perfect. There are no tilting cakes or cracked cheesecakes or unevenly powdered pies or shakily piped cookies. Decorative touches include ceramic turkeys, real pumpkins, and, in more than one case, actual stalks of corn.

The grandest of all, of course, is Kiki's table, festooned with multiple levels of shelving, Pinterest-worthy decorations, framed oil paintings, and such professional-looking confections that I'm almost positive she hired a caterer to make them and pass them off as her own, something she actually joked about in one of her emails. Set so close to her table, ours looks even more pathetic than it is.

I stare in horror at the Valentines' table, wondering what— if anything—I can do to spruce ours up at such late notice. When Kiki said in her email(s) to "have fun with your table decor," I assumed she meant we shouldn't leave it bare. I didn't realize she expected us to make it look like Thanksgiving threw up on it. The whole point, I thought, was to put our time and effort into the food, so that's what Scout and I did. We worked every day after school in the kitchen for the past week, hoping to produce as many yummy things as possible to raise money for the local soup kitchen we're sponsoring with today's proceeds.

I notice Scout looking back and forth from the handprint turkey she drew and colored, pinned to the front of our drop cloth, to Kiki's Thanksgivingpalooza and want to melt into the floor. Jet covers his gaping mouth with his hand as he scans the room and sees one outlandish setup after another. His eyes water with the effort to hold back his laughter.

I'm not laughing. This is a disaster.

Quick-stepping it over to him, I shield my lips from the rest of the room and mutter near his ear, "Go out front and snag that half-barrel of mums by the doors."

He pulls back from me to look me in the eye and verify I'm serious. Seeing that I am, he starts to protest, but I merely say, "Quickly. Before customers start arriving. We'll put it back when everyone else leaves."

Before he can offer any more objections to the plan, I push on his shoulder to nudge him forward. Catching Kiki watching us, I smile brightly at her and say, "Looks like he has to make more than one trip, after all. Forgot something in the trunk."

"I was wondering where all of your decorations were," she says with an equally bright smile as she adjusts the gerbera daisies scattered here and there amongst the dishes and ephemera on her table.

"I got distracted by all the food," I say.

She looks me up and down. "It happens, I suppose."

When Jet returns with the mums, I direct him where to position them—as a sort of barrier between Kiki's table and ours—sighing with relief that their dark maroon color doesn't clash as much as with our drop cloth as I worried it would. It looks very Asian Indian. Kiki reminded us multiple times that there would be no "Pilgrims and Indians" themes, which always struck me as sad that people had to be told, but my inadvertent rebellion cracks me up. In fact, with the addition of the flowers, ours is suddenly the classiest and most on-trend display of the room. It's the Marie Kondo of bake sale booths. And yes, it "sparks joy."

There's no more time to do anything about it, anyway, as the doors have been opened to the public, and customers are already trickling in, eager to purchase the holiday desserts they won't have to bake themselves.

The first few people hit Kiki's booth, then walk right past ours without pausing. The next few pause, but we get no takers. At a lull in the action, Kiki leans over and says, "It's so sweet that you let Scout help you with the baking."

"Larissa didn't help you?" I make sure to inject enough sarcasm into my tone that she knows I know that even *she* didn't help with the baking.

Examining her perfect nails, she sighs. "No. Larissa spends as little time with me as possible. We aren't nearly as close as you and Scout are. And because I'm the stepmother, Paris practically hates me. She'd live with her mother if she had life as good there as she does with us."

Shame washes over me. Here I am, getting in my digs about her professionally-made pies when she might have preferred a fun day like Scout and I had yesterday. And why? Because I'm jealous of some table decor? How petty!

For the first time, I realize she's here alone. In fact, Jet and I are in the minority as a couple, and nobody else brought their children.

I clear my throat and will the blush to recede from my face and neck. "I'm sorry," I say, keeping it generic to cover both her situation with her daughters and my own sins.

She waves me off. "It is what it is. They'll appreciate everything I've done for them when they're older. When they have kids of their own, they'll understand."

This is obviously a consolation to her, so I don't blurt what I'm thinking, that it's a lot of work for a payoff that may never happen.

I mean, historically, it's true. My mom grew about a thousand times in my estimation after Scout was born. However, if I'd never had kids—as I'd originally planned—I'd like to think I'd still have had a good, close relationship with my mother, and not because of all the things she's done for me over the years, but because she's my mom, and she loves me. And I love her.

I smile, hoping it doesn't seem too sad or pitying. I want to say something, but everything I consider seems wrong. If I tell her why Scout and I enjoy spending time together, it sounds like I'm bragging or rubbing it in. If I commiserate about how difficult kids can be sometimes, it sounds disingenuous, considering what she already knows about my relationship with Scout. If I merely agree with her that her daughters will appreciate her someday, I'm buying into a promise that might not come true. Anything deeper doesn't seem appropriate for the setting. Then again, if I say nothing, it's obvious I don't agree with what she's said.

Eventually, enough time passes that I miss my chance to say anything, so it goes to the last option by default. More customers come by, and someone actually picks something from *our* table. Scout provides the background information on the pumpkin bread, coming just short of including the part about it falling on the floor when we turned it out of the pan. The floor was clean, so the five-second rule applied, and we agreed nobody needed to know. I'm pretty sure she would have told that part, too, though, if Jet hadn't stepped in and directed Scout's attention to our next customer.

The next time we get a break in the action, Jet takes the opportunity to walk around with Scout and look at the other tables, then texts me from across the crowded gym that Scout needs the bathroom, and he's going to take her. The inevitable awkward silence falls between Kiki and me, so I mention how impressed I am by the community turnout for the event.

She sniffs. "Yes, well, I wish the proceeds were going to the school, but…"

I wait for her to finish with something charitable but realize I'll be waiting forever after she lets her sentence trail off indefinitely. "It's for a really good, important cause," I finish for her.

With a shrug, she avoids my eyes while rearranging the few dishes she has left on her table. "I suppose. There's no cause more important than our own children's education, though."

I mentally test out that theory and find it faulty. "Our kids have us, though, to fund that education. It's nice that we're doing something for those in the community who need it."

Again, she shrugs, but this time she adds a tight, condescending smile and crinkles her eyes—or tries to—at me. It's an expression that clearly states, *"You're so cute, with your charitable spirit,"* and it pisses me off.

"No, really," I say, as if she's patronized me out loud. "We should probably dedicate our fundraising efforts to more community causes."

"We do a toy drive at Christmas. Which reminds me, Maura, I'll need you and Jet to really step it up for us at that event. I was hoping you'd organize—"

"I really can't, Kiki. Sorry. I mean, we'll definitely participate in whatever way we can, but that'll be a busy travel time for Jet, and I'm trying to get the theater rebuilt and back up and running before the first of the year. I'll be up against a lot of deadlines, too."

"I see." She chuckles. "You make it sound as if you're hammering the nails yourself."

Trying to keep it light, I reply, "Not quite; I've hired someone else to do that part. It's all the other parts that will eat up my time and attention."

She sighs. "Everyone's a critic, but when it comes to actually doing the work…"

"Under any other circumstances, you know I would."

A group of women about our age approaches us, oohing and aahing over Kiki's table but ultimately selecting items from mine. Ha! Take that! Substance finally beats style. They'll be much happier with my granny's raspberry thumbprint cookies, chocolate chip banana bread, and snickerdoodles than they would be with that flawless pumpkin cheesecake made with zero love. I commend them on their choices and point them to the cashier's table when one of them asks.

As soon as they're gone, Kiki says, "Back to your suggestion that we do more community service, anything more than what we already do would make us look like a charity, and we're not. We're a school."

"An extremely wealthy school funded by private patrons, high tuition, and government subsidies."

"Government subsidies, my foot." Her disbelief and disdain drip from her words. If she weren't too good for it, she would snort.

"Ursuline gets them. I've checked."

"Oh, I know we do, but they're a drop in the bucket."

"As they should be." I can't believe this woman. The people who get the most always want more. "Like I said, tuition and donations cover the rest. Very well, I might add."

"You've checked that, too, I take it."

"Of course."

"Because you and Jet are such civic-minded, salt-of-the-earth folks."

There's no doubt that, coupled with the country accent she uses to say it, she's insulting us, but I reply, "I guess so, if that means we do our homework and care about where we spend our money."

"Some of us don't have time to research where every penny goes."

"We don't—"

"But I'm *so* glad that Ursuline was worthy of the Knox stamp of approval."

"That's not—"

"You, Maura Knox, are a snob."

"Excuse me?!"

Heads swivel our way. I try to smile reassuringly so everyone will go back to their business. Some do, turning toward the goods they were previously admiring or continuing with their transactions at the cashiers table. Many others, however, continue watching what they sense to be some brewing drama.

Lowering my voice, I move closer to Kiki. "That's pretty rich, coming from you, but please, enlighten me."

"You're an intellectual and emotional snob. You don't want me to elaborate any further than that, trust me." She simpers. "Let's leave it there, and you can do your own soul-searching."

The absolute gall of this woman sends my blood pressure

into orbit. It pulses in my eyeballs and temples. "Like I'm going to spend a minute analyzing why you think that about me," I say through gritted teeth. *More like hours and days and months.* "I don't care, Kiki." *Easy, breezy, untruthful.*

"Mmm-hmm."

With a carefree roll of my shoulders, I take a deep breath. "I don't. Your opinion of me is none of my business. Maybe you should keep it to yourself from now on." *Maybe I'm born with it; maybe it's make-believe.*

"And maybe you should stop psychoanalyzing my child at sleepovers."

"What?" The outraged word echoes and bounces off the gymnasium floors and metal-beamed ceiling.

The people still here who had decided to stop watching are back with intention. Those who never stopped chomp harder on their metaphorical popcorn. Some murmur to the others to get them caught up. Some snicker. Some merely stare with their mouths agape.

Rather than shying away from the attention, Kiki seems to delight in it. Her red lips widen in a Joker-like grin. "Oh, yeah, Mommy Feelings. I heard all about it. How you really set my five-year-old straight. It's not your job to teach my child how to behave toward others."

"You're right; it's yours! Maybe you should try it sometime. Then your daughter wouldn't be an insufferable brat who bullies her classmates into being her friends."

Someone in the crowd says, "Oh, no she didn't." Another says, "Uh-huh. Truth."

All signs of amusement gone, nostrils flared, and lips pulled back from ultra-white teeth, she spats, "How dare you!"

"How dare I? How dare you? Your daughter has been

terrorizing mine since the first day of school and blackmailing other kids to do the same so they won't be her next targets. That's the product of great parenting there, Keek. Brava." I slow-clap.

She rearranges her features into something better resembling her usual haughtiness. "Terrorizing? Blackmailing? Methinks someone watches too many movies. Kids learn early nowadays how to be tough and get what they want. In boys, that's called 'leadership'; in girls, we call it 'bossy' or 'aggressive.'"

I plunk my hands on my hips, feeling every inch a Wonder Woman. She's not going muddy the very real sexism and misogyny waters with this argument. Not on my watch. "No, in both it's called 'bullying,' and there's a zero-tolerance policy for it at this school. You're lucky we haven't reported it and had your little darling expelled."

"Are you threatening my child?"

"I'm explaining to you what could have happened but hasn't—yet—because Jet and I believe in second chances."

"Oh, *more* charity from the Knoxes. Bless you." She presses her hands together and bows, and for a second, I have to resist the urge to push on the back of her head and grind her face into that plate of meringue tarts in front of her. "Maybe your 'little darling' should grow a thicker skin and stop being such a baby. Maybe you should let her."

Without my noticing, Jet and Scout have slipped back into the room and sidled up next to me. "What's going on?" he asks quietly with a nervous chuckle.

"Kiki and I were just having a little chat about all sorts of things. Mostly parenting styles."

"Uh-huh. And why is everyone watching?"

"It got a bit heated."

"Are you talking about me?" Scout asks in a tiny, quavering voice.

The rage storm in my brain and body dies down slowly. My pulse returns to a normal rate. My eyeballs and temples stop pulsing. Kneeling in front of her, I say, "It's okay, sweetie. We're just trying to get to the bottom of this whole bullying thing."

"Everyone's staring at us. She said I was a baby. In front of everyone."

"No, that's not—"

Before I can finish, Jet reclaims one of our daughter's hands and says tetchily, "Let's go wait on the playground, Bump."

Looking up at his face, I confirm that the temper tempest has passed from me to him, but I'm shocked and dismayed when he directs his angry eyes at me. "When you're finished and need help packing up, you know where to find us."

———

Scout's tears and her and Jet's hasty exit seemed to snap everyone in the gymnasium out of their drama-porn trance. As soon as attention was no longer on us, both Kiki and I fell into a silent stalemate that eventually led to both of us retreating behind our tables and pretending the other wasn't there for the rest of the event.

Well, almost. Just as I was texting Jet that I had everything packed up and ready to take back to the car, Kiki said nonchalantly while folding her drop cloth and draping it over the two large paintings nested against the wall, "You know, I'm not sure Richard's decision to hire Jet is working out. It would be different if Jet were good at what he does, but..." She smiled sympathetically. "We both know that's just not the case, don't we? *Everyone* seems to know, in fact, except Jet."

I wish I could say I defended him. I wish I could say I told her where to go with her childish insults and not-so-thinly-veiled threats. Neither of those things happened, though. I merely stared at her, feeling as if my intestines were packed in ice, while she continued to consolidate her belongings for the fewest number of trips down to her SUV.

*This is how Scout feels every time she's bullied by Larissa*, I thought. The only thing I could focus on was how helpless I felt and how humiliating it was, how I couldn't get the vision of myself standing there, impotent, mute, and stupid, out of my head long enough to think clearly. My mind flashed to a scene hours later in the Valentine household, where Kiki was regaling her family with the story, doing an impression of me that included stuttering and just one word: "Duuuuuuh." The shame at the mere idea of it was so powerful and paralyzing that I could do nothing but stand there, dumb.

By the time I'd conceived of any response at all—a very inarticulate, short, profane one, at that—Jet and Scout were back, so I remained silent. The last thing I wanted was to humiliate either of them more than I already had.

My public feud with Kiki was a much-discussed topic of conversation in the Knox house for the rest of the weekend. I finally got to explain myself, in vague terms in front of Scout but in more detail—albeit not completely detailed—in private with Jet. Scout has decided that Kiki is a meanie, just like Larissa. Jet's less-than-warm silences tell me he hasn't taken as simplistic a view of things.

Despite my worries about the possible repercussions of the bake sale imbroglio for Scout, it's almost a relief to drop her off at school on Monday morning with strict instructions to tell a teacher or staff member if Larissa gives her any guff. It's less of a relief to drive back to the house, where I find Jet waiting for me on the driveway.

"I think we both need some fresh air and sunshine," he says, getting into the car before I can pull back into the garage.

All of which has led to me to this trail, climbing fifty bazillion rock stairs (okay, more like three hundred) to reach the top of a three-hundred-fifty-foot peak. But now that I'm here, I'm glad. I suddenly feel amazing. Maybe I should exercise more.

Nah. It's probably the view working its magic on me.

"Whoa," I say when we reach the top. Lowering myself to the concrete patio behind the safety railing, I pull my knees to my chest and look out over the city.

Jet sits next to me and wraps his arm around my shoulders. "Pretty neat, huh?"

"That's one way of saying it."

He sighs rapturously. "Came up here with some friends in college once. There was an open-air benefit concert, or something. And a buddy of mine from the team got married up here, too."

"I bet that was beautiful."

"I didn't cry or anything." He leans against me in a modified nudge, and I almost topple sideways but catch myself on an outstretched arm at the last second. He straightens and pulls me fully upright once more. "Anyway. I've been here a few times since we moved here."

Surprised, I turn my head to look at him. "Alone?"

He nods, his eyes unreadable behind his sunglasses.

"Oh. I didn't realize—"

"It's close to work." He points out the building from where

we are. "It's great exercise and a good place to think. Puts things in perspective." He squeezes my shoulder in his hand and gestures with his free one at the vista before us. "It's not *that* high, right? I mean, it's not a mountain, or anything."

"Felt like it, climbing those stairs."

Jet nods at the vista, "I come up here and imagine what this view was like before all those buildings went up. Hundreds, thousands of years ago."

Gazing out, I try, too. "Beautiful but boring. It's probably much more interesting now."

He tilts his head and squints. "I guess. But not as clean."

Since I can't debate that, I let him have the last word and turn my attention to the rest of our surroundings. Every once in a while, I spy a few people on the trails below us, but we're the only two at the lookout. I bet this place is heaving on the weekend; not so much on a Monday, mid-morning. Jet obviously knew that and picked this spot well.

After a few minutes of contemplative silence, I ask, "What else do you think about up here?"

"How lucky I am."

"Naturally."

"I'm serious," he says with a laugh.

"That's because you're pathologically grateful."

"You say that as if it's a terrible thing."

"Not terrible, just... not me."

He shrugs. "Whatever makes you happy."

I shake my head, laughing at the contradiction. "It doesn't. That's the point."

"Then choose to be more grateful."

"Oh! Is that what I've been doing wrong all these years? Good to know."

Again, silence descends while we survey the view and

retreat to our own thoughts. Then Jet removes his arm from around me and says, "What are you not telling me, Maura?"

"Huh?"

He merely raises his eyebrows expectantly, so I reconsider his question. In the context of the topic that has consumed our family conversations for the past thirty-six hours, it doesn't take me long to understand exactly what he means.

I swallow painfully, wishing I had been given the opportunity to pack a water bottle. The moment of truth has arrived. Actually, it's arrived several times in the past couple of months, but I've slammed the door in its face so many times, it's become a habit. Even now, I wonder how weird it would be if I stood up and ran back down the hill. Would that prevent this awful moment one more time? Probably not. It would just delay it. Jet would catch up to me and force the issue again. There's no wiggling away from it this time.

I can't look at him when I say it, though, so I fix my gaze back out on the view, finding a particularly shiny building to stare at, retinas be damned.

"So, uh, the things is, there's a component to the bullying that I haven't told you about. Scout didn't want me to tell you, and honestly, I didn't want it to be a distraction for you." I stop, hoping that will be good enough. Like, *There's some stuff you don't know and probably shouldn't know, for your own good* would actually work.

"I'm listening," he says, dashing those hopes.

"Okay. Shit. This is really hard to say out loud."

"Just say it, then. You're freaking me out."

"Larissa's been teasing Scout about *you*."

"Me? Oh, man. What did I do? Did I say something dumb at the birthday party?"

"No. Well, maybe. I don't know. It's not about that, though."

"Then what?"

*All right, Maura. This is it. You are the wax technician at the salon. You've applied the wax to the pubic area. You've pressed the cloth strips over the wax. Now, it's time to let 'er rip. The faster, the better. Let's go.*

"Larissa makes fun of how you announce games and tells Scout that her dad will fire you if Scout doesn't do or act exactly the way Larissa wants her to."

He says nothing. But I know from experience that there's no feeling the first couple of seconds after that strip comes off. Eyes closed, I wait for him to feel it, really feel it.

"I see," he says stoically.

Peeking through one eye, I try to gauge how he's actually feeling and confirm that it's not good, based on his pale complexion and bobbing Adam's apple. I wrap my hand around his. He pulls away.

"I'm sorry. It was shitty for me to agree not to tell you. I just thought— It didn't make sense to worry you."

"I'm her dad. It's my job to worry." Finally, after several more seconds, he rubs his face and chin and says, "Shit."

"Yeah." Again, I reach for his hand. This time, he lets me hold it. When I stroke it with my thumb, though, he stops the movement with his other hand.

"No."

"Okay."

He clears his throat and attempts a smile my way. "I mean, I'm fine. I don't need…"

"Right. Got it."

Color returning to his face, he stares into the distance.

Finally, he sucks his reddening cheeks into his mouth on a huge inhale before saying, "I need to tell you something, too."

"Me?"

He nods, and I can tell he's giving himself a similar pep talk to the one I gave my inner wax technician.

"Larissa makes fun of you, too."

Icy embarrassment drenches me like a winning coach's Gatorade shower. "What? How does she make fun of *me*?"

"She calls you Mommy Feelings." As if his discomforture on my behalf is too much for him, he flips his sunglasses to the top of his head and covers his eyes with one of his hands.

Mouth agape, I take in this information. "Mommy Feel—" Hang on. That's what Kiki called me at the bake sale when she scolded me for having that heart-to-heart with Larissa. "Because I had that talk with her at the sleepover?"

He bobs his head. His shoulders start to shake, and for a second, I think he's crying. The sound that finally comes out of him when he releases it, though, is decidedly mirthful.

"It's not funny!" I say, experiencing a full-body blush.

"Yeah, it is," he manages through his laughter.

"Shut up!" I shove his shoulder, but to my annoyance, he hardly moves. Damn his core strength. As his amusement continues, I cross my arms over my chest.

"Mommy Feelings!" he says, fully giving into fits of giggles.

"Fuck you," I say with a grudging smile as I start to see the humor in it. "You're so mean."

He wipes his eyes. "Sorry," he says, trying to sober up— and failing. "It's just— They role play at recess. Larissa pretends to be you, and the kids go to her and get 'advice.'"

"Shut up. You're making this up now."

"I'm not!" Now he does calm down, his reddened eyes

widening earnestly. "It really upsets Scout. It's humiliating for her."

"These are kindergartners! How—"

He scratches his eyebrow. "Yeah, I know. It's gotta be stuff Larissa's hearing at home."

I confirm his theory by quickly ripping off one more wax-backed strip and telling him what Kiki said—paraphrased, of course—while we were cleaning up after the bake sale. Before he can dwell on it too long, though, I bring us back around to my own disgrace. "Oh, my gosh. Why didn't Scout tell me?"

He levels a look at me that clearly conveys what a stupid question that is.

"Right," I say, biting my lower lip. "The same reason she didn't want to tell you they were making fun of you."

During the ensuing pause in our conversation, I run through nightmare scenarios in my head and hold back tears at the thought of Scout dealing with the teasing and taunting every single day at school, thanks to both of us.

I'm assuming Jet's thinking similar thoughts until he starts laughing again. Just when I'm about to admonish him and remind him our daughter's pain isn't funny, he says, "During role-play, I wonder if Mommy Feelings tries to make me feel better about sucking at game announcing."

A chuckle escapes me, but I choke off any others. "Stop."

"Okay, I'm done," he says, returning his sunglasses to his nose.

"I feel so bad for Scout." Guilt piles on top of the chagrin, and I feel an almost overwhelming and dramatic urge to throw myself off this hill.

Interrupting my impulse, Jet says, "Come on, now. You're not the only one they're laughing at. Like, I'm not stupid. I know people are super-disappointed that I didn't turn out to be the next Lorenzo Walker." When I have no words of reassurance to the contrary, he continues, "That blows, all by itself. It kills me, though, that Scout's suffering because of it, too."

Taking his hand and weaving my fingers between his, I say, "What's done is done, in my case. As for you, you're learning and improving."

It sounds lame and insincere to my own ears, so I'm not surprised when Jet shoots me a long-suffering look and says, "Babe."

"Don't call me babe."

"Sixteen million viewers aren't diggin' me. They can't *all* be wrong."

"Oh. You, uh, have figures on that?"

"They're called 'ratings.' And complaints pour in every week."

"Ouch."

He shrugs and sighs, "It is what it is. I suck."

"Now, I wouldn't go that—"

"Maura. I suck. You don't have to pretend anymore."

"I wasn't pretending. I was giving you time and space to learn."

He kisses my knuckles. "And I appreciate that. But this part of the The Plan ain't workin'. They've, uh, decided not to renew my contract."

"Oh."

"Yeah."

"And you were going to tell me this... when?"

He looks down at our hands. "Soon. Now. I mean, I just found out yesterday."

Yesterday. So, he wasn't still mad at me about the bake sale fiasco. He was quiet because he'd been, effectively, fired.

"Why didn't you tell me right away?" I ask.

Again, he shrugs. "I just needed some time to let the sting wear off, I guess. I mean, I'm kind of relieved now. But it still sucked to get that email."

"They fired you in an email? That's shitty."

"Nah. Richard was giving me a heads up. I've got a meeting this afternoon. I'm supposed to act like it's the first I'm hearing about it." He looks up at me. "Richard's not a bad guy, you know?"

"He just talks about things maybe he shouldn't in front of his witchy wife?"

"Yeah. Maybe." He sighs. "I really thought I'd be good at this. I like people. I like talking about football. I love analyzing plays on the fly. I mean, even though I suck, I still have fun up there in that booth. That's the worst thing about it. I love it. But loving something doesn't make you good at it."

"I learned that the hard way about scriptwriting," I say quietly. "So much fun. But I can't write movies worth a damn."

That earns me a sympathetic smile. "The worst, isn't it?"

"Yeppers."

With a cocky smirk, he says, "You can't be awesome at everything, I guess."

"Oh, champ. I'm sorry."

He looks down at his knees for a second but quickly raises his head and shoots me his "L.A. smile," which immediately makes both of us laugh, even though it reminds me of the brave face he showed me after his Super Bowl loss, a terrible memory.

My chest tightens with disappointment at how all of this has turned out. Nothing has gone the way we hoped it would.

Jet snaps me back to the present by clearing his throat.

"Anyway, I gave Scout the same advice I've been giving myself: keep being yourself and trying your hardest, and do your best to ignore the jerks."

I let go of his hand and lean back on my straight arms. "About that. Do you really think that's the best strategy for her? Talking to Richard and Kiki might be pointless, but maybe we should have a sit-down with the principal and Scout's teacher or counselor or *someone* at the school."

"We can't fight her battles for her all the time, Maura."

"This isn't 'all the time.' This is *this* time. In kindergarten. If this were high school, I might agree with you. By then, she might have the emotional skills to tune out the jerks. Now, though… She's practically still a baby."

"She's not. And one way to make sure they keep calling her 'Baby' is to jump in and try to save her."

I throw my head back and groan at the crystal-clear sky.

"You know I'm right," Jet says, looking back at me.

I keep my eyes on the sky. "No, I don't, actually. That's why this is so crazy-making. What you're saying makes sense, but I can also think of a million examples of when doing nothing led to terrible headlines and people saying, 'Why didn't that kid's parents intervene?' "

"I don't think we're anywhere near that point yet."

"Yet."

"Which means it's okay to wait and see."

I lower my head. "For how long, Jet?"

He opens his mouth, then closes it.

I take advantage of this hesitation and throw out some scenarios. "Do we wait until she starts losing sleep? We're there. Do we wait until she becomes moody and irritable? We're there. Until she loses interest in her favorite subjects and activities? Until she's diagnosed with depression and/or anxiety and has to go on medication? Until the bullying becomes physical? When is the 'right' time to intervene, and when is it too late?"

He runs his hand through his hair and scrubs the back of his neck. "I don't know! I don't know, okay? I just know that my gut is telling me right now to hang back and let her figure it out."

"Sit back and watch her implode?"

"No! Of course not! We support her at home. We give her advice. We—we— I don't know— Show her that we believe she can overcome this, that she's strong and can bounce back when shit's hard."

"How do we know it's not too hard, though?"

He bangs a fist on his thigh. "I don't want to be those parents who rush in too soon."

Straightening, I sit forward once more and grasp his upper arm. "I don't want to be the ones who step in too late! I can't watch her suffer, Jet. I won't."

"Sometimes we don't have a choice. I'm figuring out that's the hardest part of being a parent. You can't shield your child from every hurt they're going to face."

"But shouldn't we try?"

"No, Maura. No, we shouldn't."

I scoff. "That's our job!"

To my frustration, he merely kisses the top of my head, inhaling and exhaling a while with his nose against my hair. Finally, he pulls back and says, "Our job is to raise a good person, not protect her from every possible negative thing in life. Good people know how to deal with negative things in positive ways. And you don't learn how to do that when someone else fights every battle for you."

I lower my head and rest it against the soft space between

his chest and shoulder. "I get that there are things in life that happen that you can't predict or prevent. But we know this is happening. It seems wrong not to do something about it."

Separating slightly from me, he places his hands on my shoulders and pushes me back far enough that he can look down into my eyes. Again, he moves his sunglasses to the top of his head so I can see the conflict and pain in his. "We *are* doing something. We're teaching her to deal with it."

"Fine, but I'm going to give her teacher a heads up about what's happening, so she can keep an eye on things. It's ridiculous that nobody's noticed." I clench my jaw.

"And if the teacher decides to take action based on what she sees…" The left side of his mouth rises, and his eyes sparkle. "Well, that's out of our hands, isn't it?" He pulls me in for a hug, and I cling to him like a sock on a fleece pullover straight from the dryer.

"I hate this," I say through a tight throat. "This feels so shitty."

He rubs my back and rests his chin on top of my head, resuming his survey of the city below. "Don't fight it, Mommy Feelings. I'm here for you."

"I hate you so much right now."

## TWENTY-FIVE

## RESULTS

Jet picked up Scout from school on his way home from his meeting with the big wigs at Football Network, so it isn't until after we put her to bed that he has a chance to catch me up on the specifics of what happened.

Even then, I spent a little longer with her, reading aloud a chapter of *Harry Potter*. Then we talked for quite a while after our reading when she mentioned that one of her friends at school, who is transgender, doesn't like *Harry Potter*, because the author has said some mean things about transgender people. That led to us discussing the concept of separating an artist from their works when the artist says or does things that clash with one's belief systems. Try explaining to a five-year-old the complicated flow chart that leads to still reading *Harry Potter* but never watching another Roman Polanski film.

Before I could botch it too badly, I simply said, "We all have a line that we don't let people cross. Your friend has decided that what this author did was a deal-breaker. I still think the characters and stories in this series have a lot to teach us. They're bigger, to me, than the author. But I respect your friend's choice and understand why they feel that way."

She seemed satisfied by that, to the point that I earned a long hug and a kiss on my nose before she burrowed into her covers.

By the time she's settled, I find Jet lounging on one of the loveseats in front of a crackling fire in the sun room, clutching a cut glass snifter of Scotch in one hand and petting Torzi, snug on his chest, with the other.

"Don't you two look cozy?" I say, firmly sliding the door behind me and making sure all of the other doors connecting the patio to the house are securely shut, as well. The last thing I want is for Scout to overhear that her dad has been fired, in spite of everything she's endured, thinking she could prevent it.

He smiles lazily and nods to the glass of wine he's poured for me and set on the coffee table. "Not as cozy as I hope to get with you pretty soon."

Oh, wow. Maybe that's not his first glass of Scotch. Or second, even.

I take up a similar position to his on the opposite loveseat and reach for my wineglass, taking one long gulp and closing my eyes.

"Did you and Scout solve all the world's problems?" Jet asks.

"Feels like it. How about you and Torzi? Are you doing your part to make the world a better place?"

"Does farting count?"

"No, it absolutely does not."

"Then Torzi's slacking, as usual."

"And you?"

He gestures to the can of air freshener resting on the floor under the coffee table. "I'm in damage-control mode."

"Gotcha." I drain the rest of my glass and set it down, out of the way. "Speaking of, what's the damage at Football Network? Don't leave me in suspense any longer."

Lazily petting the dog, he sips his Scotch and smiles enigmatically. "Oh, I've been dying to tell you."

"So do it!" I sit up and place my feet on the floor, elbows on my knees.

"Okay, okay."

As if reading from the ceiling, he stares up at it and says, "Richard sent me that email, so I knew what was coming, but I decided on the drive there that it wasn't going to go the way they thought it was going to go. I—"

"Who's they? Who was there? Where did the meeting take place?"

"A bunch of pompous asses you've never met. We were all crowded into Richard's office." He turns his head to look at me." Do you want me to tell the story, or what?"

"Yes. Sorry. I'm just anxious."

"Well, you're going to love this, so sit back and relax. Get another glass of wine."

I shake off the suggestion of more alcohol but scoot back into the cushions and rest an elbow on the loveseat arm, folding my legs out to the side of my body.

When I've gotten comfortable, he continues, "I just kept thinking how awkward it was going to be for everyone if they got me in there and said, 'Knox, we've decided not to renew your contract,' or 'It's not working out,' or some other euphemistic way of saying, 'You're fired.'"

"Shhh... Don't say that last word too loud around here."

He waves me off. "She can't hear me. She's sound asleep by now, and we're shut off in here, just the two of us and Torzi. And his farts." He picks up the air freshener and squirts some into room for good measure. "Anyway, I thought, if I go in there and take control of the room, they're saved the awkwardness of fi— letting me go, and I'm saved some face, right?"

"Okay. So… you quit?"

He shakes his head. "Not quite." Setting down his glass on the coffee table and shoos the dog from his chest. "Yeesh. That's enough cuddling, stinky old man." He sprays the air one more time toward Torzi's retreating butt and says, "Don't sit too close to the fire, boy."

The dog ignores him, as usual, and hops up into the chair closest to the fireplace, circles a few times, and harrumphs into place, curled up nose to tail.

"Good luck with that position," Jet mutters.

I roll my hand. "Can we get back to the story, please? You're killin' me, Knox."

He laughs. "Sorry. So yeah, I get there, and as I'm walking through the building, I can tell everyone knows why I'm there, right? I mean, their faces… Erin looked at me like I was about to get a death sentence. She might have even been crying. Or almost."

I click my tongue. "Poor Erin."

"You mean, because she has to work with me every week?"

"No! Because she's so nice, and she obviously likes you and respects you."

"Sure. As a person. As a co-worker, I think I've been a nightmare for her, but anyway." He runs his hand through his hair, leaving it standing up in spikes around his forehead, then rests his arm on top of his head. "As soon as I got into Richard's office and all the bullshit handshakes were done, I came right out with it and said, 'Listen y'all, before we start, I want to let you know I won't be renewing my broadcasting contract.'"

My mouth falls open.

When my reaction remains silent, Jet looks at me and laughs. "See? I told you you'd love it. Baller move, right?"

I cover my mouth and giggle.

"I know!" He brings his arm down and pulls it into his side in a pump as he bites down on his lower lip. "Uhn!" he grunts.

"What was their reaction?" I finally manage to ask.

"They all just kind of looked at each other, and Richard tried to say something, but he sounded like Yosemite Sam. When nobody else was looking at us, I winked at Richard, and then I said, 'I'm sorry to drop that on you guys, but it's something I've been thinking about for a while, and I didn't want to start talking about something else here today, without us all being on the same page.'"

I shake my head at him. "You are somethin' else, champ."

He cackles at the ceiling.

"But really, like you said, you were kind of doing them a favor."

"Exactly!"

"You'll still finish out the season, right? That's almost two months. If you'd been released from your contract, there could have been hard feelings with management and weirdness with your co-workers. You were smart to do what you did."

"I can be smart sometimes."

"You're smart most of the time."

"Just not when I'm mic'ed up."

"It's probably the microphone's fault."

"I blame the teleprompter. That thing's evil. It's had it in for me from the word, 'go.'"

For a few seconds, I study his profile, his spiky hair, the dimple peeking out in his cheek as he smiles at the memory of his face-saving victory. While I watch, though, his expression fades, and eventually he stares into the fire, his forehead crinkled, the corners of his mouth turned down.

"What is it, champ?" I ask.

"Huh?" He snaps out of his trance and attempts to toss a smile my way, but it's definitely half-hearted.

"You look worried all of a sudden. Did something else happen?"

"Nope. That was it. We all shook hands again, and I pretended it wasn't weird that they didn't have anything else to talk about in the meeting that they called, and we left the office, all smiles. That confused some people, I bet. I didn't stick around to talk to anyone; I wanted to get to the school to pick up Scout."

"Have you heard from Erin since? A text or anything?"

"Uh-uh."

"Don't you think that's weird?"

"Nah. If she knows, she's already part of talks to figure out who to put with her next season. If she doesn't know, then she'll assume she's stuck with me again, and she's probably rip-roaring drunk at the thought."

"Come on!"

"I wouldn't blame her."

I don't know that I would, either, to be honest, so I move on. "Then why so serious?"

He sighs. "Nah, it's nothing. I was just thinking. Like, what's next? I'm super-relieved that the decision not to call another season has been made, and all, but now I've gotta figure out something else."

"There's plenty of time for that."

"Hmm. I guess." He doesn't sound convinced in the slightest.

Having stiffened into the position I've been sitting for the past several minutes, I try not to wince unattractively as I lower my legs, and sit up, then limp two steps across the room to his loveseat, where I stand over him.

He looks up at me and smiles, taking my hand and kissing it. "Hey there, beautiful."

"Hey. Wanna get cozy?"

He pulls me down on top of him. "I do, actually. It's like you read my mind."

We arrange our long limbs and bodies to get comfortable against each other on the smallish sofa. Finally, we settle, and I snuggle up to his chest, my head under his chin. He sighs contentedly and kisses the top of my head while rubbing my lower back with his thumb.

"You smell much better than Torzi."

At the sound of his name, the dog jerks his head up and blinks at us.

"Low-low bar. Is that what passes for foreplay nowadays?"

His laugh rumbles through his chest to my ear, and I look up into his twinkling eyes. "This is just a cuddle," he says. "The foreplay's later."

Damn it if my insides don't jump and wiggle at that promise. Playing it cool, I simply say, "You're full of saves today, champ."

Less than a week after my short but ultra-sweet email to Scout's teacher tipping her off to the not-so-playful goings-on during recess and asking that she pretend she noticed it without any nudging from me, Scout says immediately upon entering the car after school, "Larissa got taken to the principal's office today for being mean at me."

While I suppress a fist-bump and merely make mild noises of interest in the front seat, Scout regales me with the full scene, including how Larissa resisted arrest by digging her heels into the mulch and screaming about her PTA president mommy and very important daddy. It's all I can do not to laugh out loud. Instead, I say, "Wow. I guess nobody's above the rules, huh, Bump? When you're not nice to people, you eventually have to suffer the consequences."

"Are consequences like Karma?"

Flabbergasted, I manage to say, "Sort of, yes."

"Because Neville said it was Karma."

"Neville is unusually enlightened for a kindergartner. I take it he's not one of the ones who's been laughing at you?"

"No! Neville's my friend. He takes turns with me on the swing and tells me jokes so I won't cry when Arya and Larissa and Catlyn call me Baby and say things about you and Daddy."

"That's really nice." I glance at her in the rearview mirror and revel in her triumphant smile. "So, you didn't have to tattle after all, huh? Your teacher finally noticed Larissa picking on you?"

She nods and pulls on the curled silky end of her braid. "And Arya and Catlyn, too. They were being super-quiet, so I don't know how she heard, but she did. Maybe she got a hearing aid. Or one of those listening ear thingies, like Hermione has in *Harry Potter*."

"Did Arya and Catlyn get in trouble, too?"

"They had to sit in time out in the classroom, but they didn't go to the Principal's office. This time. Miss Itrie said next time they would. Then she said, 'I'm watching you.' And that was kind of creepy, but whatever."

"Good. Sounds like you had a decent day, then."

Her smile fades. "I guess. But what if…"

I wait.

Since my talk with Jet at the lookout, I've thought a lot about what he said, about how anticipating our daughter's every need and trying to prevent every hardship is not only impossible but harmful. I've only ever focused on the "impossible" part of that job, seeing parenting as a venture in which some measure of failure is the only outcome because of that impossibility. Whether we *should* try was never questioned by me until now. Now that I've essentially been given permission to let go of that struggle, I suddenly have both hands free to do what I've actually always wanted: to raise a good person.

What kind of adults do children who've never had to work at anything become? Entitled. Self-centered. Unsympathetic. That's not who I want Scout to be. I've always worried our financial situation was the biggest obstacle to Scout's personal growth. Jet reminded me that adversity comes in many forms, and resilience can't exist without it.

Even though I can tell from her voice and my frequent glances at her that she's is conflicted, struggling with her thoughts and how to express them, I don't rush to finish Scout's sentence or to reassure her that what she's worried about won't happen. I merely drive. And wait.

Finally, she says in a wobbly voice, "What if Larissa's dad fires Daddy because Larissa got in trouble?"

We haven't discussed Jet's job situation with Scout yet, since we don't even know what it means yet. Will Jet permanently retire and be a stay-at-home dad? (That's what I'm rooting for, but he doesn't seem all that pumped at the prospect.) Will he try to go back to playing? (Dear God, please, no.) Will he hunt for coaching positions. (Most likely, based on what he's said so far.) If so, where? (High School? College? Pro? West Coast, East Coast, Midwest, North, South?) There are still too many questions to burden Scout with what little information we already have. We're waiting until we have something definitive to tell her.

Here and now, I honestly answer, "We'll be okay. It's not the end of the world."

"It's not?"

"No. Think about it. Getting fired hurts sometimes. It can be disappointing or even a little embarrassing. But it's not a disaster. People don't die from it."

She thinks about it for a second, and I'm almost sure she's going to challenge that assertion, but instead, she says, "Not like Pompeii. The volcano, not the gerbil."

"Nope. No volcano *or* killer gerbil."

When she giggles, I take it as my cue to relax and change the subject. "So what do you think? Enchiladas for dinner? A little salsa verde?"

"Yummers! Yes, please!"

Sounds like we'll have a lot to declare we're thankful for this Thanksgiving.

## TWENTY-SIX

## CONSEQUENCES
### FOUR MONTHS LATER

"I don't wanna."

"Come on. It's not a big deal. One hour—two, max—and we're out of here."

"'Coffee with Kiki.'" I wrinkle my nose. "It sounds like a miserable local access morning show. I just— I don't think I can handle her today."

"We promised we'd be here." Jet pinches my pinkie between his forefinger and thumb and gently tugs, as if to lead me from the public dining area of the European-style coffee-house to the private room where Kiki's holding today's PTA "brainstorming sesh."

I stand my ground, hands wrapped around my thin porce-lain cup of steaming coffee. "Let's just grab a table outside, instead."

"Tempting, but no." He sips his drink and grunts apprecia-tively at the taste. "Damn. That's good." After another, longer drink, he says, "That would look really weird." Stepping aside to let some other parents pass with their orders on the way to the reserved room, he nods and says hi.

Neville's dads pause long enough to ask, looking somewhat worried, if we're coming. Jet reassures them we'll be there in a minute, and as soon as they move on, says, "See? People are counting on you."

I roll my eyes. Ever since my standoff with Kiki at the bake sale, I've been the unofficial spokesperson for all of the parents not part of Kiki's clique. And even some of the clique, at times, when they were too afraid to publicly defy their queen. When news got around that I found a way to have Larissa reprimanded for her bullying without turning any of their kids into tattletales, I was elevated to a sort of embarrassing hero status.

Of course, that meant that Kiki also knew for sure that I was the whistleblower, so things have been—shall we say—tense between us. Every PTA meeting is a minefield. After months of this, combined with my real job and getting the Knox in Kansas City back up and running, I'm tired.

"They need to learn how to stand up to her themselves."

"They're learning how to do just that—from you."

"They can't keep relying on me, though. We might not even be here next year."

"We don't know that yet." When I level a "Seriously?" look at him, he bobs his head sideways to concede. "Okay, probably not."

As I suspected would be the case, Jet and his agent, Tom, have been in touch every day, sometimes multiple times, as they try to figure out together what the next best move is for Jet's career. The problem definitely isn't a lack of offers; rather, the abundance of choice—and the spectrum along which they fall—has proved problematic. Jet's paralyzed by indecision. It's a completely new experience for him, the guy who used to making split-second choices on the field. Sure, not all of them panned out, but the next opportunity was never far behind. This situation is obviously different. He's a lot more cautious after the Football Network section of The Plan had to be ceremoniously burned.

Most nights after Scout goes to bed, we confer on the couch and discuss the list of options available to him. It seems like new opportunities are added every day. Coaching. Team management at the corporate level. Acting. Guest starring on reality talent shows. Some of Football Network's rivals even want him, although none for calling games. He's been offered everything from sideline reporting gigs to technical consultant positions. One sports network in particular has been coming at him hard, trying desperately to make him their in-studio go-to quarterback analyst.

Everyone who wants to keep him in front of the camera thinks they have the expertise to "fix" him, and they all have different theories as to what the root of the problem is. Because broadcasting was Jet's original post-playing dream, he's tempted to believe them. But which one? What if they're wrong? What if they're *all* wrong? What if it's just not meant to be, no matter what?

Then there are the actual playing offers. Unfortunately, the Chiefs have moved on with their latest ingenue, another first-round draft pick they chose at the tail-end of Jet's career, a virtual kid who lit it up and took the team all the way to the Super Bowl—which they won—his first starting season. Jet and I couldn't be happier for the guy, even if that means it slams the door on a Kansas City comeback for Jet. He doesn't really want to play, anyway. Most days. Some days, he does, though. Fortunately, I think he remembers what an all-in, every day job it is. If your heart's not completely in it, it won't work. The last thing he wants is to give some foundering team hope only to come on board and bomb because he just doesn't have what it takes—mentally or physically—anymore.

So we wait. I keep telling him he'll know the perfect offer when he gets it, and if he can't decide now, then it hasn't arrived yet. Sort of like dating. If you try to force it with a relationship that's not exactly what both of you want and need, in the interest of being with someone, anyone, it's not going to end well.

Meanwhile, Scout's been loving having her dad home all the time, even if he is on his phone a lot. He tries to limit that to when she's at school, and being on West Coast time helps. By the time he picks her up from school, the people he's typically dealing with are ending their work days, two to three hours ahead of us. That leaves plenty of one-on-one time, goofing off, experimenting in the kitchen (being a stay-at-home dad means he's in charge of dinner, and it's been interesting), having deep, philosophical conversations that I sometimes overhear—and covertly record on my phone—and simply being together unlike they've ever had the chance to be.

I think he likes it more than he wants to admit. He thinks he *should* be bored with it, *should* be more interested in his prospects outside of the house. Because he's a man? Because stay-at-home parent was never part of The Plan? I don't know. All I do know is that he's damn good at it, much better than I've ever been, strange dinner experiments notwithstanding. The mere mention of him retiring for good, though, and continuing this way always leads to him shutting down. For some reason, it's not something he's willing to seriously consider.

Then again, I don't blame him, when attending events like today's are part of the job description. He'd take another traveling job just to avoid PTA meetings. Maybe I would, too. We could make Gloria our PTA proxy.

Unfortunately, I didn't think of that before now. Now, I'm here. And this is happening. Rubbing my thumb back and forth on the rim of my coffee cup, I say, "It feels ridiculous for me to be making demands—"

"They're not demands; they're suggestions. And they're not just yours. A lot of people have given you ideas." He finishes his coffee and looks sadly into his empty cup, then says, "I'm getting a refill. When I get back, we're going in. So pull it together, Richards."

Him calling me by my maiden name makes my lips twitch in an almost-smile that's determined to defy my sour mood. "Fine. But I'm not going to enjoy it."

"You don't have to. That's what next week is for."

At his mention of our spring break getaway, just the two of us, while Scout stays with Ned, Gloria, and her cousins, my face breaks out into a full-on grin.

"There she is," Jet says with a proud pat to my shoulder. "Eye on the prize, babe."

He walks away to my muttering, reflexively, "Don't call me babe," while I continue to fantasize about the Greek villa we've rented for seven glorious days.

Six minutes later, I find myself seated with him and twenty or so other parents on one side of a bunch of smaller tables scooted together to make one long one. Kiki sits alone on the other side, ubiquitous clipboard at the ready.

"Who's ready for spring break?" she says, sticking out her tongue and making a face. "Everyone, right? We're almost there! Cabo, here we come! Am I right?"

We all humor her with sounds of agreement, although I think she's the only one who's taking her kindergartner to

Cabo San Lucas at a time of year when college students are down there partying as if the world's about to end. Not judging, just saying… It wouldn't be my first choice. Or tenth.

"Anyway, before we can relax and have fun, we need to do a little bit of work. That's how it always is, right?" She picks up her pen and scoots her teacup aside. "So. Brainstorming sesh!" She beams brightly across the table at us. "Let's talk about next year's PTA fundraisers and events!" Pulling a small stack of papers from under her note page, she slides them to the person at the far end of the table. "Take one and pass them down. Couples may need to share."

When the pile finds its way to me, in the center, where everyone so helpfully saved seats for Jet and me, directly across from Kiki, I take one and position it so Jet can see it, too. It's a calendar, with some entries already filled in.

"As you can see," Kiki says before everyone even has a copy, "A lot of things are already filled in, as they're annual events, like Oktoberfest, the Holiday Shoppe, et cetera. But we still have quite a few months with no events, and many of our recurring fundraisers benefit the community, not the school, so we need to make up the shortfall. In addition to the usual educational field trips and outings throughout the year for various grades, the fifth graders and eighth graders are staying a weekend at Disneyland next year for their matriculation rewards, and the senior trip was just decided…" She pages through more paper under her top note-taking sheet until she comes to the one she needs. With a gleeful grin, she announces, "Cancun! Now, we can't let the kids down, can we?"

I squirm in my seat when several pairs of eyes swivel toward me, as if I need reminding that this is one of my cues. I clear my throat, "Uh, Kiki?"

Her smile drains from her eyes but remains on her lips. "Yes, Maura? You have some fundraising ideas?"

"I do. But first, about those big trips…"

She blinks expectantly while I take a deep breath and gird my loins.

"Would it be unreasonable to ask parents to pay for their children's tickets. After all, we're getting group discounts for everything, and—"

She taps her finger against her chin and tries to arrange her Botoxed features into something akin to perplexity. "Do you have a fifth, eighth, or twelfth grader, Maura?"

"No, Kiki. You know I don't."

"I didn't think so," she says with a fake tinkling laugh, "But I never want to assume that situations can't change in an instant. Jet was an NFL player, after all. Could have all kinds of surprises in the background that could pop up, right?"

Jet, slumped in his chair and looking at his phone, sits up straighter at the mention of his name and laughs along good-naturedly with some of the others' nervous titters. "Nothing like that in my 'background,' Keek. I was usually too busy sitting in ice baths after games to participate in any groupie fun."

She tilts her chin down and clicks her tongue sympathetically. "Ouch. Poor you. Well, in any case, I guess what I was trying to ask, without being too blunt about it, was, 'Is it really fair to ask people to do something you wouldn't be expected to do, yourself?'"

"I would be willing to do that, though. And I think most Ursuline parents would."

"*Most* is the key word there, Maura. We do have some students…" She lowers her voice to a stage whisper. "On scholarship." Looking down the line of parents before her, she says, "Of course, none of their parents are here today."

I swallow. "They're not here, because they're working jobs that don't allow them to take an hour or two off on a Friday morning for a 'brainstorming sesh.'"

"Exactly. If they were here, though, they'd tell you that they can't afford to pay for those trips, and if they don't have to pay, it's not fair to ask the other parents to pay, which is why the PTA has always funded these outings."

Her blinking smile and look down at her still-blank note sheet signify the topic is closed, that my question was asked and answered, and we're moving on.

"I talked to most of them ahead of this meeting, though, and they all said they were willing to pay a portion—as much as they could. The parents who can easily afford it said they'd be willing to supplement the ones who can't." This bit of information brings her head back up so fast, I worry about her neck. Not really. Really, I hope she has a crick in it for the rest of the day.

"What's that, now?"

"I called people. On the phone? And I emailed the ones I couldn't get ahold of."

"Scholarship information is— Well, it's confidential."

"Not really. I mean, it's not shouted from the roof of the building or given to just anyone, but when I explained to the administration what I was trying to do, they agreed to give me the contact information."

"What *are* you trying to do, Maura?" With precision, she sets down her clipboard and clicks her pen on top of it. Leaning back, she folds her arms over her chest. "Because from where I sit, it looks like you're, once again, going behind my back, undermining my authority, and subverting time-honored traditions and processes."

"No. I'm doing what you refuse to do: figuring out better ways of doing things so that everyone benefits, including the larger community that Ursuline is a part of."

"Here we go…"

"Nope. Not gonna get on my soapbox."

"Thank God." She picks up her pen and writes my name down, then "Class Trip Funding," which she underlines three times. "If you're so smart, you get to organize collecting the money for those trips."

"Fine. Done."

She laughs and shakes her head, adding one more line underneath the note. "I don't think you understand what a logistical nightmare it's going to be. But good luck with that. We'll be back to having the PTA pay for the whole enchilada the next year, mark my words."

"Doubt it. With online crowdfunding, it'll be a breeze. We'll have a grand total goal, and everyone will know what the per-student price is. If we're falling short close to the deadline, we can make an appeal to the wealthier parents or pull funds from the PTA account."

"Sounds like socialism to me," she mutters, begrudgingly writing it down.

I roll my eyes. "Fine. We could hold an impromptu fundraiser, then. Something quick and easy to organize—like a bake sale."

At those last words, she narrows her eyes at me. "Hmmph. We'll see, I suppose. I'm willing to try it. I *am* open to new ideas, you know. Hardly anybody gives them to me, though. It's all, 'Kiki will think of something.'"

I look around at the other parents. "Interesting. I haven't

had that experience at all. The PTA members I've talked to are full of ideas."

"Maybe they should bring them to the PTA President." She straightens her spine and pulls down on the bottom of her leather jacket. "Anywho! Speaking of ideas, let's hear 'em, all you creative parents!"

And like that, without my having to say another word, every single person on our side of the table pitches at least one new concept. By the end of the meeting, when Kiki's furiously scribbling the final notes in the margins of her paper, one parent helpfully passes her a blank sheet from their day planner. She takes it with a shaky smile and "thanks," and continues writing.

The best part: every single one of the plans requires the PTA split the proceeds evenly between the school and a local non-profit organization.

Strike that. The best part is that I didn't have to do as much talking as I feared, *and* now that the meeting's over, I can focus on my much-needed vacation.

## TWENTY-SEVEN

## RESET

I stare at nothing in particular as I stand/float with my chin resting on my arms at the edge of the private heated infinity pool that fills up the entire back "yard" of the Greek villa where we're staying. On this, day four of our vacation, I've finally remembered how to do nothing. To think of nothing. To stare at nothing. It's all too bright to focus on for too long, anyway. Everything is sun and sparkling sea and bright white structures made from modern materials simulating the mud bricks of ancient Greece. It's dazzling and blinding.

For the first couple of days, I couldn't tear myself from this view of the sky before me, the rough, brown land around me, and the Mediterranean below me. Now, though, it's as if I've become one with the landscape. I am Greece, and Greece is me.

There are hundreds of other villas like this one surrounding us, but from here, I can't see them, and they can't see me. It's an amazing feat of architecture that makes me feel as if I'm the only person here. Even the boats below seem like images on a screen, not actual watercraft captained and occupied by people like me.

A small splash behind me and rippling of water against my shoulder blades serve as another reminder I'm not alone. I turn just enough to watch Jet walk across the pool, arms lifted to keep our drinks above the surface. Arriving next to me, he hands me the tall, thin glass tumbler containing the cloudy white cocktail and clinks his glass against mine. After a lingering thank-you kiss, I take an exploratory sip, and my suspicions are immediately confirmed.

I cough quietly. "How much *tsipouro* did you put in this?"

"Enough," he says with a naughty smile before taking a drink of his. "Mm. The perfect amount. I made it just like the guy at the bar."

"Just like him?"

"Well... Maybe not *just*. I didn't measure anything."

"It's... strong."

"But delicious."

"Of course, it's delicious. Are you trying to get me drunk?"

"As if I need to." He sets down his glass on a nearby ledge and tries to take my drink from me, but I pull it back for a few more hasty gulps before relinquishing it. He puts it next to his own and snakes an arm around me. I float against his sun-warmed body and kiss him again. And again. He tastes like sweet grapefruit with a hint of vanilla. Even without that, though, I can't get enough of him. The feeling appears to be mutual.

Pool sex isn't my favorite, so I lead him out of the water and onto one of the more sheltered chaises in the striped sun and shade of a pergola. While still attached to my lips, he pulls the gauzy curtain behind him, another reminder that while we may feel isolated, we're not, and steps out of his swim trunks. It's still early spring and the air temperature away from the pool is a bit nippy, creating goosebumps on our exposed skin. Nevertheless, I eagerly peel off my wet scraps of clothing, too, and submit to his expert ministrations while gazing through drooping lids at the bright blue sky through the white wooden beams above.

Afterward, both sweating and panting, we pull a second chaise over, butting it against the first, and he collapses onto it. We both stare longingly at our drinks, left way out of reach at the other side of the pool. "That was poor planning," I say breathlessly, knowing we're both thinking it.

One arm across his forehead, he waves off our self-criticism. "I'd rather have water right now, anyway. I need to rehydrate after that."

"Me, too."

Still, neither of us moves.

After a few more seconds, he rolls onto his side to face me and grins. "That was nice."

"Nice? It was more than 'nice' for me."

"Me, too. I just didn't want to be gross about it."

I laugh, and he joins in, then thumbs one of my nipples. "I'll be ready to go again here in a minute."

"You will not."

"I will if I keep looking at you."

"Shallow." My guts betray me by doing somersaults. "I'm more than just a piece of meat."

"I know. That's what makes you even sexier."

"Stop." He really is making me blush, and I both love it and hate it at the same time, a seriously discomforting experience. "I'm going to get a pitcher of water."

I move to rise, but he holds me in place by cuffing his hand around my wrist. "Wait." Settling back into the cushions, I do just that.

He threads his fingers through mine and looks down at our joined hands. "I've been thinking..."

"Not allowed. We're on vacation."

One corner of his mouth lifts, but he doesn't laugh or even smile, like I expect, so I realize he's about to say something important. I sober and quiet, shifting so that I can look into his downcast eyes. He helps by looking up.

"I've been thinking about so many things lately. Like, I feel like my head's about to burst with all the stuff bouncing around up there. Just so many options and decisions and—"

I will myself not to interject, not to say anything at all, as reassuring or well-meaning as it might be. Instead, I take a deep breath and patiently defer to him, let him figure out what he wants to say and how he wants to say it.

"I've had so much *fun* the past few months, being home with you and Bump." He smiles, but the shine that enters in his eyes contradicts—or maybe reinforces—his expressed joy. Blinking and sniffing, he continues, "It's just... I don't know. I feel like there's something more I need to be doing, you know? Like, it's selfish for me to be like, 'This is it. I'm done.' Maybe not selfish, but lazy."

I nod but squeeze my fingers against his to let him know it's a nod of understand, not of agreement. There's nothing lazy about him.

He pokes at his eyes, then widens them and blinks several times, as if to dry them. With a final, determined sniff, he says, "The truth is, though, I like it. A lot. Too much to go back on the road all the time, even for just a night here and there. I don't want to do that anymore. I've already missed so much." He swallows hard. "It didn't seem like it at the time, because it was in little pieces, you know? But those little pieces add up, and they've added up to enough. Maybe too much."

"Nah," I say through a tight throat. "You didn't miss anything important. You've been around for all the big stuff."

"Mostly. So far. Luckily. But my luck's gonna run out eventually, and I'm going to miss something big because I was in some hotel eating room service alone and studying stats or plays. I don't want to do that anymore."

"So don't."

"What does that leave, then? What else do I know how to do?"

"So much," I whisper, drawing closer to him, so close that we could almost touch noses. I do, in fact, briefly tap the tip of mine to his and withdraw a little so we don't have to cross our eyes to look at each other. "You know how to fix Scout's hair the way she likes it. And cook her favorite meals. And make her laugh harder than anyone else in the world. Cheer her up when nobody else can. Come up with hilarious 'conversations' between Pompeii and Joey, with separate voices, and everything. Answer her craziest, most out-of-left-field questions. Explain complicated football rules to her. Talk her through tough stuff. Get her to stop crying when she's hurt."

He rolls his eyes, but his smile betrays his pride. "Yeah, okay. That's just being a dad, though."

"Just being a dad? *Just* being a dad? You say that like it's easy."

"It is. For me. With her. She's incredible."

"Yeah, she is. But so are you. You're not 'just a dad.' You're an amazing parent."

"And I love it. I really do."

"I can tell. So if that's what you want to do for a while…"

"Tom says I need to choose something, get back out there before people lose interest."

I nudge his foot with mine. "But if you don't care that people have lost interest, what does it matter?"

"I do care, though. I hate that I do, but I do. I don't like being just another guy. There. I've said it." He even blushes to underscore how shameful he thinks it is.

Pushing some damp hair from his forehead, I say, "That's not the worst thing."

"I guess not. It means that I don't want to be a full-time parent, though."

I laugh. "Uh, too bad, champ. No matter what else you and I do, we're stuck with that job."

"You know what I mean. I want to have *another* job, too."

"So what's it gonna be? God knows, Tom's given you *plenty* of choices. The list is a mile long."

"Not after you take 'traveling' off the table."

"True. So that narrows it down even further. Makes it a little easier to decide."

"What if I don't like any of the things on the official list, though?"

My ears perk up. "Is there an 'unofficial' list?"

Again, he looks down at our hands. "Sort of. I've been kicking around an idea."

"Well, out with it, then! Don't keep me in suspense!"

"It might be dumb, and it might not even work."

"So? If it doesn't work, you try something else. And if that doesn't work, you take what you've learned from that and try something else. There's no such thing as wasted experience. Take it from the queen of 'failing up.'"

Thirsty beyond belief at this point and starting to get chilled again, I disengage and stand, pulling my cold, wet swimsuit back on so I can decently emerge from our little love tent.

He sits up and does the same, and as he's tying the drawstring at his waist, he says, "I think I want to be a private consultant."

We step back into the full sun, and I lead the way toward the house, walking backward and squinting at him. "Oh? And what would that entail?"

He shrugs. "I don't know. Whatever I want, I guess. I could focus on quarterbacks, or I could keep it open to whoever wants or needs a little extra one-on-one coaching. Or even just someone to talk to." He holds open the back door for me. "It doesn't have to be play coaching. It could be sort of *life* coaching, figuring out how to balance a personal life with the professional life, how to stay out of trouble. You know, stuff like that."

Opening the fridge, I take out the water pitcher and top it up from the kitchen tap, then pour two tall glasses and hand one to him. "You'd be so good at that."

"You think so?"

"Yes! Your own life is your résumé."

"I haven't done everything perfectly."

"Nobody has. But you can take the things you've learned and pass them on to young players, especially rookies."

"Players at any age, really. I've been through every stage."

"That, you have."

After gulping down one full glass each, we refill them and, wrapped in warm fluffy robes, return to the patio, where we sit at the edge of the pool and dangle our feet in the crystalline water.

I think about his proposal for a while, then say, "It could definitely work. You have the connections, you could work from home, and you're not relying on whatever income it would generate, so you could start slow, with one or two clients. Coaches could refer them to you."

"Yeah."

"What's holding you back?"

He smiles over at me, closing one eye against the sun. "Nothing, I guess. I wanted to run it by you, though, to make sure it wasn't stupid."

"It's not stupid at all! It's kind of brilliant, actually. I'm jealous I didn't think of it."

He laughs and grips my hand on the concrete between us. "I definitely don't want to make any decisions this time without talking them through with you."

"I appreciate that. Tends to go a little smoother when we're both reading from the same page of the playbook."

As the sun moves lower in the sky, turning the white stone around us into a soft tangerine tint, he sighs contentedly. "All this has made me hungry."

"Me, too." I push our now-empty glasses out of the way and lean back on my arms. "But I could also totally take a nap."

"It's too late for a nap."

"Never."

"Yeah, it is. C'mon. Let's go get ready for dinner."

Keeping a tight grip on my hand, he stands, splashing me in the process, and tries to pull me up from the patio, but I resist, holding fast to the edge of the pool.

He tugs again, but carefully, so he won't yank my shoulder out of its socket.

The same time I decide to relent and loosen my grip on the smooth, painted stone, he pulls again, this time harder. Stumbling to my feet, I fall against him, both of us laughing as he loses his own footing and steps sideways into a puddle. That causes him to twist and slide, and I screech as I realize what's going to happen. Jet topples into the pool on his back, and I belly-flop on top of him. When we resurface, I splash him in the face, and he grabs me around the waist, pulling me under again.

Someday we'll grow up. But I guess for now, we're just not ready.

THE END

## ALSO BY BREA BROWN

The *Secret Keeper* series:

- *The Secret Keeper* (Book 1)
- *The Secret Keeper Confined* (Book 2)
- *The Secret Keeper Up All Night* (Book 3)
- *The Secret Keeper Holds On* (Book 4)
- *The Secret Keeper Lets Go* (Book 5)
- *The Secret Keeper Fulfilled* (Book 6)

The *Underdog* series:

- *Out of My League* (Book 1)
- *Rookie of the Year* (Book 2)
- *Opportunity Knox* (Book 3)

The *Nurse Nate* series:

- *Let's Be Frank* (Book 1)
- *Let's Be Real* (Book 2)
- *Let's Be Friends* (Book 3)

Stand-alone novels:

- *Daydreamer*
- *The Family Plot*
- *Plain Jayne*
- *Quiet, Please!*

## ABOUT THE PUBLISHER

Thank you for your time and attention! If you enjoyed this book, we hope you will leave a short review on the site where you purchased it to let other readers know of your experience.

To be notified about new titles and special contests, events, and sales from Wayzgoose Press, please visit our website at

http://wayzgoosepress.com

or sign up for our mailing list by clicking here. (We send email infrequently, and you can unsubscribe at any time.)